Praise for

STORMING HEAVEN

"Bears witness to a turn-of-the-century struggle that failed to avert the future. The book's triumph lies in the authenticity of these voices, in their ability to make real these undiminished lives."

JAYNE ANNE PHILLIPS

"This is the gripping story of a real conflict.... Denise Giardina tells the miners' stirring story with a fierceness and passion. This is a fine, moving book."

ANNIE DILLARD

"Powerful...not just names and dates, but cries and screams and warm bodies and cold bodies. It's about babies, women and men against the American government. It's about a war we never learned about in school because the American government was the bad guy. Every American should read *Storming Heaven*, and every lover of good books should know this masterful writer's voice. Anything I read after this will never be as important."

CAROLYN CHUTE

"In scope, it encompasses the spirit of humanity, from the heights of greatness to the depths of suffering with a fullness of emotion devoid of sentimentality. The beauty of the language makes us believe. The lump in our throats makes us believe."

The Nashville Tennesean

"A gutsy outrage-laced fictional reconstruction of a shocking chapter in the stormy history of the United Mine Workers...with rousing appeal... and spirit."

The Kirkus Reviews

"In a powerful political novel based on a true incident, author Giardina never loses sight of the basics—wonderful characters, a gripping story line, and authentic locales and dialogue....A sweeping, riveting story of radical politics and corporate greed."

Booklist

STORMING HEAVEN

A Novel

Denise Giardina

IVY BOOKS • NEW YORK

For Mernie King, Perk Perkins, Tricia Perkins,
and Jim Lewis

An Ivy Book
Published by The Random House Publishing Group
Copyright © 1987 by Denise Giardina

Published in the United States by Ivy Books, an imprint of The
Random House Publishing Group, a division of Random House,
Inc., New York, and simultaneously in Canada by Random
House of Canada Limited, Toronto.

Ivy Books and colophon are trademarks of Random House, Inc.

www.ballantinebooks.com

ISBN 978-0-8041-0297-1

Printed in the United States of America

This edition published by arrangement with W. W. Norton &
Company, Inc.

First Ballantine Books Edition: July 1988

Acknowledgments

Thanks to the following people who contributed to the writing of this book in many ways, large and small.

Colleen Anderson, Fred Barkey, Ann Barth, Billy Ray Belcher, Patty Flo Belcher, Bill Blizzard, Nancy Brallier, Harry Brawley, Tony Burgess, Steve Cohen, Rob Currie, Kate Fitzgerald, Charli Fulton, John Gaventa, Dennis Giardina, Leona Whitt Giardina, Frank Giardina, Joe Bob Goodwin, Dale Grimmett, Joe Hacala, Jerry Hardt, Bill Harrington, Ken Hechler, Faith Holsaert, Myles Horton, Freda Jones, Opie Jones, Tod Kaufman, Terry Keleher, Lorrie Lane, Judy Lewis, David Liden, Kate Long, Hermer Lucas, John McFerrin, Dr. Jimmie Mangus, Connie Marcum, Homer Marcum, Jim Marcum, Walter Marcum, Linda Martin, Bob Noone, Mary Kay O'Rourke, Joe Peschel, Mary Ratliff, Alec Reynolds, Paul Sheridan, Susan Small, Bob Spence, Joe Szakos, Kristin Layng Szakos, Jim Waggy, Susan Weber, Mary Beth Wells, Elmo Whitt, Ertel Whitt, Lois Whitt, Rodney Whitt, Bob Wise.

Also the West Virginia Department of Culture and History, the Library of Congress, Mayor Bob Cruikshanks and the Town of Pratt, the Highlander Center, the Episcopal Diocese of West Virginia, Sojourners Fellowship, the Kentucky Fair Tax Coalition, the West Virginia Land Ownership Study, the Charleston Gazette, and the Appalachian Research and Defense Fund.

A special thank you to George Garrett for his unselfish efforts on behalf of young writers, to Jane Gelfman for her patience and encouragement, and to my editor, Kathy Anderson.

And in grateful memory of Ned Chilton, publisher of

the Charleston Gazette, whose fighting spirit inspired the Annadel Free Press.

I am indebted to the following books and their authors: *Life, Work and Rebellion in the Coal Fields*, David Alan Corbin; *Power and Powerlessness: Quiescence and Rebellion in an Appalachian Valley*, John Gaventa; *Thunder in the Mountains: The West Virginia Mine War 1920–21*, Lon Savage; *Bloodletting in Appalachia*, Howard B. Lee; *Struggle in the Coal Fields: The Autobiography of Fred Mooney; King Coal*, Stan Cohen; *Civil War in West Virginia*, by Winthrop D. Lane for the *New York Evening Post*; *Land of the Guyandot*, Robert Y. Spence; *Sodom and Gomorrah of Today: Or a History of Keystone, West Virginia*, by an anonymous Virginia "Lad," 1912.

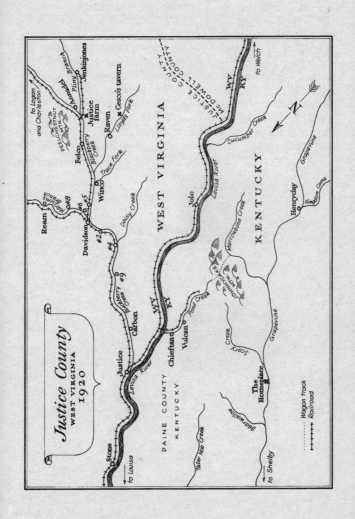

Part One

One

C. J. MARCUM

THEY IS MANY A WAY TO MARK A BABY WHILE IT IS STILL YET in the womb. A fright to its mother will render it nervous and fretful after it is birthed. If a copperhead strikes, a fiery red snake will be stamped on the baby's face or back. And a portentous event will violate a woman's entrails, grab a youngun by the ankle and wrench a life out of joint.

Me and Dillon Lloyd spoke of such things on the night Rondal was borned. It was eighteen and ninety, the year the railroad come in and took up the land, two year before the land was give out from under us to the coal company. Dillon seen it coming. We perched out on the hillside and spied for shooting stars, while Dillon told me how Rondal, his brother's first child, come into the world.

"Hit was fast for a first youngun, and the granny woman was too late. Clabe werent back from fetchin her down from Raven. Werent nary a soul to help birth him but me. He cried out when I smacked him but then he got real quiet. I held him up and he looked me right in the eye. Wouldnt look away. Them's blue eyes he's got, long and down-turned."

Dillon carved on a slab of hickory, fashioning the slender neck of a banjo for the baby. I caught curls of wood as they fell and flung them out into the moonlight.

"How you know he's goin to take to the banjer?" I asked. "Maybe he aint got the gift like you."

"I seen them hands. That one will be a picker. Them fingers was curved and he was movin them back and forth slow like. He's goin to love the feel of this here neck. And the strings will be soft. I'll git the guts from that old tabby in the barn.

3

And I'll tan its hide for the head. Hit's too old to mouse these days.''

"How can you pick on them strings when you know where they come from?''

"Dont bother me none. I wisht I could be put to some use when I die, stead of moulderin in the ground. My skin for a banjer, my bones for a scythe or a flail to clear paths in this here world.''

I loved to hear him talk that way. Dillon Lloyd was always a free-talking man. He lived alone in a cabin back up the hill from his brother Clabe. They worked the land together, one hundred acres at the mouth of Trace. Dillon's thick black hair hung down between his shoulder blades like an Indian's. People said that he had the second sight, that he could set the Evil Eye on a body. He went abroad at night, not hunting, just walking. Vernie, Clabe's wife, was scared of him. Dillon laughed at her behind her back.

When my papaw could spare me from chores, I rode my mule up Blackberry Creek to the Lloyd homeplace and spent the night. Dillon took me out after dark, coon hunting or bull-frogging, or maybe just walking. Later I'd lie alone in the loft of his cabin. The summer breeze would rush through the window and rustle the bedclothes, bearing the flailing of his banjo like the sound of the river running yonder.

When Rondal was borned, Dillon let me stay out with him all night. The moon on the wane was giving light enough to show the creek rippling silver where it joined Trace Fork. My mind's eye could see all the land—the mountain wrapped like a protecting arm around the cabin, the prickly grass in the pasture up Trace where the cows and sheep grazed, the dark fields fanning out along the bottom, soon to be dense with corn, the wall of mountain across Blackberry, the side of it rearing straight up from the creek bed.

"Bad times comin,'' said Dillon. "That youngun will suffer it. He was in the womb when the papers was signed.''

"My papaw says it too. He dont trust them railroad men. And he aint took no money neither.''

I was proud of it. My papaw, Henry Marcum, had refused to sign the paper giving the minerals to the railroad. He hadnt knowed what the minerals was, but when he heard they was on his land, he wanted to keep them. Still he was scared, like most people. The railroad men claimed they owned all the land, had bought it off somebody in Philadelphia whose papaw had fought in the Revolutionary War and been give it as a gift. According to them, they owned most of Justice County, and McDowell County, too. Then they come around, fat, smooth-faced men in black suits, and vowed they'd leave us the land if we'd sign over the minerals. Vernie signed one day when Clabe was gone hunting. Clabe didnt chastise her.

But Papaw sucked loudly on his teeth when he heard what Clabe and Vernie had done. Wouldnt no good come of it, he said. He'd already wrangled with the railroad men. When he told them about the deed he held at the courthouse, they laughed at him. *Junior patent,* they kept saying. *Senior patent is what we own. That takes precedence. Ask any judge.*

The judges we was supposed to ask was a way far off, so most folks signed. The railroad men vowed they'd not bother us no more. We'll see, Dillon said. He sat on the mountain on the night of Rondal's birth and said it again. We'll see.

THE RAILROAD MEN SPOKE TRUE—THEY DIDNT BOTHER US NO more. Instead they give the minerals over to the coal companies and the coal companies took our land two year later. Omar Kane, sheriff of Justice County, come around and said everyone had to move, that he had an order. *American coal took a lease from the Richmond and Western railroad. Railroad owns the mineral. Mineral owner has precedence over the surface owner.* He tacked a notice on Clabe's cabin door, on Dillon's, and most everyone's on the holler. When he passed us by, my papaw was pleased with himself.

"I told them other durned fools, but they wouldnt listen. Hit's what comes of bein greedy, Cincinnatus. You remember that."

Papaw Henry always called me Cincinnatus, only person that did, Cincinnatus Jefferson Marcum, after the two greatest men that ever lived.

"Farmers and freemen," he called them. "You be just like em, boy."

Papaw had the naming of me because my daddy died of the pneumonia before I was borned, and the childbirth took my mother away right after. I was sent to school at Justice in the

winters. Papaw had it in mind that I would read for the law
someday.

"Cincinnatus, fetch some honey jars up the hill."

That was the last thing Papaw ever said to me. The jars was
dusty and I went to the well to wash them while he climbed
the hill. Mamaw and me heard a shot. We run and found him
toppled over into one of the hives. We was both stung all over
when we pulled him out of there by the legs. He was shot once
through the head.

Sheriff come round in three days and nailed the notice to
vacate on our cabin door.

"What gives you the right, Omar?" Mamaw said.

Sheriff wouldnt look at her. "Henry set his mark to a paper,
didnt he?"

"His mark?" I said scornfully. "He didnt have no call to
make no mark. My papaw could read and write."

"I dont know about that," Sheriff muttered.

I wanted to kill him. He was the same man I had known all
my young life, Omar Kane from Justice town, who give me a
molasses candy when Papaw went to the polls to vote. I wanted
to get my squirrel rifle and shoot him. When he rode away and
I had not done it, I despised myself for a coward.

The fields was half plowed when we packed to go, leaving
the homeplace the Marcums settled in 1801 when they first
come to West Virginia, on the little creek called after us, Marcums Branch. We left my papaw buried atop the ridge behind
the cabin in the Marcum family cemetery. They wasnt no
preacher due for a while and we knew that this time he'd not
come by for the summer funerals, so me and Mamaw each
said our own goodbyes and trusted the Lord would hear them.
I read a little from the scripture about folks raised up on the
Last Day. I throwed the first dirt on with my hands, then shovelled the hole full. I pictured the Last Day, when Papaw would
come busting through the very dirt I piled on him. He would
fly straightway to strangle Sheriff Kane and all the smooth-
faced railroad men.

WE WASNT SURE WHERE TO GO. SOME FOLKS HAD LEFT FOR
Kentucky or Tennessee to look for farms to buy there. Others heard tell they was mountains like ourn out in Missouri

and Arkansas. But most was living makeshift until the new coal camps was built. The men was promised jobs cutting the timber, putting up the houses, and then working the mines. But mamaw said she wouldn't let me do that. I didnt care to no how.

We finally settled on moving to the Justice farm. Ermel was Papaw's cousin and, like Papaw, he hadnt signed no paper for the railroad. So far, nobody had bothered him. Even before the coal companies come, Ermel Justice held more land than anyone on Blackberry. His fields stretched more than a mile up past where Pliny forked off. At the forks, Ermel had set up a mill to take advantage of the rush of water. He also built a blacksmith's forge and a general store. Folks come from Peelchestnut Mountain, from Pliny Fork and Lloyds Fork to trade with Ermel, a tithe of meal for the miller, a gallon of linn honey for bought goods. The post office inside the general store was named after Ermel's wife Annadel, who was postmistress.

Ermel's great grandfather built the two-story log farmhouse in 1818. The porch was added in 1852 by his papaw, who had so many younguns to help with the chores that he could afford to sit in a rocking chair on a soft summer evening and survey his holdings.

Ermel was glad to have me because his one brother was gone off and all he had was little younguns. He had to hire out to work the land. He let a few other families settle in as well, Garmon Tackett and Tennis Farley and Everett Day. He wanted Clabe and Vernie and Dillon, but Vernie was bound to go back to her people on Island Creek, acrost Peelchestnut. And Dillon wouldn't have no more to do with Blackberry. He planned to head back into the hills. He come to visit us once more and brung little Rondal, two year old, with him.

Dillon vowed he was going way back in, beyond Daisy.

"That will be hard livin," Ermel observed.

"Our people allays lived hard," Dillon replied. "That there is what makes us."

"You keepin that moonshine still?"

"Maybe."

Ermel rubbed his chin. "All this new trade comin in, they'll be a call for liquor."

"I might trade," Dillon said. "Long as I dont have to set

foot on this creek. Hell, you wont even find a coon in the
holler time all that mining starts up. I cant bear to see it, all
mud and ugly, men sellin their souls for the almighty dollar."

"Take me with you!" I pleaded. "I dont want to see it
neither."

Dillon just laughed. I was so hurt, I went off to the creek
and cried. By the time I got back, they was leaving. Rondal
run up to me on his bow legs and stretched out his arms.

"Hwing me, C. J.!"

I held him by the wrists and swung him round and round.
When I set him on his feet, he staggered and fell. I picked him
up and held him clost to me. He was still for a moment and I
felt the rise and fall of his chest against mine. Then he set his
hands to my shoulders, pushed himself back and looked at
me. Something passed between us then, I vow it, though he
was only a baby. Rondal was marked at his birth and easy
marked every day after.

"You tell your daddy not to stay on Island Creek," I said.
"You tell him to bring you back to Blackberry."

He smiled and poked my nose with his finger.

I WORKED RIGHT BESIDE ERMEL IN THE FIELDS. I CRAVED THE
company of a man, an older man, to take the place of Dillon
and papaw. In the afternoon we would stop work, come set
on the porch steps and take a glass of cold cider from the
springhouse. Annadel had hung leatherbritches on one end
of the porch, row after row of drying green beans dangling
on strings, thick as a screen.

No one come for his land. Every day we expected to see
the sheriff, and Ermel kept his rifle close by at all times,
but the sheriff never come. Later we heard from a new man
come to trade at the store that they was no coal in reach of
the forks. That saved us. The railroad did come in 1893 to
negotiate a right-of-way up to the head of Pliny Branch,
where American Coal would build a camp. Ermel sold the
right-of-way, but he never signed away his mineral rights
and nobody never claimed he did.

"We're still yet here," Ermel would say.

He would rub his balding head. Ermel is the kind of man

who shows sun, and his scalp was raw-looking all through
the summer, like it had been scrubbed with a wool carder.

"We're still yet here," he'd say again. "Hit wont never
be the same though."

I got riled when he said that, though I never let on. I tried
to tell myself that nothing was changed, except that my
papaw was gone. On Ermel's farm it was easy to think it,
most of the time. But when I would pause in the field, lean
against my hoe, and the wind would stir and bear a shriek,
thin and ghostlike, from up Pliny—the death cry of some
huge tree, fallen to make mine timbers and houses for
American Coal—then my dream of sanctuary on the farm
seemed a mockery and a reproach.

ONE DAY IN THE SPRINGTIME, ERMEL TOOK ME ON THE NEW
train to Justice town. Lumberjacks had shaved the mountainsides for fifteen mile, sliced the trees into boards or
strewn them about in tangled heaps. The bushes was growed
up, the flanks of the hills gashed and sticky with mud. At
the mouth of Marcums Branch, long stone buildings rose
from the oozing ground, and on the ridge where the Marcum cemetery had been, a tall structure of wood stood like
a giant tombstone. Ermel said it was a coal tipple. He talked
the whole time, while I sat with my arm acrost my belly to
hold it still, because of the jostling of the train.

"Damnable thing is, business at my store has never been
better. I make more in a week than I used to all year. No
sense in farmin much this year. I'll be makin money outen
this mess anyhow. They're a blastin and a tamin the mountains, and I'm a gittin rich." He shook his head. "I'm glad
my daddy has passed on so he cant see it."

When we arrived at Justice, I jumped down from the
train, wobbled along the station platform, and lost my
breakfast beside the baggage rack.

THREE YEAR LATER, VERNIE LLOYD'S PEOPLE LOST THEIR
land on Island Creek to another coal company, and Clabe
brung his family back acrost Peelchestnut Mountain. They
come the way they left, in a mule-drawn wagon laden with

their belongings. Little Rondal set up between his mother and father on the buckboard, and Vernie held two younguns on her lap, Talcott and Kerwin, the baby. They stopped over with us for the night. Ermel laid out a salty brown ham in their honor. Isom, Ermel's son, and Rondal, who was the same age, glared at one another acrost the table. Isom screwed up his round face and stuck out his tongue, trying to establish his territorial rights. Rondal pursed his lips defiantly and made a fist. Isom laughed to show he didn't care and attacked a heap of fried apples.

"I seen you added to your store," Clabe said.

Ermel replied with a shrug.

"We're doin a right smart trade these days," said Annadel. She looked sideways at Ermel. "He dont like to talk about it."

"I dont like what they're doin," Ermel said. "I dont like makin money offn it. We was doin all right before all this here happened."

"Well, the folks need a place to trade," Annadel said mildly. "All else they got is them company stores, and them is dear. You should see their prices, Vernie. Twenty-five cent for a pound of coffee."

"I swan!" said Vernie.

"Them miners cant trade with me no ways," Ermel said grumpily. "They git paid in that company money, got to trade at the company store. Scrip, they call it. Aint no good to me. Most of my trade is with the other folks that come in here with them."

We moved out onto the front porch. The sun disappeared behind Peelchestnut, and the dense evening light lingered like it come from no source and was drawed gentle into the purple mountain. Annadel bounced her baby, Pricie, on her knee and sang beneath her breath, deedle-um deedle-um deedle-um day. Pricie had red hair, the color of the flames on the hearth.

"Look, girlie, at the lightnin bugs," Vernie crooned.

She caught two, and set one each on the bare arms of Kerwin and Pricie. The smooth baby skin glowed golden. The river rustled nearby. Rondal ran in circles before the front stoop. He stopped, teetered on tiptoe, and plucked a lightning bug from the dusk. Trapped in his fist, it lit the crevices between his fingers like a woodfire in a mysterious cave.

"Where yall goin to settle?" Ermel drew on his pipe.

"Back to the homeplace," said Clabe. "Or what's left of it."

"Winco."

"That's what them coal companies call it. Reckon I'll go down the mines there. Leastways we'll be back on our land."

"You aint goin to like what you see," said Ermel.

"Lookee here!" cried Isom. He pried open Rondal's fist and grabbed the lightning bug. Holding it careful by the head, he cut its body in half with his fingernail and stuck the luminous tail on the back of his middle finger.

"Lookee here! I got on a ring!"

Rondal flew at Isom and knocked him down. Isom kicked, and punched Rondal hard in the belly. Rondal yelled.

Clabe and Ermel hauled them up like sacks of meal.

"What the hell?" said Clabe.

Rondal sobbed. "He kilt my lightnin bug."

"I's just showin him how to make a ring," Isom said. "He lit into me."

"You should have asked Rondal first," said Ermel. "Now you beg his pardon."

"I beg your pardon," said Isom, his anger already spent.

Clabe shook his son. "Cryin over a damn bug! Now you tell him you're sorry."

"I'm sorry," Rondal said, not meaning a word of it.

I picked him up and held him in the light of the lantern hanging on the porch post. He looked ornery, his lips pressed together, his eyes long slits. I grinned.

"Danged ifn this boy dont put me in mind of Dillon."

"Law, I hope not," Vernie said fretfully. "Dillon's my kin by marriage, but he never was right in the head."

Two

RONDAL LLOYD

EARLIEST THING I RECALL FROM WHEN I WAS A BOY IS daddy coming in from the mines and taking his bath. It always scared me when he came in. It would be way after dark, and I'd be asleep with Talcott and Kerwin in the bed in the front room. Most nights he'd come in quiet, just lay himself down, coal dust and all, on a mat behind the cookstove in the kitchen, so as not to track dirt into the rest of the house. He would be back out before dawn anyway, so there was no need to bathe. But on Saturday, Mommy boiled water, rattled coal in the buckets to throw on the fire, pulled out the Number Three wash tub. I could never sleep through the noise. I always lay on the side of the bed next to the door, so I could hang my head over the edge and watch her. Daddy would stomp onto the back porch, peel off his boots, and bang them against the steps to knock off the crusts of mud and coal dust. He stripped off his clothes and left them in a heap for Mommy to wash the next day. She never washed his mine clothes with the rest of our things. Then Daddy came inside. His face and hands were black and shiny; the rest of him was pale and waxy like lard. The whites of his eyes were vivid. He tossed his pay envelope on the kitchen table.

"Snake again," was all he would say, meaning he hadn't been able to mine enough coal to pay off the bills at the company store, that he still owed for food and doctoring and his work tools and blasting powder, that his paycheck had a single wavy line where the money figures should have been. But I learned about those things later. At that age, I thought he meant he had seen a copperhead, and that was why his eyes looked so wild and frightful. I lived in terror of snakes.

Daddy sank slowly into the round tub of hot water, moaning as he went down. The tub was just large enough for him to sit in if he drew up his knees under his chin. The edge of the tub scraped his backbone just above his fleshless buttocks. Mommy stood over him pouring water from her pots and kettles. She scrubbed his face like he was one of us babies but never got all the coal dust off. His face was gray on Sundays like a newspaper photograph.

We lived in Winco, West Virginia, once our homeplace. American Coal Company owned our house. Richmond and Western Railroad owned our land. Mommy never talked about the old days, but Daddy told me how it used to be. Our cabin had set on the same piece of ground as the company store, which was three stories high, wood painted white with black trim, with stone steps trailing up to plate glass windows. "American Coal" was painted in gold on the glass door. Daddy said the cabin used to creak when it was windy, but the company store stood firm and unyielding. The railroad track, its ties oozing tar, ran through Mommy's vegetable garden. Most of the houses were built around the hill where the cow and sheep had grazed.

"The creek was clear as glass, and we used to git trout outen it, and bullfrogs," Daddy said. "You aint et till you had frog legs. Now the creek wont run clear till kingdom come, I reckon. We let it git away from us."

We never ate trout or frog legs, but mostly beans, biscuits, and gravy. The creek water was black with mine drainage and raw sewage, and acid stained the rocks orange.

On Sundays in the spring, Daddy and Mommy took us for walks up around the mountain, searching for wild mustard, poke, and creasy greens for supper. Mommy carried Kerwin on her back. She had broad cheekbones and brown hair pulled back in a bun so that the top of her head appeared flat. We followed the road the company had gouged out of the mountainside. Mommy said there had only been a path there once. The Negroes lived in the houses on that road. Their houses were tinier than the small ones the comʌany provided for white people. Each Negro family was crammed into two rooms of a four-room double house. The company never painted these houses, and so they were streaked with black. In summer the windows stood open and faded pink or green curtains flapped out in the breeze. The colored people had no porches, so they hunched on their front stoops when they wanted to take some air. Their outhouses were not built over holes, but hung out over the hillside. One night a man broke his arm when white boys toppled over the privy while he was inside.

Skinny yellow dogs barked and lunged at us as we trudged by those houses, and the colored people watched us silently from their stoops. Mommy always walked with her head down, never speaking, for she didn't like the colored people. Daddy said they never would have come if the coal company hadn't brought them in.

When we were past the colored houses, we'd start gathering greens. Talcott and I took turns holding the paper poke. Sometimes we went farther up the mountain to the Lloyd family cemetery. Daddy carried a scythe and cut away the weeds from the graves.

One day we climbed to the cemetery but were stopped by a gate and barbed wire fence strung across the road, and a sign which read, NO TRESPASSING. PROPERTY OF AMERICAN COAL.

We never went to the cemetery again.

I ATTENDED THE WINCO SCHOOL AND DID WELL. WHEN I was in the third grade, the teacher, Miss Radcliffe, invited the ten best students to her apartment for oatmeal cookies. She lived in the clubhouse, a building most of us had never entered. It was reserved for the unmarried teachers, nurses, and bookkeepers of the company.

Miss Radcliffe, tall and gray-headed, led us single-file up the stairs and ushered us into her rooms with the air of a genie revealing a treasure. We tiptoed across a rug Miss Radcliffe said was oriental and settled in miserable silence upon her purple-striped sofa and chairs. Miss Radcliffe smiled proudly as we craned our heads to take in the high cherry bookcases with glass doors, the purple-flowered wallpaper, the grandfather clock with gold trim on the door.

She served the cookies on bone-white china, and we had hot tea served in delicate cups with handles so small that even a child could not get a proper grip without being burned. Miss Radcliffe talked about the importance of an education, about how we had the obligation to raise ourselves above our parents and save our mountain people from ignorance. She reminded us that Abraham Lincoln had been as poor as we were. Then she gave us our assignments for Class Day, when our parents would visit the school. I was to memorize the first two paragraphs of the Declaration of Independence.

Cookie crumbs kept falling down the front of my overalls and I couldn't fish them out without spilling my tea. I was afraid they would drop on Miss Radcliffe's carpet when I stood up, and she would call me "slovenly," one of her favorite terms of disdain. When the grandfather clock struck four, we escaped. I wrapped three cookies in my bandana to share with my brothers after supper, and ran down the hill to our house. When I went inside, I smelled grease. Mommy was scraping the bacon leavings in the iron skillet for gravy. I scuffed my bare feet across the gritty wood floor, sprinkled with coal dust despite Mommy's daily scrubbings. Yellowing newspapers plastered the wall to keep out the cold.

Talcott and Kerwin wrestled on the bed in the front room.

"Yall lookee here," I said. "I got a surprise treat for after supper."

When they reached for the bundle I held it high above my head.

"After supper," I said.

I stuck the cookies beneath my pillow, dared them to touch it. Then to show I was not so strict, I hugged Talcott to me and tickled his belly. He wriggled and laughed. The back of his neck smelled of dried perspiration, sweet like a field in summertime. I sighed, lay back on the bed, and was glad to be home.

OUR HOUSE WAS ONE OF THREE THAT SAT IN THE BOTTOM beside Trace Fork. A narrow strip of grass and a fence of wood and wire separated the houses. Daddy put up a swing on the front porch where Mommy could sit of an evening and shuck the beans that she grew in the company garden. Ivy grew on one end of the porch, and flower boxes full of red and white petunias lined the bannisters. Coal dust speckled the flowers. Each day Mommy splashed the petals with water and gently wiped them clean with a dry cloth.

Daddy didn't work on Sundays. He would have liked to, because he was paid by the ton and would make more with an extra day's work. But the mine owner, Mr. Davidson, who was an Episcopalian, said the miners owed the Lord a day of rest. At first Daddy slept on Sundays, but as I grew older he spent most of the day drinking.

Sometimes C.J. Marcum, a friend of our family, paid the train fare to bring Talcott and me to Annadel. Annadel was seven wooden buildings put together so poorly they all leaned in opposite directions—Ermel Justice's store, stable and smithy, three private dwellings, and two taverns. The main town straddled the forks of Blackberry half a mile from the Justice farmhouse. C.J. and his mamaw, Missouri, still lived at the farmhouse at that time.

Talcott and I loved to play with Isom Justice and his sister Pricie. We climbed the mountain behind the Justice farm to a cave overlooking the railroad cut. Inside, we crouched together, the rough stone wall chafing our backs where we leaned. Isom told haint stories. When he stood close to the cave's mouth, framed by the sunlight beyond the darkness, the ridges and peaks of his curly mop of hair formed a silhouette like a miniature mountain range.

"Who-o-o!" he cried at the climax of the story. He rolled his head upon his neck and waved his arms. Pricie would scream with fear and delight. But Isom could never match the shrieking of the trains that roared through the cut and blew their whistle on the approach to Annadel. These were like the cries of evil fairies Mommy sometimes warned us about, the henchmen of the Unseelie Court seeking lost souls. Even I was frightened of the trains, but we couldn't bring ourselves to abandon the cave above the tracks.

Often we would swing across the fifty-foot precipice on grapevines. The vines, gray and scaly, creaked like an old wooden floor as they bore our weight out over the cliff. We launched ourselves from a moss-covered root, and if we misjudged our return, our bodies slammed into the broad oak that harbored the vine. Too shaken to swing out again, we must wait to be hauled up to safety.

I helped with the blacksmithing, taking turns with Isom cranking the blower. The blower kept the fire roaring, the fire where Ermel laid his slender lengths of black iron. The hot irons glowed orange and appeared fragile and clear as glass. Ermel plucked a length of iron with his tongs, laid it across the anvil and tapped it into a graceful curve with his hammer. Then he dipped it into a tub of cold water where it sizzled and spat before surrendering in a cloud of steam. A line of finished horseshoes hung beside the tub.

"You remember, boys," Ermel said, "anything will bend if you put enough fire to it. You remember that."

Sometimes C.J. and Ermel took us squirrel hunting. Isom and Talcott were better shots than me. Talcott, Ermel claimed, was the best he had seen. Besides the squirrels, we shot rabbits, and possums for baking with sweet potatoes. I would take some dressed back home to Mommy. It was the only meat we got except bacon and an occasional chicken or ham on holidays.

I loved to hunt, to tramp through the woods with my friends, to climb the mountains far away from the coal camps and wonder which mountain my Uncle Dillon lived on. But I didn't like to shoot the squirrels, though I was ashamed to admit it. Isom always whooped when he hit one. Sometimes I would have a squirrel in my sights and remember what it would look like dressed out, naked and long limbed like a skinny little man. I would miss on purpose and the others would tease me for being a bad shot. Then I would be mad and go out of my way to shoot another one, never wavering as I pulled the trigger, then feeling a wave of remorse when I retrieved the warm body. I dressed my squirrels quickly and cut them into pieces, for then they were not something that had lived, they were meat that would feed Mommy and put color in her cheeks.

We always ate a big supper before we went back to Winco, and we played music afterwards. I took my banjo that Uncle Dillon made me before he went off. Garmon

Tackett taught me to play, and Isom learned the fiddle from
Ermel. We liked especially to play "Sally Ann." But the
first song we learned was "Boil That Cabbage Down," because it was easy. Talcott, not yet big enough for the guitar,
sang along. Isom sawed the fiddle hard, elbow flying to and
fro. I learned to flail and drop my thumb. *Boil that cabbage
down, bake that hoecake brown.*

I took my banjo to school one day and picked and sang
"Cripple Creek" for Miss Radcliffe. I hoped she would let
me pick instead of reciting the Declaration of Independence. But she only said "How nice," and pressed her lips
tightly together.

C.J. Marcum used to come visit on Sundays, sit on the
front porch with me and sip iced tea he brought up from
Annadel.

"One of these days . . ." he was always saying. "One
of these days we'll git that land back. One of these days
you'll go off to school and come back and help your people."

C.J. and Miss Radcliffe were the only ones who talked
about "my people." I wasn't sure who "my people" were.
Were they my kin, most of them scattered when the land
was lost? Were they the old-timers who had been around
before the companies came in? What of the Italians and the
Poles and the Hungarians and the Negroes, hauled in by the
trainload to dig the coal? Were they my people too?

I studied the Italian children in my school. They were
different from me, talked different, smelled different. While
we brought biscuits spread with sorghum for our dinner,
they ate hard white bread soaked with olive oil. Their skin
was darker, their hair shiny and thick like a groundhog's
coat. They wore garlands of garlic around their necks, instead of asaphidity bags, to ward off colds. They were bigger than we were, for their difficulty in understanding
English caused them to be held back in school. Big Italian
boys beat me up on several occasions.

I asked C.J. if they would be returning to Italy "one of
these days." He rubbed his square chin.

"I reckon they's land enough for all," he said after a
time. "I like to think we can live together ifn we have to.

Hit wont never be the same, but we'll have to do the best we can."

C.J. hated the coal camps, had as little to do with them as possible. He rarely went to Jenkinjones, at the head of Pliny, although it was only two miles from Annadel. He passed through Felco, then the largest camp, on the train, and only came to Winco to see me. He usually brought a newspaper with him, the *Justice Clarion*, or the *Charleston Gazette* when he could get it. He said there were things going on in the world I would never learn in a coal operator's school, and was always pointing out stories about revolts in the Philippines or strikes in Massachusetts.

"I fret about you growing up here," he said. We sat on our porch swing. "Company runs everything, makes all your daddy's decisions for him, even gits his mail. Hit's like Russia with that there Czar. Your daddy aint a free man. He's like a slave."

"Aint nothing he can do about it," I said defensively. I didn't like to think I came from a cowardly daddy.

"Aint nothing he is doing about it except drinking," C. J. said. I shushed him, afraid Mommy might be listening and send him away. "Hit eases his back," I whispered.

C.J. pushed back and forth hard with his legs. I looked anxiously at the ceiling to see if the swing would hold. C. J. was a big man, over six feet tall and two hundred pounds, and his end of the swing tipped lower than mine so that I was jerked back and forth each time he pushed off.

"What you learning in school these days?" he asked.

"I'm a-memorizing the Declaration of Independence for Class Day. Can I practice on you? 'When in the course of human events . . .' "

I spoke proudly and confidently. I had already practiced before the class and Miss Radcliffe said I had "presence."

I stopped breathless with "the pursuit of happiness" and waited for his praise.

"That it?" he asked, like he was disgusted.

I nodded, hurt.

"Aint it just like them," he said. "Where's the rest of it? Where's the part about overthrowing the government?"

"I dont know nothing about that. Miss Radcliffe just wrote this here out for me on a scrap of paper."

"Declaration of Independence says we got a right to overthrow the government when it gits worthless," C.J. said grumpily. "I'd like to hear about that there sometime."

I wanted to hear that I had presence, but C.J. was in a bad mood the rest of the day. His parting words were a vow to bring me a copy of the complete Declaration to read.

In fact, his visits became less frequent after that. A company policeman told him he came too often; the company did not like outsiders to be such regular visitors. He was welcome only once a month, and then he must tell the police he was there.

C.J. TRIED TO SAVE ME FROM THE MINES. IT WAS LIKE HIM to think that he could. Daddy started taking me with him when I was ten. The law said you had to be fourteen, but the company looked the other way. Daddy thought if I helped, he might get out of debt to the company store. C.J. came down to argue with him.

"They aint never going to let you out of debt," he said. "The bastards is weighing you light as it is. They'll keep right on no matter how much coal that boy loads."

"It will help," Daddy insisted. "Denbigh says hit could mean as much as fifty cent more a day. And he's taking Talcott on as a breaker. We'll do a lots better."

"What about Rondal's schooling?"

"What about it? He cant eat them books."

"He could be a lawyer or a doctor someday."

"Someday. You're a-talking twenty year down the road about something might as well be a fairy story. Boy aint smart enough for that."

"That boy is plenty smart. You just aint around to see it. They got you stuck in that hole so you dont know what's going on in the world."

"Damn it, C.J., I know what it takes to live. Look at my woman. She aint nothing but skin and bones. She dont eat no supper half the time sos the younguns can have some. Schooling takes money, and I aint got none. Have you?"

My heart sank when C.J. shook his head.

"No, I aint got it right now. Maybe in a couple years. Ermel talks about setting me up with a store in Annadel."

"Then tell me about it in a couple years. Right now, I cant see wasting no more time on schooling when they'll just be teaching the boy what that boss wants him to know anyhow. Hit's got nothing to do with us that I can tell."

I didn't sleep that night, and hid under the bed the next morning when I heard Daddy get up. I hoped he would think I had run away. But Talcott was awakened by Daddy's swearing and said, "He was just here. The bed is still yet warm." Daddy looked all over, went out on the front porch and hollered, stuck his head under the house and rousted out the dogs. It was Mommy found me and dragged me out from under the bed. Daddy took the belt to me.

"Later we git started, longer we got to work. Otherwise theys one less biscuit on the plate. You git that through your head, boy."

I went to the mines with a sore back from his strap. I had on my first pair of boots. They were too large and rubbed blisters on my heels before we even reached the tipple. I told Daddy and he said, "We'll tell your mommy to put you on two pair of socks next time."

An early morning rain fell as we walked past the out-buildings—the engine house, the supply house, the black-smith's and new powerhouse, all built of solid brown blocks of stone with high windows of thick cloudy glass. Daddy and I held Talcott's hands. We took him to the breaker boys' shed. Here the chunks of coal came trundling in on conveyor belts, and Talcott would sit beside the moving line and pick out pieces of slate to be discarded. The shed was drafty and the roof leaked. Drops of water left hissing round craters in the coal dust on the floor. Some of the boys were already at their places, hunched on wooden boxes beside the conveyors like they had been working all day, even though the coal hadn't started to run yet. The boss man paced back and forth, a stick in his hand, ready to strike the shoulders of any boy who missed a piece of slate.

"He's going to hit me with that there stick," Talcott whimpered. He was only eight years old.

"You just do what the man says." Daddy sat him down on a stool. "Dont you back talk him. Mommy put a piece of dried apple pie in your dinner pail, special for your first day. Dont let nobody else git a holt of it."

We left quick before Talcott could commence to crying. Soon after we walked into the drift mouth, we passed the underground mule stable.

"Can I pet one of them mules?"

"Hell, no. We aint got time to pet no mules. This is the coal mine, this aint Ermel's damn farm. Besides, them mules is mean. They'll take your hand right off."

One mule was led out in front of us and I gave its flank a furtive pat. Its hair was sticky with sweat and dust. The skinner saw me and yelled, "Git back fore you git your head kicked in!" Daddy grabbed my arm and pulled me along behind him.

"Git offn that track. You got to git in the habit of watching out for cars, or you'll git run over."

I shrank against the ribs of the tunnel, walking so close that I kept bumping into the wall and staggering. I was afraid some invisible force would drag me into the path of an oncoming coal car. Once I looked back. The drift mouth was small, a milky gray circle that promised the dawn.

"Say goodbye to the light," Daddy said. "Hit will be dark when we come out of here."

It wasn't really light outside. But the weeds had smelled strong and green in the spring dew, mourning doves and meadowlarks had cried for the sun to rise, and a breeze ruffled the fine hair at the nape of my neck. Now there was no movement of air except the unnatural breath of the trap doors opening and closing in the tunnels. The smell was like the inside of our coal stove, but damp and decaying. Ahead of us, lamps bobbed like monstrous lightning bugs. Here and there an arm swung free from the darkness and disappeared again. I felt the mountain hunkered over us, pressing down, and it was hard to breathe.

"Daddy, I cant do this."

"Other younguns do it. You aint nothing special. You'll git used to it."

I knew there were other children in the mine. Boys at my school were always dropping out to go to work. I would lose sight of them for weeks, then they would reappear on a Sunday afternoon, some with chaws of tobacco bulging in their cheeks, looking hard and wise like little old men. I felt ashamed when I thought of them. Daddy was right. I was due no special privileges.

I knew the boy on the first trap door we came to. He was an Italian who went to first grade with me. His job was to pump the trap door all day long, keep the air moving. He had to open the door for the mule trains too, and keep out of the way so he wouldn't be run down. When the light from my cap reached his door, I saw he had been writing on it with slate. DO NOT SCARE THE BIRDS, he had scrawled, and beneath that a picture of a canary with fancy swirls on its wings. I raised my hand to him. He nodded briefly as he hauled on the door.

We walked almost two miles in. It was low coal so that Daddy and his buddy must always crawl, but I was short for my age and could walk if I bent over. I was called on to fetch and carry the tools, the auger, rod and black powder. Daddy stretched out on his belly and showed me how they would work.

"This is called our place and that there is the face of the coal. We drill in there with our auger and then we tamp in the powder and dirt and the needle. Tamp it in tight as a virgin's ass. Then we pull out the needle and stick the squib in the hole and light it. Then we git for cover on our hands and knees. You stay put out of the way while that's going on. You'll help us load the coal after it blows."

Daddy's buddy, Joe Kracj, crawled in and was listening but not understanding a word. He was a foreigner. I couldn't see his face in the dark because of the carbide lamp on his head, and it occurred to me that I might work with him all day and never recognize him outside the mine.

"You git down when the coal starts to blow," Daddy said. "Put your head down. You'll know hits a-coming when I holler out like this."

He leaned back and yelled, "Fi-i-i-yah! Fire in the hole!" He laughed. "I allays do the hollering cause hit just dont sound right when ole Joe does it."

I went back where Daddy showed me to wait while they drilled. I tried not to think of the mountain pushing down on us. To distract myself, I bobbed my head up and down and watched the light from my lamp skitter across the ribs and timbers. It was quieter than I had expected. Puffs of coal dust danced in my lamplight. I heard a steady plopping of water, like a banjo played with only one note. My eyes were heavy with the darkness. I longed to see the mine lit just once, to possess a magical eyesight that could see the men all at their places; Daddy crawling on his belly in the number four coal; others drilling upright in the number five; the skinners driving their mules; the trappers opening and closing the trap doors. I felt them trying to breathe together as one, in unison with my own heaving chest. The air was still and our breathing could not move it. The mountain pressed down, uneasy at the violation of its entrails. Daddy hollered. The air blew apart. I bounced onto my belly, covered my ears with the heels of my hands. The earth stroked my chest, my thighs.

Daddy emerged from a billowing black cloud.

"Come on, boy, time to break it up and load it."

I jumped up and hit my head on the roof.

When we left the mine at the end of the day I was so weary from shoveling coal that I could not walk very fast. When we came for Talcott, he could not stand up, but sat hunched over on his bench. Daddy picked him up and he cried out.

"Dont worry, son," Daddy said. "You'll git toughened up."

I heard Mommy crying in the kitchen that night before I slept.

"What am I supposed to do? I'm a-scairt to hug my own babies for fear of hurting them. I seen bruises all over Talcott's back where that boss man hit on him. Aint no mother supposed to let such things happen to her younguns."

"Shut up!" Daddy said. "I can take care of them boys."

I closed my eyes.

THE PAIN IN MY BODY SETTLED INTO A DULL ACHE. I WENT on. For the first time in memory, I spent time with my daddy. I came to realize that he was glad to have me with him. He had few ways of showing it. We seldom spoke underground. We were too busy with our picks and shovels, straining to load as many tons as we could, for the more we loaded, the more we were supposed to earn. But when we left the mine, Daddy sometimes pulled off my cap and gently rubbed his knuckles back and forth across the top of my head. He could never bring himself to touch me with the fleshy palms of his hands. But I knew he loved me.

It was Mommy I missed now. I only saw her on Sundays, except for a few moments in the early morning and late at night. Even on Sundays she seemed more distant. She went to church and stayed all morning, or worked in the garden and told me not to come bother her.

One Sunday when she was outside, I got the idea of reading the newspapers covering the walls. I missed C. J.'s visits with the *Justice Clarion*, missed the books at school. The newspapers were new; Mommy had put them up that very week. I brought a wooden chair from the kitchen and set it by the front door, lit a kerosene lantern, and stretched on tiptoe to read the headlines near the ceiling. When I had read halfway down the wall, I got down and stood on the floor, then hunkered down to study the articles near the baseboard. I worked my way around the room, even removed the calendar with the picture of Jesus given out by Ermel Justice's store so I could read beneath it. I was wedged in tight behind the black pot-bellied stove, my rear end pressed against the pipe, engrossed in an account of how European companies would soon be mining coal in China, when there came a sizzle and pop and a burst of acrid smoke. The heat from the lantern's chimney had set the wall on fire.

I squirmed from behind the stove, ran outside to the rain barrel, returned with a bucket of water. I dashed the water against the wall. A gaping black-edged hole was left in Mommy's clean newsprint wallpaper, but the flames were dead.

I went to find her in the garden.

"What you doing down here?" she said. She was clearing a patch for fall planting.

I told her what I had done. When she didn't answer, I said, "You going to switch me?"

"Why should I?" She chipped at the ground with her hoe. "You done gone in the mines. Aint no switch going to faze you none. Your daddy done made a man outen you. I cant do nothing with you now."

I wished she would whip me about the bare legs with a briar switch, like in the old days, then weep at the sight of the scratches, hug me and feed me an apple butter biscuit. But I was left lonesome to chastise myself.

ONE OF MY JOBS IN THE MINE WAS TO KEEP AN EYE ON OUR canary. We were always in danger from black damp, an odorless poison gas that collected in pockets where we blasted. We kept the bird in a small wooden cage at our place. If we hit a pocket of black damp the bird would fall over dead, and we would know to run. It didn't take long for black damp to kill a man.

I grew fond of our bird, and named him Butterball. He was a sooty gray color from the coal dust, but I could ruffle his feathers with the tip of my finger and reveal tufts of yellow down. I began taking his cage with me to the dinner place where we met other miners to eat our bait. The other boys teased me at first, but then they started to bring their birds too. We argued about whose bird was the best.

One of the Negro boys, Antoine Jones, had the biggest bird of all. He named him Tiger. The others agreed Tiger could lick any bird in the mine. But I wasn't so sure. Butterball was small, but he jumped around constantly and had a bald spot on his scalp from hitting his head on the top of the tiny cage. I pointed this out to the others.

"He's like a banty rooster," I said. "He's born to fight."

"My daddy raises fighting birds," Antoine countered. "He aint lost a cockfight in years. And he taught me a lot. Your bird couldn't beat Tiger."

Tommy Slater proposed a fight. The loser would have to give the winner his bait to eat. I was reluctant because bird fights were supposed to be to the death. But I couldn't back down since I'd done too much bragging. We unlatched the doors, stuck the cages together and shook them sideways until Butterball was coaxed into the bottom of Tiger's cage. He fluttered his wings and pranced nervously in one corner.

"Git up on the perch!" Antoine urged. "Git up there and fight, you coward!"

"He aint no coward!" I protested. "Tiger dont know what to do neither."

Tiger sat on the bar and craned his head.

All the boys started yelling. "Come on! Fight, you cowards! Sic him, Tiger!"

The birds just sat.

"We got to make them mad," Tommy Slater said. He picked up the cage and shook it. Tiger clutched the wooden perch and Butterball flew against the bars in a panic. "Come on! Fight!" Tommy shook the cage harder, up and down.

"Stop it!" I jerked the cage away from him. Tiger stood up in the bottom of the cage, wobbling like he was drunk. Butterball lay still, his head twisted sideways.

"He's dead!" Antoine shouted. "Your bird is dead! Tiger wins!"

He opened my dinner pail, sorting out the biscuits and side meat. I didn't care about the food. I reached into the cage and picked up Butterball as gently as I could. His head fell across my finger. I wrapped him in my bandana, concentrating hard on being neat so the others wouldn't see me cry. When they were busy talking, I slipped back to Daddy's place to be alone.

That night I took Butterball down by the creek to bury him. But I decided it would be cruel to put him back under the ground, so I made a pyre out of twigs, laid the stiff body upon it, and set it on fire. It burned quickly. A breeze bore away the gray flakes of ash.

THE NEXT DAY WE WENT INTO THE HOLE AFTER WE SHOT the coal, on our hands and knees, Joe Kracj first, then me, then Daddy. Like we always went in. Suddenly the air cracked; Daddy gripped my ankle and dragged me backwards; thunder filled my ears and a steaming slab of rock sat where Joe had been. I screamed. Daddy kept dragging me backward. I screamed again and again.

I sat beside a prop while they dug for Joe. Daddy sent me away but I crawled back in to see if I could help. A gritty fist stuck out from beneath the slab of rock. They broke the rock up and lifted it away. His arm was mashed flat and spread wide like the body of a frog run over by a wagon wheel. Daddy turned away, cussing, and saw me.

"Jesus God! Didn't I tell you to git?"

"Take him on home, Clabe," someone said.

He carried me out. The women had heard the whistle blow and gathered at the tipple to learn who was killed. Mommy was there. She came forward, her face wild.

"What are you doing down there?" She shook me. "I done lost you. Coal mine will git you sure. You're bound to git kilt. I seen it coming."

She kept shaking me. I tried to cry out for her to stop, but no words would come. Daddy carried me home, undressed me, bathed me and sat me before the stove. He paced up and down.

"It happens," he said. "Hit's one of them things. Joe's number was up, that's all. When it comes, you cant stop it, no matter where you are."

I opened my mouth to speak but still I could not. I was mute for three days. My tongue felt like it had swelled to twice its normal size, and it pained me to swallow. Talcott crept to where I sat beside the stove, plucked at my sleeve.

"Why cant you talk none, Rondal?"

I shook my head and concentrated on breathing, afraid that if I didn't think about it, I would stop.

C.J. heard what happened and came to see us.

"I'm setting up my store next month," he said to Daddy. "Drug store. Let the boy come to me. He can go to school, work the store in the afternoons, send the money back to you."

"What do you think, Vernie?" Daddy asked.

"I dont care," Mommy said in a flat voice.

"He's still yet my boy," Daddy said. "He dont want to leave home so young. Besides, I need his help. He cant make as much in no store."

"Twenty-five cent a day," said C.J. "Hit's something anyhow. Ask him. Ask him what he wants to do."

"He cant talk," Mommy said.

"Ah-h," I said. "Ah-"

They all looked at me.

"Ifn that boy leaves," said Daddy, "I'll take Talcott in. Hit comforts me to have my boys around."

C.J. walked to the door. "You got to talk, Rondal. You got to say what you're going to do. Hit's your choice."

I motioned for a pencil to write with.

"No," C.J. said. "You got to say it."

So I tongued the words as though speaking a new and exotic language.

"C.J." I said. "C.J. Take me."

Talcott ran away from home the day after I left. Daddy found him below Felco and wore him out with his strap.

Three
CARRIE BISHOP

YOU HAVE SEEN OLD PHOTOGRAPHS, BROWN AND SWEET-looking, as though dipped in light molasses. My memories of the Homeplace in Kentucky are like that. Sweet, bitter-sweet.

When I was ten years old, Ben Honaker lent me his copy of *Wuthering Heights*. I loved it, just for the name of it, even before I read it. It has the sound of a lost and precious place, Wuthering Heights. I learned from that book that love and hate are not puny things. Nor are they opposed. Everything in this world that is calculating and bloodless wars against them both, wars against all flesh and blood, earth and water.

Even now, when I whisper that name, Wuthering Heights, it is the Homeplace I see. My people crowd around me, Ben and Flora, Miles, Daddy, Aunt Jane and Aunt Becka. And I see myself, waiting for Heathcliff, waiting for some-one to come from outside, bearing with him both passion and menace.

I knew he would come from the outside, because Daddy and Aunt Becka said I would never find a man on Scary Creek or Grapevine. I was too forward, they said, too stub-born. I was not pretty like Flora. Flora looked like the princess in children's stories old folks tell—white skin, rosy cheeks, and black hair. She took after Daddy and Aunt Becka's side of the family, which was part Cherokee. I took after my dead mother's side. Freckles splashed my face, my shoulders, my arms. My nose was a trifle large, my hair drab brown.

"Carrie takes after the Mays," Aunt Becka said to Daddy one night when we were in bed before the hearth and supposedly asleep. She was Daddy's oldest sister. "She's even got her Papaw Alec's nose, poor child. Hit wouldnt look so bad on Miles."

I couldn't sleep for worrying and went straightway up the river the next morning to the Aunt Jane Place. Aunt Jane May lived at the mouth of Scary Creek where it flowed into Grapevine. Aunt Jane was both my grandmother and my great-aunt. She was Daddy's aunt who had married Alec May, and their daughter Tildy was my mother.

I cried out my hurt feelings to her. She sat composed, her hands laid flat on her lap so the blue veins stood up in ridges.

"Dont you pay no mind to your Aunt Becka," she said. "That woman will wrap her tongue around any kind of silliness. You're the picture of your mother, and I love to gaze on you for it."

"Am I ugly?"

"Course you aint ugly. You favor your Papaw Alec a heap, too. His face had character. They wasnt no forgitting what he looked like, no more than you could forgit the mountains. When I stand on my porch and look at those mountains, I still yet see him everywhere."

Uncle Alec had been dead for a long time, killed in the War Between the States.

"You think he's a ghost?" I asked. "You think he still yet comes around here, and that's why you cant forgit him?"

Aunt Jane smiled. "Maybe. Sometimes I feel him close. But ifn he's a ghost, he's a contented one. He walks for joy, not for disquiet."

I began to watch for him then. I thought he walked abroad in the fog. The mists rose from the river each morning to cling to the mountaintops, and in the evenings, after a rain shower, patches of fog ran like a herd of sheep up the hillsides. I would go out then, breathe the air and feel it clean the bottom of my lungs. A path wandered behind the cabin down the riverbank. Grapevine was broad and green, slow running, never more than waist deep on a grown man save during the spring thaw. I waded into the water, my skirt hiked to my thighs. Silver explosions of trout churned the water and minners darted fearlessly about my legs. I came abreast a stand of cattails and halted. The sweep of Grapevine curved away north, its path to Shelby and the Levisa hidden by the far mountains layered one after another, the mist dancing up their flanks. Every way I turned the lush green peaks towered over me. Had it been winter or spring, they would have been iron gray, or dappled with pink and white dogwood, sarvis, and redbud, but always they would be there, the mountains, their heights rounded by the elements like relics worn smooth by the hands of reverent pilgrims.

I swept my arm up and flung water like beads of glass.

"Hey, Uncle Alec," I whispered.

MY SISTER FLORA WAS SIXTEEN WHEN BEN HONAKER CAME to teach. She was the oldest pupil, and the tallest. She sat in the last desk of her row so she wouldn't block anyone's view. The new teacher noticed her right away. He was only twenty years old and Scary Creek was his first school, yet he moved gracefully between his desk and the chalkboard as though he had always belonged there. He was tall and slender, his hair was the color and texture of corn silk, and thin on top. He told us he had come from just over the mountain on Tater Nob Creek, that he had been to the normal school at Louisa. I was inclined to fall in love with him, but noticed how he kept watching Flora. I took stock of my tender years and decided it would be nice to have a new brother, for I was tired of Miles.

On that first day, Ben Honaker read aloud the "Midnight Ride of Paul Revere," and his voice rose and poured forth a torrent of heroic deeds. When he finished, he closed his book with a satisfied thump and smiled at Flora. During the arithmetic lesson she finished quickly and he checked her work approvingly. He asked her to help the younger students. Later he gave us a geography lesson. He spoke of the fabled land of Persia where the earth quaked and buildings and rocks tumbled down about the heads of the people. I tried in vain to imagine an earthquake on Grapevine, the river roiling, the mountains moving like bones beneath the skin. But it seemed impossible that our land would turn on us.

He held Flora back after the others had been dismissed. I sat on the stoop to wait for her.

"Why are you still in school?"

"Because I like to learn." Flora's voice was soft and shy.

"A girl as smart as you should be off to the normal school, or maybe even to Berea."

"I dont want to go way far off from home. Dont want to teach neither. Hit would upset me too much when the younguns did wrong. When I was helping them with their lessons today, I couldnt stand to have them make a mistake. I felt like hit was my fault. And I couldnt never fuss at them."

"What do you like to do?"

"I like to grow flowers. I like to take care of the animals. And I like to read. I like to read a pretty word and say it out loud. Me and my brother and sister all likes to read."

I took this as my cue to step inside the door and call attention to myself.

"That there is Carrie," said Flora.

"Oh, yes. Carrie likes geography."

I grinned. "I like to hear all them outlandish ways folks do."

"Would you girls like to borrow some of my books?"

He opened a chest in the corner, just an old battered trunk, but a treasure chest to us. Flora chose a book of poems by Keats, and I picked *Wuthering Heights* because I liked the name. We hugged them to our breasts as we walked the two miles to the Homeplace. The trees were beginning to take on their autumn colors, frosted with bright reds and yellows as though spattered with wet paint.

"Florrie, that teacher is sweet on you."

"Naw," Flora said, and blushed.

But it was true. Ben Honaker wasted no time in courting her. Soon he took supper with us three times a week, and walked Flora to church on Sundays. I was glad to have him around, for he was a contrast to our daddy, Orlando Bishop. Daddy was a cold, quiet man; he was sparing with his praise and his expectations were high. He took for granted that we would do well with our chores and our schoolwork. Anything less than our best was reason for disdain. He seldom rebuked us with words, but his black eyes would be contemptuous. There was no approaching him then.

Miles was the oldest of us children. He detested farming and barely tolerated his chores. Daddy knew it and they clashed often. When they were at it, the rest of us knew to be silent.

Miles hated to hunt, was uncomfortable with guns even though he was a fairly good shot. He didn't mind killing things so much, but would rather be curled up with a book. Daddy would make him go anyway, and if he came back empty-handed, would berate him before us all at the dinner table. I longed to go hunting, but Daddy only laughed when I mentioned it.

"Aint fitting for a girl," he'd say.

I knew that many of the girls at school could handle guns, but that didn't convince him. He said we were raised better than that.

Miles and I finally came to an agreement. He would secretly teach me to shoot. Then I would take over his hunting chores. After that, Daddy was not so mean to him, but Miles was still restless and dissatisfied. At seventeen he was done with Scary Creek School. He should have gone out to get himself a piece of land, or married and settled in on the Homeplace. But he claimed he wanted to leave. He wanted to go to Berea but was afraid to ask Daddy about it.

Ben came to his rescue. He acknowledged there was nothing wrong with a man who did not like to farm and said as much to Daddy. To our surprise, Daddy said mildly that Ben may be right and that Miles could go if he wanted. Miles was admitted to Berea for the next year. He was a great deal easier to live with after that.

ONLY AUNT BECKA WAS UNHAPPY WHEN BEN AND FLORA announced their engagement. It wasn't that she disliked Ben. He praised her cooking, and she enjoyed serving his favorite meal of chicken and dumplings. She declared that Flora could do no better for herself, if she must marry. In other words, Ben Honaker was just fine, for a man.

Aunt Becka was married once, for a month. It was well before my time, but I had the story from Aunt Jane. The man carried Aunt Becka away to Chloe Creek in the next county, and she showed up on the front porch of the Homeplace one month later, having walked all the way and slept in the open for three nights, the last in a pouring rain. Aunt Becka took her own name back again. It was said later that her husband took off for Arkansas or thereabouts, where he no doubt became a bigamist.

"Was he mean to Aunt Becka?" I asked Aunt Jane.

"Law, no, child. He was just more man than your Aunt Becka wanted."

Aunt Becka and Aunt Jane did not care for one another. That was why Aunt Becka lived with us at the Homeplace instead of the Aunt Jane Place where there would have been more room. Also Aunt Becka claimed we needed a mother. I would have preferred Aunt Jane or Flora for a mother, but Flora was always hurt for Aunt Becka's sake when I said it. I was surprised then, when I found her crying in the loft after her engagement announcement. She said Aunt Becka had frightened her.

"How'd she fright you?"

"I cant talk about it," Flora sobbed. "You aint old enough."

"Well, then, I know what hit's about. She was telling you scairdy things about men, werent she?"

When she wouldn't answer, I knew I was right.

"You aint got no call to be scairt of Ben, do you? He's just Ben."

She sniffed. "Course I aint scairt of him."

"Dont pay Aunt Becka no mind," I said. "Aunt Jane says men are just too much for her."

"Aunt Jane shouldnt say such things to you."

"But hit's true. And you know why? Hit's because Aunt Becka aint got no hair between her legs."

"Carrie Lee! Why ever would you say such a thing?"

I knew to shut up, that this piece of information should have been kept to myself. I had learned it by accident. We never saw Aunt Becka naked, for she jealously guarded her privacy. The Homeplace consisted of one large room and a smaller loft reached by steps on the outside of the cabin. We children slept in the loft during the warm months. In winter we spread our featherbeds on the floor before the

hearth and wrapped ourselves in our mother's multicolored
quilts. Daddy slept in the four-poster in one corner. If
strangers stayed overnight, we got under the covers and
pulled off our clothes. But if it was just us, we stripped
down without a thought—until we started growing hair. It
happened first to Miles, then to Flora, and I waited expectantly for it to happen to me. Then I saw Aunt Becka.

Aunt Becka's bed stood in the corner beside the supper
table. At night she draped quilts from the rafters so she
could undress alone. Even in the heat of summer she slept
behind the wall of quilts. She was equally secretive about
her bath. We had to all troop outside when she was bathing.
In good weather we sat on the front porch until she was
done. In the wintertime we saved our outside chores until
Aunt Becka's Bathtime, as we came to call it. It was then I
saw her naked. Daddy and Miles were cleaning out the sta-
bles and Flora was gathering eggs. I sneaked to the window,
scratched a clearing on the frosty pane with my fingernail,
and looked in. I didn't expect to see anything unusual; I did
it because Aunt Becka didn't want me to. Then I saw that
Aunt Becka was hairless.

At first I thought this was merely interesting. But soon I
began to worry. I was as bald as she was. Suppose I didn't
grow any hair. Suppose that was why Aunt Becka didn't get
along with men. I confided my fears to Aunt Jane.

"Law," said Aunt Jane, "hit's just the way she's made,
child. And you're too young to be fretting about sprouting
hair. Hit will sprout when the time comes."

We were in Aunt Jane's root cellar, picking preserves for
supper, for I would be eating with her. The jars gleamed in
the lantern light. They held peaches, pears, sauerkraut,
green beans, tomatoes, jams.

"Pickled corn," I suggested.

"If hit's sour, I'll eat it," she agreed.

She didn't say any more about Aunt Becka then, but when
we were eating she said, "Your Aunt Becka is funny turned,
but she's a good woman. And she's kin. Aunt Becka cant
help the way God made her, and she has a right to be the
way she is. I should never said things about her to you
before, and I wont never say them again. As for you, you
just be like your own self. And ifn Aunt Becka dont like it,

you and her might not git along. But God help the stranger tries to hurt you, cause Aunt Becka would tear them limb from limb. Whip anybody tried to harm a hair on your head. Dont never forgit it.''

I remembered her words after I spoke to Flora, and was sorry. I thought of them again the night before Flora's wedding. It was Old Christmas Eve, and Aunt Becka sat us before the fire, as she always did, fed us roasted apples, and told us how the animals in the barn, the cows and mules, knelt in homage before the Baby Jesus on that night, and spoke to one another. I had not noticed before how wrinkled Aunt Becka was becoming. She sat beside Aunt Jane, placid, and they were like the lion and lamb reclining together for a time. It pleased me to think of our animals in the barn waiting together for Old Christmas, kin like we were. We were flesh of one another's flesh, and we would live together until we died, then we would be together in Heaven. Mother would be with us as well. Heaven would be a place very much like Grapevine, lacking only an angel of death.

I couldn't sleep that night for thinking about it, and of Ben and Flora, soon to be wed. When I was certain everyone slept I crept from bed, pulled on my wool dress, and wrapped myself in a quilt. Outside, falling snowflakes struck my cheeks. It was a pitch dark night but I knew my way to the barn and never once stumbled. I lit the lantern hanging inside the door. The animals shook their heads and their gargantuan shadows leaped like a flight of blackbirds.

I shivered from the cold. A heap of fresh hay stood in an empty stall and I went to it, burrowing deep, but with the animals still in my sight. It was nearly midnight. I craned my neck and waited for the slow sinking of the heavy animal bodies. When the time came I was sleepy. The rustling of the cows and mules as they went to their knees, and the sighs that escaped them as they shifted their weight, seemed to me to be the voice of God.

ONE WINDY NIGHT IN MARCH THERE CAME A POUNDING ON our door. I had been sound asleep and didn't quite wake up. I heard someone say, ''mortal ill.'' Later Daddy carried me to Aunt Becka's bed.

"They's a sick boy needs to lie beside the fire," Aunt Becka whispered.

"M-m-m," I answered, turned over, and slept again.

I saw the boy the next morning, before I went to school. He was wrapped in quilts like a cocoon so that only the top of his head showed. All I could tell was that he was black-haired. His breathing was slow and raspy. Aunt Becka made an onion poultice.

"Is he going to die?" I asked.

"Hush," she said, and nodded toward a man sitting forlornly at the table. "We aim to do everything for the poor youngun we can."

"Who are they?" I whispered.

"Drummer and his boy. Now you go on down to the Aunt Jane Place. She's making your breakfast. And you go there after school, too."

"Yes, ma'am. I'll say me a prayer."

I dreamed about him all day, a black-haired waif like Heathcliff at Wuthering Heights. He would be handsome, dashing, and I would be his Cathy.

Flora came in the next morning after sitting up with him through the night.

"I'm afraid the pneumonia is going to carry that boy off," she said wearily. "His fever aint broke yet and he's hot as a stove. Hit's got to wear him out. He's a fighter, though. Hit pains me to hear how hard he tries to breathe."

I was so distracted in school that Ben gave up on me and sent me back to the Aunt Jane Place. Flora was asleep and Aunt Jane was gone, so I walked to the Homeplace. Aunt Jane stood at the well.

"Help me fetch some water," she said. "The fever appears to be breaking."

HIS NAME WAS ALBION FREEMAN, AND HE WAS FOURTEEN years old. He was to stay with us all the spring and summer. His daddy was bound for Ohio and back to sell his wares— drumming, we called it. But the doctor from Shelby said Albion must stay in bed at least a month, maybe longer, to guard against a fever of the heart. Albion's father decided to come back through Kentucky in the fall and get his son.

He gave Aunt Becka a new cooking pot for the boy's keep, and promised Albion would be a good hand to work once he was better.

Albion cried when his father left. I was disappointed, because it did not seem brave of him. Heathcliff would not have cried. Nor was Albion handsome. He was slight of stature to the point of scrawniness. Aunt Becka guessed that he had often been hungry. His hair was unkempt, "nappy," Aunt Jane called it. He had a gap between his front teeth, and one was the color of used dishwater. When he grinned I was put in mind of a chipmunk. But his eyes, at least, were fine, brown and warm as coffee.

He was shy with us for a long time. Flora was the best with him. We sat and listened while she drew him out to talking, her voice low and gentle. He said his mother had died only a few months earlier, also of a fever. They buried her on a hillside. No, he didn't know where exactly; it was in Harlan County. They had been on the road since he was eight years old. His daddy lost a farm on Blackberry Creek in West Virginia.

"Daddy cant afford no land of his own. Says he cant work for nobody else. So, he's a drummer."

"How do you go to school?" Flora asked.

"Aint never been."

"Cant read at all?" asked Ben.

"No, sir."

"I can teach you."

Albion traced a quilt pattern with his fingertip.

"Dont know as how I'm anxious to learn."

"Why ever not?" Aunt Becka said sharply.

He ducked his head. "I'm afeard I'll learn so much new things I'll forgit what I know. I know lots of stories and all. Got em stored in my head. New things might run em clean out."

"Aint you wanting to learn about new places?" I asked.

"I been lots of places," he said softly. "I want my own place. Maybe then . . ." His voice trailed off.

"I reckon that's enough questions," Flora said. "We're a-wearing this poor fellow out."

He smiled at her gratefully, sank back onto his pillows, and closed his eyes.

He stayed in his bed until barefoot weather in May. Then one day he wobbled outside, sank down onto the front stoop and turned his face up to the sunshine. Soon he was walking around, and by June he was helping with the chores. Mostly he worked with me, caring for the animals and thinning the corn.

Our cornfield covered five acres of bottom land between the Homeplace and the Aunt Jane Place. I moved ahead of Albion along the rows, stooped to pull the smallest shoots and toss them aside. I paused often to wait for him because hoeing was slower work. Albion put me in mind of the scarecrow spread-eagled on its high post. His shirt was too big and slipped off one shoulder as he hoed. His bony, pointed elbows punched the air. He sang as he hoed about a noble lady who left her rich husband to run off with the gypsies. *I wont go back, my dearest dear, I wont go back, my honey, for I'd rather have a kiss from gypsum's lips than all your land and money.* He sang of Barbry Allen and how she spurned her lover so that he died brokenhearted, and how Barbry died soon after. *Daddy, Daddy, dig my grave, oh dig hit deep and narrow, young Jemmie died for love today, and I shall die tomorry.* A thorn grew from Barbry's grave, and a rose from her sweet lover's, and the two twined together. That's how the rose got thorns, Albion said.

"Florrie loves roses," I said. "She grows them rambling roses all over the front porch. But I like weeds best. They're all wild and tangled up."

He grinned. "I like weeds, too. Whole big fields of iron-weed." When we finished in the cornfield, I sat down and stuck out my legs. The dust was high up on my calves and gritty between my toes.

"Aint time yet to git the cows," I said. "Let's go fishing."

Albion was the only boy I knew who apologized to the fish he caught. He smiled at the first tug on the line, took an uneasy pleasure in hauling in his catch, then crooned, "Poor thing," at the fish flopping on the line. Once he caught a fish that had swallowed the hook and bled from the mouth. He cried out and dropped it.

"Kill it! Hit's a-suffering terrible! Wont you do something, Carrie?"

I tugged, but the hook was caught solid. "Lay it out and it will die by and by," I said. But he was still upset and fretted so about the pain it was in that I began to cry. I pulled again and the hook came out with another gush of blood. I tossed the fish back into the river and it swam feebly away, trailing a pink stream behind it. I wiped my slimy hands on my overalls.

"Maybe hit will live," I said.

He told me I was brave, brave enough for ten men, and I felt better. It was clear to me now that he wasn't Heathcliff. But I liked him anyway.

We fished a lot that summer, and swam in Grapevine, and called the cows home in the gentle evenings. Albion and I became inseparable. I even coaxed him into starting school in August when the corn was laid by. He expected his father in October, he said. There was no sense in starting school. Ben promised he would be reading by then. Still he was reluctant, until I pointed out that if he didn't go to school we wouldn't have nearly so much time together. He agreed then.

"I dont reckon I'd mind learning to read the Bible," he admitted. "I heard it read out loud and hit sounded fine."

One day after school in late August we walked the creek, our dinner pails filled with apples we had gathered along the way. Aunt Becka had promised to bake apple pies. The rocks were slippery beneath our bare feet and we fell often, usually on purpose, and sat down backwards in the middle of the stream. Sometimes we spilt our pails and chased the apples down little waterfalls on our hands and knees. We managed to salvage most of them, and swung full pails as we followed the path that skirted the cornfield and crossed the fallow field behind the barn.

Then we heard a distant cry of "Mad dog! Mad dog!"

We froze and Albion clutched my arm.

I saw Miles near the barn. He held a shotgun and waved his arm wildly. "Run for the trees! Climb a tree!"

Albion pointed. "There!"

A yellow dog trotted toward us from the riverbank. It snapped at the air.

"Oh, lordy!" I dropped my pail and ran. But I stopped,

for Albion was not with me. He stood rigid and watched the dog.

I ran back to him. "Come on!" I screamed, and tugged at his arm.

"I can't!" He sounded about to choke. "I'm scairt to turn my back on it!"

The dog was so close I could see the white flecks about its jaw.

"Run, damn it!" he whispered fiercely. He was crying. He broke away from me, walked toward the dog. It saw him, broke into a loping run. Miles's gun cracked, the dog's hind legs kicked the air, and it lay still.

Miles ran up, knocked Albion down, stood over him.

"You durned fool! You nearly got my little sister kilt!"

Albion stood up. Miles pushed him down again.

"Miles, you stop that!" I yelled. Flora and Aunt Becka ran out of the house. Aunt Becka gathered me into her arms and Flora helped Albion up.

"You aint being fair, Miles," she said. "He put hisself between her and the dog. I seen it from the window."

Miles trembled all over. "What if I'd missed? I'd never have forgive myself. Hit's been a year since—"

He broke off and turned away. It was a year since he'd been hunting, I knew.

When Daddy came home from helping Clinard Slone build a fence, he praised Miles to the high heaven. He examined the carcass before he burned it, said, "You took him clean, son. Couldn't have done better myself. We're a goin to miss you around here."

Miles looked frightened instead of pleased. He was to leave for Berea in a week.

"Maybe I should stay here," he said feebly.

"Dont be silly," Ben said quickly. "Hit's only school. Aint like you wont never be back. Besides, I'm here now. We'll be just fine."

At suppertime, Albion was nowhere to be seen. Aunt Becka set his portion back in the warming closet, and I went to look for him. I found him beside the river, seated upon a rock, his head buried in his arms. When I spoke his name he turned his face away.

"We had a good supper," I coaxed. "Trout and fried

taters and cornbread. And apple pie with cream. Aunt Becka saved yourn still yet warm if you come on.''

When he did not answer, I was uncertain what to do.

"You weren't no coward," I whispered. "You was brave. Miles was just het up is all. He was scairt to think hit was all on his shoulders.''

I eased up behind him, slipped my arms beneath his and wrapped them around his chest. I felt him stiffen and nearly let him go, but when he moved, the ribs of his thin chest rubbed against my bare arms and I felt the hurt in him. I tightened my hold and rested my cheek against his back.

"That poor old dog," he said. "He couldn't help it if he were mad. I looked him right in the eye. He weren't hating us. He was suffering. How could God let it be?''

It was not in my nature to chide him for questioning God's purposes, as Aunt Becka might have done, so I said nothing. He rubbed the back of my hand with the tips of his fingers.

"I was scairt," he said. "Hit was like if I turned my back, he'd be on me right then. But if I kept a-staring at him, I might see where he hurt. I didn't want him kilt.''

"Florrie says you got a tender heart.''

He sighed. "Florrie is good to me. I wisht I could stay here all the time.''

We watched the river. Mosquitoes teased the surface of the shallows and minners flicked back and forth, chased by their shadows. Albion tore open a milkweed pod and scattered the soft white insides. Some of the seeds were borne away on the water. Others flew on the wind like pale fairies and settled in the brake to take root.

IN OCTOBER, FARRIE WHITT CALLED FOR A CORN SHUCK-ing. Already the women of Scary and Grapevine were putting up their fruit, vegetables, and apple butter. Now the corn would be shucked and stored for the animals and for grinding into yellow meal. In November the hogs would be killed, strung up by their hind legs and slit down the belly, the bloody carcasses festive against the gray mountainsides. The slabs of meat would be salted and hung to smoke, and the winter could be faced with security.

Of all the shuckings, I liked Farrie Whitt's the best because he lived at the head of Scary Creek and so the journey was longer and more adventurous. We set out in the wagon just after noon. Halfway up Scary, shadow swallowed the sunlight. Here the mountains closed in and smelled strong and damp, like a wet animal. At the head of the holler, they gave way grudgingly, offering Farrie's family their bit of earth. Until then, for the last mile and a half, there was no bottom land, only the creek and the rutted road twisting side by side, finally merging into one. The sun did not touch this place save when it stood directly overhead, and in winter the ice grew thick on the rocks even during the thaws. This was my favorite part of Scary. I turned on my belly when the wagon rode the creek and watched the churning water through the cracks between the floorboards. The mountains hovered close and sheltering, like a quilt upon my back.

When we arrived at the Whitts', I took Albion to the molassy making. This was the province of the old men. Their hands were too stiff with the rheumatism to shuck corn, so they sat on their chairs beside the sorghum pan and wielded their skimmers, pausing to stoke the fire. The green juice, squeezed from the cane at the wheel, was poured into one end, where it grew a thick skin like the scum on a stagnant pond. Clyde Baisden skimmed the top and sent the foaming juice on its way through the labyrinth of the pan. By journey's end, the sorghum was a thick golden syrup helped along by old Homer Whitt's wooden paddle.

"This uns a light batch, younguns," said Homer. "Have a taste."

We stuck our fingers beneath the pan where the molasses dripped slowly into a bucket. It was warm, sticky and light as Homer promised, sweet with a tangy green flavor. Mighty fine, we agreed. We lingered, for the fire beneath the pan warmed the whole area, until supper lured us away.

The women set out the food on tables inside the cabin: fried chicken and salty ham, mashed potatoes swimming in butter, green beans cooked with hunks of fatback, hot pickled corn, biscuits, yellow cornbread, boiled cabbage, sweet potatoes, green poke sallet in bacon grease, fresh kale, squirrel meat with dumplings, venison steaks, groundhog, red-eye gravy, milk gravy, stack cakes, apple pies. Albion piled his plate several inches high, a look of reverence on his face. He followed me outside and we sat down against Farrie Whitt's watering trough. When we were done eating, it was difficult to stand up.

Afterwards the older women cleared away the food and washed the dishes, and the old men returned to the molassy making with a jug. The rest of us went to the bonfire near the heaps of corn and set to work stripping the silk and parchment shucks from the ears. The boys worked especially fast so that they might be the first to find a red ear and steal a kiss from the girl of their choice. Amos Preece, a boy from Scary School, pulled so hard and carelessly at the shucks that he sometimes snapped the ear in two. He was sweet on Ila Mae Slone and had never declared himself, but everyone knew it, and Ila Mae neglected her own shucking to watch the cobs as he uncovered them.

"Red ear!" Vance McCoy called, but he did not have it. It was Albion, sitting astraddle a milk bucket, who turned the dark thing this way and that in his hands.

"Hit's the drummer's boy!" They laughed and teased. "Who's your girl here, drummer? Reckon you got one in every holler."

He looked around briefly and ducked his head. He was shy with girls; they laughed at school about how quiet he was, how homely. He daydreamed often, so that he did not hear when Ben called upon him. He was not good at the games the boys played. He was a stranger to Scary Creek, he came from beyond, bearing some taint of misfortune, and everyone knew it.

"Kiss Clary Leach," someone yelled. "That's Miles's girl. That'll fetch him back from Berea."

"Kiss me," Ila Mae Slone said. She made a face to show how distasteful she would find it and broke into gales of laughter. Albion stared at the ground, frozen to his seat, holding the ear out at arm's length as though it were cursed.

"Kiss Florrie," I whispered. "Hit don't matter that she's married. Ben wont mind."

He stirred, set the red ear at my feet.

"I dont want to kiss Florrie," he said.

He leaned over and brushed my cheek with his lips. I

shivered, folded my hands in my lap and tried to look like
a lady.

Everyone except Ben and Flora hooted with laughter.

"Carrie's a LITTLE girl! Cant you kiss nobody but a
little girl?" Amos Preece taunted.

Albion stood up. "You're just jealous," he said. "That
girl you was going to kiss has got more mouth than a bull-
frog."

He picked up his bucket, gathered an armload of corn,
and walked away.

"Big for his britches, aint he?" Ila Mae said. "And him
ugly as a mud pie."

I hesitated before I followed him, for it seemed to me a
choice from which there would be no retreat. They belonged and he did not, and to leave their circle and the
warmth of it would mean that I possessed the power to cast
myself into the outer darkness where moved the misfits, the
lost, and the brave.

But I followed him. His kiss had marked me, and I was
called out. I found him near the smokehouse, sat beside
him and spread my skirt daintily around me. We shucked
corn by ourselves for quite a while, never saying a word.
Then Ben came and sat with us.

"Yall done sulking yet?" he asked.

"We aint sulking," I retorted. "We just dont want to be
round no mean people."

"Aint you being a little hard on em? Most of em didnt
mean no harm. Amos was smart-alecky, but Albion was
right, Amos is just mad because he didn't git the red ear
first. And you know how Ila Mae is. She's allays sour as if
she ate a bait of persimmons."

I giggled and looked at Albion.

"I reckon we ought to go back," he said. "I shouldn't
have got so riled."

"I didn't say that," Ben said. "You had a right to be
riled. But they aint no reason to be all by yourself because
of it. You're like kin now. Come on back and set with us."

Flora smiled at our return and indicated we were to sit
beside her. Most of the corn was shucked and Farrie Whitt
told a haint story around the bonfire. We ate popcorn, and
Aunt Jane brought down taffy that the women had pulled

from the new molasses. I looked around the circle at the smooth faces glowing in the firelight. Then I thought, what agony to truly be cut off from them.

We stayed past midnight. Aunt Jane, old and tired, took Albion and me to the wagon long before, and snuggled in the back with us beneath piles of quilts. Albion and I did not sleep. We lay side by side, our faces so close that I could see the whites of his eyes even in the dark.

"How did you lose your homeplace?"

"The railroad took it."

"How?"

"They just took it."

I had never heard of such a thing, but knew Albion was not one to lie.

"How can that be?"

"They wasnt nobody to stop them. Now I aint got no place. Aint no place to be buried when I die. Just be out on the mountain somewheres, like Momma. Wont nobody know where I am."

"Why dont you stay here?"

"My daddy wouldnt stay. He vows to go back to West Virginia some day and settle. But he aint got enough money yet."

"Where will yall go when he comes back?"

"We go down toward Georgia in the winter. Hit's a bit warmer."

It hurt me to think of him with only his father, hungry and cold, most likely.

"Will you come back?"

"I hope so. I'll come back and marry you when I'm bigger. And I'll git me some land, maybe here in Kentucky."

"And we'll build us a house out of wood with a big porch, and paint it white."

"And have six younguns."

"All right. Can I have another kiss?"

He kissed me lightly on the mouth and we fell asleep.

The wagon jolted us awake when we started back down Scary. The sky was punched full of stars. We turned on our backs and all of heaven stretched out over us. The mountaintops hung upside down; as the wagon dipped and swayed they reached out and grabbed the full moon, then let it pop up again, like a fish teasing a cork bob.

Albion's father came the next week and took him away. I followed their wagon for a time as it trundled up Grapevine toward the ridge that led to the Levisa and West Virginia. Albion was pale and quiet.

"Come on go with us, girl," Thomas Freeman said jovially.

His words were terrible to me. I walked along until we reached the mouth of Scary. Then I stopped. It was the boundary of the Homeplace, a mystical boundary. I feared to cross, feared I would be cast out as Albion was with no place of my own. I waved goodbye, my arm heavy as lead. Albion was lost to me. I loved him, but it was not enough to hold him. I first began to understand what I have learned since, that there are forces in this world, principalities and powers, that wrench away the things that are loved, people and land, and return only exile.

I ran to the Aunt Jane Place to lay my head in the lap of the old woman and weep.

Four

ROSA ANGELELLI

YES, I KILL THAT BUTTERFLY. BUT I SAVE ALL THOSE OTH-
ers. I let them go. I throw them into the air and they fly
away.

Mama, why do I ever leave Sicily? You hold me on your
lap and pat my cheek. You feed me oranges.

The butterflies live in our trees, purple and gold. I chase
them and have one in my hands. The legs are strong, they
pluck at my flesh and I am afraid they will hurt me. My
hands break the wings. I do not mean it. My fingers are
slick with powder from the wings.

I cry because it is dying.

Papa laughs. Silly, he says. Stupid.

Mama cleans for the big people in Palermo. She polishes
the floors. She comes home and combs my hair.

You do not pick up the butterfly, she says. Do not touch
with your fingers. The dust comes off and the butterfly cannot fly.

I sob, I broke the wings.

Bambina. She kisses the top of my head. It was so pretty.
Is that why you are sad?

Senore Davidson keeps butterflies in cases. I polish the
cases. The butterflies are prisoners, the pins hold them
down. I want to tell Mama about them but she is so far
away.

Mario brings me here. And Papa. Mario comes to West
Virginia to dig the coal and be rich. I don't want to go. I
don't know Mario very well. Papa says go.

I have eight children, he says. How can I feed them all?

49

You are the oldest. You go and send back money. How else can a woman help?

Mama cries. Rosa is like my sister, she says.

Mama takes me to the boat. Papa does not come.

I will see you again, she says. *Bambina.* I will see you again.

Senore Davidson brings Mama to stay with me in this place. There is a white bed for her here, in this room.

Mario digs the coal for Senore Davidson at Felco, and that is where I go to live. I watch the names from the train. Carbon. Winco. Felco. I like the name of Felco because it sounds Sicilian. I think of home. The olive trees, the orange trees, Mama. The towns in West Virginia are all the same— the houses are white and they have eyes. Their windows are black, eyes that do not sleep, that need rest.

Mario takes me to his house. The floor sags. When we speak the house speaks back. We have our iron bed, one chair and a table. Mario says it will be better. He saves the money. I cook our first dinner, pasta slippery with fresh tomatoes and peppers. We have *baccala* on Sunday for our wedding. Special. The priest comes to our house because there is not yet a church. We cannot talk to him because he is the Irish. I wear a white chemise with the cutwork on the front. Mario comes into my bed and I think of Mama, I want her to comb my hair once again.

The women watch me when I go to the store. They are very pale and their dresses are faded. I wear a red skirt. They turn their heads and whisper. Little boys cry, Dago, Dago.

I tell Mario and he is angry. I kill them, little sons of bitches.

He drinks wine. He doesn't like me to drink it, but I pour a little into my cup when he is gone. The Tally wine is sweet. Sometimes we have the Spanish wine, sour as an olive. The water is bad here. The house is so cold. The wine warms me. But Mario measures how much is in the bottles and he hits me.

Do you think I am made of dollars? And what shall I do with a woman who is *ubbriaca*?

Mario whips my babies. Francesco says he will not go in the mine. Lazy, Mario says. He ties him to the fence, pours the slops down his back, sets the pig on him. Francesco bleeds and bleeds, my sheets are bloody. How? says the doctor. He slip and fall down the slate pile, I say. Cut his back.

My hair is still black. I catch it with a net, like black lace. I make it myself. I watch for the butterflies to return. Then I will leave this place.

Five

C. J. MARCUM

I NEVER THOUGHT MUCH OF ISOM JUSTICE WHEN HE WAS A boy. Oh, I like Isom well enough. A body can't help it, him always with a grin on his face and acting silly. But he never has been serious about nothing, wasn't then and ain't now. Not the union, not the land.

Rondal is crazy about Isom. He always looked up to him. I never could figure it. Sure, Isom always had everything he ever wanted. His daddy has money. Ermel built the Hotel Alhambra in Annadel, fanciest hotel in southern West Virginia, yellow brick, stained glass windows, mirrors and carpets inside. He built the Roxie Theater and give it to Isom to run when he growed up. The women always hung around Isom, especially them flashy whores. But take away the money and that laugh of his, and Isom Justice can't shine Rondal Lloyd's shoes. That's the way I always seen it. But Rondal can't see nothing in himself.

Whenever them two boys was in trouble, you can bet it was Isom thought it up. Not that Rondal don't have a good mind. But he weren't cut out for trouble-making. He paid attention to his schooling and did real good at science. His teachers said he was curious-turned. I sent him over to talk to Doc Booker, the colored doctor, who is a friend of mine. Rondal didn't want to go at first, said his daddy didn't hold much with Negroes. But he finally went and come back with an armload of medical books and some old doctoring tools. He took to catching frogs, smothering them in bottles and cutting them up with them instruments, right on the kitchen table. Violet had hissy fits when she found a pile of frog innards in a coffee cup.

Me and Violet done well for ourselves in them days. We got married in 1901, the year after my mamaw Missouri passed away. Thereafter we had two little girls, red-haired like their momma. Violet was a Stacy, Annadel Justice's second cousin. She is good to Rondal, loves him like a son. Fact is, I never missed having no boys because I think of Rondal as mine. He worked in the drugstore with us, run the soda fountain all on his own after school.

Isom got a hold of Rondal after supper. Rondal started his homework at nine o'clock, but before that him and Isom would go to the hotel. They'd shoot pool in the gambling room. Gambling is illegal in Justice County, but the sheriff at that time was one of Ermel's best customers. They was a room back in behind the hotel lobby. Inside Ermel had pool tables, slot machines, and dice boxes. The door was bolted and they was a panel at eye level that slid open from the inside so that Elmo Bowen, the bouncer, could see who was there. Isom got in any time he wanted by banging on the door and hollering, "Hit's me, Elmo!"

The Alhambra was a sore point with our family and the Justices. Annadel hated it, partly because of the whore-houses and saloons beside it, partly because of the gambling. I heard her and Ermel fight about it many a time.

"You should never of sold Everett Day that land for them whorehouses," Annadel would say. "I dont like my young-uns growin up around that."

"What you want me to do, keep all the land to myself, tell everybody when they can go take a crap on it, like them coal operators do?"

Truth was, Ermel was into politics even back then. The coal operators controlled the Republican Party and held all the local offices at that time. But through business connections, Ermel knew every bootlegger in the area and had already got himself on the county Democrat committee. He seen the Alhambra and the whorehouses as a way of saving the county from the Republicans.

I wasn't happy with what he was doing. I wished he would have kept on farming his land. Of course if he had, I wouldn't have no drugstore, nor money saved up. I wouldn't have no icebox nor electric nor water inside my house. It keeps me awake at night wondering if I done sold my soul for them things.

I TRIED TO FORBID RONDAL GOING TO THE ALHAMBRA WITH Isom. But Ermel took it like I hurt his feelings, so I shut up about it. Ermel has been good to me. So I just told Rondal no drinking. He said sometimes Sam Gore, the bartender, slipped them whiskey watered down. I whipped him for it and went to talk to Sam. Sam promised he'd stop it, and keep an eye on Rondal, too. I felt better then, because Sam is a man to trust, not like a lot of white men I know.

They's a lots of Negroes in Annadel, and I like about most of them. The Jim Crow don't go here. Ermel ain't happy about it, but he admits that colored people's money spends just as good as white people's. And he'll say, "It's a hell of a lot easier to deal with a nigger than a damn dago. At least a nigger speaks English."

I was scairt of the Negroes at first. It was something different. Then Doc Booker come on the city council with me. One night we got drunk together after a meeting and Doc started cussing the coal companies. After that we got on just fine.

Doc told me a lot about history that I didn't know. The Negroes, they been kicked around. They know what it is. The white man, he's a little slow to learn. You got to kick him about ten times solid, till his teeth is all knocked out and his balls is black and blue, before he catches on that he's been whupped.

We got four Negroes on the council now and Doc Booker was mayor twicet before me. We got Negroes on the police force, and colored and white mix in the hotel and in the whorehouses. The *Justice Clarion* claimed Annadel is like "Sodom and Gomorrah, a den of violence, drunkenness, depravity, and miscegenation." Last couple of years they added "radicalism" to their list. What they don't like is that this here is the one place in all these coalfields where a man can be free, speak his mind, do like he pleases. Sure we got problems. The police is busy most nights breaking up fights, and Doc does a lots of business on people that been shot. But it beats what happens other places.

One thing I tried to teach Rondal is to respect the coloreds and the foreigners. He was raised up wrong that way. And I'll say this for Isom, it don't make no difference to him the color of a man's skin, nor how much money he has. Isom likes everybody.

DOC BOOKER TENDS THE COLORED PEOPLE AT JENKINJONES as well as Annadel. The coal camp doctor at Jenkinjones won't see Negroes, and Lytton Davidson didn't want to pay for a doctor just for coloreds. That is the only reason Doc Booker is allowed to hang around Jenkinjones.

Winter of 1904 when they was real bad cholera, Doc begged medicine from my drugstore for his patients at Jenkinjones. Later on, when the danger was over, he took me on his rounds to meet some of the folks I'd helped.

When we got off the train at Jenkinjones, a mine guard stopped us. The brown handle of a pistol showed at his belt.

"What was you doin on the nigger car?" he demanded.

"Dont I look nigger?" I held my hand close to his face. "See them half-moons under my fingernails? That means nigger blood."

"What?" He glared at me suspiciously.

"Aint you never heard that? Ask Doc here."

"That's right." Doc nodded his head solemnly. "You got one drop of Negro blood and it show up in your fingernails."

We left the man anxiously studying his own hands and hiked up the creek toward colored row. The massive brick company store blocked our way, straddled the narrow holler like a setting hen squatted down to guard a nest full of eggs. We passed it on a path that rimmed the creek bed.

I sat on rickety chairs, in little rooms whose walls were blackened with soot from stove chimneys, while Doc pressed his stethoscope to chests that heaved patiently. Sometimes he would look at me while he listened and raise his eyebrows. His eyes, what you call the whites of the eyes, was actually yellow, like they was stained with tobacco juice.

"What this boy been havin to eat?" he would ask.

"Cornbread and gravy. He spit it up."

"Can you git a soup bone?"

"Maybe I ask the store. Nothing to go with it, though, till the garden come in."

They never paid Doc. They didn't have no money. Doc talked while we dodged around septic mud puddles between the houses.

"I judge half the houses here got a baby buried in the back yard where the mother give birth before her time, mostly in the winter. The mother be hungry and the baby be born weak. The mother wont have much milk. And take a look in the cemetery here. Aint nobody buried there that lived past fifty. You look. I give you ten dollars if you find more than two or three old people buried there."

Foam gathered along the edges of Pliny Creek, and the smell of sewage was strong in the wet spring air. We passed by a row of white peoples' houses. A woman come out on her porch.

"Yoo hoo!" she hollered.

We stopped.

"You a doctor?"

"Yes, ma'am."

"I got a youngun doin poorly. Can you look at her?"

A neighbor woman was hanging clothes on the line in her yard. She watched us climb the rickety front steps.

"Ethel, dont you let no nigger touch that child. No tellin what he'll do."

Ethel ignored her and stood with arms folded across her chest as we entered the house. The child lay wrapped in a blanket on a bed in the front room. They was four beds there, and no other furniture.

"Doc Boreman claims she's took with the flux," she said.

"So I see. 'Pears she's had it quite a spell."

"Doctor aint been back in a month. Cant git him to come. Hit's the drink is what it is. He lays drunk up in that office and dont see nobody."

"He may do that for the same reason I'd like to do it," Doc said, a tad too charitably, to my mind. "I can give you some medicine, but the main thing that child needs is good food. And I know you aint got it, so what good do it do for me to suggest it?''

The woman sat on a bed and clasped her hands acrost her belly. Her hands were big, her knuckles knobby.

"My man's already workin sixteen hour a day. They's eight younguns."

"Honey, I know it. It's the same story I hear on colored row."

Doc give her some calomel I had donated. When we left, the neighbor woman was still in her yard. She was heavyset, and her hands was on her hips. Her only protection against the stiff wind was a thin brown sweater buttoned crooked up the front so the top button hung empty. Two boys was with her.

"Git on home, nigger," she hollered. "We dont like you comin in here."

A rock sailed past our heads as we walked down the road.

Doc held his bag on his lap during the three-mile ride home, as though it was a comfort to cradle it there. That bag is the only fancy thing about Doc. It was a gift from a doctor at the Freedmen's Hospital in Washington, where Doc studied medicine after he graduated from Howard University. His full name is printed on the side in gold—Toussaint L'Ouverture Booker, M.D. The bag is made of shiny black leather, in contrast to his shoes, which are scuffed white across the toes.

He leaned across to me and lowered his voice.

"I belong to the Socialist Party. You heard tell of it?"

I nodded my head.

"I git a newspaper from them, the *Appeal to Reason*. It come out of Kansas. They's a lots of sense in it."

"I dont know," I said. "I always thought a man should own his land. I'd have to think about that there socialism."

"Hell, let him own a little bit of land. Long as everybody got some that want it. But the man that does the work should own the coal mine. He should receive the fruit of his labor, like the Good Book say."

"Aint many folks here would go along with it. How would socialism git that woman back yonder to share the fruits of her labor with a Negro?"

"I aint sayin that would be easy. But what's called for is

education. Education is the key, education and necessity. That woman Ethel need a doctor for her youngun, she dont care if it's a Negro. She got a sick baby, that's all. When you git right down to it, these folks wont have no hard time with socialism. Hell, they been socialized for years. They git the crumbs from under Lytton Davidson's table, and them crumbs is parceled out pretty equal. They got socialized soup beans, socialized cornbread, socialized gravy. What we got to work for is socialized pork chops."

I laughed. "I can go for that."

"I want to start me a newspaper. And I want you to help."

I whistled. "That would take some money."

"Let's go talk to Ermel. He got the money."

"Ermel? Payin for a socialist newspaper?"

"He wont give a damn whether it be socialist or not, long as it aint for prohibition."

Ermel laughed when we put the proposition to him, said he'd think about it. Nothing happened for over a year. Then the *Justice Clarion* announced it would no longer accept advertisements from his businesses, because "they flout the laws of propriety with regard to the separation of the races, and promote an unhealthy atmosphere by the dispensing of alcohol and the operation of gaming devices."

Ermel was furious. We promised him free advertising if he would help us buy a printing press. And in 1906, the *Annadel Free Press* was born, with Doc Booker as editor and me as business manager and associate editor.

In the meantime, I become a socialist. Doc give me a lot of books by Karl Marx to read, and I fell asleep every time I tried to read one. They was just too dry for me. But I voted for Eugene Debs.

Six

CARRIE BISHOP

I HAD A DREAM THE NIGHT MILES CAME HOME FROM BE-rea. I dreamed one of Flora's quilts hung on the clothesline to dry. It was the double wedding band, neverending loops of purple and red on white backing, paths leading back into themselves, mountain paths that refused to run straight. The quilt did not sag on the line but was taut as if nailed onto an invisible wall. Something moved at its center; it was the point of a knife thrust from the back. The knife cut easily as through butter, with no sound of tearing. I knew Miles held the knife.

"Why are you cutting up Florrie's quilt?" I asked him.

"To make little covers for the baby's bed," he answered cheerfully. "It's all for the new baby."

Miles always said "it" now, never "hit."

"It sounds ignorant to say 'hit.' They shamed us out of it at school. Same with 'aint.' Educated people don't use those words."

Ben sat by the fire and whittled. "Chaucer said 'hit,'" he observed.

Miles looked startled, then said, "That's different."

"Why?" Ben asked.

"He's been dead a long time. He was *medieval*." He said this last word as though it described a very disgraceful condition. "This is the scientific age."

It rained all that September evening. Daddy, Miles and Ben sat up late, deep in conversation about what Miles called "business affairs." I listened from the front porch.

"Subsistence farming," Miles said. "That's what this is.

59

You can't make it on subsistence farming any more. The economy is changing. Prices are going up. It's the miners' wages doing it. They see more cash than you do, Daddy, a whole lot more. When Pond Creek opens up over here, you won't be able to make it without more cash."

Miles planned to move to Pond Creek in November to become superintendent of a new coal mine that was owned by a Boston family, relatives of one of his professors at Berea. That is what education is about, Miles said. To prepare mountain youth to take their place in the modern world. We must not be left behind, he said. Who better to oversee a coal mine than someone who had grown up in the area, someone who understood the men he would supervise? Miles had spent the summer in Boston getting acquainted with his employers and learning what he called their "business philosophy."

He wanted to buy Daddy's trees for his coal company.

"We'll be building houses, using timbers inside the mine. A coal company always needs trees. Daddy, it will be more money than you've ever seen. You can even build a new house for Ben and Flora and their children. You get some of the boys from Scary next winter and cut the trees, float them down to the sawmill at Catlettsburg. We'll pay you cash right there. I can draw up the contract first thing when I start work."

Daddy spoke so low I couldn't hear what he said. But he came out on the porch after a while to smoke his pipe and take a breath of air.

"You going to do it?" I asked.

"Aint much to do that time of year no way," he said.

"I dont think you should. The trees is too pretty."

He looked at me. "Where's the women?"

"Gone to the Aunt Jane Place."

"Why aint you with them?"

"I wanted to hear yall talking."

"Aint nothing for a girl to hear. Go on down there with them."

I ignored him, as I did more and more in those days. He was usually scornful of me as well. It had started not long after Albion left, when Daddy learned I was doing most of the hunting. He led me way up on the mountain, pretending we were going to hunt together, then he took my gun and left me without a word. I sat and cried for a long time and listened to the report of his gun on a distant ridge. Then I stumbled down the mountain alone.

He told me he didn't expect me to find a husband. I was not "deferrin" enough, my tongue was too sharp and I was too forward in my ways. I didn't believe him. Aunt Jane was not "deferrin" and she had been married. Most of the women I knew on the creeks were strong and fiesty and they all had men. Still he hurt my feelings. I held myself distant from him and from other men who might treat me the same.

The boys I knew didn't interest me. I still waited for Heathcliff and felt nothing for Arley Whitt or Billy Good. None of them paid attention to me either. Aunt Jane said I had my nose up in the air. Flora said I was too shy to flirt properly. Only Aunt Becka said nothing, and her silence frightened me. Did she think us kindred spirits?

I rocked back and forth after Daddy went inside. Rain hammered the roof and drowned out the voices of the men. Spray from the bannisters left tiny wet spots on my cheeks. I closed my eyes and pretended they were the kisses of a man. I couldn't see his face, but he would be brave and charming, and I would marry him. I put my finger to my lips and pretended he had touched me.

"I love you," I said softly, to no one.

FLORA'S FIRST BABY WAS DUE IN MAY. BY THE TIME THE men began cutting the trees she was too large for her regular dresses. She and Ben lived with Aunt Jane. Ben had stopped teaching when Miles left home so he could help Daddy work the land. Now he was timbering and would ride the logs down the river. Sometimes, we heard, trees fell on men, or ran them over as the trunks were dragged to the river. And the trip to Catlettsburg would be the most perilous part of all. Flora fretted so over Ben that she became distracted. Aunt Jane took to gathering the eggs each day, because Flora would drop them or rattle them so hard in the basket they cracked.

From the Aunt Jane Place, the distant axes sounded like

slow woodpeckers. The men cleared the mountainside down Grapevine from the Homeplace. Daddy planned to use it for a new ground or pasture. They cleared it rough. The tree stumps, some of them five feet across, were fresh and raw like proud flesh, and the falling trunks smashed the dogwoods and rhododendron. Trimmed branches fell in untidy heaps and the gashed carcasses of white oak and poplar were dragged to the riverbank. There the men wielded their cant hooks and called to one another in a strange language they had only just learned, crying of tie poles and chain dogs. They slid the logs over the bank and into the water. The logs would float in a pen until high tide when the men would lash them into rafts for the trip downstream.

We cooked all day to feed the men who had come from all over Scary and Grapevine to work on the hillside. We grumbled as we worked.

"I'm scairt for this here baby," Flora confided. "Hit's a-trying to grow all the while they're a-cutting and slashing. Hit's aiming to be borned while its daddy is putting himself in mortal danger. When them trees holler and crash down, this here baby kicks."

Aunt Jane shook her head in agreement. "They's something about it aint right. Hit's one thing to clear for a new ground, but this here, I dont know."

"They aint nothing wrong with providing for your family," Aunt Becka said. She was always especially fond of Miles. But even she spoke without conviction and her forehead was wrinkled with worry.

I hated the ugliness of the cleared mountain. But most of all I was angry about missing school to cook. I thought about my neglected books lying in the loft and burned with resentment at the bedraggled men who trooped in to dinner each midday. It often rained that winter, and the men shook themselves like dogs before they came into the house, so many of them that the four of us women had to stand bunched together in the corner near the stove until they went out again, and make do with the scraps they left.

"Put up with it now," Miles said when he came for a visit. "This time next year there'll be a big new house."

I resented his part in this disruption, but I couldn't be

too angry with him. When I complained about the school I had missed, he looked at me thoughtfully.

"You like school, don't you, Sis? You ought to go off and study like I did."

"I'd love to," I said. "I want to be a nurse. They's a nursing school over at that new hospital at Justice."

"I'll pay for it, if that's what you want to do."

"You mean that?"

"Sure. I haven't got a wife or children to worry about yet. Why shouldn't I help you out? That's what family is for."

I daydreamed about nursing school. When I mentioned it to Daddy he laughed. I knew it meant nothing to him, but I also knew he wouldn't oppose it as long as he didn't have to pay for it.

THE THAW CAME IN MARCH. THE RIVER WAS UP, LASHING at the lowhanging branches of trees, running so wide and fast that the whole earth seemed to move with it. The men roped the logs into rafts and prepared to leave. We gave them cool goodbyes, for to cling and weep would be to acknowledge the danger they would face.

We didn't cook elaborate meals while they were gone. We were weary of cooking and food did not interest us anyway. We sat around the table at the Homeplace and nibbled on sliced ham, cold biscuits, and boiled eggs. Sometimes we opened a jar of preserves.

We fed the animals, milked the cows, chopped wood. Aunt Becka hitched up our mule Mag and plowed the vegetable garden. I would come laden with water buckets from the well or from bringing in the cows and see Aunt Jane walking beside Aunt Becka, talking earnestly to her and sometimes draping an arm across the younger woman's shoulders.

School was done for the year. I tried to read on my own to make up for what I had lost, but it was hard to concentrate. It was unsettling to have the men gone. I had no doubt that we women could take care of one another. But I missed their maleness. They were kin and a vital part of our kinship had been torn away.

* * *

A MAN PASSED THROUGH ON HIS WAY TO LETCHER COUNTY.
He had been down the river. He told us a man had fallen
from the rafts on the Levisa and been killed. He heard the
man was from Paine County, but he didn't recall the name.

"Happened four days back," he said.

"Nigh to Louisa. They went on to Catlettsburg," he said.

"Probably werent one a yourn," he said.

We shoved his food at him. He slept in the barn and left
the next morning.

"He was likely mistaken," said Aunt Jane. "Besides,
they's a heap of men in Paine County that run logs."

Flora began to cry. She sat hunched forward so long that
I wondered if a baby could be squashed inside of its mother.

FLORA SPIED THEM FIRST. "THEY'RE A-COMING!" SHE HOL-
lered.

We found her on the porch, clutching a post, her belly
pressed against it. From a distance the men seemed to float
over the bottom land like ghosts. They were too far away
to tell who was who.

"Oh, lordy," Flora prayed, "please let Ben be all right."

They came on slowly.

"There's Ben!" I cried. "I spy Ben!"

Flora pressed her hands to her cheeks.

"Who else, child?" Aunt Becka pleaded. "Your eyes is
better than mine."

"There's Farrie Whitt, and Clarence. And there's Mos-
coe and Amos Maynard. Vance McCoy. Lee Slone. And
Miles! Miles has come back with them."

"Where's Orlando?" Aunt Jane asked.

Flora raised her head. "Where's Daddy?"

We stood still for a moment. Aunt Becka staggered down
the steps, almost fell.

"Where's my brother?" she cried. "Where's my little
brother?" Then Ben was with us, he said our daddy was
dead. Flora and I clutched one another and wailed.

Aunt Jane, who knew what it was to lose husband and
daughter, remained calm.

"Aint you brung back his body?" she asked.

"We had to bury him right there. We wasn't near no place and he was all tore up. They was a blockade and he was throwed off and caught between two rafts. Hit was all we could do to git the corpse out of the river. We went on to Catlettsburg, sold the logs, and come on back here with Miles."

Aunt Becka commenced to keening. "Orlando's gone. Oh, Jesus, he's gone, my poor little brother that I carried in my arms oncet. And all for a handful of silver."

FLORA WENT INTO LABOR THAT NIGHT, THREE MONTHS BE-fore her time. I stayed at the Aunt Jane Place but couldn't sleep, and sat watching the lights burn in the windows of the Homeplace. I thought of my father. Had he lived and another of us died, he would have been no comfort. He would have kept his own counsel and gone out to tend the cows. I was not sure that I had loved him. I mourned his death, but it was because no one else could be Father, and because there would be no more chances to earn his love.

Miles came up sometime after midnight.

"I thought you'd be awake," he said.

I nestled against him. His shirt smelled of sweat.

"The baby's dead," he said. "It was a boy. Lived less than an hour. Ben held him when he died." He began to cry. "It's my fault. I should never have talked Daddy into selling his trees."

"How could you know what would happen?"

"Aunt Becka thinks it's my fault. I'm scared she hates me."

"Course she dont. Aint you her kin? Aint we all kin?"

"I love you, Carrie."

I patted his back. "I love you, too, Miles."

"I loved Daddy. I did. I swear I loved him."

"I know it."

WE NAMED THE BABY ORLANDO AND BURIED HIM IN THE May cemetery at the mouth of Scary Creek. He lay next to Tildy May Bishop, our mother. It was as though he had been conceived for just this purpose, a stunted effigy to lay in place of his missing namesake.

Flora did not go to the burying and did not leave her bed until a month afterward. When she finally ventured outside, she would have nothing to do with caring for the animals. She was afraid, she said, that she would accidentally do them some harm.

Ben built a house of wood with the money from selling the trees. It had six rooms and a large front porch all painted white. Ben said it was the last thing our daddy did for us.

Seven

ROSA ANGELELLI

I POLISH THE GLASS CASES WHICH HOLD THE BUTTER-
flies, in Senore Davidson's big sunny room with all the
books.

Look, he tells me. He points to the butterflies. I catch
this one in this place, and that one in that place. Gold.
Africa. Purple. Louisiana. He goes everywhere for the butterflies.

Rosa, he says. You should know some of these names.
They are Latin. Your Italian language is from Latin.

I shrug my shoulders and smile. Still, I do not know it.

See this one. I go all over the world for it and never find.
Then I catch it here, on Blackberry Creek. What do you
think of that?

I look at it. Argynus Diana. I will name my daughter
Diana. Now I have only sons.

We move to the town of Davidson. It is better, Mario
says. New town. Bigger house. Mario works outside the
mine. He does not go down in. It is because he plays the
baseball. What an arm, says Senore Davidson.

There is a sign above the bridge in Davidson. Francesco
reads it to me. American Coal Company. Man Hours Lost
Due To Accident, 1909. Safety Is Our Motto. Beneath that,
the numbers. They change the numbers every day. My babies go down in and I pray.

There is a priest in Davidson, a church. Our Lady of
Victory. We live at Number Six. It is one mile to the church.
I stop on my way to clean for Senore Davidson. My little
baby Luigi is with me. Francesco, Antonio, Carmello go to

school. I smell the incense in the church. It is like my mama's scent. Our Lady of Victory. I light the candle every day. I leave the penny. I steal the penny from Mario.

At Easter we walk through the streets. My babies, their faces shine. We bear the relics, the bones, the blood, the images, all wrapped in gold. There are many priests; they wear red or white. They stop to sip wine. I go home and bake eggs in my bread, eggs whole in their shells.

Francesco comes home from the mines. He is so dirty. He bathes but his face is not clean. His eyes are dark all around, like the ones in the moving pictures. Here, bambino, I say. I dip the rag in turpentine and wipe the soft skin beneath his eyes. It burns, he says. He squeezes my hand.

Senore Davidson has hearths of marble. Like the big house my mama cleans in Palermo. Rosa, he says, you are my best maid. Better than in Philadelphia. He smiles. His face is round. His hair is gray, but his face is like a little boy.

He comes to see me here. Once.

He lives in Philadelphia sometimes. He lives here sometimes. His wife will not come. Dirty, she says. How can you stand these people? Come home. And he goes. But he comes back. I must run my business, he says. If I don't look after my interests, who will? Eh, Rosa?

I wear my white chemise when I work for him. He stretches out his hand and touches the cutwork. So pretty, he says. *Punto tagliato*, I say. I do it myself.

Rosa, will you stitch the pillowcases? he says. Make them pretty.

The butterflies speak to me. Their mouths are very small, but still I hear them speak. Take care not to break the wings, they say. They sound like mama.

Mario plays the baseball. The grass smells sweet when it is cut. The ball runs through it like a snake. Home plate, they cry. Home plate.

The ball leaps but Mario has it. He flings it away as though he cannot bear to touch it. That is why he is so good, Antonio says.

I like to hit the ball, Mario says. I like to hit the son bitch and watch it fly away.

Mama sends the reliquary to me. She saves the money to buy it. I carry it in from the wagon. "Now God is in the house," I tell Luigi. Mario throws the baseball to Carmello. It skips across the rocks. The pieta is inside the reliquary, behind the purple glass. The holy water is inside, and the candles. The priest gives me Christ's body to live with us. Mario comes in with my babies. We eat pasta and butter. I put on my brocade vest. I light the candles and tell my beads.

Holy Mary, Mother of God, pray for us sinners now and at the hour of our death.

The candlelight dances on the glass. Mario sits in the corner. He says nothing. He holds the baseball, strokes it with his fingers. The candlelight flows over his trousers like water.

Eight

RONDAL LLOYD

SOMETIMES I WISH I COULD GO BACK TO AGE SEVENTEEN and start all over again. I'd study medicine, wear a tie, and go around tapping people on the chest and saying, "Mm-hmmm." Would C.J. have been satisfied then? I doubt it.

From as early as I can remember he preached two things to me—medicine and the United Mineworkers. He never understood that I couldn't have both, that I had to choose. Whichever I picked, C.J. was bound to be disappointed.

Isom was drunk the night C.J. and I had the argument over whether I would study medicine or go down in the mines. I had been drinking too, as much as Isom, but I was never so cold sober in my life. I walked straight to the house from the Alhambra without a stumble, and took Isom right into the setting room with me. C.J. and Violet were making fudge with the girls. C.J. stood up, angry.

"Aint I told you never to come in like this when you been drinking?"

"I aint drunk," I protested.

"I am," Isom said, "but I'll be quiet as a mouse."

"Violet," C.J. said coldly, "put the younguns to bed and go make some coffee."

Isom snatched off his hat as the girls left. " 'Night, Gladys."

Gladys, who was five, giggled and waved at him. He was a great favorite of hers, always teasing her and bringing her candy. She often proclaimed she would marry him some day, and he would clasp his hands to his chest and cry, "I'm a-pining for ye, Gladys."

When they had gone, C.J. stirred the coal fire with a poker.

"We got to talk," I said.

"You know I'm ready any time. But wouldn't you rather be sober?"

"I can say what I got to say right now. I cant be a doctor, C.J. I aint going to Huntington."

His face fell, his shoulders slumped and he looked as crushed as I had known he would.

"Why ever not?"

"He'll take on airs ifn he goes down there," Isom said.

I told him to shut up.

"Why'd you haul me over here if you dont want my help?" he said plaintively. But he sank down on the maroon sofa and ate a piece of fudge.

"Look here," I said. "If I go off, I'll be gone for years. When I come back things wont be the same. I wont be the same. Folks will treat me different."

"They'll treat you with respect."

"They'll treat me different. Look at Doc Booker. You cant tell me folks treat him like any other nigger. They treat him like a dressed-up nigger."

"You dont use that kind of talk in this house."

"I am making a point, goddamn it!" I waved my arms. "You are so damn pure, C.J. You got so many standards and ideals. Well, maybe I picked up some of them. Maybe I picked em up because I love and admire you. And maybe I decided I want to help bring the union in here. Aint no doctor going to bring in no union."

"Look at Doc Booker and the paper."

"What about it? Aint no ten million Doc Bookers going to bring in the union. Hit's coal miners will bring in the union. If I aint one of em, how can I help?"

"I aint no miner. You saying I cant help?"

"I'm saying they aint a miner on this holler that you got an in with. And I'm saying they is all kinds of missionaries up in Boston can come down here and be a doctor for all us poor folks on Blackberry Creek. I'm saying we got to bring the union in for ourselves."

"Rondal, you're still yet a youngun. Ten year from now you'll look back and regret it if you dont take this chance to better yourself. I lay awake at night sometimes and think about the chances I missed.''

''I got to do what's best for me. I cant live on what happened to you.''

''He goes off, I'll lose my best buddy,'' Isom said from ⟨the co⟩⟨uch⟩. ''Hell, even if he comes back here, he wont be ⟨no f⟩⟨un⟩ no more.''

C.J. glared at him. ''Hit's one reason I want him to go. Git him away from these whorehouses and such.''

''Git him among quality folks,'' Isom mocked. ''Like them coal operators.''

I was frightened at the anger on C.J.'s face. I had always assumed he loved Isom as I did, but at that moment I thought he hated him.

Then he leaned against a chair, looked down at his hands, thoroughly beaten.

''I been saving money for your schooling,'' he whispered.

''C.J., I cant pay you back for all you done. But dont make me go. I'll be so lonesome. This here is my home. Dont send me away.''

He was crying. I had never seen him cry.

''Oh, God, C.J. I aint meaning to hurt you. Werent it you taught me about the union, about the coal operators? Aint they made this place a burden to bear? I'm scairt if I go off, I wont never settle here again. Hit would be too easy to turn tail, like Uncle Dillon.''

He raised his head. ''Dillon never turned tail. You heard that offn your buddy there. Dillon's living the old way.''

''We aint got the old way no more. We got the new way. That's what I got to live. Only I cant bear to think I disappointed you. Say you aint disappointed.''

''I aint never been disappointed in you. You do what you got to do.''

He took a long time to say this last, and his voice held no ring of conviction. I felt like Judas. C.J. went into the kitchen to sit with Violet.

''Hey, dont worry,'' Isom said. ''You're growed up now, and he aint even your daddy. He aint got no say so over you.''

* * *

THERE WAS NOTHING I COULD HAVE SAID TO HURT C.J. Marcum any more than to tell him that he carried no influence with coal miners, that he was not one of them. If I hadn't been drinking, I would never have said it. But it was true. It was ironic, for C.J. had been on Blackberry all his life, before the companies came in. But it made no difference. To the miners, he was an outsider because he didn't share their life. He was a businessman; he had money.

I was more at home with the miners than C.J. was. To them, I was Clabe Lloyd's boy, even if I did live at Annadel. Isom and I spent time with them in the beer joints and whorehouses. We first ventured into Everett Day's when we were fifteen and lost our virginity to a pair of amused colored girls. We were regulars for a while until Ermel found out and called us into his office at the hotel.

"So you boys want the clap," he said.

We smirked and studied our hands.

"I go to Lizzie Mae ever time," Isom said. "She aint got the clap."

"So she says. If she aint got it now, she will have. You boys want your peters to shrivel up and fall off, just keep on going to Everett's."

That scared us and we decided to take his advice. Isom was smitten with a new colored girl at Everett's named Aquanetta Jones. He set her up working the ticket office at the Roxie and she promised not to run with other men. I settled into an affair with Ruby Day, Everett's daughter. She wasn't a whore but her daddy's business had certainly made an impression on her. She made few demands on me, and I liked that.

Daddy came up occasionally and I bought him a beer. It was the only way he could afford it.

"You come on back home anytime," he always said. "You was a good buddy when you was working with me."

But Talcott was the member of my family I saw most often. He came to Annadel every Saturday and stayed the night, for he was courting Pricie Justice, Isom's little sister. Talcott, Isom and I had formed a band and played for pay in the places round about Annadel and up Lloyds Fork.

Isom played the fiddle, Talcott the guitar, and I picked the banjo. We called ourselves the Blackberry Pickers. Some folks said we were the best in the county.

Talcott was saving the money he made from playing because he wanted to marry Pricie and move into his own house. He was sixteen, she was fourteen. We were drinking beer at Cesco Thompson's on Lloyds Fork after a performance, and Isom had gone off to play cards, when Talcott told me of it.

"What does Ermel say?" I asked.

"I dont care what her old man says. We're gitting married."

"Dont you think you ought to ask Ermel?"

He shrugged. "I reckon. But sometimes he says things about me hanging around too much. Maybe he thinks a coal miner aint good enough for her."

"Naw, Ermel aint no snob. Maybe he just thinks you're too young. Besides, you dont have to stay down in the mines. Ermel can take you on to work for him."

Talcott lit a cigarette, tapped his fingers on the table. "I aint interested in no soft job. I like it down there. Aint nobody on my back."

He looked older than me. Pouches hung beneath his eyes and his nose was long and pinched.

"If I hadn't left home," I said, "you wouldn't have worked in there with Daddy all these years."

"Hell, I'd a gone in there sooner or later. What's the difference?"

"You wasnt never mad at me?"

"Hell, no!"

He sucked on his cigarette. A blue heart was tattooed on the back of his right hand.

"Any of the boys at Winco talk about the union?"

He laughed. "Union? That's just a bunch of fellers in offices up at Charleston. I dont need them to fight my battles."

C.J. blamed Isom for my decision, but Talcott was the main reason I decided against going away to school. At the Justice farm he borrowed Isom's pistol and practiced with it, shooting at bottles, squirrels, possums. Once when Annadel went to wring the neck of a chicken for dinner, he shot it in the head before she could catch it. At the Alhambra he pulled a knife on a drunk who heckled his singing. "Shit!" Isom yelled, and floored him with one punch. Talcott jumped up and was after him, but Isom kept leaping out of his way and laughing until Talcott wept with rage. After a while he wore himself out and calmed down. I took him to the station and put him on a train for Winco.

"Goddamn Isom," he said, almost cheerful. "He's lucky I didn't slit him open."

"He's lucky," I agreed. I hugged him to me.

"You're a good brother," he mumbled.

I left him once. I wouldn't do it again.

WHEN I FIRST WENT BACK TO WINCO, MOMMY MADE IT clear that there was no room for me at the house. I tried not to show how hurt I was and went to live at the boarding house for single miners. They gave me a tiny room beside the kitchen that always smelled of hot, greasy dishwater. At least I didn't have to eat there, but stopped by the house each morning to eat breakfast and pick up my dinner pail.

Mommy grew kinder as she saw how my return stretched her credit at the company store. But it was a remote kindness that offered me little comfort. I saw her only at meals. She would pour my coffee, stand behind me while I ate my eggs and bacon, heap seconds of fried potatoes on my plate. Then she went to the corner and said not a word. When I mentioned it to Talcott, he said, "Hell, she's always like that. She dont love nobody but Jesus."

That wasn't quite true. She adored our little brother Kerwin. He was fourteen and she kept him in school despite Daddy's repeated claims that he should be working. I was jealous. But I would not have wanted to be the meek creature Kerwin had become. He took his religion after her. They went to church together on Sundays and spent all day at it. In the evenings he read the Bible to her while she mended our clothes. He grew up skinny and round-shouldered with a thin face and wavy light brown hair. I never heard him raise his voice.

When Mommy invited me back into the house at last, I

knew it was because she saw me as a powerful weapon in her fight to keep Kerwin at home.

IT WAS FEARSOME GOING DOWN IN THE MINES AGAIN. I spent the first month in terror of a roof fall, and talked little so I could listen to the grinding and moaning of the coal seam. But time brought disregard for danger and even a mocking sort of courage. I would look up after the powder had blown and dare the son of a bitch roof to come down.

I saw C.J. most Saturdays. He usually heard us play if we were in Annadel. It was awkward at first, but there was too much between us to keep us apart. Once he said, "The money is still yet there if you change your mind." Then he didn't mention school again.

ISOM AND ERMEL CAME AFTER ME ONE SPRING NIGHT AS I was about to hop in bed with Ruby. I pulled my pants back on and went outside with them.

"Talcott and Pricie have run off." Isom did all the talking. Ermel just stood behind him, grim and quiet. "Gone to Virginia, we reckon. Hit's easy for younguns to git hitched down there. We're going to fetch em back. Want to come?"

We took the train to Grundy but we were too late. When we got back to Justice County on Sunday afternoon they were at the farmhouse.

"Dont be mad, Daddy." Pricie cowered on a chair and twisted a handkerchief in her lap.

"We're old enough," Talcott said. "I got me a house in Felco and a job. I'll take real good care of her."

Pricie's red hair stuck out all over her head from where she had slept on the train. She took Talcott's hand.

"I'm going to have a baby, Daddy," she said shyly.

"Jesus H. Christ," said Ermel.

Annadel sat on the back stoop and flung cracked corn at the chickens. I hadn't noticed before how loose and stringy the skin was under her chin.

"Why couldnt she fell for you? You're such a steady

feller. You'll make somethin someday. I had hopes for the two of you."

"Law, Annadel, I aint no kind of feller for a woman to settle with. I can be mean as a striped-ass snake to a woman. Talcott there, he works hard."

She shook her head. "What will happen to them younguns?"

"They'll do all right. They both got kin that loves them."

"Is that there enough in this day and age? I just dont know." She smiled, a bleak smile. "Well, hit's done, aint it? We'll just have to git behind them now."

Mommy was upset too, but not for Talcott's sake. She met me at the door when I got home and pulled me into the kitchen where Daddy sat slumped over a cup of black coffee.

"Yall aint taking my boy down in that hole."

Kerwin stood by the stove and stirred a pot of soup.

"Talcott loaded a heap of coal," Daddy said wearily.

"This boy cant load no coal. He's too skinny. Look at him. Jesus has set his mark on him. You cant have this boy."

"Mommy, we aint said we was taking him in."

She rounded on me. "Nor dont you think you will, neither."

"I want him in school," I said.

"That damn Talcott," Daddy said. "Why'd he do such a durn fool thing?"

"I dont mind going in," Kerwin said in a small voice. "The Lord will watch over me. Aint it so, Mommy?"

She started to cry.

"You aint going in," I said.

I WORKED TWO YEARS IN THE MINE, BIDING MY TIME. THEN I wrote to the union in Charleston, the state capital, and begged them to send us an organizer. I sealed the letter in one of the Flat Iron Drugstore stationery envelopes and posted it in Justice so that it wouldn't get into the wrong hands.

A month before I wrote the letter, I watched two dozen blue-uniformed guards get off the train at Winco. They worked for the Baldwin-Felts Detective Agency in Blue-field. C.J. said their presence meant that the union was making plans to move into the Levisa coalfield. Davidson and the other operators would be taking no chances.

American Coal had always employed its own policemen, frightened little bullies who liked to throw their weight around. We always laughed at them behind their backs. The Baldwin-Felts guards were different. They were not local men, and they were professionally trained. While many of them had been policemen in Virginia, others had been taken off the streets of big cities and boasted openly of prison records. We came to call them "gun thugs." They would beat a man for no other reason than he had met their eyes in what they judged to be a forward manner. Gatherings of more than two people who were not family members were forbidden. A colored man at Felco who came home drunk one night and threw red dog at a Baldwin guard was shot to death.

To counter the rumored union activity, Lytton Davidson built a model coal camp at the mouth of Marcums Branch. Main Davidson had tennis and basketball courts, paved streets, a theater, YMCA, and a new high school built by the company. Smaller branches of the new town clustered around the mine portals on down Blackberry and up Marcums Branch. These last towns had no names and were called by the numbers of the portals—Number Ten, Number Eight, Number Six.

"Aint that just the way a coal operator would name a town?" C.J. complained.

It near killed him to watch all this going up on his land. Davidson miners weren't allowed to come to Annadel, and the postmaster kept out the *Free Press* and other questionable materials, including Ermel's Democratic Party campaign literature.

"Your mommy wants to move down there," Daddy said. "She wants Kerwin in that new high school. I reckon we could. I got good standing, far as I know. I hate to leave this land, but hit aint been ourn for a good while. Likely wont never be."

"You'll go without me," I said. "I aint moving."

"They take care of you better down there."

"I'd rather take care of myself."

I told the union about all this when I wrote my letter. Nothing happened.

"You should have wrote the Socialists," Doc Booker said. "That union gits lazy."

I CAME AWAY FROM THE PAYROLL WINDOW ONE WINTER evening and a colored man fell in step beside me. He was a new man who had been around only a few months.

"You Lloyd?" he asked.

"That's right."

"You the one that wants to ride the goat?"

I stared at him and he grinned. He had a large nose shaped like a triangle and a gold tooth.

"What you mean? This some kind of Masons?"

"Naw! I talking bout the *goat,* man. Aint you the one hollered for the goat? It's a fearsome thing you done. You best recall it."

It began to dawn on me what he meant, and it near took my breath away.

"Oh, lordy," I whispered. "You're here."

A gun thug saw us talking and walked toward us.

"Up on the hill behind Cesco Thompson's," the Negro said. "Tonight at ten. Bring a few good men."

He walked on into the evening, fading into the grayness.

"What did that nigger want?" the gun thug demanded.

"Borrow money," I said.

"Aint it just like a nigger?"

ONE BY ONE WE ARRIVED ON THE HILL BEHIND THE TAV-ern. We were seven in all. The Negro, who called himself Johnson, was already there.

"Yall here to ride the goat?"

We mumbled that yes we were ready.

"But how do you know you're ready till you know what it is?" said Johnson. "Let me tell you about it. Some of you belongs to the Redmen, the Odd Fellows, and the like. You got all them secret words, all the mumbo-jumbo. But brothers, this aint no club. We got to stay secret for a while to survive, and when we finally show ourselves, we got to stick together to live. This here is life and death. This aint no Mason lodge, this is the United Mineworkers.''

I shivered at that name, to hear it spoken aloud in that place. Johnson paced slowly, stopped in front of each of us.

"The union means brotherhood. That's something them operators cant never take away—brotherhood. I worked the mines down in Pocahontas, Virginia, twenty year. I know what it is. My daddy was a slave. I know what that is. When a man got the money, a man got the land, a man got the guns, you cant beat him. No, you cant. Unless you got brotherhood. When you stick together, the man cant beat one down cause he knows they's more where that one come from and they'll whip his ass.''

He lapsed into silence. We waited. A cold wind rustled the dead leaves. I strained to see if anything moved; the darkness pressed against my eyeballs.

"You scared, aint ye?''

I started at the sound of his voice.

"You scared,'' he said again. "You wondering, did any gun thugs foller us out here. I'm scared too. But dont we risk our lives ever damn day in that mine? And why should you risk your life, git your body broke up, see your little children go hungry, just so Mister Davidson can live high? You digging the coal! He setting in a big house on his ass! He run your life! He do your thinking! And you as good a man as him.''

He reached into his pocket.

"I got cards to sign. Thirty-five cent dues. Take the pledge, sign the card, you in the union. It aint easy. You got to be ready to die for each other. We dont want no yellow-bellies in the union. You in that Klan, we dont want you in the union. Union is for white and Negro alike. Union is for foreign. Union is for Catholic. Anybody want to be a free man and fight for it, union is for him. Here is the cards, boys. Take the pledge and they are yours. Who want the pledge?''

I stepped forward. "Me.''

"Raise your hand.''

I repeated the words after him. I pledged that I would not

reveal the names of union members to the boss; that I would not take the job of a striker; that I would cease work when called on to do so; that I would never wrong a brother or see him wronged. The others hesitated.

"Thirty-five cent is a lot of money," said William Thomas.

"Union cant operate without money," Johnson answered.

"Ifn I git put out, where will I go?" asked Amos Toler. "My old woman's expecting. Aint them operators got a blacklist?"

"We all taking a chance," said Johnson.

"Theys some of the boys aint interested."

"We got to change their minds," I said.

In the end they all took the pledge, the Pinkards, Junebug Slater, Homer Knox, Amos Toler, William Thomas. We left the way we had come, silently and separately.

WE AGREED THAT ONLY JOHNSON AND I WOULD RECRUIT new members at first. It was a frightful thing to approach a man, to read his eyes as you talked to him and wonder if you had misjudged him. It was even more worrisome to learn from Johnson that union officials in Charleston didn't think the Levisa coalfield was ready to be organized.

"Why'd you come?" I asked.

"I knew they was a Socialist paper down here. I met Doc Booker in Charleston last year. Thought I'd give it a try."

When I asked Doc Booker about this, he said, "That's right. Them union officials say, 'They's a bear in the woods. It be too dangerous, so let's send a colored man, see if he come out without the bear eat him.'"

After a week I had spoken to eight men. On Friday a gun thug met me and Daddy on our way to work at the drift mouth. He pointed his rifle at my head and grinned.

"Where's your union card?"

I stepped back. The gun barrel poked me in the chest.

"What's this?" Daddy said.

"Git on out of here, old man. This is between me and your boy."

"I dont know what you're talking about," I said.

"Hell you don't. You got ten seconds or I'll blow a hole in you. Where is it?"

My head felt like it would burst into flames.

"In my shoe," I managed to say. I had slit the instep with a razor and worked the card down inside.

"You kill my boy you'll have to kill me too," Daddy said.

The guard laughed. "Go on home, old man. We're going to teach him a little lesson." He pushed me with the rifle barrel. "Let's us take a walk down to the powerhouse."

Daddy yelled after me, but I couldn't understand him. F gun thugs met us at the powerhouse, dragged me inside. The boss man, Malcolm Denbigh, an Englishman, stood beside the huge coal-eating furnace that provided the electricity for Winco. Johnson was with him. His arms were tied behind his back and he stared down at his feet.

"We've had our eye on you for a while, Lloyd," Denbigh said. "You run with a crowd of red agitators at Annadel. Now you've brought this union nigger here. What do you think we ought to do with you?"

My knees gave out. Hands gripped me like iron pinchers and held me up.

I tried to say, God, Johnson, I swear I didn't tell.

One man threw open the furnace door.

Shall we throw this white boy in, cook him black as a nigger?

Their mouths opened. They were laughing.

Who else took the pledge, son? Who else?

A rifle butt struck me in the belly and I doubled over. They dragged me over to the furnace, made to lift me, then pulled me back and threw me against the wall. I struck my head.

I'd rather kill a nigger. It's more fun.

I looked. Johnson's face was terrible. His eyes had turned to stone.

They lifted him off the ground. He began to sing. It didn't really sound like singing.

"No more moaning!" he screeched. "No more moaning!"

He twisted his head so that the muscles of his neck stood out like ropes. His mouth curved in a smile.

"No more moaning over me!"

An orange sheet of flame belched from the furnace. Johnson's head fell back, I met his eyes, I knew he did not see me, that he was ripping his soul from his body and soaring away with it.

"And before I'll be a slave—"

They tossed him inside the furnace and slammed the door. They raised me up.

"Go on home," Denbigh said. "You've got twenty-four hours to get out of Justice County or you're dead."

I stumbled outside and vomited. Somehow I made it back to the house. Mommy and Daddy were in the kitchen and Daddy met me at the door.

"Thank the Lord! Your head's a-bleeding. They beat on you?"

I nodded.

"What kind of trouble you got yourself in?" Mommy demanded.

I looked at Daddy. "I got to git. Out of the county in twenty-four hours."

Mommy came closer. "You're a leaving."

I gasped for air. I went to my bed and stuffed my belongings into a pillowcase. Two shirts, socks, and a change of underwear, a Bible and a copy of *Huckleberry Finn* that C.J. gave me, a comb, pocket knife, toothbrush, watch. I knotted the laces of my good shoes and hung them around my neck, picked up my banjo, hugged the pillowcase to my chest and went back to the kitchen. Mommy waited for me.

"You are good for nothing," she said.

"Vernie!" Daddy said.

"You have ruint your brother over some foolishness. He'll go down the mines. He'll pay for your sins."

"Vernie!"

I brushed past her. "Daddy, I love you. Tell Talcott and Kerwin goodbye."

I went out the screen door. A gun thug stood in the yard and watched me go. I walked the five miles to Annadel, following the railroad track.

* * *

"HUNTINGTON OR KENTUCKY,' C.J. SAID.

"Kentucky."

"Huntington's safer."

"Kentucky's closer."

We glared at one another.

"What did you think?" I said. "You think they was going to let us do all this without a fight?"

He covered his face with his hands. "I dont have to enjoy it, do I?"

"So they throwed Annadel up to you?" Doc Booker said. "I reckon we got to protect ourselves better."

"I reckon you better," I said.

"I'll go with you," Isom said. "Make sure nobody bothers you on the train."

"Your mommy and daddy must be tore up," C.J. said.

"Yeah," I said bitterly. "They're real tore up."

He raised his head at the tone of my voice.

"It's you I'll miss," I said. He smiled.

"Talcott?" Isom asked.

"I aint talked to him. You better watch he dont kill nobody over this."

"We can still yet play music in Kentucky," Isom said. "Aint that far."

"Sure," I said.

We rode the train to Justice, the gun thugs following all the way. We went into a cafe on Court Street and bought some ham sandwiches. Then we gave the thugs the slip in a dark alley. Around midnight we found a swinging bridge across the Levisa.

"What's your name?" Isom asked.

"Lloyd Justice."

"Good." Isom grinned. "They's a passel of us Justices in these parts. One more wont make no difference. You write my daddy. Aint nobody will mess with his mail. He's got friends, you know?"

We shook hands.

"Dont git a new fiddle player," he said.

The bridge was an old one, not well kept up, and some of the slats were missing. I went slowly, gripping the railing and swaying, bearing on my shoulders the death of Johnson, the abandonment of my brothers, the renunciation of my mother. I stepped onto the firm ground of Kentucky. Isom was a shadow on the distant shore. I waved to him. Then I headed south toward Pond Creek.

Part Two

Part Two

Nine

CARRIE BISHOP

I HAVE TRAVELED OUTSIDE THE MOUNTAINS, BUT NEVER lived apart from them. I always feared mountains could be as jealous, as unforgiving, as any spurned lover. Leave them and they may never take you back. Besides, I never felt a need to go. There is enough to study in these hills to last a lifetime.

Justice town, where I went to nursing school, is different from Grapevine. Grace Hospital is built so high up the hillside that I could see much of Justice and Paine counties from my window in the nurses' quarters. I loved to rise early in the morning and watch the mists rise like ghosts from the far hilltops.

In Justice town, the houses stabbed pillars of stone and wood into the flesh of the hillside and clung there like a swarm of mosquitoes. The buildings were too closely packed for trees to grow. The clamor of trains and autos and people chased away the bullfrogs and hoot owls and other sounds of night. But I loved to wander the streets on a Saturday afternoon; to watch gentlemen and their well-dressed ladies come and go at the train depot; to poke my finger into a fresh octopus or squid at the Italian grocery, or buy a strange-smelling cheese to carry back to my room; to sit in the dark of the Odeon Theater with the gray flickering of the moving pictures teasing the faces of the people around me.

Pond Creek, where I worked for Miles after I finished school, was different yet again. The holler was narrow and twisty; it seemed to squeeze me and say, "Stay a while, but never rest easy." Vulcan, the coal camp where Miles and I lived, was wonderfully dark, like a painting in a book I once saw of a Spanish town called Toledo, with a sky that looked as though demons streaked across it. Sway-backed houses grew right up around the tipple like toadstools about a tree stump. The camp was divided into little colonies—Negroes in board and batten shacks down in Colored Bottom, mountain people in squat four-room houses on Tipple Hill, Hungarians in tall thin double houses up Hunkie Holler. None of the houses sat on foundations, but instead balanced on small piles of bricks set at each corner. Clouds of black bug dust whipped through the streets, and when the wind was right, the sulphurous fumes from the burning slag heap above Hunkie Holler choked the air in the narrow bottom. Orange slate, called red dog by the miners, littered the streets, carelessly scattered about to keep down the mud. Vulcan was a challenge for me, an adventure, like Florence Nightingale in the Crimean.

I moved into the big house on the hill where Miles lived, above the noise and dirt, three stories and fifteen rooms, green shingles outside with white gingerbread trim and scalloped eaves. From the bottom it appeared to be a castle, floating behind its brown stone wall on a moat of green grass. I was uncomfortable living there, for we had not known chandeliers and crystal drinking glasses on Grapevine. After a few months I moved into two rooms in the clubhouse at the foot of the hill. Miners were not allowed to board there; it was reserved for the "better sort" of employee. Although I knew I should disapprove, I accepted this distinction. It added a touch of the exotic, as though I had set down in imperial India amid the sahibs and the natives, and all this in Paine County, just across the mountain from where I had been born.

I lived an independent life in the clubhouse. Miles, noting that I was an orphan, had taken upon himself the role of guardian. When I lived with him he was insufferably bossy.

"A woman has got no business living by herself," he said when I told him I was moving.

"Half the people in that clubhouse is unmarried women."

"They're old women. Spinster schoolteachers and such. A young woman is different. I know how these miners are."

"Do you, Miles?" I smiled sweetly. "How are they?"

He turned red. "You know what I mean."

"No. Tell me."

"Durn it, Carrie—"

"Now you look here. I am a nurse. I seen more naked men than you got working in that mine. I give em baths. I been on my own for three year of school, nobody telling me what to do. I lived in Justice town where they's bars and whores. Just what do you think you're protecting me from?"

"Well—"

"I dont like rattling around in this house. Hit's big enough for all of Scary Creek to live in. You want somebody in here with you, git married and have a passel of younguns. But I want me a place of my own."

"What if I say no?"

"Then I'll go somewheres else. They's a need for nurses anywhere I choose to go. I might go to New Orleans or New York. Or Paris, France or Peking, China. You dont know where I might run off to."

There was nothing he could say to that, and I got my two rooms on the back corner of the second floor beside the fire escape. They had high ceilings, long narrow windows, rich oak floors and walls of gray wainscoting. I hung green and blue curtains, bought a green bedspread and blue rugs. I also purchased a gray metal electric lamp from the company store, and painted pink flowers around the base. These were the first things I had bought with my own money, and I was very proud.

Still I ate supper with Miles, and sometimes stayed the night. It was a comfort, from time to time, to sleep under the same roof as kinfolks. Miles was usually pleasant company. He was happy with his work, but lonesome. He had been in love at Berea, but never heard from the girl after he graduated. Clary Leach, back on Scary Creek, was out of the question, he said.

"They aint nothing wrong with Clary," I said.

"Aw, what would she do with a big house like this?"

"Same as you do. Look silly."

"Come on, Carrie. She's not educated."

"That dont mean she's stupid. If you're gitting uppity, go on up to Boston and marry one of your old rich boss's daughters."

"You know what? I've been thinking of going to that Episcopal church in Justice. Those are good people to socialize with."

I went with him once. The building was solid stone and stained glass with red doors, just like the churches in *Wuthering Heights*. I loved to walk by it when I was in school. But during the service, I got tired of standing when everybody else stood, and kneeling when they knelt, and looking up prayers in a book.

"God could bung them people over the head and they wouldnt know who done it," I said. "They'd have to look it up."

"I like it," he said. "It's a dignified service."

Miles worked hard at being dignified. He never went outside the house without his hat, tie and starched collar. He had been to Boston, he said, and seen how they lived. He said it the way other people describe their religious experiences. Every Friday he sat at his desk and wrote to the mine owners; every Monday he went eagerly to the post office to receive their letter to him. In June he made his second pilgrimage to New England. I helped him pack and saw him off at the train station. He waved to me through the dusty glass window, his face bright and eager as a child's.

When he returned two weeks later, I went to the big house for supper. Miles picked disinterestedly at his ham, prepared by the widow woman who cooked for him.

"They took me to their summer cottage in Maine. Cottage! It was bigger than this house. We had lobster. I ate my salad first, real slow, so I could watch how they got at that lobster and not let on like I was ignorant. It wasn't too hard to eat."

"What's it like?"

"Like a great big old crawdad."

I giggled. "Was it good?"

"Oh, my! I wish we could get it here. You dip it in melted butter. One of these days I'll take you up there and buy you one."

"One of these days mules will fly. In the meantime, I'll enjoy this here ham and sweet potatoes."

He had come back with his corn-colored hair parted in the middle and cut short, "like they wear in Boston." He looked very young. After dinner we went to sit by the fireplace and he smoked a cigar he brought back with him.

"We had Baked Alaska for dessert," he said.

"Well, while you was having Baked Alaska, we was having typhoid."

"What?"

"Typhoid. We had five cases while you was gone. Two died and one is like to go any time. Hit's the season for it."

He sighed. "I reckon I got to come back down to earth, dont I?"

"I been looking around. The privies is built over the creek and that's where most folks gits their water. With this many folks living cramped together, you got to build new privies, deep ones, and treat them with chemicals. That, or bring water into the houses. If you dont, you'll keep right on gitting typhoid."

He frowned. "I don't know if they'll approve that. They aren't spending any money on living facilities right now. They're talking new tipple. Privies or plumbing would take some money."

"Sounds to me like they got some money."

He wrote, after much prodding on my part, and asked permission to install new sanitary facilities at Vulcan. The answer came back in a week. There was no money in the budget for such frills. As for disease in the camp, it was caused by the filthy habits of the miners and their families.

I was furious. "They built this here camp. They built the privies where they are. Anybody on Scary Creek will call you a fool ifn you build your privy next to your drinking water. Is that how they do things in Boston?"

"Don't be silly, Carrie."

"Dont call me silly. Who do them people think they are? And what are you going to do about it?"

"I've done all I can do. I took a risk bringing it up to them in the first place. They don't like to be bothered by details."

"And that's all you got to say?"

"That's all I've got to say."

He was my brother, so I said no more, tried to smother my anger. Two more typhoid cases died. I was silent. Each of us has our price, I thought bitterly. Miles has not walked behind a plow in six years, and he will do what he must to stay here. I have lost my mother and father, I have no husband and am not likely ever to have, and family means all the world to me. I'll not turn on my kin.

I was restless through those summer nights, and often rose at dawn to look out my window. Scores of miners walked to the drift mouth. From that distance they appeared gray, and slow-moving, and transparent, as though they could pass through the mountainside and disappear.

JUNE WAS BALMY, A BLESSING BEFORE THE SWEATY HEAT of July and August. In good weather I especially missed the Homeplace. I was used to taking walks in the evenings, searching out berries or poke, or fetching the cows. Vulcan kept me penned in. There was no way to get away from the sights and sounds of coal mining without trudging three miles up the creek. I walked farther than that on Grapevine, but here it felt oppressive. My legs would not take me so far. On pretty days I scanned the blue skies out the windows of the doctor's office and thought myself a prisoner.

On such a day late in the month I had the office all to myself. The doctor was gone to see about a hard birthing on Turnhole Holler where the Italian miners lived. It was a breech birth, long and drawn out, and we had been expecting it. The call came just before noon, and the doctor would not be back until late that night.

Only two people sat in the waiting room, neither of them seriously ill, so I sent them home, then retired to the back office to eat my lunch and read a book. I was so absorbed in the mysteries of *Jane Eyre* that I started when a knock came on the door frame and stared stupidly at the black-faced man who stood there.

"We brung up a hurt feller," he said.

"Oh, no! The doctor's gone for the day. Is he bad?"

"Dont know, ma'am. Hunk of slate fell on his foot."

"I'll see to him then. Thank you for helping."

He tipped his cap and left.

The man sat on the examining table with one leg dangling and the other propped on a stool. He listened to his own heartbeat through my stethoscope.

"What are you doing?"

He looked sheepish and draped the stethoscope over the back of a chair.

"Sorry. Hit was right where I could reach it and I couldnt resist."

I smiled to show I wasn't angry. "I'd think you'd be in too much pain to be fooling around."

"It does hurt. Like hell. I was trying to git my mind off it."

"I have to examine it. It's going to be painful."

"Right."

The foot was purple and swollen to twice its normal size. I washed it gently.

"Good thing they took your boot off," I said.

"Had to cut it off, even so. I know it's broke."

"I got to check anyway. You hold onto something."

He gripped the back of a chair. "This here is a nice office. Lots of instruments."

"Yes, we've got most things we need."

"You been nursing long?"

"Just a few months."

"Where'd you st—Ow! Jesus!"

I palpated his foot, felt the bones pull apart like a chicken wing. I stood up.

"Broke," I said.

His face was pale, the skin drawn tight with pain. It was a handsome face, square, with high cheekbones. His hair was brown and curled on the back of his neck, and he had a full moustache.

"What's your name?" I asked.

"Justice. Lloyd Justice."

I wrote it down.

"And whereabouts you live?"

"I board with the Widder Schoolcraft in the main bottom."

"Schoolcraft? Didn't she have a typhoid case recently?"

"That's right. One of her younguns took sick and died.

You come to visit the house one day, she said. I was down in the mines.''

"I remember now."

"Betty was that little girl's name. Sweet youngun. You know what causes typhoid, dont you?''

His voice was no longer friendly and his blue eyes were cold. I tried to fill out the rest of the form.

"Yes, I know."

"You're a health officer and you aint done nothing about it?''

"That aint true. I had words with my brother over it."

His eyes narrowed. "That's right. He's your brother. I heard that but I'd forgot it. Stupid of me, weren't it? Reckon I'm fired now. Will you fix my foot before you send me packing? How do yall do it hereabouts?''

"Dont be silly. I dont care what you have to say." I bent over the form, tried to look busy. "What do you know about typhoid anyway?''

"Enough. I wanted to be a doctor oncet."

"Is that so?" I tossed my pencil on the counter and glanced at the clock. "Tell me about it on the train. We got fifteen minutes to git over to the platform. I'll fetch you some crutches.''

"Train? What for?"

"I got to take you to Grace Hospital in Justice town."

To my surprise, he looked frightened.

"What's wrong? You aint scairt of hospitals?"

"Where's the doctor? Why cant he set my foot right here?''

"He wont be back until after midnight, most likely. We got an agreement with the hospital. Whenever the doctor aint available, I take the patient in to Justice on the train. I know you're in pain but it's only seven miles. It's better than waiting for him.''

"I cant go to Justice."

"Why ever not?"

"I just cant go, that's all."

He slid off the table, grimaced, and wavered on one foot. I stood in front of him and folded my arms.

"This here is foolishness," I said sternly. "If you dont git that foot tended proper, you wont never walk again.

Now as you said, I am the health officer in charge here. And if you dont come to Justice with me, you wont never work again neither, here or any other mine. Nobody wants a gimpy miner. You understand that?''

His voice trembled with anger. "They's a doctor at Chieftan camp. Why cant we go to him?''

"That's a whole different coal company. Besides, Doctor Redman is a lots busier than we are. By rights they ought to have two doctors in that camp, big as it is.''

I went to the closet, selected a pair of crutches.

"Please," he said.

"You come with me or I'll have somebody fetch you. It's simple as that.''

We barely made the train. When we sat down I found that I was trembling. He was obviously in terror of something, and I knew I must seem cold and heartless. But I didn't know what else to do. Doctor Harless would be furious if I let the foot go untended, and I would have to live with the knowledge that a man might be crippled.

I turned from the train window and looked at him. He sat rigid, the crutches upright between his legs, and stared straight ahead.

"You mad at me?'' I whispered.

He started to answer, ran his fingers back through his hair, and looked away.

"What are you scairt of?''

When he didn't answer, I turned back to the window. The train approached Chieftan, the last stop before Justice.

His hand, still black from the mine, gripped my arm, soiled my white uniform. I pulled back, but he leaned closer.

"I like the way you talk. Sounds like you're from around here. Is that so?''

"I was raised over on Grapevine. Lived there all my life until I went to nursing school over at Justice.''

He was searching my face for something, a sign, an answer. The train stopped at Chieftan.

"Come on!'' He was out of the seat before I had time to think. Five or six people went by before I could enter the aisle. By the time I gained the platform he had crossed the station yard and lurched along on his crutches toward main

Chieftan. When I caught up to him, he rounded on me before I had a chance to speak.

"You ever seen a man die?"

I was so astonished that I could only nod my head.

"You seen a man murdered?"

"No," I whispered.

He leaned closer. "Would you like to see me murdered? If I go to Justice, that's what will happen. I been told never to set foot in that county again, or I'm dead."

"Why? Did you kill somebody?"

He touched my cheek. "No, I aint killed nobody. I used to make whiskey over in West Virginia. They's a man in Justice thinks I took some of his trade. Says he'll shoot me ifn he catches me back acrost the river. That's all."

He dropped his hand, and his face was pale. "I feel faint," he said.

I led him back to the platform and sat him down with his head between his legs. A company policeman came by and asked what was wrong.

"He'll be all right," I said. "I'm taking him to see Doctor Redman. But I would appreciate a cup of water for him."

He revived some after he drank his fill.

"Will this doctor see me?"

"He's a good man. I'll try to talk him into it."

He smiled. "I aint even asked your name."

"Carrie. Carrie Bishop. Now ifn I dont git you to a doctor soon, they'll be cutting that foot off. Can you walk now?"

"I think I can make it."

Doctor Redman was an elderly man whose white hair had turned yellow at the temples. He listened to my vague pleading, asked no questions, and set the foot after only a half hour's wait. The cast would stay on two months, he told us, and the crutches should be used for another six weeks.

"You may have a permanent limp, young man, but a slight one. Shouldn't keep you from doing anything you want to do."

"Thanks, Doc. How can I go about paying you?"

"I don't want any pay. Just promise me you're not getting this young lady here into some kind of trouble."

"On my honor."

Before we left, the doctor gave Lloyd a shot of morphine for the pain. By the time we got back on the train, he was drowsy, and he fell asleep before we reached Vulcan, his head dropping to my shoulder. I roused him with difficulty and we wobbled drunkenly toward the Widow Schoolcraft's house. The widow came outside and helped him into the yard. I stayed at the gate until he disappeared inside the house.

A WEEK PASSED WITHOUT ME SPEAKING WITH LLOYD Justice, but he had taken up residence in my daydreams. I was touched by his confession that he wished to be a doctor. He was obviously intelligent and sensitive, a poor boy trapped in the mines. In the mornings I spied him from my window, swinging along on his crutches toward the tipple. I had talked Miles into giving him a job picking slate so he could pay his room and board at the Widow's. I pictured him in the breaker shed, hunched all day over a conveyor belt, leg propped on a stool. He was so vulnerable, his potential so precious, I would have loved him for that alone.

I decided Lloyd Justice and Miles must become friends. They would put their heads together over a bottle of Miles's bourbon. Lloyd could give Miles a firsthand account of the miners' health problems. Miles would explain how troublesome the Bostonians were, but Lloyd possessed a great deal of charm and would convince him at last.

One evening I stopped by the Widow Schoolcraft's on my way to visit Miles. Lloyd lay flat on his back on a bed in the front room. He sat up.

"Look who's here."

"I come to see how you're doing."

"All right. It aches sometimes and itches like hell, but it aint too bad."

"That's good." I was suddenly shy and looked down at my hands. "I had an idea. I wondered if you'd want to come up to the big house for supper. I'd like you to meet my brother."

"What kind of game you playing?"

I looked up. "I aint playing no games. I thought you

could tell him about how the miners see things, and about the typhoid. They aint too many of the miners he knows on a personal basis."

"Sit down here." He patted the side of the bed. "Does he know some of the miners?"

"Well, they's two or three comes to see him from time to time. They sit and talk and smoke cigars."

"What do they talk about?"

"Dont know. Miles allays sends me out. Business, I reckon. But I bet they dont say too much to him."

"Same ones every time?"

"I only seen two or three."

"Who?"

I hesitated.

"Look," he said. "I got to watch out for my reputation. If the boys think you're too cozy with the boss man, they may not trust you. Tell me who your brother talks with, and I'll know if they're respected by the others. I'll know if I can come visit and not lose no faith."

"Well, Tom Mace is one."

"Do tell."

"And Anse Crenshaw and that Negro with the beard, Albert something or other."

"That all?"

"That's all I ever seen come."

He nodded his head contentedly. "Well, I never would of thought it of them boys. Aint that interesting to know." He smiled at me. "Reckon if they can visit, so can I. When should I come?"

"I'll have to let you know. I aint asked Miles yet."

"You aint? What makes you so sure he'll say yes? Most boss men wont fraternize."

"I done told you, they's some he sees. Besides, I'll tell him you're my friend."

"Oh. That should do it then."

His eyes seemed to mock me, but then he smiled again. "You are something. I reckon you could talk a bear down outen a honey tree."

Maybe, but I had a time convincing Miles.

"You've got no business being friends with a single miner," he said. "I had a look at that fellow at the tipple.

He's got a swagger even with that cast on. There's just one thing he wants from you.''

''What?''

''You're not baiting me this time, Sis. I'm warning you, that's all.''

''What makes you think he wants something from me? Aint nobody ever wanted it before.''

''That's because you're so muleheaded. It's not becoming.''

''Go to church ifn you want to preach.'' I stomped out, slamming the door behind me. Then I stuck my head back inside. ''I'll just invite him to supper at my place.''

I knew that would do it. He let out a sigh and said Lloyd could come to supper on Saturday.

Miles served roast beef and cherry pie. Lloyd had three helpings, and I noticed him wrap a fresh-baked roll in his bandana and stick it in his pocket. Then we went to sit in the library. Miles opened a box of cigars, made an elaborate display of choosing two and cutting them. He had a special cutter shaped like a guillotine, a present from Boston. He was never quite easy with it and had sliced his finger on several occasions.

Lloyd sat on the sofa and looked around the library with its bookshelves and piano.

''I reckon you didn't grow up in a room like this,'' he said.

''No,'' Miles agreed. ''No, of course not. My father was a simple mountain man.''

''Simple my foot,'' I said. ''You never figured him out.''

''You know what I mean,'' Miles said. He gave me his down-the-nose look, which meant I should behave myself. ''Daddy wasn't a sophisticated man.'' He smiled at Lloyd. ''And there's nothing wrong with that, of course. I'm proud of my background.''

Lloyd smiled back. ''Reckon it's helpful in your job. You come up like the rest of us. You know what it is to do a hard day's work.''

''Yes. The company likes that. That's one reason I was hired.''

''They like to know how their miners think.'' Lloyd was reared back on the sofa, blowing smoke at the ceiling.

"That's smart. We're a pretty cantankerous bunch, independent like. Dont take kindly to hard bossing."

"I've helped them appreciate that in Boston," Miles said. "They have to respect the independent turn of mind of the Appalachian miner."

"Make the men mad, they might do something out of spite," Lloyd agreed. "Like agitate for the union."

Miles tried to look relaxed, but I saw right through him. He kept tapping his cigar against the ashtray long after the ashes had dropped. "You hear much about that?" he asked.

"Now and then," Lloyd replied. "I dont put much count in it. Hit's just a hothead shooting off his mouth." He flicked his own ashes. "Now and then."

Miles frowned. "Anything recent?"

"Not since the first week I was here. And the feller who said it, I dont think he even knows what a union is. He was just mad at a boss that day. I better not say nothing more about it. I aint wanting to get a feller in trouble over losing his temper."

"Sure. I understand how people speak out in anger. No sense in making a big thing of it."

"Man talking union, that aint no cause to fret yourself. Most of these men seem real happy."

"I'm sure they are. This is a good company."

"And not that I'm for the union," Lloyd continued. "I was raised to look after myself. I dont want nobody telling me when I can work and when I cant. I know if I want to work or not. If I dont like the boss, that's my privilege. I'll say goodbye, move on."

Miles cleared his throat. "Yes, I certainly agree with you. I approach this job the same way. Unfortunately, some people bring ideology into it. The union claims to be concerned about the miners' welfare, but what they're really after is a change in the economic and social order."

"What do you mean by that?" I asked.

"Well, you know"—he waved his arm vaguely—"the idea that uneducated and backward people are capable of running the mines." He looked at Lloyd. "Of course, I didn't mean to imply—"

Lloyd smiled to show he wasn't offended. "You mean socialism."

"That's the fancy word for it."

I didn't like the way the conversation was going. "They's some of those uneducated people got more brains than you, Miles. Just because Ben sent you to Berea—"

"I admit I'm lucky. If I hadn't gone to school, I wouldn't deserve to be in the position I hold now. But education is the key to progress."

"Hit's the twentieth century," Lloyd said.

"Exactly. Our grandchildren will see the year 2000. And look at all the new inventions—electricity, the telephone, the motorcar. The world is changing, Carrie, changing for the better."

"And we got to change with it," Lloyd said. "We got to adapt."

"Exactly!"

"Hit's the age of the machine. Folks got to adjust or they'll get crushed like a miner in a roof fall."

"Well," Miles said, "that's a pretty strong image. It's more like they'll be left behind. But I can see you think about things."

"I do some reading," Lloyd said modestly. " 'The machine is the new messiah.' Henry Ford. I read what them educated boys say." He smiled at Miles like a pupil impressing the teacher.

"Lloyd is interested in medicine," I said quickly. "He wanted to be a doctor. And he aint happy about the sanitary conditions in the camp, neither."

"Now, Miss Carrie, you're going to get me in trouble."

"Not at all," Miles said. "You're entitled to your opinion. I'm glad to listen to grievances."

"You do anything besides listen?"

"If I can. In this case, I can't. I've already tried."

"Cant fault a man for trying, can you?" Lloyd said.

I brought up school again, but Lloyd said he couldn't afford to go and wouldn't be beholden to anyone who might help him. Miles didn't make any offers. I told myself it was a good beginning and tried not to be disappointed. I listened while they talked amiably about the company's plan to open new mines. Miles asked if Lloyd ever thought about being a foreman, and Lloyd said he'd think about it. He asked if he could escort "Miss Carrie" back to the club-house, and Miles agreed.

"You didn't say much," Lloyd said as we walked along. "I thought you'd be more of a talker."

"I'm sort of quiet," I said. "Unless I'm riled."

"I've got acquainted with your brother. When can I get acquainted with you?"

"Come to supper tomorrow night."

"Would Brother Miles approve?"

"It aint none of his business."

He grinned. "Looks like I'll be eating good this week-end."

HE SHOWED UP ON MY DOORSTOOP AT FIVE O'CLOCK, HIS cap in his hand and his hair still damp from a washing. He handed me a paper bag full of poke and wild onion.

"Flowers from the mountains," he said.

"Let's take them downstairs. I talked Mrs. Hairston into letting me use a cookstove in the big kitchen."

I had four pork chops, wrapped in slick white paper, specially cut by the butcher at the company store. I simmered them in flour and butter, mixed cornbread and baked it in an iron skillet, fried potatoes and wild onion, tossed the poke salad. When I was finished we bore our treasure upstairs on trays, along with a pitcher of cold buttermilk. We sat down at the table and looked across at one another. There was an awkward silence.

"You usually say grace?" Lloyd asked.

"No."

"Good." He heaped potatoes onto his plate. "You feed a man real good, Miss Carrie."

"You can stop calling me Miss Carrie," I said. "Miles aint around."

He smiled. "I was just being polite like my mommy taught me."

"Where is your mama? You never told me where you're from."

"I was born and raised in Justice County, over in West Virginia. Blackberry Creek. We had some land there oncet. Company took it."

I remembered Albion Freeman, who had spoken of stolen land in West Virginia. I had not thought of him in years.

"They do that a lot? Steal land, I mean."

"Sure. All over. Steal it or put the pressure on to buy it. Same thing, far as I'm concerned. How do you think your brother's company got this here land?"

"I just figured they bought it."

"Oh, they did. Everything legal, but sinful as hell. This here is fine cornbread."

"Thank ye. Hit's my Aunt Jane's recipe."

"Aunt Jane. What's she like?"

"Real old. Fiesty."

"That where you git your meanness?"

I giggled. "Some say we're peas in a pod," I said.

We finished off with a chocolate layer cake I made the night before. Lloyd leaned back in his chair and moaned.

"I got to git up and move," he said. "Maybe all that food I et will settle down into my hollow leg. You want to go for a walk?"

"Sure. Dont let's fret about the dishes. I'll cover em and do them tomorry."

We went outside and wandered down the road toward Chieftan, past a row of double houses. We'd had no rain for two weeks. The holes in the road were dry, and coal dust lay thick on the dandelions that grew up by the fences.

"You was awful sweet to Miles," I said.

"I'm sweet by nature."

"You are not. I was watching you close. You was laughing at him the whole time."

Lloyd grinned. "You watch too close," he said.

We passed by the company garden. People worked their corn, chinked their hoes against the rocky ground.

"I git tired of all that talk about education and progress," he said.

"Aint you interested in bettering yourself?"

" 'Bettering yourself.' Now there's a phrase for you. You think your brother is a better man now than he was when he was hoeing corn?"

"He's happier."

"That aint the same thing. He's happy at everybody else's expense. Progress is always at somebody's expense. Hit means putting everything in order till they's no room to breathe. Progress means cleaning everything up. But I like things dirty.''

"You sound like a radical. You didn't sound like one last night.''

"I didn't want to git throwed out before I finished my cigar.''

We passed the houses, walked half a mile in the blue evening to the curve between lower Vulcan and upper Chieftan. Lightning bugs decorated the stickweeds and gnats bit my ankles and bare arms.

"We better turn back,'' he said. "Aint nothing to see in Chieftan.''

I turned obediently, my arms clasped across my chest.

"How come you aint married?'' he asked.

"I just aint found the right man,'' I answered, shamed to tell him that I feared no one would want me, that in my three years at school no one had come courting.

"You look to me like you're too independent,'' he said. "You wouldnt take to a man bossing you around.''

The way he said it did not sound like a reproach.

"I can take care of myself,'' I agreed proudly.

"Sure you can. I'm that a way, too.''

"I know. I like a man to talk the way you do.'' I was afraid that sounded too forward, so I changed the subject. "Who are your kin? You still aint told me about them.''

"Aint much to tell. My daddy's a broke down old coal miner. I got two little brothers. One of em's married, got a youngun. He's the only one I see much of.''

"What about your mama?''

"She dont care much for me. Aint never been able to please her.''

I felt a tenderness for him then, and an anger at his mother.

"Did I tell you I pick the banjo?''

"No, you never told me that.''

"I pick in a band with my brother and a buddy. We play all over in Kentucky. Inez. Warfield. Louisa. Even over to Shelby oncet. Call ourselves the Blackberry Pickers. I'll take you to hear us sometime.''

"I'd love that.''

His crutches tapped the road.

"You like nursing?"

"Hit satisfies me to help sick folks feel better," I said slowly. "And the human body is such a miracle. I study it and I think, 'How could it all work?' I seen babies borned. I seen dead bodies cut all apart by my teachers until they werent nothing left and I wondered what it was that run that body, that made them muscles move and them lungs breathe. Hit's like an invisible fire running through us. Hit dont surprise me that the fire goes out. Hit's where it come from that makes me ponder. And how we could feel things and think things, and us just a mess of muscle and fat. And if the fire comes from somewhere, then hit surely does go somewhere."

"You ever seen a youngun die?"

"First person ever I saw die was a youngun. A Negro girl name of Charlene. I nursed her two weeks before she passed on. The day she was took bad, they had to go hunting her mama. She cleaned house for a big shot in Justice town. He wouldnt even let her stay by her youngun's sick bed. When Charlene took to breathing hard, I knew she wouldnt make it until we could fetch her mama. But she did. She just stared up at that ceiling and breathed until her mama walked in the door. Then she turned her face to her mama and died. I walked right out of that room. And I aint been scairt to die since, not since I seen how that youngun did it. I just wonder where we go, and what it will be like."

"And it didnt make you mad?"

"I werent mad. I was just perplexed. But I did git drunk that night. Only time in my life I drunk liquor."

He laughed. "I'd like to seen that." Then he grew quiet. After a time, he said, "I seen men die. Seen my dad's buddy die when I was just a youngun. Made me mad as hell. Not mad at God, mad at the company. And I seen a union organizer murdered. Gun thugs throwed him right into a furnace. Seemed like he leaped right outen his body before they threw him in. Like he went off somewheres else."

"A union organizer?"

We stopped walking and stared at one another.

"That's right," he said.

He took my hand, led me on down the road a ways, stopped again.

"Carrie, can I come up to your room and set for a spell?"

My insides quivered. "Sure," I said.

Dogs charged from beneath houses and barked as we walked back down the rows. Lloyd sang softly, an old fiddle tune.

> "Polly's in the garden sifting sand,
> Sue's in bed with the hog-eyed man.
> I'm going home with Sally Ann,
> I'm going home with Sally Ann."

He turned to me.

"Your name Sally Ann?"

I giggled. "Hit's Carrie Lee."

"Close't enough."

My thoughts were all awhirl as we climbed the clubhouse steps. What would I say if he did this or that? When should I say no? What would Flora advise? What would a good girl do?

I looked at his face in the lamplight, felt the weakness in my legs, and knew it would be impossible to say no to him.

I sat down on the sofa. He will go to the chair, I thought. But he sat beside me, lay back on the lumpy cushions.

"You ever been kissed, Carrie Lee?"

"No," I whispered.

"Hit's about time."

He put his arms around me, pulled me closer, and kissed me on the mouth. Then his moustache tickled my neck and he slipped one hand inside my blouse. Every muscle in my body relaxed and in one magical moment I was on my back and he stretched full length on top of me.

"No corset, thank God." He smiled against my cheek.

I followed what he did, unbuttoned his shirt and ran my fingers through the hair of his chest.

"I aint sure what to do," I said.

"You're doing just fine. Do whatever you want to do."

"I dont want you to think I do this all the time, just with anybody."

"Honey, I know better than that." He lifted my skirt, caressed my thigh. "You want me to stop?"

For a moment Aunt Becka's face was close to mine, frowning in disapproval. I was astonished this was happening so fast, that I was letting it happen. But then I tasted his mouth again, so sweet.

"No. Dont never stop."

He tugged off my skirt, my blouse, pulled my shift over my head. Then he stood up, leaned against the sofa, and awkwardly undressed. Together we struggled to pull his pants over the cast on his foot. Then he lay back down beside me and slipped off my underpants. I marvelled at the smoothness of his skin, the smell of him, as though I had never encountered a human being before. I clung to him with a fervor I had not known I possessed.

"You are a hugger," he said, and I held on all the more tightly.

He encircled my wrist with his finger and thumb. "So small." He guided my hand to his groin. The skin was softer than a baby's. I thought I must be the first to make such a discovery, that I had stumbled onto something precious. I longed to cry out that I loved him, but the words would not come. We had not yet spoken of love. I knew a moment of pain, but it was fleeting, and I balanced on a great promontory, I scaled the heights to be touched by God and would never be the same again.

He was spent, his hair damp against my cheek. His heart fluttered wildly in his chest, like a bird trying to escape a cage.

"I feel your heart beating," I said.

He raised his head languidly, propped himself up on his elbows. "That's what you done to me."

"It was my first time," I said shyly.

"I never would have knowed it."

I wasn't sure if that was a compliment. Then he kissed the tip of my nose.

"I reckon you're just a natural."

"I think hit's because I'm with you. You was so gentle. I felt—I aint never felt this for a man before. Hit was so special."

He kissed me as though to quiet me. He had remained

inside me and now he rose, moved, came again, affirmed what had gone before. Later we stood naked in the moonlight. He was just tall enough for me to bury my face in the silk-smooth skin of his neck.

"I want to wake up beside you," he said.

We went to the bedroom, rested awhile, then loved again, drowsily this time. Afterward he fell asleep, snoring softly. I giggled into my pillow. Listening to Lloyd's snores would be part of loving him, too. I lay sleepless throughout the night, my mind wandering from one scene to another—here we courted on the front steps of the Homeplace, and my kin would take me aside and tell me what a fine man he was; there we stood up before the preacher at our wedding. I saw Lloyd pace anxiously while he waited the birth of our first child. I saw him old, his hair and moustache turned to white but his eyes still a lively blue.

I watched him wake up in the morning, heard the catch in his breathing. He turned his head and threw his forearm across his eyes. He seemed to remember something, then he turned to me and smiled.

"Morning," he said, and pulled me to him.

"Morning. You slept good last night."

"Sure did. The sleep of a contented man. How about you?"

"No, I didnt sleep a wink. Couldnt. Had too much on my mind, thinking about everything that happened."

"Uh-oh." He kissed me and got out of bed. "We better git dressed. The widder has likely set a place for me at the breakfast table."

"You can eat breakfast here. I'll run downstairs and bring something up."

He stumped into the front room on his crutches and dressed. I put on a nightgown and stood in the doorway. He buttoned his pants and looked up.

"I dont want you to take this too serious," he said.

I felt as though a cold hand grasped my throat. "What do you mean?"

"Just what I said. I aint the kind of man to fall in love with a woman. Dont know why, but that's the way it is."

"But I thought—"

"I never said I loved you, did I?"

I didn't want to answer him. "No. You didnt say that."

"What happened last night was nice. But dont expect nothin more from me. My life is crazy. Hit aint no kind of life to drag a woman into. And I aint no kind of man for you. You deserve more, somebody to pay you lots of attention. You'll find somebody like that, I know it."

"Dont you dare tell me what I deserve and dont deserve. I dont want nobody mooning over me, nor no rich man throwing money at me. I just want somebody to love me, somebody I can love."

"Then I surely aint no man for you," he said. "I aint never loved a woman and never will. I got nothing to give you. Absolutely nothing."

"Why didnt you tell me that last night?"

He came closer. "I didnt think it would make any difference. You wanted me. Aint that the truth?"

I blinked back tears and nodded my head. "But hit werent all I wanted," I said.

He took me in his arms, pressed my face to his shoulder with one hand.

"Carrie. Carrie. I wasnt wanting to hurt you. We should never have done what we done."

"That's easy to say now. You got what you wanted." I pulled away from him. "This mean I wont never see you again?"

He shrugged. "We might get together again sometime. If the time's right. I cant never say about nothing too far in advance. I'm picking the banjo in Inez next weekend. And the week after in Paintsville. Not to mention working my job. You see how my life is."

He kissed me goodbye and left. I sat beside the table and wept. Aunt Becka spoke loudly in my ear. You see. Just like a man. Now look what you've done. You're a fallen woman, and see where it has got you.

"Damn him," I said. "Damn him, damn him, damn him."

But I said it without conviction for I loved him. I believed in God and what Aunt Jane called His purposes. God had brought Lloyd to me, as surely as He placed us both in the mountains. I had freely given him, without a thought, what I had hoarded for years.

I could not bring myself to bathe, to wash away the smell of him. I dressed and walked through the July heat to the big house.

MILES QUESTIONED ME OVER THE NEXT FEW WEEKS, SAYING I seemed "all mopey and dreamy eyed."

"It's that fellow, isn't it?" he said once.

"Maybe it is," I said. "Maybe I took a shine to him. But he aint interested in me, so that's that."

"Just as well. He's nice enough, but you've got an education, and he doesn't seem interested in one. You can do better than a coal miner."

Twice I waited in the doctor's office until I saw Lloyd leave the tipple, so that I would be sure to meet him on the way home. He was always friendly, and told me how good I looked. But he didn't mention spending time with me.

MILES AND I SAT ON THE PORCH OF THE BIG HOUSE AFTER supper and ate strawberry ice cream from the company store. A light rain fell and washed away the August heat.

"Between the store and the electric, I'm gitting spoiled living here," I said. "But I still yet miss the Homeplace. I want to go visit pretty soon."

"I miss the family," Miles said, "and I miss the land. But I don't miss working it." He turned his spoon upside down and licked the back of it. "Carrie, do you understand why I came here?"

"I reckon so."

"I could have gone a way off somewhere, made my mark in Cincinnati or Lexington or Charleston. But I didn't want to leave these hills. That meant coal. Oh, I could have set up some kind of little business in Shelby or Justice. But to really be successful, I had to go into coal. You understand that, don't you?"

"I dont know that I understand why you got to be that big of a success. But what are you trying to tell me?"

He fidgeted in his chair so much that I knew there was more. He leaned forward, laced his fingers together.

"You know how they are in Boston. You know how they

feel about the United Mineworkers. They'd close this place down before they'd see the union come in here. You know that, don't you?''

I set down my bowl of ice cream. "Go on."

"One of my miners got drunk in Justice yesterday and let out that he had joined the union. Some of the Baldwin guards roughed him up and he told them who the organizer is.''

I pressed my lips together and sat up straight. "Who is it?'' I asked.

"It's Lloyd. Only his name isn't Lloyd Justice. It's Rondal Lloyd.''

"Oh, God, Miles! You wont hurt him? You wont let them hurt him?''

I tried to recall what I'd heard of organizers, how they were beaten, sometimes killed. Another thought came to me, almost as frightening.

"You wont make him leave?''

"I can't have it, Sis. Those guards got me a list of everybody that's joined. It's over half the mine. By the end of summer, they'd be ready to walk out on me. He's figured out who my informers are and avoided them, because I haven't heard a word about this until now.''

"Your informers," I said. "So that's why them men come to visit you. That is low down, Miles.''

"How the hell else am I supposed to know what's going on?'' He stood up and leaned on the porch rail, his back to me.

"Lots of operators would have beat him half to death by now, Carrie. You got to understand my position. The Baldwin people have got a lead on him. Seems they know him from before, over in Justice County. I've already warned him what I know, told him to get out.''

"Damn you, Miles.''

"Carrie, I've got to fire all those men. I've got to put them and their families out of their houses. How do you think I feel? If he hadn't come in here, those people would still have jobs.''

"If you'd let them have the union—''

"Carrie—''

"I know. Boston wont let you. You aint no man, Miles. You aint got no backbone nor principles."

He walked to the door. "He'll be leaving soon as it gets dark." He went inside.

I ran down the hill to the Widow Schoolcraft's. The rain had stopped and the fresh air cut my lungs. Rondal sat on the front steps.

"I figured you'd be by here," he said.

"Why didn't you tell me? I didn't even know your real name."

"Why should I tell you? Why should I trust you with my life?"

"I trusted you. I trusted you with my life, and more."

"If that's what you did, you're a damn fool. Hit aint my job to justify your faith in mankind."

I sat down beside him so I wouldn't have to look at him.

"Where you going to?"

"I'll hike up to the head of Pond Creek and cross over onto Marrowbone. Hit's safer to go west, I reckon. I was thinking to head in that direction anyhow if I had to run."

"How far west?"

"Colorado. They's a big fight in the coalfields out there. Taking on the Rockefellers." He held my hand, ran the tip of his finger along the lines of my palm. "I tried this twicet, and made a mess of it both times, aint I? I cant git no help from Charleston. The leadership up there aint worth shooting. I got to git out and learn how to do this better, meet Debs and Mother Jones and all them."

"Take me with you." I cringed at the sound of my voice, begging.

He smiled, kissed my hand, stood up and hobbled inside. I followed him. The widow sat in her front room stitching a quilt. Her eyes were cold when she looked at me.

"How you going to manage with them crutches and all?" I said. "What if them guards catch up to you?"

"I got a gun. I can take care of myself."

"What will you live on?"

"I'll do odd jobs. Jump trains. I got ten dollars saved up. I'll git by."

He picked up a pillowcase full of clothes, stuck it under

his arm against one crutch and swung out into the dusk. I ran after him.

"I got five dollars. Take it." I folded the bill and stuck it into his shirt pocket.

"All right," he said softly. "I'm obliged."

"Please let me go."

He touched my cheek. "I'm sorry I drug you into my life. I never should have done it. Maybe if things was different—"

He set his hand to my forehead, smoothed back my hair, then turned away. I watched him cross the bottom.

"I love you!" I cried.

I thought he paused, but it may have been some trick of the fading light. I heard the tapping of his crutches even after he was no longer visible. Then I ran up the hill, tore into the house. Miles stood in the parlor by the window.

"I hate you!" I screamed. "I hate you! You aint no brother of mine, you aint worthy to be kin, and I never want to see your face again!"

I went back to my room, sobbing with hurt and rage, and packed my things. I left the furniture, taking only my clothes, my books, and the electric lamp. I went to the station early the next morning. Farther down the tracks I saw Miles with all his men standing in a bunch. He was reading from a list, and the men separated to stand on one side of the track or the other. I wondered which side was the union men. When the train from Justice pulled in, four men with rifles got off.

I rode the train to the head of Pond Creek and hired a farmer with a mule team to take me and my belongings to Grapevine.

Part Three

Ten

C. J. MARCUM

THE DAY AFTER THE LETTER COME FROM RONDAL, I attended the monthly meeting of the Annadel Political and Social Club.

Our club started meeting in 1912 during the miners' strike on Paint Creek in the Kanawha coalfields. They was sixteen of us altogether, including Doc Booker, who was mayor at the time, Ermel and Isom Justice, Sam Gore the bartender, Everett Day, the entire town council and several policemen. We started by drinking together on Sunday afternoons, lounging in the gambling room of the Alhambra with our feet propped up on the tables, sipping Pabst Blue Ribbon and shots of whiskey. After a while we always talked about the strike. The Paint Creek miners and their families lived in tents for a year, even through the dead of winter. They was shot at, some was killed, and they shot back. The governor declared martial law and jailed folks for speaking their mind. We followed it all and wondered if it was coming to us one day.

When the strike was done with, we argued about who had really won.

"Course hit was a success," Ermel declared. "They got the union recognized, didnt they?"

Doc Booker disagreed. "Union was already recognized there for years, before them operators tried to bust it. Them people starved and froze and died all winter, just to stay where they was."

"The gun thugs smashed the press at the socialist newspaper in Huntington," I added.

119

"So what?" Isom tilted his head back and tossed down a shot. His adam's apple jumped.

"You'll think so what when it happens here," I said.

"Aw, I seen some of them socialists from Huntington. They wear ties and talk about nonviolence. Them kind is easy pickins."

We didn't always get along at our meetings. We was all so different from each other. Me and Doc was socialists. Ermel by that time was one of the big shots in the Democrat party machine, close to getting his man elected as circuit judge. Sam Gore was a Republican out of loyalty to Abe Lincoln. Isom weren't nothing, far as I could tell, except he liked to argue and drink his daddy's liquor. We had fights all the time and we loved it.

We took turns suggesting what we should talk about. Doc wanted to discuss the Brussels Congress of the Second Socialist International. Isom said that sounded dull, but we talked about it anyhow and he stayed perked up most of the time, especially when we wrangled over the fighting in the Balkans. Isom is real interested in the Balkans because he says they sound like West Virginia.

We talked about Woodrow Wilson, the Niagara Convention and the Ku Klux Klan. Then the coal strike in Colorado caught our eye. It was Paint Creek all over again, the strikers throwed out of their houses, the tents, the gun thugs and martial law. Then the letter come from Rondal.

"He's out there," I told the club proudly. "He's in Ludlow workin for the union. He even met Mother Jones and Eugene V. Debs."

"Hot damn!" Isom said. "So my banjer picker's all right."

"He's all right so far," I agreed. "This here letter is near two weeks old."

I read the letter out loud. Rondal's last words were, "You better get ready. This is coming your way some day." When I finished reading, my fingers trembled.

We followed the news from Colorado every day, and featured it on the front page of the *Free Press*. When the miners took Trinidad, we threw a party. Isom, drunk, sent a telegram to Mr. Felts of the Baldwin-Felts Detective Agency, telling him "what a fine job your gun thugs is doing stop keep up the good work stop John D. Rockefeller.'' But we sobered up considerable when word come out of Ludlow. The gun thugs and the U.S. Army attacked the tent colony there, shot people, set tents on fire and burnt women and children to death.

We fretted about Rondal, but they was nothing we could do. It was after the strike failed that another letter come and we knew he was safe. He was downhearted, he wrote, he was going to Chicago to see the city of Haymarket and Pullman, of Jane Addams and Altgeld and Clarence Darrow. We wasn't to fret, he said. He had in mind to watch the Chicago White Sox and stay out of trouble.

"He wouldnt go to school in Huntington because he didnt want to go far away," I said, "and now he's in Chicago. What's goin to happen to that boy?"

"He aint a boy no more," Doc said gently. "He must be twenty-four by now. And he always had a good head on his shoulders. You see if he dont come back."

I knew Doc was right. These mountains has got a powerful pull. They let a man wander so far and then they yank him back like a fish on a line. I knew Rondal would sleep uneasy as long as he was away, and the hills would bring him home.

THE ANNADEL POLITICAL AND SOCIAL CLUB began to talk less and less about the world outside and more about Justice County. We all knew we had to do something, but we disagreed on how to do it.

Ermel was deep into the Democrat party. He was connected with every bootlegger and roadhouse owner in the county. Me and Doc wasn't too happy about it, and not only because we was socialist. It just seemed to us like a bootlegger wouldn't have no principles. The Republicans got their votes when the operators looked over the shoulders of the miners in the voting booths. Ermel's crowd took in everybody else by promising a school board job for cousin Myrtle or threatening a busted still for brother Otis, or buying votes. Nobody never talked about getting back the land. It was just grab this and grab that.

I thought we in Annadel was better than that and we

ought to go our own way. Rondal's warning raised fear in
me. We had to prepare ourselves. I told Doc Booker. He
brought it before the town council and we voted to put a
few more men on the police force, but that was all we done.

I tried to reason with Isom, so he would talk his daddy
out of his crooked dealings. He wouldn't listen.

"Them coal operators aint angels, C.J.," he said. "You
got to reckon with it. They's socialists in England and Russia and the Sahara Desert for all I know, and they all get
together and talk. But that dont mean a diddly-squat in
Justice County. Aint nobody pays us no mind. We got to
do for ourselves."

Sometimes I thought we was saying the same things but
not matching up. Isom, he never lost no land. He aint had
kinfolks killed. He thinks he can do anything and get away
with it. He is his daddy's boy.

After the club got going, I tried to get Talcott Lloyd to
join. We set on his front porch at Felco one warm Saturday
evening and ate a fresh huckleberry pie sent down by Pricie's mother. Talcott is touchy where Ermel and Annadel is
concerned. He suspects that they send Pricie money, and
resents it, but when fried chicken shows up on the supper
table, he don't have the gumption to ask where it come
from. By his own lights, he tries to pay Ermel back by doing
work around the farm some Sundays and by going hunting
with Isom. Him and Isom is both crack shots and they sure
bring home the critters. Isom sends me squirrel meat about
oncet a week. I'll take squirrel over a chicken leg any
day.

That evening, Pricie come out on the front porch, one
baby holding to her hand and the other riding up on her hip.
The younguns' mouths was smeared blue with huckleber-
ries.

"We're goin to Gloria's," she said.

"Aint you better clean up them younguns before you take
them out of here?"

"I run out of water. We'll stop down at the pump."

"Dont you stay gone all night."

"I dont never, do I?"

They walked barefoot across the red dog, walked as

straight and steady as if they'd had on shoes. Folks in the camps, their feet bottoms gets tough as hide.

I told Talcott about the club.

"Why'd I want to come to somethin like that?" he said. "I aint got no education."

"You dont need no education. Sam Gore belongs and he aint got no education."

"Yeah, but he's a nigger."

"Lookee here, we talk about what's happenin in the world. Anybody can have an opinion."

"Opinion? Sure, I got lots of opinions. So what?"

"You ought to be able to say what they are. You ought to hear what other fellers thinks."

"Why? They aint got no more say-so than I do. Why do I want to waste a Sunday afternoon talking about some far off thing that dont have nothing to do with me?"

"Hit will expand your mind," I said. "Hit's like an education of itself, the way we talk. And Ermel supplies the beer and liquor free."

"I dont need no free beer and liquor offn Ermel. I can buy my own."

We ate another slice of pie and I helped fetch jugs of water from the pump. The water was thick and brown.

"I hope you boil this," I said.

Talcott shrugged. "Sure. Skim that stuff offn the top. Looks like nigger piss, dont it? Hit's either this or rainwater with wiggletails in it. Pricie likes the rainwater but I never could abide a damn bug."

"Aint nothing wrong with rainwater," I said. "We got a good well at Annadel, but we catch rainwater too."

"You have it," he said.

I couldn't get nothing else out of him on any subject. Ever since Rondal left, it was like he'd closed himself off behind a wall of stubborn. His daddy had moved to Number Six Davidson so Kerwin could go to the high school. I couldn't figure why Lytton Davidson would let them in up there, knowing that Rondal was 'beirn. But Doc said it would give them a way to keep up with Rondal. He couldn't visit his family without Davidson knowing it.

* * *

WHEN THE BIG WAR COMMENCED, WE COULDN'T WAIT TO sink our teeth into it at the club meeting. I took a hard time because I'd been predicting they'd be no war.

"They's socialists in all them countries," I'd said. "Hit's international. A workin man in England aint goin to fight a workin man in Germany. Not for some capitalists, he aint."

Even Doc disagreed with me on that.

"People is people," he said. "We all got the devil in us."

"Hit's them Balkans got their dander up," Isom declared. "They got tired of bein bossed around by them Austrians."

"Naw," said Doc Booker. "The real reason they fightin this war is over all them colonies in Africa. The German imperialists wants what the British imperialists has got."

"Oh, hell," said Isom. "What do them Croatians and Serbians know about Africa? They started it."

"And we'll finish it," Ermel declared. "Wait and see. They'll be American boys over there before this is all over."

"Your man Woodrow says not," I teased him.

"He aint my man just because he's a Democrat. He'd need ten sets of balls before he could stand alongside William Jennings Bryan."

Sam Gore went to the bar to fetch some liquor.

"What would ole Abe say to this?" Isom asked.

"He'd say, 'America, the enemy is within.' " Sam raised a glass.

Behind him the door exploded and a score of men with drawn pistols poured into the room.

"Hands up! You're under arrest!"

"What the hell?" Ermel stood up.

"Them's Baldwins!" Isom cried. "I know that bastard there."

"Shut up!" the leader said. He was a tall thin man with fleshy lips and a high, thin voice. "You're under arrest for seditious activities." He smashed a whiskey bottle with his rifle butt. "And for selling whiskey on Sunday."

"I aint sellin it," Ermel said. "I'm treatin my friends here. And you got no right—"

The man walked up to him and pointed the gun barrel at his temple.

"What you say?"

They tied our hands behind our backs and marched us to the train station. Annadel ran up just as we was boarding.

"Go git Roscoe," Ermel called. She nodded mutely.

We was scared and quiet when they checked us into the county jail at Justice. All except Isom, that is.

"What is this?" he kept saying. "You cant do this."

They hit him once and Ermel told him to pipe down. But he started up again when Doc, Sam and the other Negroes was set aside for separate cells in the back of the jail.

"That's right!" Isom yelled. "Git them socialist niggers away from us good white men. Aint nothin worse than a red black man!"

Doc snickered and a guard pushed him.

"Son, you aint in Annadel," Ermel said.

We was four to a cell, and only two cots. You couldn't call them cots really because they was no mattresses, just the wire frames that grilled our hides if we stayed in the same position more than five minutes. And burlap sacks for cover. And the electric lights on all through the night. And hard-boiled eggs with cold fried baloney for every meal.

I slept until my neck ached and my head felt like the metal frame of the mattress had grown into my skull. Then I heard singing from the colored section. I sat up.

"What's that?" Isom snickered. " 'Swing Low Sweet Chariot'?"

"No. Listen."

It was the "Star Spangled Banner." They sung it through and started it again. By the third time, a guard stalked past our cell, muttering to himself.

Isom laughed his high cackling laugh. "Jesus God! That's the worst song in the world!" He kicked Everett Day, who slept on the floor. "Wake up, Everett. Let's help em."

We waited until they reached the beginning and started in. "Oh, say can you see, by the dawn's early light!"

A guard ran up, banged on the door. "Shut that up!"

"O-oer the la-a-and of the freeee!"

We took shifts, sung it over and over again. Isom rocked back and forth on his heels, waved his arms in time to the music.

"Aint it fun bein seditious?" he said.

"—and the ho-ome of the bra-a-ave!"

After seven or eight hours, it weren't so much fun. We tapered off a bit, but we managed to keep it going. Finally they let us out, cussing all the time. Annadel waited in the hallway along with Roscoe Titlow, one of Ermel's Democrat cronies. Roscoe was a short man with close-cropped gray hair and a face that looked like it had been gnawed on.

"We been here since four o'clock," Annadel said.

Isom hooted. "Hit was the singin done it! Where's them red colored people? I want to shake somebody's hand."

The Negroes was brought up shortly. We hugged and jabbered, our voices cracking.

"All right, boys," Ermel declared. "Hit was fun. But hit werent the singin done it. Hit were Roscoe here."

Roscoe nodded his head. "Me and the sheriff had a little talk."

"And the sheriff live beside the jail," Doc Booker said. "Could he hear the singin?"

"He heard it," Roscoe admitted. "Said it was drivin him crazy."

We cheered, slapped backs, and headed for home.

WE LAUGHED ABOUT OUR JAIL STAY, EVEN LONG AFTERwards, but we cried when we got home. They had broke into our newspaper office, smashed the press and scattered type out into the street.

"Never mind," Ermel said. "I'll help you start again."

But it would be six months before we put out another edition of the *Free Press*. In the meantime, Isom come to me and Doc and said, "You're right. We got to do something. And I got an idea."

"What's that?"

"Make me Chief of Police. Between us, we'll make sure nobody can never come into Annadel and do this again. One thing I want to git straight, though. I aint no socialist, nor never will be. I dont care to see the government run these here mines."

"Hell," Doc said, "you think I want to see Woodrow Wilson in charge here? That man got his head so far up his ass he hear his heart beat."

We already had a Chief of Police but he was tired of Annadel's wild Saturday nights and agreed to go work for Ermel at a raise in salary. Isom took over. First thing we done was impose a one cent liquor tax. Then we joined the American Rifle Association and started to stockpile Krag-Jorgensen rifles.

Eleven

CARRIE BISHOP

I WENT BACK TO THE HOMEPLACE, AND BECAME PREOCCU-pied with the simple matters of living and dying. Aunt Jane passed away and her namesake was born to Ben and Flora.

Though my parents were both dead, I felt like an orphan for the first time. Aunt Jane was the last of the old people, born of the first settlers, wed and brought to the childbed during the War Between the States. For me she was a strong post to lean against. All my people knew about Rondal, but Aunt Jane alone took to her grave the knowledge of every-thing that had passed between us.

Flora and Ben grieved, but they had their first baby after two miscarriages, little Jane, and they could not feel totally bereft. They were continuing Aunt Jane's line. I was happy for Flora, but at night I wept for myself. Only Aunt Becka was as shaken as me by Aunt Jane's death. The women had a stormy kinship, but they had grown closer the last few years, Flora said.

"I think Aunt Becka was allays scairt of Aunt Jane. But Aunt Jane was feeble here of late. She lost some of her vinegar. They drawed close't at the end."

"They was two old women alone," I said. "Like I'm going to be."

"They's worse things. You could be married to some ras-cal. Aunt Jane and Aunt Becka got on all right by their-selves."

"Maybe. But I dont want Aunt Becka latching on to me now that Aunt Jane is gone."

"Shame on you! Aunt Becka will be lonesome."

"I know. And I dont want to see it. I'm too scairt of it for my own self to keep looking on it in her."

"What about Aunt Jane? She lost her husband young, only had one youngun by him, and then lost the youngun too. She got on. She lived a full life. You cant say she werent happy."

"Least she had a husband and a youngun for a time. Least she had them to remember on. That way she belonged here."

"Carrie Lee, you stop that feeling sorry for yourself! Hit aint pretty to see. This here is your home and allays will be."

It was a cold January day. We made biscuits in the kitchen beside a frosted windowpane. Flora flung her arms around me, careful not to touch me with her flour-dusted hands. I didn't tell her that I feared we would lose the Homeplace some day. I tried not to think about it myself. It was bad enough to dread a long life without the love of Rondal and hope of children. But if there was no place of my own to be, no ground where my bones could be laid beside my kin's, would I not be the most miserable creature in God's world?

Flora still held me tight. "God has picked out a man for you somewhere," she whispered.

"What if He aint? What if He dont mean for me to git married?"

"Then you got to accept God's will."

Her answer infuriated me. It was the answer she would give, the answer that all my people would give, all except Miles. But when I realized that, I was not so angry. It took a strength of will to give such an answer. If I could not say such words, if I could not overcome my selfishness, there was nothing left except to go off and turn my back on all I had come from.

I still prayed to God, as Aunt Jane and Aunt Becka had taught, even though I never really liked to go to church. The only church on Grapevine or Scary when I was a child had been the Holiness church at the mouth of Bearwallow. Daddy didn't care for the Holy Rollers and all their noise. He wanted a church where he could sit quiet, but there had been no preachers raised up for that sort of thing in our vicinity. Aunt Jane wasn't much of a churchgoer either, but she took me occasionally to Bearwallow. I was fascinated by the joyful whooping and the shimmying dances, but always left downhearted because we had not gotten the Holy Ghost the way the others had. When I mentioned this to Aunt Jane, she said, "Everbody gits the Holy Ghost in different ways. Me, I git it when I'm working the garden, when I see the food God gives us spring outen that rocky ground. I may not whoop and holler, but I swing my hoe in praise of the Almighty."

"Maybe I git it down by the river," I mused. "Sometimes they's something special I feel when the sun lights the mountainsides and everthing looks so clear." Then I remembered Old Christmas. "I got the Holy Ghost one time in the barn!" I exclaimed, and told her about the animals.

She nodded her head. "You see there," she said, satisfied.

After she died, I took armloads of spar grass and cockscombs to scatter on her grave. Burying grounds, too, would be places to receive the Holy Ghost, places where God danced with the spirits of the departed while they awaited the great raising day. At the cemetery, my people whirled around me, all the Bishops and Mays and Thornsberrys, baby Honakers, and even Daddy, come from afar and dancing slow, reluctant.

I settled back into the rhythms of the Homeplace. Miles, uneasy and quiet, had come home for Aunt Jane's funeral. We had little to say to each other. He returned the next year with a bride named Alice Collins, plump and curly-haired, the daughter of the bank president in Justice. She was not impressed with the Homeplace and I knew we wouldn't see much of them. Then I was sorry for Miles, even though he was married. I thought he would lose his strength, like Samson shorn of his hair. But I would be as tough as Aunt Jane.

Ben subscribed to the *Courier-Journal* and it brought news of the rest of the world. I read of the strike violence in Colorado and fretted over Rondal, but an inner voice told me he was still alive. The war broke out overseas and we shook our heads and wondered at the reports of it. I nursed sick people all up Scary and Grapevine, and as far away as Henryclay, and delivered babies. At night we talked, told stories to the children, Jane and baby Luke, and turned the logs on the fireplace.

Then Albion Freeman returned.

HE WALKED THE EIGHT MILES FROM KINGDOM COME, ABOVE Henryclay, where he lived. He had just moved up from Knott County to preach at a Hardshell Baptist church and to farm a piece of land near the head of the creek that didn't seem to belong to anyone.

"What was you doing in Knott County?" Ben asked.

"I was preaching there, too. Only some of them didnt like the word I was bringing. I felt a call to come up this way anyhow. They aint no place I was ever happier than here in Paine County. I wanted to see yall again."

They invited him to spend the night and we sat around the table after supper. I let the others ask the questions. I was a little frightened of him. He had been a slender, sharp-faced boy. He was still lanky but he had grown tall, over six feet, with a black stubble of beard, wiry hair that trailed over the collar of his shirt, and a long nose. His fingers were large and so gnarled they looked like he dug a corn patch with his bare hands. He kept looking at me, quickly, shyly. I studied my coffee cup.

"You're awful quiet, Carrie," Ben said once, and I wanted to smack him.

"I'm listening," I said.

Albion went on with his story. His daddy had taken the consumption and a warm climate seemed to ease him, so they wandered out of the mountains into the foothills of Georgia. They sharecropped a farm near Marietta. His daddy died in 1913 and Albion took off into the mountains again.

"The Lord has lead me hither and yon," he said, "but seems like He has allays aimed to bring me back here."

"How come you aint never married?" Flora asked.

"Aint settled in one spot long enough." He looked at me again. "You aint never married neither."

Rebellion made my voice sharp. "No, I aint. I dont never intend to git married."

"Remember how we used to talk about marrying each other when we grew up?"

"We was just silly younguns," I said. Aunt Becka kicked me beneath the table.

Flora put the children to bed and Ben took Albion to the parlor while Aunt Becka and I did the dishes.

"Why'd you kick me?" I asked.

"Cause you was being mean to that poor boy. Shame on you!"

"Well, he seemed to me like he was presuming some things. I dont like presuming."

"He werent presuming nothing. He was trying to be nice. And ifn you would be sweet to him, he might take an interest. A preacher would make a good husband."

I rattled the dishes in the washtub. "I dont think so. I think preachers is dull. Besides, why are you so anxious to find me a man all of a sudden? You done without by your own choice."

"Because you aint happy, that's why. Way things are, time you git my age, you'll be bitter."

When we went into the parlor, Flora and the men were discussing the crops we planted that spring.

"I put in a little patch of tobaccy, first time ever," Ben said.

Albion shook his head. "It's a heap of fuss."

"But hit's a little cash."

"I got me a goat and a couple sheep. That there ewe is going to lamb real soon."

"Oh," Flora crooned, "I love a little lamb."

"I'll bring you some of the wool offn it."

"You work that place all by yourself?" I asked.

He seemed touched that I had finally shown some interest, which irritated me further. "Hit aint a big place," he said. "You wouldnt think it was much."

I was supposed to say that I'd like to see it, but I didn't. After a pause, he said, "You'll have to come visit."

"Wouldnt that be nice?" Flora exclaimed. "Carrie, you should go some Sunday and hear Albion preach."

"I aint much of a preacher," Albion said. "But I sure would be tickled ifn you'd come visit."

"Flora and Ben would have to go too," Aunt Becka said.
"Hit's a long ways. You'd have to stay the night Saturday."

"I'd be honored," Albion said. "And hit would mean a lot to introduce you to my congregation."

"How about Sunday next?" Ben asked.

"Fine. We'll kill a chicken and have a big dinner after church."

"I'll bake a cake," Flora said. "Wont it be fun, Carrie?"

I crossed my legs and folded my arms. "Sure," I said.

HIS FARM WAS A CABIN, BARN AND THIRTY ACRES TUCKED away in a cove on Kingdom Come. It had belonged to an old man who died without heirs and it had stood empty for a year before Albion arrived.

"Hit was a crazy man lived here," Albion explained. "Went out of his mind after his wife died of the childbirth and kilt his own baby son. That was back during the War Between the States. He come back here after he got out of prison. He was allays standoffish with folks, wouldnt give no help nor ask for any hisself. Come time for him to die, no one knew he was gone for two weeks. Family up the road, Thornsberrys, say he come a tapping on their window late on Halloween. Next day they found him in the barn. Hung hisself from the rafters."

"Oh, lordy," Flora said. "I aint going in the barn."

"No need to." Albion patted her hand.

"Aint you scairt of being haunted?" I asked. I tried to sound like I didn't believe his story.

He smiled. "I am haunted. But I aint scairt of it. Sometimes I feel an uneasy spirit, but I speak to it, soothe it. I tell it to talk to that baby. Folks hereabouts are happy to have a preacher living here."

The night was unusually warm for April and we sat on the front porch. A chorus of peepers cried from the creek.

"Frogs is hatched," Ben said. He smoked his pipe contentedly.

I sat on the step with my knees drawn up under my chin and studied the barn. It was like a dark portal in the gathering dusk, a doorway to perdition.

"Do you think that man is in Hell?" I asked Albion, who perched on the bannister.

"I reckon I aint told you. I'm a No Heller."

"A what?"

"A No Heller. Hit's a kind of Hardshell Baptist. The Hardshells, you know, they believe God has it all set out who will be saved and who wont. Some go to Heaven, some to Hell, and they aint nothing a body can do about it. Me, I'm a No Heller. That's why I left Knott County, because they didnt want to hear the No Hell preached. They reckoned they was bound for glory and they didnt want to hear about no sinners coming with them."

"You mean you dont believe in Hell?" I was shocked. "What about the bad people?"

"Who is the bad people? Hit's us, Carrie. I believe in the Fall. I believe in the first sin, that it taints all of us."

"What about the man that kilt his baby? You and me wouldnt do that."

"Who's to say what we wouldnt do? We aint lived our lives yet. We had it easy compared to some folks."

"What about the coal operators that stole your daddy's land?"

"What about Miles?" he said softly.

I stiffened, stared into the darkness. "What about him?"

He came down to sit beside me. Ben and Flora had gone inside without my noticing.

"I shouldnt say I dont believe in Hell," Albion said. "Hit's real. We all of us live in it sometimes, and maybe will after we die. Oh yes, hit's real, and hit burns, just like the others preach. But one day Jesus Christ will wade right into Hell and haul out the sinners. Haul them out kicking and screaming. And I'll tell you what. The folks that stays in Hell the longest will be the ones that vow they dont belong there."

"I dont know," I said. "When I think on dying, it's Heaven scares me more than Hell. Hit allays has worried me that Heaven sounds so dull. Nobody does nothing wrong, which means we aint got no choice but to do right, and everybody sits around staring at them golden streets and twiddling their thumbs. Hell sounds a lots more interesting."

"Naw," he said. "I dont reckon that the God who thought up all this here peculiar world would come up with nothing dull. Think of what would make you content."

"I'd be content ifn everybody I loved was together in one place."

"But aint you been hurt by the ones you love?"

"Yes," I whispered.

"See there. And ifn them people hurt you ever day for all eternity, you wouldnt care, because they'd always be there. Even that man that kilt his baby, he'll be with that baby for all time. I tell him that, and he moans about it. But ifn it werent so, he would vanish in the twinkling of an eye. That baby wont let him go, though. That baby has got a toe hold on him."

"And the ones that wander all alone on this earth? The ones that lost their faith to believe?"

"Jesus will haul them out," he insisted. "Jesus will save ever last one. That there is Jesus's job. When this feller here died, hit were Jesus took him to tap on the Thornsberrys' window. Hit were Jesus brung me to soothe him." He stood up and stretched. "We'd best git to bed. I got to bring the word tomorry, and you got to hear it. I aint sure which takes more strength."

He slept in the loft and I had a cot in the main room where Ben and Flora shared the only bed. I drifted off to sleep but was awakened by Flora's anguished cries from some nightmare. Ben murmured to her, and then I heard the comfortable sounds of lovemaking. I fell asleep.

CHURCH MET IN THE KINGDOM COME SCHOOLHOUSE ONE mile up the creek. The congregation consisted of only three families, but all with numerous children. Altogether there were perhaps thirty people.

Albion's preaching style was strenuous, but not as much as a Holy Roller. He waved his arms and paced back and forth, but he didn't leap. When he stood still, he had a way of cocking his head to one side that I had not noticed before.

He preached from the eighth chapter of *Romans*.

" 'For the creature was made subject to vanity, not willingly, but by reason of him who hath subjected the same in hope. Because the creature itself also shall be delivered from the bondage of corruption into the glorious liberty of the children of God.' ''

He cradled the Bible in his big hands, glanced up at us as though he would ask some question. But he read further, and his voice rose.

'' 'For we know that the whole creation groaneth and travaileth in pain together until now.' ''

He rocked back on his heels.

"Gro-oaneth and travaileth in PAIN!" He whacked the Bible. "Together! Until now! Until now! And now—now Jesus saves the sinner. He saves the earth. He puts back what has been tore up. He heals what has been broke. He makes all things new. He drags the sinner outen Hell and arms him with truth and justice and righteousness, and together they storm the very gates of Heaven!"

"Amens" rose on all sides. Albion set down the Bible, clutched both hands to the sides of his head and paced. He halted.

"You say 'Preacher, how do you know this?' But dont the Bible say, 'the Kingdom of Heaven suffereth violence, and the violent take it by force'? The violent have took this here earth, but the meek shall have it by and by. And first, the groaners and the travailers must take Heaven. Hit wont come easy to them, oh no. But Jesus Christ shall lead and no mountain shall hold them back, brothers and sisters, even if it were ten times the height of these hereabouts. No flooding river shall keep them from crossing. Neither height nor depth''—he flung his arms wide—''shall separate them from the love of God, nor keep them outen Heaven.''

He wiped his face with a red bandana when he was done and sprawled back in his chair, his arms dangling over the sides. A thin-faced woman with a plum-colored birthmark on one cheek stood to lead the singing.

"We're floating down the stream of time, we have not long to stay," she called out in a practiced monotone, and we took up the tune, repeating her words after she lined them.

"Then cheer my brothers cheer, our trials will soon be o'er. Our loved ones we shall meet, shall meet, upon the other shore. We're pilgrims and we're strangers here, we're seeking the city to come. The lifeboat soon is coming to carry the jewels home.''

After church the four of us ate a big dinner at the farm and sat out on the front steps. Albion dragged a large box filled with dusty bottles from beneath the porch.

"What's that?" Ben asked. "Cider?"

"Wine. I make wine."

"Law," Flora said, "I aint never had wine except some dandelion oncet at Clinard Slone's."

"I didnt think preachers drank," I said.

"Now, now. Jesus changed the water into wine, didnt he? I reckon he dont mind ifn I make a little myself."

He ranged the many-hued bottles from deep purple to pale yellow along the porch railing. They glowed in the sun like they were lit with electric lights.

"This here is wild grape." He read the labels from the darkest to the lightest. "Blackberry. Huckleberry. Plum. Peach. Pear. Dandelion. Rosehip. Watermelon."

"Watermelon?" Ben laughed.

"That there come all the way up from Georgia. Hit is strange, I'll guarantee."

"Think you got enough kinds?" I asked.

He grinned. "Ifn hit rots, I make wine outen it."

He opened a bottle of rosehip, pear and blackberry, and we took turns sampling. The rosehip, pale yellow, tasted strong and medicinal. The pear was better, pink-tinted and sweet. But the blackberry was best of all. I drained my cup and asked for more.

"Tastes better the more you drink," I said.

Albion filled my glass. Soon we were all giggling. Ben told a preacher story.

"They's a preacher at our church over on Tater Nob that cant read. Name of Peter Rowe. Old man. Has a brother name of Kenzebee that has been to school. Peter, he is a proud man, wants to read his own scriptures, lead his own singing. After all, it was him the Lord called, he says. Lord dont make no mistakes. So Kenzebee, he stands behind Peter and whispers what Peter ought to read out. Peter, he lines the hymn and they sing it back to him.

" 'I am a poor pilgrim of sorrow,' Kenzebee whispers.

" 'I am a poor pilgrim of sorrow,' Peter hollers out. The congregation sings it back to him.

" 'Cast out in this wide world to roam,' says Kenzebee. Peter hollers it and the folks sing it. They just sing to shake the building down.

"Then Kenzebee cant see the words.

" 'Move your finger, Peter,' he whispers.

" 'Move your finger, Peter,' hollers Peter.

"Folks sing about half the line and start looking at each other. Kenzebee's all het up.

"He says, 'Now you played Hell!'

"Old Peter sings out, 'Now you played Hell!'

"They just stopped the service right there."

We hollered laughing.

"Pull our leg again," I said to tease Ben.

He raised his hand. "I swear it happened. I was right there in the pew."

"You and everbody in east Kentucky, many times as I heard that story," I said.

We laughed again and Albion poured more wine. Then Flora remembered that she and Ben had planned to stop at the mouth of Marrowbone to visit friends.

"But you stay here, Carrie," she said quickly and stood up. "You just come on before sundown and meet us there. Yall have fun now."

I started to protest but Ben was up as well, he had their hats. They were both grinning like sheep-killing dogs.

"I'll walk her down to where yall are when the time comes," Albion said.

I sat still in the rocking chair and watched them weave their way across the bottom. Flora clutched Ben's arm as they crossed the swinging bridge.

"You want to go for a walk?" Albion asked.

"I'd rather sit. My head feels like it might float off somewheres."

"Dont have no more wine."

He pulled up a chair and sat beside me.

"You didnt want to stay, did you?"

"I aint sure what I want. I'm all confused."

"Why?"

"Because I aint sure what you want. Because I cant think

straight with all this wine in me. Ben and Florrie think they know what's good for me. But I dont know myself. How can they?''

He held up his hand. ''Hold on. That there is too much to chew offn one plate. Now, in the first place, all I want is to git to know you again. As to what Ben and Florrie want, I reckon they want you to be happy, that's all.''

''They want me to git married.''

''And you dont want to?''

''I told you, I dont know what I want. Only thing I know is I wouldnt marry just anybody.'' I clutched the arms of the rocker and pushed back and forth.

''You're a-missing somebody, aint you?''

I nodded my head and started to cry. He took my hand, held it between his two rough ones.

''I allays knew you'd love fierce,'' he said. I leaned against him and wept on his shoulder.

''I'm sorry,'' I said. ''Hit's that ole blackberry wine.''

''That's all right.''

''They was a feller I met on Pond Creek when I worked for Miles. A union organizer. I aint never heard from him. I dont even know where he is.''

''He aint never forgot you.''

''Course he has. He dont love me. He said so.''

Albion leaned over and kissed the top of my head.

''You air a silly,'' he said.

I took the hiccups and he fetched me a dipper of water.

''I'd like to court you,'' he said. ''Ifn you'd allow me to.''

''I cant allow you. Hit wouldnt be fair to you. They's things you dont know.''

''Like what?''

''Like I aint the kind of woman men expect to marry. Especially not a preacher.'' I looked over the blurred green and brown landscape. ''I aint pure. I done give myself to someone else.''

''I dont care about that.''

''Well, I do. I couldnt be all yourn. They's a part of me that will allays belong to him. Hit's a part you wouldnt never share. I cant help it. That's just the way I'm made.''

''I dont want to take away the part that's hisn. I want my

own part. Hit will be mine because I'll share your life different than he did. Carrie, I been watching you this live long day, and I know I can love you."

"I dont know if I can love you back."

"Let's court. Hit can be slow. They aint no need to rush."

I was trapped. "Let's walk to Marrowbone," I said.

It was almost four miles to the mouth of Marrowbone. Albion told me about Georgia, and I talked stiffly about nursing school, about Pond Creek. I kept stepping on rocks and turning my ankle. When we reached the mouth of the creek, I stopped and folded my arms across my chest.

"They's a lot of water passed under the bridge since we was younguns," I declared. "You see how I changed. I dont know why you'd want to court me anyhow. I'm gloomy a lots and stubborn, and bad moods come to me. I reckon they's plenty of girls in that church of yourn that would be proud to have a preacher."

"May I kiss you?"

"No!"

He looked hurt and I was shamed at my own coldness.

"You can come see me," I said.

"When? Next Friday night?"

"All right. But I wont have nobody mooning over me like an old puppy dog."

I walked away toward the cabin where Ben and Flora waited and left him standing in the road.

ALBION VISITED THE HOMEPLACE EVERY WEEK, OR ELSE I saw him on Kingdom Come. I made it clear that there would be no kissing, only hand-holding. I thought he would give up and go away, but he didn't. After three months of his kindness and patience, I let him kiss me, and to my surprise I enjoyed it. By Christmas I began to think that I might want to love him after all. I looked forward to his visits and came to acknowledge the quiet contentment I felt when I was with him.

Still I was uneasy, and told myself I must study him some more. I was not sure what he felt for the Homeplace, how he would act when the companies came for it. He did not even own his own place at Kingdom Come, but spoke of God owning it. When American Coal or Imperial Collieries stripped it away from him, would he turn the other cheek? And sometimes he spoke of God calling him to preach in the coal camps of Justice County, his father's home. I could not imagine him in such a place. He would preach Jesus dragging the coal operators out of Hell and die of broken down lungs before he reached the age of forty. That might please Jesus, but I could not bear it.

I forced him to court me longer while I fretted and waited for something I dared not name.

SOMETIMES I WAS CALLED OUT TO NURSE AT HENRYCLAY or Kingdom Come. At such times I would board with the Thornsberrys. We decided we were distant kin, for my grandmother Bishop had Thornsberry as a maiden name, and Aunt Becka bore some resemblance to old Pappy Thornsberry.

"Reckon my paw and your mamaw was sprung offn brothers," Pappy said. "My papaw was Lonzo Thornsberry."

"That might have been her uncle," I mused. "I heard the name. But that one aint in our cemetery."

"Lonzo's buried with my people," Pappy agreed.

I was staying at the Thornsberrys' in May of 1917 when Albion brought word of a dance at Kingdom Come schoolhouse to raise money for new books.

"Hit's tomorry night. You want to stay over and go?"

"Sure. I aint danced in a long time."

Next day I washed the best dress I had along and dried it in the sun. I washed my hair and tied it back with one of Alice Thornsberry's green ribbons. Albion whistled when he saw me and held my hand all the way down the creek.

It was dusk when we arrived, and the school house was lit up like a jack-o-lantern. We heard fiddle music and the soft thumping of feet on the board floor. I squeezed Albion's hand.

"Listen there! Aint that the happiest sound you ever heard?"

"For a fact," he agreed. "I'm already dancing in the road here."

He gave a little slide and skip. Albion was a good clog dancer. It was a cause of scandal to the Regular Baptists on Marrowbone Creek, whose preacher didn't hold with dancing. When confronted once in Henryclay with a Regular Baptist pining after his soul, Albion pointed out in the same calm way he defended his winemaking that King David "danced before the Lord with all his might" in the streets of Jerusalem.

"He werent wearing much neither," Albion added. "Reckon I can dance with my clothes on."

"Hit's for such sin that Jesus paid the price with his blood!" the Regular Baptist had cried.

"Praise the Lord!" Albion answered with equal fervor. "Aint it good to know we're bought and paid fer?"

He heard later that the Regular Baptists had prayed for an hour the next Sunday that he might be saved. He shook his head and said, "What a bait of time taken away from thanking God."

Outside the schoolhouse, men gathered to take the air and smoke their pipes or spit tobacco juice. They hunkered down on their haunches and rocked back and forth.

"Good band, preacher," said one.

"Sounds like it." Albion squatted down. "Where'd Ralph git them from?"

"Heard them up in Inez last month. Called the Blackberry Pickers."

I stiffened. Albion was still talking with the men. After a moment I slipped over to the doorway and looked inside. Three men played "Soldiers Joy"—a round-faced fiddle player, balding with a fringe of curly hair around the back of his head; a thin, sallow guitar picker. And Rondal, flailing the banjo.

Pappy Thornsberry stood inside the door. "Aint seen a banjo picker yet that cracked a smile. You ever notice that, youngun? Now that fiddle player, he appears to be having fun."

I moved past Pappy toward the center of the room, bumped into several dancers. Rondal held his shoulders back, the banjo resting on the slope of his abdomen. He stared over the heads of the dancers, pursed his lips. The others nodded at him and stepped back; Rondal took up the melody. His hand moved across the banjo head as though he were rousing it, scratching and stroking. The fiddle came back in, strong and harsh. Rondal dropped his head and retreated. His eyes swept over the dancers and he saw me. He stared, still flailing, and then he smiled slightly and nodded his head. He looked away, but he still smiled.

"Who's that feller?"

Albion stood beside me.

"Hit's—he's just—" I stopped for his eyes brimmed with hurt.

"Hit's all right," he said. "I understand. You ready to dance?"

The desks had been pushed against the wall and a square dance formed. The band played "Handsome Molly," and Fred Combs stood by them to call. Around we went, and Rondal flashed into my vision each time Albion swung me. After the dance we went to the dessert table and Albion bought me a slice of sugar-dusted apple pie. We didn't speak. Dancers swirled past, their feet banging the floorboards and skittering on across, their legs swinging loose at the knees like doors on hinges. One old man, Mr. Pauley, danced by himself, a shuffle step with an occasional lunge like a chicken pecking. He hooked his thumbs around a pair of bright red suspenders. Behind him Rondal scanned the room with studied disinterest.

Albion and I danced again. Then he went to talk to someone in the corner, came back to me.

"I promised Mildred Combs I'd look in on her granny. She's ailing and didnt feel up to coming tonight. I'll be back in about an hour." He squeezed my hand, let it go. "You'll be just fine," he said.

He walked away, his shoulders slumped. Well good, I thought. Ifn you dont want me bad enough to fight, you wont git me.

I sat beside Granny Thornsberry, asked her about planting camomile, but didn't hear her answer. The band stopped playing and a cake auction commenced. The band members leaned their instruments against the wall and stretched. Rondal started toward me and I looked away.

"Well," he said, close by, "hit's been a long time."

I looked up. "Yes. How you been?"

"Fine sometimes. Not fine others." He pulled over a chair and straddled it backwards. "You come with your husband?"

"No, we aint married. He wants it, but I aint sure."

"You aint changed much."

"You neither."

"I got a few gray hairs now." He ran his fingers along his temple. "That's what Colorado done to me."

"Was you there when them women and children got burned up?"

"I was there."

"Where are you these days?"

"I work at a sawmill up in Martin County. Wolf Creek."

"No more organizing?"

"Time's a coming. Aint much can be done while this here war's on."

I was relieved that he had not given up, then ashamed that I would want him to be doing such dangerous work.

"You want to meet my brother and my buddy?" He took my arm and helped me up. They sat near the stove and shared a whole rhubarb pie between them.

"Isom Justice," Rondal said. "My brother, Talcott Lloyd. This here is Carrie Bishop. I knew her over on Pond Creek."

"I wondered how you found a good-looking woman so quick. Honey, you're the best-looking thing I've seen this boy with." Isom sized me up with his snapping brown eyes. I would never have believed a word he said.

"This here is one of our last times to pick," Rondal said. "Talcott is going in the army."

"I hear the fighting is gitting bad," I said.

"Be safer than a damn coal mine," Talcott said.

"He'll be all right," Isom said. "They'll hear he's a miner and set him to work digging trenches. He wont even git to carry a gun."

"Hell, better not be that a way," Talcott said. "I aim to learn some things while I'm in there. They teach you to use them machine guns like old man Davidson has got squirreled away."

Fred Combs waved his arms from up front. "Band back up here," he hollered.

"Hey, boys," Rondal said, "what if I want to dance with this here woman? Can I do it?"

"Dont see why not," Isom said. "They's bound to be some feller here can pick a banjer for one or two numbers."

"I want 'Sally Ann,' " Rondal said and winked at me. "You recall that there song, dont you?"

His shirt was open part way down his chest and I could see the curly brown hair.

"I recall," I whispered.

"Myself, I got fond memories of it," he said.

They found a man from Marrowbone to pick the banjo. Fred Combs called for a circle dance and we joined it. Rondal danced hard, vigorous, banged his right boot on the floor.

> "Circle up four around that floor,
> "Circle around that ole barn door."

His fingers dug hard into my waist. We spun around for a corner swing.

> "Back to your center with an elbow swing,
> "On to your partner with a turkey wing."

He caught my eyes each time we passed.

> "Birdie in a cage, aint she sweet?
> "Hear that birdie go tweet tweet tweet."

They circled up and threw me inside. No way out even if I tried.

> "Birdie out and old crow in,
> "Six hands up and gone again."

Rondal pranced into the center and punched the air with his elbows.

Isom sang counter to the tune, Sally Ann Sally Ann Sally Ann Sally Ann.

Oh-h-h, ha-a-aw! Pappy Thornsberry called from the corner.

> "Chase that rabbit, chase that squirrel,
> "Chase that purty girl round the world."

We tore off in opposite ways, touched strange hands all round the ring. Then Rondal had me, swung me high.

> "Sue's in bed with the hog-eyed man,
> "I'm goin home with Sally Ann."

When the dance ended, Rondal said, "Let's go outside," and pulled me along behind him. We stood just beyond the door. He drew me into his arms and I rubbed my lips against the soft skin of his neck. The smell of him was strong and familiar, mixed with the scent of the honeysuckle that bloomed beside the school. A moth brushed against my cheek.

"Damn miller," Rondal said, and waved it away.

"He's drunk on honeysuckle," I said. I kissed his neck. "You got a woman?"

"I see a woman in Inez. A redhead."

"You love her?"

He shrugged.

I gathered all my courage. "I love you. I allays have. I'd a married you in a minute ifn you'd asked me."

"I never asked you," he said proudly.

I pulled away.

"Hit's been four year," he said. "Cant you forget? We was just two nice people that wanted to be together that night."

"Dont speak for me! I made a choice and I wont have it made light of! And now you bring me out here and git me all stirred up. Why? Just to prove that you still yet can?"

He leaned back against the wall like he was exasperated.

"You was lonesome then," I said, "and you are now. I can tell it. Why wont you let me love you?"

"All right. I am lonesome. That make you feel better?" He turned his face away. "Carrie, you ask too much. You would take what I do so damn serious. I like a woman to help me forgit. With you I'd never git away from it.''

"You dont know that. You've never given me a chance."

"I aint ready to give you a chance. I aint ready to give nobody a chance." He nodded toward the door. "Let's go back inside."

"No. Hit's too close in there. I dont feel very good."

"Suit yourself. But I got to pick some more ifn I want to git paid."

Inside I watched him put his arms around Isom's shoulders. They laughed together. I turned up the road toward Albion's, stumbling in the darkness. Once I fell and skinned the palms of my hands. At last I reached the barn. The rough board door opened with a rusty scream and I went inside. A bat flapped past my head and then all was still.

"Old man," I whispered, "I know how you felt."

I groped past the mule and the milk cow, found an empty stall and huddled in the corner.

"Come git me!" I called out. "I dare you. Make me crazy like you."

The sleeping cow breathed with a slow, regular snuffling sound. My eyelids were heavy. I leaned back against a bale of hay. Albion would not find me here. No one would ever find me and I would never need to be with anyone again.

WHEN I WOKE IT WAS STILL DARK. A HAND RESTED ON MY shoulder and a light blinded me.

"Carrie? Thank the Lord! I was worried to death trying to find where you'd gone, and when I saw you a laying like that— you was—your head was all rolled back like—''

I sat up and rubbed my stiff neck. Albion set down the lantern and knelt beside me.

"Why'd you have to find me?" I moaned. I burst into tears. "Leave me be."

"No. I aint leaving you alone. You had enough of that. And so have I. You aint the only one that's been crying tonight. I been doing nothing but walking and crying ever since I seen how you looked at that feller. I been fooling myself, I reckon, because you aint never looked at me that a way, and I doubt you ever will."

"You mean you aint seen Granny Combs tonight?"

"I aint seen Granny Combs. I walked to the head of Kingdom Come and back down to the school. Since then I been looking for you."

"I wanted to be with that old man that kilt himself. I know how he hurt."

"No. Hit's a different hurt. You dont want to be like him."

I shuddered. "Hit's what I'm scairt of. To be like him."

He held the lantern to my face and I put my hand to my eyes.

"Why'd you leave that feller tonight?"

"He didnt need me there. I tried to tell him how much I love him. But he wont hear it. He cant let himself be loved."

"You're just like him," Albion said. He pulled my hand down, held the lantern closer. "You want to love your own way. You're scairt of something else."

He blew down the lantern's chimney and the flame popped and died.

"I got to tell you something," he said. "I come to a decision while I was traipsing this holler tonight. I've talked for a spell about leaving here, going to West Virginia. I been scairt to say too much to you for fear you wouldnt go with me and I'd never see you again. But the call is stronger and louder. I got to go, Carrie."

"When?"

"Soon as I'm able. I plan to go down the mines. I know hit sounds crazy when I got such a good life here. But my daddy allays aimed to make it back there. He raised me with that notion. And God keeps telling me to do it, too. I'm a preacher, pledged to bring His word to the lost. There's where they are, Carrie, over yonder there. I hear them crying out in my sleep. I got to go."

He stood up.

"I wanted you to go with me. As my wife."

"What about the Homeplace? Aint that my land? Ben and Florrie need me."

"Talk to God about it. Stay in the barn ifn you need to."

"Out here? In this haunted place?"

"It's where you come to be," he said. "I'll be up at the house."

I sat still, my hands in my lap, and waited for God to speak, fearing I would hear the old man instead. Nothing. "Hit aint Old Christmas," I said aloud. I tried to imagine Albion selling the animals and setting out alone for a coal camp. I saw him disappear into a dark, gaping hole, not to mine coal but to preach the Gospel. And, God help me, I saw Rondal, another prodigal returned for a different reason, drawn, as he must be some day, to Blackberry Creek. I knew then that I loved them both, and that there must be a reason for it.

I gathered my skirt about me, rose up and walked to the cabin. Albion sat on the porch.

"He makes me feel alive," I said. "But I'm at home with you. I want to go with you."

He held out his arms and I went to him. He set his hand to my breast, then took it away.

"We'll wait," he said.

Twelve

C. J. MARCUM

THE COAL OPERATORS STARTED THE BASEBALL LEAGUES. I heard tell of baseball, but I never paid it much mind before that.

Davidson had a team, and Felco, Carbon, Chieftan, and Vulcan. They was a separate league for Negro miners. I thought baseball was silly, even wrote an editorial saying so in the *Free Press*. Every Sunday in the summertime, the miners and their families went to the ballfields. You couldn't never get that many of them out to talk about something serious, like politics. And yet, when it come time to swat a little white ball, there they'd all be. Even worse, the baseball games caused the miners to turn on each other instead of cooperating. The Vulcan miners despised Carbon, Carbon detested Felco, they all hated Davidson, which usually had the best team.

"You think the operators dont know that?" I wrote. "They love to see the miner fill his head with such foolishness. They love to see him fret about anything except who will control the mines."

So when Isom wanted to get up a team, I was agin it. It was a typical Isom Justice idea, pure foolishness with nary a bit of use to it.

But I couldn't help linger by as they built the ballfield at Annadel. It took up the whole bottom above the whorehouses. They filled in pools of black water, cleared a mess of chiggerweeds and planted the whole thing with a scrubby grass. The fan-shaped ballfield, bounded by its wood plank fence, fit perfectly where the creek runs in hard by the hill-

150

side near home plate and falls away to open up room for
the outfield. Centerfield is higher than the rest of the field,
for the mountain begins its rise there and the ground swells
up like they is something ready to bust through. I watched
them build and was took with a hankering to play that centerfield. But I didn't say nothing about it for two year.

Annadel plays in the Independent League for teams that
ain't owned by coal operators. Jolo is in that league, and
Justice, Stone, Logan, and War, Iaeger and Davy down in
McDowell County. Annadel come in third the first two year
in the league and won the championship every time after
that. The first season we won it all was the year I joined
up, and maybe that had something to do with it.

Isom had kept after me to play. "Big as you are, I bet
you could hit a few homers."

"Ifn I wanted to," I replied. I thought baseball was beneath me. But I went to the home games anyway. I was
elected mayor in 1915 and it was my duty to attend all such
civic functions. That's what I told myself. It was a long time
before I admitted I loved baseball.

In 1916 I attended a Wednesday night batting practice.
Afterward Isom let me use his glove and he hit grounders
to me. The ball jumped offn his bat with a crack and slid
past me. I chased it.

"Dont worry," Isom hollered. "I got a bagful. Git in
front of the next one, block it with your body ifn you have
to."

"Hell!" I protested. "That thing's hard as a rock."

"Most it will do is knock your front teeth out. Then
you'll look like a ball player. Come on. Keep your glove to
the ground unless the ball hops at the last second. Then you
got to foller it all the way."

The ball skipped off my glove and struck me hard in the
chest.

"Grab it quick! Throw it back!" Isom screamed.

Furious, I lunged at the ball and flung it. It sailed past
Isom and rattled around the wooden bleachers.

"Damn!" Isom said. "That there is an outfielder's arm.
But let's try a couple more grounders."

Two balls skittered past me, one right between my legs.

"Shit!" I muttered.

Then there come a ball that jumped halfway to me, ran on, and leaped again just before it reached me. I followed it with my eye, poked my glove at it and caught it with a smack that set my palm to tingling.

"Good!" Isom yelled. "Had it all the way!"

I wiggled my shoulders around, cocky-like, and turned the ball over in my hand. It was hard but warm. Throwed with enough force it could kill a man if it hit him in the head. But I had stopped it, damn straight I had. I admired the smoothness of its skin.

"Back up and I'll hit you some flies," Isom said.

I stood high upon that centerfield and felt like I was riding the hill, a frozen wave that would crush everything in its path once it was unleashed. I learned to judge the fly balls and seldom missed one. Then I throwed the ball to home plate, pretending they was a coal operator standing there and the baseball sliced him right in half.

I took batting practice, swung viciously.

"Level it out," Isom said. "Smooth it out. You aint tryin to bash in somebody's head. Watch the ball in."

After while he couldn't get one past me. I didn't care where the ball went, over Isom's head or straight up in the air. It was soothing to beat on that ball.

"You swing at ever damn thing," Isom complained. "Real pitcher would tie you in knots." But he sounded happy. Then I hit three straight pitches over the left field fence.

"C.J., you got to play," he pleaded.

"Aint I too old to start this?"

"Thirty-six," Isom said. "We got two guys older than you. You can play a few year."

They give me number 33, a gray flannel uniform trimmed in red. We are the Annadel Redlegs, named after Cincinnati. My first year in the Independent League I hit twenty-five homers. Little boys followed me around town, and I'd set them down and tell them about how the coal companies stole the land.

BY 1918 FOLKS WAS WONDERING WHO HAD THE BEST BASE-ball team in the Levisa coalfield—Davidson of the Miners

League or Annadel of the Independent League. (Actually, I reckoned the best team was the Justice Cardinals of the Negro League. We played them in pre-season games and they took three out of four.) Lytton Davidson wasn't happy with the idea of our teams playing each other. He had put too much money into his ballteam to be embarrassed by Annadel. Davidson was from Philadelphia and was buddies with the owner of the Athletics. He hired on a full-time manager, Tiny Sanders, a former A's coach who washed out on account of his drinking. A Davidson miner who played ball got special treatment, like outside work or a foreman's job down in the mine. Mario Angelelli, the legendary Davidson shortstop, had not seen the inside of a coal mine in ten year, and his son, Carmello, the second baseman, was a section boss even though he was only eighteen. This was to be Carmello's last year in the Miners League. Tiny Sanders had arranged a tryout with the Philadelphia Athletics and they agreed to pick him up for the 1919 season.

The main reason Davidson didn't want to play us was politics. Like all the coal operators, Lytton Davidson hated Annadel. "Redlegs" was too tame a name for us, he said, because we was red right up to the tops of our heads. Besides that, it was humiliating to see Negroes and white men playing on the same team, and to risk seeing white men beat by coloreds. Sam Gore was our best pitcher, Doc Booker played first base, and five other Negroes was on the team as well. Davidson never would have played the game if there hadn't been such a clamor from the fans. All the American Coal Company miners wanted to play us bad, and Davidson didn't like to look a coward, so in late August of 1918, after we both had won our leagues again, a game was set. Davidson wouldn't come to Annadel to play. That's all right, we said, we'll beat you anywhere.

The Davidson field is up Marcums Branch, not a quarter of a mile from where our cabin set. We'd had a canebrake in that field, I recalled, and a molasses wheel. It all looked so different now, with the ballfield, the electric wires, the houses climbing the holler and on out of sight. Lytton Davidson, the man who stole it all, set in the dugout and watched while his boys took warm-up. He was short, with a fleshy, babyish face. I tried to feel hate for him, but it didn't seem worth the effort, like trying mightily to despise a worm. You aint got to hate somebody in order to whip them.

Nearly everybody I knowed in the world was at that ballgame, including Clabe Lloyd, who coughed and spat with every other breath. He stood with Talcott behind the outfield bleachers.

"How's it goin, Clabe?"

"Hit aint, but I aint complainin." His laugh ended in a wheeze.

"Workin hard?" I thought what a stupid question it was, but everybody always asked it.

"Hell, yes. That there youngun I got for a buddy aint as good to work with as this one here." He put a purplish hand on Talcott's shoulder. "Oh, Kerwin tries hard. I aint complainin. But you know."

"Kerwin here?"

"Him and Mommy wouldnt come," Talcott said. "Ball games is the Devil's playground, Mommy says."

"I seen that preacher Freeman from Felco over by third base," Clabe said.

"He lives down the row from me," Talcott said. "He dont believe in Hell so he can do anything he wants to. Wonder ifn we can git him to save Mommy?"

"You cant git saved but oncet," Clabe said.

"Kerwin been saved six times," Talcott answered. "He gits saved ever time nobody else does. Says it hurts the preacher's feelins ifn nobody answers the altar call."

Talcott wa. just back from the war, where he'd spent six months in the trenches. He hadn't changed much, and when I asked him once what it was like over there, he shrugged and claimed they was nothing he hadn't seen before, and that a German's head was a lot bigger target than a squirrel's.

"Yall better git a seat," I said. "Them bleachers is fillin up fast."

"Wont be much to see," Talcott said. "Davidson will kick your ass."

"Maybe."

"Hey, I know. And I aint happy neither, cause I bet five

dollars on you yesterday. Pricie like to clawed my eyes out over it. But Daddy here told me this morning they done brung in a ringer.''

"What?"

He smirked, pleased to be the first to give me the bad news.

"Look at number 21. Aint never seen him before, have you?"

"Mickey O'Malley," Clabe said. "Sits the bench for the Philadelphy Athletics. Power hitter. Two homers this year as a pinch hitter."

"They cant do that!"

"He's a coal operator," Talcott said. "He can do anything he damn well pleases."

"Davidson claims that feller is on the payroll," Clabe said. "Goin to dig coal first thing tomorry. Course he'll likely come down with a sore back from this here ball game and quit the mines."

"Me, I'm goin under the bleachers here with my buddies, drink a little moonshine, and kiss my five bucks goodbye." Talcott patted my back sympathetically and went off with his daddy.

I told the boys. You aint never heard such cussing.

"We got to protest," Doc said. "We got to leave the field if that ringer plays."

"That's what he want," Sam Gore said. "Then he can say Annadel is scairt of Davidson. He can say niggers is scairt of white men."

"But you cant pitch to no goddamn Philadelphy Athletic," Isom moaned. "He'll take you so far up the creek you wont never git back."

"He's just one man," I said. "He gits four bats, maybe five. Ifn they aint nobody on base, we can walk him intentional. If they are men on base, well, we can score seven or eight on them, cant we?" I looked around, clapped my hands. "Well, cant we? We got eighteen offn Iaeger! We can get six offn Davidson."

"Hell yes!" Isom cried. "Hell yes!"

They was nothing for it but to play them. The bleachers was packed behind home plate and in the outfield, and the fans was four deep along the fence down the baselines. The

Justice Clarion had sent a sportswriter and a photographer. Our families was there, Ermel and Annadel, Violet with Gladys and Evelyn, Sam's wife in the colored section in left field.

We come to bat first, and I knew we was shook. Isom and Sam struck out, and Antoine Jones, one of our town policemen, popped up to Mario Angelelli at shortstop. We was a gloomy bunch when we took the field in the bottom of the first.

Sam walked the first man, Carmello Angelelli, and the Davidson fans sensed a rout. Mario Angelelli bunted back to the mound and Sam throwed him out, but the runner advanced. Joe Tibbs, who usually batted cleanup for Davidson, swaggered to the plate and waggled his bat. But he smacked a line drive right to Doc at first, and Doc almost caught Angelelli off the bag at second. That brung up Mickey O'Malley.

They was no swagger to him. He was all business. He took a practice cut, squeezed the rosin bag, tapped the toe of each shoe with his bat, and stepped right in. Even from centerfield I could tell he had two inches and fifty pounds on me. The crowd hushed. Sam turned and looked at us, and I knew he would pitch to him. I hunched over and talked.

Hum tha hum tha hard baby hum tha

The pleadings rose from all over the field like foreign folks praying to some outlandish god. Sam reared back, his red cap bright in the sunlight.

O'Malley rode the first pitch over the left centerfield fence. It bounced off the railroad track across the creek and disappeared in the bushes on the mountainside.

OK Sam OK only two only two

The Davidson right fielder popped up to third and we retreated to the dugout, shaken. We poked each other to make sure we was still yet alive.

"C.J. up!" Isom hollered.

I stepped in to face the Davidson pitcher, Froggy Lester. Froggy was all right. He worked at Felco oncet and come to Annadel to drink his beer and shoot his pool before he moved to Davidson. I pretended he was Lytton Davidson. He worked me to three and two, and I sent a high fastball over the left fielder's head and all the way to the fence. I went into second standing up. Acrost the way I heard Violet shrieking above the noise of the other Annadel fans. She stood and waved her arms. I raised my cap.

Doc sacrificed me to third and a long fly by Ralph Day brung me on home. We couldn't do nothing else and trailed 2-1 going into the bottom of the second. But scoring had relieved the pressure, like puncturing a boil. Sam settled down and started in to pitch the game of his life. I never seen him throw so hard before or since. He struck out one in the second, and three straight in the third. When O'Malley come up in the fourth, Sam took a while with his pitch. O'Malley went after the first one again, but this time it carried high into the deepest part of centerfield and seemed to drift in the wind. I got under it, leaped, caught it as I banged against the fence. Lytton Davidson stood up in the dugout, stuck his hands in his pockets, and turned his back. I held the ball high over my head and brought it off the field like a trophy of war. Isom leaped on my back.

"Holy shit! What a catch!"

"We may win this jump!" Antoine Jones bounced up and down.

"Well," I drawled, "that's one quarter of Mister Davidson's investment that he done lost."

"It was inside," Sam gloated. "He got trouble inside. His wrists aint strong, I can tell."

We all laughed because we knew, especially Sam, that O'Malley had hit the hell out of the ball, that the wind held it up and even then it had been close.

Still we was stirred up enough to make our move in the fifth.

With one out and one on, Isom hit a home run over the right field fence and we went ahead 3-2. Then Sam singled and Antoine doubled him home. I flied out but Antoine went to third and Doc hit one over the first baseman's head. 5-2. Tiny yanked Froggy and a new pitcher warmed up.

Talcott Lloyd pushed his way through the crowd near the dugout.

"Isom! C.J.! You're a-doin it! Shit, you're fuckin em ten ways to sundown! Shit!"

He reached out and grasped our hands.

"Ever damn miner from Felco is rootin for Annadel! You better believe it! Davidson dont tell us what to do!"

"You wasnt so cocksure before the game," I teased.

"Hell, I didnt know you'd hit Froggy like that. Damn, you boys owned him."

"Come on and sit the bench," Isom said. "Bring us luck."

"Naw! Me and my buddies is workin somethin up. We got our pistols with us, and after you win, we're goin to shoot em off. Scare the hell outen old man Davidson."

"He'll fire your ass!" I said, alarmed.

"Dont care! I'll kick his."

We watched him sort his way back through the crowd.

"Damn fool crazy when he's drinkin," Isom said. "And sometimes when he aint drinkin."

"He worse since he come back from France?"

"Let's just say he dont seem to care about much." Isom spat a brown stream of tobacco juice. "One thing he aint done yet is beat Pricie. Long as that's so, he's still yet my kin by marriage."

Sam Gore tired in the seventh. I could tell the zip was gone offn his fastball, and he hung a curveball that Carmello Angelelli slashed for a triple. Carmello's daddy homered and it was 5-4, Annadel. Then Joe Tibbs took four straight balls and trotted to first base.

We gathered around Sam, who kicked at the mound and wouldn't look at any of us. His eyes glistened with tears.

"Had to expect it," Doc consoled him. "You cant shut down them Angelellis forever."

"Arm's hurtin," Sam muttered. "It's weary."

"Better bring in Antoine," said Ralph Day, our catcher.

"Jesus!" said Antoine. "O'Malley up."

"Wait!" Isom held up his hands. "I got an idea. Let Sam pitch to O'Malley."

"You crazy?" We screamed it together.

"But look here," Isom insisted. "We know O'Malley can hit good pitchin. What we dont know is, can he hit bad pitchin. I bet he cant. He been in the majors too long."

"Play ball!" the umpire cried.

The Davidson fans cheered, clapped impatiently, rhythmically. A group in the corner of the first base bleachers chanted, "Choke niggers choke! Choke niggers choke!"

"You want him, Sam?" Isom asked.

"Sure I want him."

"Give him change-ups. I mean real change-ups, like a girl would throw. Put an arch in it, drop it in."

"Sam," Doc said. "You dont have to prove nothin. Walk him if you want to."

"And move Tibbs into scorin position?" Sam shook his head.

The umpire strolled toward the mound.

"Let's break it up, boys," Isom said. He swatted Sam on the rump.

I backed up all the way to the fence. Sam stood watching O'Malley, his arms dangling at his sides. The fans still chanted. O'Malley stepped out of the box, came back.

Sam didn't lunge off the mound. He took a tiny step, lofted the ball in a high, slow arch. It looked like it had been thrown underhand. As far away as I was, I seen O'Malley's mouth hang open.

"Strike!" the umpire cried.

The second pitch was just the same. O'Malley watched it, hungered for it, his shoulders bunched tight and the bat held high. He started to swing, realized it was too soon, checked, then swung half-hearted. The ball was already past him.

The stands was in an uproar. Lytton Davidson charged out of the dugout but was persuaded to return by Tiny Sanders. Then Sam Gore reached down for one last fastball.

He blew it right by him.

O'Malley went down on his knees like he was praying. Sam ran straight for the dugout and we all piled in after him, hollering and carrying on. The veins of Sam's forehead stuck out.

"You see that white boy beat the air!" he yelled. "I struck me out a Philadelphy Athletic!"

Sam went to bat and promptly struck out himself, but he didn't mind. We added a run in the top of the ninth to go up 6-4. But in the bottom of the inning things started falling apart.

Antoine replaced Sam on the mound and had control

problems. He had walked two in the eighth but got out of the inning without any runs scored. In the ninth he walked the leadoff batter, then give up two singles. It was 6-5, two on, no outs. Carmello Angelelli flied out to center, and my throw held the runners. But Antoine walked Mario Angelelli to load the bases. Joe Tibbs come to the plate. The fans rose to their feet. Ralph Day walked to the mound to settle Antoine down, went back to his squat.

Antoine struck Joe out.

That left two outs and O'Malley. Ralph called a conference.

"Walk in the tyin run, or take a chance on him cleanin the bases."

"I aint walkin in no tyin run," Antoine declared. "We play to win, dont we?"

"Hell, yes," Isom said. "Let's go for it."

Back in centerfield, I wet my finger, held it up. The wind was still blowing in, a hopeful sign.

Ay batter ay batter batter batter

Antoine threw two balls, both high and outside. The Davidson fans commenced their clapping.

The next pitch, a curve ball, hung like it was drapes and O'Malley was on it. There was a crack, and the ball towered over the outfield. The wind had it again but it would do no good this time.

A second crack. The ball disappeared. Black fragments sprayed in all directions. Something struck my upturned face and fell to my shoulder. I plucked at it, held it up. It was a singed strip of cowhide.

The crowd was stunned into silence. I heard a high whoop beyond the outfield fence.

"Ball game's over!"

Talcott Lloyd held his pistol high over his head. He whooped again.

"Ball game's over, Mr. Davidson! You dont run things no more!"

All hell broke loose. I was scared that the Davidson police would shoot Talcott, but when I leaped the fence I saw him toss down the pistol. He spied me and yelled, "C.J.! Did you see that shot? Them's ten to one odds, brother! Hot damn!"

He was still laughing when the police wrestled him to the ground and handcuffed him. The stands emptied and fist-fights broke out. I dodged some irate Davidson fans and got back onto the field. The teams stood in a bunch near home plate. Sam Gore and Joe Tibbs wrestled on the ground. Lytton Davidson, surrounded by police, yelled at Isom.

"Just what I expected! You people are crazy! You can't do things this way!"

"He was a goddamn ringer!" Isom screamed back. "He werent legal in the first place!"

Tiny Sanders throwed down his cap and stomped it.

"It was a home run!" he yelled at the umpire. "It's 9 to 6!"

I pushed my way between them. "Hit never cleared the fence. I was under it. Hit never cleared the fence."

"It would have!" Davidson's face was beet-red. I never seen him up close before. He was so short he barely rose up to my ɔits.

Isom grabbed the umpire, spun him around. "O'Malley's a goddamn ringer," he repeated.

The umpire throwed up his hands. "I'm a-callin this here game! You bastards can tote it home in a poke!"

Davidson opened his mouth to speak but thought better of it. He glared at me.

"This is my property," he said in a voice like ice. "Get off it. I want you and your team on the first train out." He turned to a policeman. "Clear this field. Send these people home."

We separated Sam and Joe Tibbs, who were rolling on the ground and doing little damage to one another. Sullenly we gathered our bats and gloves, tossed them into canvas bags.

"We beat them bastards," Antoine said. "I know we did."

"Damn straight," Isom agreed.

Most of the Davidson players had retreated to their dug-out, unsure whether or not to leave. Carmello Angelelli, a slender boy with dark brown skin, stood outside, his black cap in his hand and his hair wet and shiny. I wanted to talk to him, to say hell, son, none of this here was personal. Good game. Good luck in the American League.

I raised my hand. He smiled, raised his in reply.

* * *

THE BALDWIN GUARDS WENT TO TALCOTT'S HOUSE THAT
very night and put Pricie and the younguns out in the street.
They tossed their furniture from the porch, broke most of
it. Pricie took the younguns to live at the farm. Talcott was
in the Justice jail. He got one year for disturbing the peace
and brandishing a deadly weapon. Ermel's friends, who now
controlled the county judge, got him out after he'd served
two months, and Ermel put him to work at the hotel. But
by that time, the Davidson baseball team had been ripped
apart and tossed to the wind.

Thirteen

CARRIE BISHOP

WHEN ALBION FIRST SET EYES ON THE TALL, NARROW TIPple at Felco, he said, "That there is my church."

I thought it looked more like something built by the Devil. It sagged and screeched and spewed clouds of black dust that settled over our tiny house. The day after I washed windows I could write my name on the pane. If we went barefoot in the house, the soles of our feet turned black and we smudged the white sheets when we got into bed.

We had been married at the Homeplace on a warm spring day when all the earth smelled sweet. Though I knew we would be moving to the coal fields, I had dreamed of a neat little house with boxes of red flowers on the porch. Flora, who stood by me at the wedding, gave me seeds for planting from her prettiest flowerbeds, and cuttings from her rose bushes. But our house was near the coke ovens, and the sulphurous fumes killed anything I planted. Our narrow strip of yard was gritty with cinders.

But Albion was happy. The first time he went in the mine, I fretted the whole day long. I cooked chicken and dumplings special for supper, and bread pudding, but I expected he would be too tired to enjoy his food. I dragged out the number three washtub, filled kettles with water and set them on the stove, paced by the kitchen window anxious for the sight of him. When he came home he was weary, and leaned against the door frame, but his eyes were alive. He talked the whole time I undressed and bathed him.

"I knowed it would be all right, soon as I got inside. I felt easy, like they was nothing to fear. And guess what I

163

seen, over by the haulage way? Mushrooms! Growing up just as pretty as you please, there in the dark and the dust. I tell you, hit was a sign from God. He was saying, 'See here how the least of these creatures can prosper in this place. And wont I take care of you?' "

I filled his plate, put the fork in his hand.

"Hit's a powerful noise when the powder blows. But when we cleared the coal out, I knelt there a minute and I thought, 'They aint never been a human being stood in this place before.' Hit was like discovering a new part of God, like being able to touch something precious. And to feel the mountain all round, to be closer to its heart than I ever did think was possible—"

I sat across from him and toyed with my food.

"And when I was picking slate I come on the outline of a fern that had growed right in the rock. You could count ever leaf on it."

"You talk to the other men?"

"We talked over our dinner pails. They was right shy about it. They're afeard of what the guards might think about meetings. So I said I'd speak to the superintendent and git permission to study the Bible over dinner. They's some are interested in it."

He wanted to make love that night but was too tired for it, so I cradled his head and stroked his temples as he fell asleep.

The superintendent saw no harm in a daily Bible study and prayer session. He thought it might uplift the men, take their minds off their petty troubles and help them work harder. The company preacher at the Felco Methodist Church was strictly Sundays only and most of the miners didn't attend his services anyway. Albion was a Godsend, the superintendent declared.

After a few months, men came to our house on Wednesday evenings for prayer meeting, and brought their wives and children. When a member of the meeting was killed in a roof fall after the boss sent him into a section the men had complained of, Albion read to them from the book of *Exodus*. One man mentioned the union, speaking quiet, his eyes skipping around the room like he feared to be arrested at any moment.

"Let's talk about it some more," Albion said, and they did. Their numbers grew until they filled all four rooms of the house, sitting cross-legged on the floor. Albion had to stand at the kitchen door and turn in all four directions to be heard when he spoke. I waited for the guards to evict us, but no one came.

"They wont be informers in this bunch," Albion said. "I know them ever man jack. They have been convicted by the scriptures."

I WAS BORED IN THE COAL CAMP. ALL I DID WAS COOK, WIPE away coal dust, and worry about where the money would come from. Albion was not the most efficient miner, and we had a hard time of it even with no children to feed. The mines were in a slump then; demand for coal was down since the war ended. Often Albion would trudge to the drift mount to find a sign posted NO WORK TODAY. There would be no pay for those days. He would come back home and make the rounds of the houses, visiting the families who were hungry and cold, praying over the sick.

I wanted to nurse those sick. But when I tried, the camp doctor complained to the superintendent and I was ordered to stop. I visited the doctor to see if I could work with him but he already had a nurse. He treated me coldly. He was from Ohio, and by his lights, I was ignorant. But as I left the office, he called after me and said, "There's a nigger doctor at Annadel who doesn't have a nurse. Wouldn't be a pleasant job, would it? But if you're really interested . . ."

We worked a garden patch the company made available, but it was only half an acre, and would yield nothing for months anyway. For many weeks we ate nothing but potatoes fried with a bit of onion and bacon grease, and that only once a day. Twice a week I dipped into our precious store of meal and baked cornbread. I took dizzy spells.

I thought of writing to Ben, but I knew that their abundance of food would do us no good, and they had little cash to spare. Besides, it would have hurt Albion to know I begged from my kin.

One night I sat on the porch and watched men work the row of coke ovens built into the mountainside below the tipple. The ovens glowed and steamed in the dark. Tiny black figures leaped and darted before the fiery pits. I knew they were mostly Negroes who worked the coke ovens, who bore the heat and breathed the noxious fumes which caused my nose to curl even at that distance. They shovelled and danced like demons at the gates of Hell.

When Albion came down the alley, banging his empty dinner pail against his leg, I met him at the gate.

"Would you mind ifn I worked for a Negro doctor?" I asked.

"I wouldnt care."

"They's some folks would look down on a white woman for it. Would you mind?"

"I wouldnt care."

"We need the money."

"Course we do. Hit would be a blessing."

Doctor Toussaint Booker took me on and paid two dollars a day, a fortune. I studied the frayed cuffs of his one suit and wondered if he could afford it, but I never asked him about it. We were no longer in the destitute class, but could now be considered fortunate. After I went to work we ate meat four days a week, enjoyed fatback in our beans, and Albion set aside fifty cents each day to give to miners with sick children. I looked back with a certain pride on the six months we lived on Albion's seventy-five cents a day. I had accounted for every single penny and every piece of scrip, and spent nary a one without thinking of ten things it might be used for and pledging to do without the nine least important. Yes, there was a pride in it now that we were a bit better off. Only those who can afford it take pride in such things, and only when looking back on them.

I went to Doctor Booker with many doubts, I am ashamed to say. I suppose that at first I looked on him with the same superiority with which the Ohio doctor had plagued me. I soon got over that. Doctor Booker was the best doctor I had ever worked with, not only because of his knowledge but because of his kindness toward his patients.

Doctor Booker knew Rondal, as did his friend C.J. Marcum, the mayor. They talked about him every time Mr. Marcum visited the office, and I listened avidly. After a time I let it be known that Rondal was an acquaintance of mine. They took it as a sign of kinship and gladly included me in their conversations. When Rondal's name was mentioned I paused at my work, and always asked questions so they would talk a little longer. I thought no woman on earth knew as much about Rondal Lloyd as I did. But the knowledge gave me shame as well as pleasure, for I was a married woman and I loved my husband.

ALBION DIDN'T SLEEP WELL IN AUGUST. IT WASN'T JUST the heat. It was the gas.

"The mine buzzed today," he complained. "Hit was like little bugs running around inside my ears."

One night he came home with the sleeve burned off his shirt and his arm blistered. I smeared grease on it.

"I stuck my lamp into the hole," he said. "The flame run right up my arm."

I daubed a wet cloth at his eyebrows, which were mostly gone.

"Yall got to stop work," I said. "Cant they see how dangerous it is?"

"They wouldnt pay us ifn we stopped work. They say hit's natural this time of year to have a gassy mine."

"Some mines blow," I argued.

"Hit's a chance. They take it."

I dreamed it all before it happened, only I dreamed it was Albion. Even though that part was wrong, I knew it was coming. I wasn't surprised when C.J. Marcum came to our office, his face white and drawn, and said, "Davidson Number Six is gone."

My stomach griped and I sat down.

"They heard the explosion all the way to Felco," C.J. said. "They're gone."

"Clabe and Kerwin?" Doctor Booker asked.

C.J. sank into a chair and looked away. "And Froggy Lester and Joe Tibbs."

"We better go down there," Doctor Booker said to me.

"I want to see my husband first. I want to set eyes on him."

"He's all right, Carrie. But go on. Meet me at the Davidson train depot at three."

Albion was in the kitchen when I arrived.

"They sent us home," he said.

I was suddenly angry at him. "Did they? That was kind of them. Too bad they didnt send Number Six home. Tell me, what does God say about this here?"

"Hit aint God's doing. All God done was give Mr. Davidson the freedom."

"Somebody better take that freedom away," I said bitterly. "And somebody ought to burn in Hell for this."

"I got to go help fetch the bodies."

I answered him coldly, for his gentleness was an affront to me. "Go on then. And dont forgit to tote that Bible of yourn."

He came to me, wanted to touch me, but he was still black from the mine.

"You'll dirty my uniform," I said. I waited for him to leave and caught the train after his.

The train I rode carried hundreds of wooden caskets. I watched them unloaded while I waited for Doctor Booker. A crowd of silent women stood near the depot; the faded cotton dresses hung limp on their heavy bodies. An Italian woman approached me. She was dressed all in white like a bride, except for a red vest, and bore an armful of red roses.

"You a nurse?" she said. She gripped my arm. "Are my babies back from the doctor? Is my Francesco very sick?"

Later Doctor Booker pointed out Rondal's mother, a slump-shouldered woman like all the others. She wandered among the rows of coffins, most of which were still empty.

I knew Rondal would come back.

Fourteen
ROSA ANGELELLI

My babies hurt their ears. That is what Senore Davidson says. The ears, they are gone first. They pop, they hurt, a little. But that is all.

Never mind, I say. We go to the doctor. The doctor fix.

Senore cries. He presses his face against my belly. The baseball, he says. My pitcher, my first base. Carmello will be in the American League.

Never mind, I say again. The doctor, he fix the ear.

I wait for the doctor. Everyone wears white. This place is very clean. Mama is here too. Her bed is beside mine. At night we whisper together.

Luigi is very difficult, she says. He makes the doctor work a long time. He is stubborn, like his papa.

They take so long I go to wait for them. I cut the roses from the bush in our yard. Francesco gives me the bush for my birthday. He is my best boy.

I carry a rose for each of my babies. Mario is angry with me.

Go home, woman, go home. He shouts and waves his hat.

Leave me, I answer. Always you whip them. But when they are hurt, they cry for mama. They love mama.

Everyone is crying, everywhere the tears. The women lean together, they sway, they do not close their mouths.

I wait but my babies do not come. Senore Davidson tells the doctor to hurry. Everyone does what Senore Davidson says. He takes me to the big house. The butterflies watch what we do. They turn their heads this way and that. They will not shut their eyes. I shake the roses at them. The thorns scratch Senore's arm. The blood tastes like salt. His hands are warm, like the hands of the priest when he signs the cross upon my forehead.

Rosa, he says, you forgive so easy.

Mario drinks too much. The empty wine bottles glow like candles. He stands before the reliquary. I am behind him and I look over his shoulder. My mama stares out at me from behind the glass.

Where is God? Mario says.

He hits the glass with his fist. His hand bleeds, the red sprinkles his shirt like holy water flung by the priest.

I gather the purple glass. Mario cries for a towel but the cut will not heal for he has cursed God. The doctor will not fix. Whenever I see Mario the blood still flows. His clothes are sticky with it. Already he is in Purgatory.

Mama shows me how to sort the broken glass. Only one piece is missing. Luigi will find it.

Fifteen

RONDAL LLOYD

ONE OF THE FIRST THINGS I DID WHEN I GOT BACK ON THE creek was try to see Mommy. She moved in with Talcott and Pricie after the explosion. They lived high on the hillside above Annadel in a blue house that straddled two spindly cinderblock pillars.

Talcott led me into the kitchen. Mommy rocked beside the stove and stared at a cup of coffee.

"Hello, Mommy," I said.

She looked briefly, then away.

"I got nothing to say to you," she said.

I stood with my cap in my hand.

"Now, Mommy, that aint fair," Talcott coaxed her. "Rondal come a long way to see you."

"Where was he when the burying was done? Where was he before that when my baby went to work in that hole?"

"Hell, Mommy—" I began.

"Oh, yes, you would be a cussing and swearing," she broke in. "Hit's a sure sign that Satan has a holt of you, and it dont surprise me nary a bit. I've knowed it since you was borned. Your Uncle Dillon helped with the birthing of ye, and he set the evil eye on you. I knowed it from the way you sucked at my breast, the way you clutched, all greedy, and bit me and drawed the blood. I knowed it—"

I turned and walked out. Pricie stood in the front room with her arms across her chest and her face tight.

"Now you know what I go through," she said.

"She aint kind to Pricie," Talcott admitted. "Blames her

for taking me away from Winco. But what am I supposed to do, put my own mother out in the street?''

"She could work in the clubhouse or take in washing," Pricie said.

"Would you do that to your mommy?''

They argued without enthusiasm, for they had lots of practice and took no enjoyment from it. Talcott was miserable at Annadel, working as a janitor at the hotel. He wanted to move to another coalfield and go back in the mines. Pricie wouldn't hear of leaving Blackberry Creek as long as Ermel and Annadel were alive.

Talcott's four children were lined up on the couch, squirming and poking one another.

"Younguns, this here is your Uncle Rondal. You dont know him but he is one fine feller. He's going to be around for a spell.''

"He got a gun?'' the oldest boy, Brigham, asked.

"Hell, yes, he's got a gun," Talcott said. "What he does, he has to have a gun.''

"Can I see it?''

"Naw," I said. "You aint got no business till you git older.''

"Daddy lets us.''

I looked at Talcott, who shrugged and smiled.

"That's up to your daddy," I said. "But I dont show nobody my gun. Hit's a big secret. You understand?''

They all nodded gravely. They were the spitting image of the way we were at their age, with their sharp eyes and narrow noses, and I yearned for a moment to have children of my own. But the feeling passed.

I saw Carrie Bishop on the street the next day. Carrie Freeman, I guess I should say, although it was hard to think of her as married. She hadn't changed. She is the kind of woman who won't, until one day her hair turns white and you notice she is old.

She'd just left Doc Booker's office when I saw her. She walked right past me, not even noticing who I was, with that intent look on her face.

I sang softly at the back of her white uniform.

"Weep no more my lady, oh weep no more today.''

She wheeled around.

"Hey, Kentucky," I said. When I approached she took a step backward.

"I heard you come back," she said. "Doctor Booker told me."

"So you're working for Doc. Aint it funny how people git to know each other." I turned and put my hand on the shoulder of Antoine Jones, who stood just behind me. "You know Antoine? He's my shadow for today. Isom's taking real good care of me while I'm in town. Let's the three of us go git a sandwich and have a little talk."

Carrie and I sat in the back booth of the Black Diamond Grill and ordered bacon and tomato sandwiches. Antoine sat across the aisle and kept his eye on the door.

"I heard your husband's doing my job for me," I said.

She nodded proudly. "They's over a hundred men that meets every day over their dinner pails in the Felco mine," she said. "They fill up the main haulage way just to hear Albion Freeman."

"Aint it something he could do that just by preaching."

"Hit aint just preaching," she said. "He's preaching God delivering the children of Israel out of Egypt. He's preaching the first shall be last and the last first. You know he goes to folks' houses and speaks the Word? They study the Bible then, too. And they study the United Mineworkers."

"I wonder," I said. "I wonder does he do it for the love of God or the love of Carrie Bishop?"

She turned all hard. "You got no right to talk about love. You told me oncet you couldnt love nobody. Dont make fun of them that do."

I traced my finger along the wooden tabletop where people had carved their initials with penknives. "I reckon you're right," I said with exaggerated politeness. "I didnt bring you to lunch to talk about silliness anyhow. I come to talk business. I'm going to have my hands full organizing Winco and Davidson. Isom and Doc and C.J. are going to work on the Jenkinjones miners for me. Hit would be a powerful help if I could trust Felco to Albion. And that's where you come in. You're in Annadel every day. You can carry messages."

She nodded, wrapped her hands around her coffee cup.

"We got to talk about some things first," she said.

"What?"

"I love my husband. But I love you too."

I always thought honesty in a woman was overrated. "So?"

"So, I just wanted you to know it. And to know that hit wont change nothing. I wouldnt never hurt my husband."

"Fine with me," I said. "Why'd you bother to tell me that?"

"Hit's a hard time you're facing. I thought it might be a comfort."

I lit a cigarette. The match burned my finger and I tossed it into the ashtray. She still ate her sandwich but I stood up. "We'd best not be seen together after this. Ifn I got a message, I'll git word to Doc." I laid five quarters on the table. "Lunch is on me. Least I can do."

It pleasured me to leave her there alone, even though I knew it hurt her. Maybe because I knew it hurt her. Her eyes reproached me. I never felt so close to Carrie as when she looked at me that way.

THE BALDWIN-FELTS GUARDS ON BLACKBERRY CREEK KNEW I was back. We did everything out in the open. We reasoned that it was easier for a man to get killed if he was operating undercover and no one knew of his presence. So I rode the train into Justice County with an escort of District 17 officials. Every newspaper in the area was notified, and many sent reporters to meet the train at Justice. The new leadership in Charleston was young, smart, and ready to take on the Levisa coal operators in a fight to the finish. We read statements about how we had come as free American citizens to invite the miners of Justice and Paine Counties to join the United Mineworkers. Then we rode on to Annadel where C.J., Isom and the whole police force was tricked out to meet us. I enjoyed all the attention, the back-slapping, the bold glances and impudent smiles at the ever-present Baldwin-Felts guards. I knew the pleasure wouldn't last long.

I had been reminded of the danger I was in by the route we took to reach Justice. The most direct way was through Logan. But Logan County was ruled by a sadistic sheriff named Don Chafin, backed by hundreds of deputies whose salaries were paid by the coal operators. Chafin wouldn't have hesitated to yank our asses off the train and shoot us on the spot, reporters or no reporters. So we traveled to Justice by way of Huntington.

Ermel set me up with a room in the Alhambra and Isom placed a twenty-four hour guard on me. It wasn't the best situation to get my work done, because anybody with a little sense could keep track of my movements. But there would be time enough for risks. I settled in to keep my eyes and ears open and to make the Baldwins wonder what I was up to.

I had time early on to spend with my buddies. It saddened me to learn that Isom and C.J. weren't getting along. Isom was in love with C.J.'s oldest girl, Gladys, and they wanted to get married. C.J. said no. I could see his point—Gladys was only fifteen. But C.J. told Gladys she would never have his blessing to marry Isom Justice. Isom was highly offended.

Each of them expected me to side with him. C.J. and Violet invited me to dinner and after the chocolate cake, Gladys went to a friend's house. C.J. started in.

"Aint you a bit hard on Isom," I said. "He's a good man. He wouldnt be my buddy ifn he wasnt."

"Good in some ways," C.J. said. "Hell, I like Isom. But not for Gladys."

"Aint Gladys got to decide what's good for Gladys?" Violet said.

"When she's older," C.J. replied. "She'll see things different when she's older. You know how younguns are. Right now she sees that shiny badge Isom wears, and she laughs at his jokes, and thinks that's all they is in the world. When she's older, she'll know they's other things more important."

"He treats her real good," Violet said. "And he's got the money to take care of her."

"Course Violet takes up for him. He's her cousin." C.J. said it like Violet wasn't even sitting there.

"What's so bad about Isom?" I asked. "What kind of feller are you looking for?"

"I'm looking for somebody serious. Somebody with a

purpose in life. Somebody with principles. You know how Ermel is. When it comes to politics, he's crooked as a dog's hind leg. Isom's his daddy's boy. Only reason he comes to our club meetings is to drink whiskey. He thinks everthing comes easy because that's the way it's allays been for him. He pokes fun at everthing me and Doc say, pokes fun at the newspaper. And besides that, he's a tomcat. He wouldnt be faithful to my little girl. He'd hurt her."

"You dont know that," I said. "He seems plumb crazy about her."

C.J. pulled on his pipe, narrowed his eyes. "Let me ask you this. Ifn you had a youngun that was set on marrying at fifteen, would you approve?"

"Dont know," I had to admit. "Hit aint been too good for Pricie."

"See there!" C.J. exclaimed, and considered his case won.

When he went in to the toilet, Violet leaned over and patted my knee.

"Hit's you he wants for Gladys," she said. "He thinks now you're around, she'll fall for you."

"Oh, lord. You know me, Violet. I cant never settle. I got nothing to offer."

She grinned. "I wouldnt wish you on no woman."

I'd said that many a time myself, but it hurt to hear it from her.

"No one would have me anyway," I mumbled.

"No, they's a certain kind would love no one but a man like you. That aint Gladys though. Gladys wants babies, and a man that will put her on a pedestal. That Isom, law, he's allays making over her. He's just got her head turned plumb around."

Isom took me drinking the next night.

"You put in a good word for me?"

"I tried. But you know how stubborn he is."

"Damn!" He slapped the table. "Dont he know we could run away?"

"Dont do that. Hit would kill him."

"How long am I supposed to wait? Hit's a killing me too."

"Is it? Aint you seeing nobody else?"

He dropped his eyes. "Course I am. Hell, I'm only human."

"You aint hurting then."

"You sound like goddamn C.J. I love her."

"You say you do. C.J. loves her too. And if yall marry without his permission, he'll cut you off. This aint the time for a feud."

He sighed. "That may be. I know we got a fight on our hands."

"Damn straight. And I need both of you."

"What am I supposed to do to win him over? Buy into them daydreams of his? I just cant. Hit's so much silliness."

"You help with this organizing, he's got to respect that."

"I already keep this here town protected from the gun thugs. You think he appreciates that? Hell, no. To satisfy him, I'd have to believe that C.J. Marcum and his brand of socialism will build heaven right here on Blackberry Creek." He sucked on his longneck, then tossed down a shot. "You know what I think? Ifn C.J. Marcum had been born in Philadelphy, he'd be just like the damn coal operators. He'd be building model towns and straightening out folks' lives for them, and bragging about how happy everybody was now that he was in charge."

"That aint fair. C.J.'s motives is different."

"Hit feels the same," he said.

"C.J. aint as bad as some," I said. "Them socialists up in Chicago fight amongst theirselves. One disagrees and goes off and starts his own group. Then somebody else argues and starts another group. Hit's as bad as a bunch of Baptists."

"True believers," said Isom. "Tell me more about Chicago."

"Aint much to tell. Hit's like a big Annadel. I told them that up there and they laughed. But hit's true. Bars. Women. The theaters flashing their lights just like the Roxie. The buildings all close together and the streets full of people, Italians and Negroes and them Poles. One thing I found out, they dont know about us down here and they dont give a damn. Even the socialists. To them we're just a passel of ignorant hillbillies. Anything we do will be done our own selves."

"Only thing I want to do is git back that land. And the only reason I want it is to shut C.J. up."

C.J. finally agreed to let Isom court Gladys one night a week if Isom would promise not to run off with her. In the meantime, I got lots of invitations to eat supper with the Marcums.

ON LABOR DAY I BOARDED THE TRAIN FOR DAVIDSON. A Baldwin-Felts guard who rode down from Jenkinjones took the seat behind me. Sweat trickled down my breastbone, tickled the small of my back. I strained to hear any movement he might make. But he sat still until we reached Davidson. He followed me down the aisle. When I stepped onto the platform, he pinned my arm behind my back, pushed me against the wall.

Two men approached. One hit me in the chest with a rifle butt. My knees buckled and I nearly blacked out. They hoisted me up and dumped me back on the train.

"You're moving on, son," one of them said. He hit me in the belly with the rifle.

I huddled there, just inside the door, all the way to Justice. No one offered to help me for fear of the gun thugs still on board. At Justice I managed to drag myself off the train and collapse on a bench. A guard watched me from a nearby doorway.

When the Annadel train arrived, I limped on board and slumped on my seat. Again, a gun thug sat behind me. This one was talkative.

"Boy, you should have kept on riding. You're awful young to die. Wouldn't you rather go on back to Charleston and lay around drunk and fuck women? Hey, redneck, you hang around here, we'll cut your pecker right off. The ladies wont like that, will they?"

At Annadel I staggered off the train and up to Doc Booker's office above the furniture store. Carrie came out to the waiting room, unbuttoned my shirt, felt my chest.

"I think it's broke ribs," she said. "Probably two." Her eyes were dark with worry.

"Could be worse," I said.

"You got to be careful."

"Hell, you love to see me risk my neck."

She backed away.

"I'll git Doctor Booker," she said.

C.J. heard what happened and stopped by the hotel.

"So much for operating in the open," I said. "From now on, hit will be at night."

"If they catch you then, they'll kill you sure."

"If I dont try, I might as well head back to Charleston."

WHO CAN SAY WHY THE MINERS WERE READY TO LISTEN TO me? They broke their backs and died of roof falls and rib rolls and gas, their children went to bed hungry, and died of the typhoid, their wives took the consumption, they themselves coughed and spit up. True enough. They stayed in debt to the company store, they had no say at the mine or freedom of any kind, they could be let go at a moment's notice and put out in the road, or beaten, or shot. All true. But it had always been that way, and they never fought back. Everything had always been the way it was, we were all pilgrims of sorrow, and only Jesus or the Virgin Mary could make it right.

So why did they listen this time? Why did they decide that Jesus might not wait two thousand years for kingdom come, that Jesus might kick a little ass in the here and now?

"Hell, it aint got nothing to do with Jesus," Talcott said grumpily. "Half of em dont believe in Jesus. They just stood all they can stand, and they dont care for it."

But I didn't think that was all there was to it when I visited Doc Booker's church up toward Jenkinjones at Conklintown. It was named the Uprising Chapel. Me, C.J. and Isom attended a Wednesday night service by special invitation of the elders. The congregation huddled on benches, their faces soft as black velvet in the lantern light. Doc, one of the elders, asked me to say a few words before the preaching. I walked to the front of the church, looked down at my toes in a fit of shyness.

"I aint no preacher," I mumbled. I couldn't remember the neat little speech I had practiced about the union and solidarity. So I told them about Johnson. The terror of the scene returned to me, it was hard to speak very loudly, and I feared I would lose them, would frighten them off.

"Hit is an awful thing to see a man die that way," I said. "Even more awful to be the man kilt. Hit was a painful death. He had to carry hisself clean outen his mind in order to face it."

They sat in silence, Johnson screaming and burning before their very eyes.

"But he went out singing," I said. "I seen his head roll back and his eyes was wide open. He was looking to heaven, ready to charge right up to the gates. He already knew about death. Everybody in this here church knows about it. You face the roof falls, you lose your younguns to the sickness. Johnson, he didnt wait for no roof fall. He went out singing."

I had raised my voice without realizing it. A woman in the back cried out, "Praise the Lord! Praise you Jesus!"

"Amen!" Others took up the cry. "Praise Jesus!"

"Johnson wouldn't be a slave no more!" I cried. "He died a free man. They's slaves today in Justice County, both white and black. Hit's time to break them chains."

I slipped back to my seat, for it was time for them to do their own talking.

"Lord!" the preacher was shouting, "we heard this before! And we are not afraid!"

A long-necked woman with her head bound in a yellow kerchief stood with a tambourine and sang, "This little light of mine, I'm gonna let it shine." She stepped from side to side in time to the music and the congregation joined her, clapping, rocking.

Way down in that coal mine
I'm gonna let it shine.

Isom clapped and sang along. C.J. tried, but he had no sense of rhythm. He clapped half a beat behind everyone else and called out in a tuneless monotone.

Doc Booker, up front, pulled a red bandana from his back pocket, waved it back and forth, tied it around his neck. It was an old sign of poor people standing together, the red badge of the union, a death warrant if seen by the gun thugs. I tied on my own bandana.

This little light of mine,

Lordy I'm gonna let it shine.

One by one the men fished out their red bandanas, knotted them around their necks.

Cant no fire burn me,
I'm gonna let it shine.

Doc placed a stack of union cards on the communion plate beside the broken crackers. When the plate reached the back of the church, the cards were gone. The pianist played a rattling version of "Precious Lord Take My Hand." They sang again and their shadows danced across the ceiling.

I sat still all through the preaching, about preparing roads in the wilderness and making straight the way of the Lord, about John the Baptist, Herod, messengers, persecutors, martyrs. The preacher, a short man in a flowered vest who worked in the Jenkinjones mine, shook my hand after the service.

"The Holy Ghost got a holt of us now," he said.

"Why now?" I asked. "Why not ten year ago, or ten year from now?"

"Hit's the fullness of time," he said.

I loved that phrase, "the fullness of time." I shivered to whisper it to myself, for I sensed I was living in it, right then. Nothing afterward would be so important, not like what was happening there on Blackberry Creek. We are put on earth for the fullness of time, we spend our days reaching it, and then we pass on. Some people die right then, with the passing of the fullness, and others breathe on, grieving all their lives that time is being strangled and they are not yet dead. I didn't fret about this last. I couldn't imagine it for myself.

In Albion Freeman's front room, I marvelled at the fullness. The house was packed with miners and their wives come to study the Bible. They sat on the floor, their knees drawn up beneath their chins to save room. Once again I was there by special invitation. I had laid out on the mountainside until dark, then sprinted through the billowing smoke of the coke ovens, a perfect cover blown over that part of the camp by a wind from the head of the holler. I stretched out in the Freemans' yard before entering the house and scanned the row for guards. None appeared, and I slipped up the back steps into the kitchen. Carrie was taking cookies out of the oven. She smiled at me.

"You'll be happy tonight," she said. "Albion has done so well."

I talked to them about what to expect in case of a strike. They listened quietly, their faces stretched tight to show no fear. After about ten minutes there came a vigorous thumping from beneath the house.

"Hit's Roscoe Blackburn keeping watch," Albion whispered to me. He led us in singing "Blessed Assurance." I wriggled back into a shadowy corner. When the hymn was done, Roscoe thumped once. We commenced talking about the union again. Albion closed the meeting with a prayer.

I stayed until everyone had left, figuring that the gun thugs would be occupied with seeing folks home. I shook Albion's hand.

"You're doing good work," I said.

"Am I?" he answered. "I aint sure. The Bible says do everything for love, and to love your enemies. I aint sure I'm doing a good job of loving the coal operators."

"Lord," I said, "Jesus Christ hisself is likely having trouble with that."

He shook his head. "He ate with the sinners and tax collectors."

"Well, ifn you can git Lytton Davidson to let you eat with him, maybe you'll figure out how to love him. Until then, it's his doing."

When I went to the kitchen Carrie was washing dishes. She turned around and our eyes met. I wanted her to tell me to be careful like she had before. Then I heard steps and spun around. Albion had followed me into the room. I felt my face flush red with embarrassment.

"I better go," I stammered.

Albion smiled.

"Douse the light, Carrie," he said. "He better not go out until we watch for Baldwins."

She followed me out on the back stoop.

"You be careful," she said.

* * *

No one bothered me since the day I was roughed up at Davidson. I worked slowly and quietly throughout the winter, and by April I judged that the majority of miners of Jenkinjones, Felco, and Winco had been organized. I slept during the daytime, usually at Ruby Day's or in various rooms in her daddy's cathouse. At night I visited taverns, churches, and even an occasional home. The Baldwin-Felts guards came to Annadel to do business, but I was always accompanied by Isom or one of the policemen.

Many a night I stayed up late with C.J., Isom and Doc to argue strategy. We knew the company would evict striking miners from their houses. The District leaders in Charleston were already getting in a store of tents for the families to live in, and collecting food. We talked about where to set up the tents. I said the Jenkinjones miners could be relocated at the ball field in Annadel, Felco miners could live at the Justice farm, Winco could go to Cesco Thompson's land on Lloyd's Fork. Davidson presented a problem, for American Coal and the railroad controlled every scrap of land all the way into Justice.

"Hell, Davidson wont come out no way," said Doc. "Why worry over where to set them?"

"They got to come out," I said. "Either that or we shut them down. We cant win no strike if Davidson keeps on working."

"Well," said C.J., "ifn we do so well that Davidson is shut down, we can just take over Davidson land. Marcum land, I should say."

"I dont care for it," Isom complained. "Not nary a bit of it. Look here, what right they got to put folks outen their houses?"

"They claim they can do anything they want with their property," I said.

"But dont we claim hit's our land?" C.J. said. "Isom's right. We shouldnt just let them git away with it."

"How we supposed to stop them?"

"With guns!" C.J. answered. "Aint we stockpiling guns?"

"What do you think them long things are they carry?

They aint hoes." I looked around the table. "Anybody got any good ideas, I'll listen. But they aint no way in hell we can stop evictions in a camp like Felco."

"Not Felco or Winco," Isom said. "But we can by God stop them in Jenkinjones."

"They got to change trains in Annadel to git to Jenkinjones," C.J. said. "I'm the mayor of this here town and Isom is the law. We got ever right to stop them."

"Damn straight," Isom said. They looked at one another appreciatively.

"I'm uneasy," I said.

"Ifn a feller comes through my town on his way to commit a crime, aint I got a right and a duty to stop him?" Isom demanded. "And aint it a crime to set a man and his family out in the road just because he joins a union?"

"I aint the one you need to convince. Tell it to the Baldwins."

"We got to fight em sometime," Doc said. "C.J. and Isom are right. This here town is ours. We start giving ground here we done whupped before we started."

"All right, all right. Ifn they try to go through Annadel, we stop em. But how? We better plan this thing out."

"I'll just arrest them," Isom said. He grinned at C.J. "Me and the mayor here, we run a clean town."

C.J. grinned back.

I was glad to see them getting along again. It was easier for them to like one another because both of them were so happy. For C.J. the time had come at last to avenge his papaw's murder and take back his land. If he was worried about how the Davidson miners would take to him setting up a farm in the middle of their coal camp, he didn't show it. There was room for everyone, he kept insisting.

Isom thought it was a lark. He couldn't wait to match wits with the Baldwin-Felts gunmen. Every time I saw him, he had a new idea about how to defend Jenkinjones.

I listened to them and went on with my organizing. The foreign miners were the last ones I reached. I had dreaded working with them because I never knew any of them well when I was growing up. But it proved surprisingly easy. Many spoke English, and those who didn't only had to hear the word "syndicato" and they perked right up. Many of them had been radicals back home or had at least heard a lot of radical talk. They joined up like flies after a mule's rump.

I couldn't believe the Baldwins hadn't got wind of it.

"Maybe they're thinking it done gone too far to stop," Doc Booker suggested. "So they figure they ride out a strike, fire everybody, and start over with new workers that dont know what's going on."

Antoine Jones and I were watching Fatty Arbuckle at the Roxie one night when Isom slipped into a seat beside us.

"Git out of this goddamn theater," he hissed. "Hit's so dark in here somebody could shoot you and nobody ever see who done it."

"Oh hell, Antoine's with me."

"The gun thugs shot up Winco."

"What?"

"Let's git out of here so we can talk."

We slipped out the fire exit into the alley. Isom explained, "You know them five houses that set on the bend there toward the tipple?"

"Right. Where Junebug Slater lives."

"Where he lived. Junebug's dead. And his oldest boy Herman, ten year old. And three others, including Vencil Ray's wife." Isom's eyes glittered in the dark. "Just a little warning, aint it?"

I felt sick to my stomach. It was one of the first places I organized. I had sat at Junebug Slater's kitchen table at two in the morning, no lamp lit and the moonlight painting everything silver, and gave six men the pledge.

Isom took me to the Alhambra and I got roaring drunk.

"You got to pull em out," he said.

"Shit. Oh shit. Why ever did I come back?"

"The dice is done rolled. They'll just be picking us off one by one from here on out. Pull em out."

"I got to talk with the District."

"Hell with the District. Send them a telegram. Tell em you're pulling out every motherfucker on this creek."

For a moment I hated him the way C.J. hated him, because it was so easy for him. He threw my arm around his shoulders and helped me to the telegraph office.

"Andy!" he yelled at the clerk. "Hit's strike time!"

I leaned on the counter, one hand splayed across my forehead. "Miners murdered stop," I mumbled. "All over stop going out stop." I stood straight, stumbled toward the door, turned at an afterthought. "Send tents send food!" I yelled. "Stop!"

Isom hugged me. "God, I love you," he said.

NEXT MORNING MY HEAD THROBBED FROM A HANGOVER. I trudged up the stairs to Doc's office. Carrie was at the medicine cabinet.

"You got any aspirin?"

She handed me two and I tossed them down.

"Tell Albion tonight. Tell him to pull them out first thing tomorry morning."

She looked out the window. "Will Pond Creek come out too?"

"We got a feller who's been signing up Pond Creek miners. I reckon they'll come out before too long. You thinking about your brother?"

She nodded her head and started to cry. My bad leg ached and I shifted my weight.

"You got anything in your house that you want to keep, you better pack it up to take with you," I said. "The gun thugs will break up everything."

"He'll be on the other side," she said. "Dont kin mean nothing no more?"

"I wouldnt know," I said.

Next morning Carrie told me Albion Freeman went to the mine early and when the others arrived, he stood at the drift mouth and poured the water out of his water bottle. Everyone else did the same and no one went in. I heard a similar story from Winco. By afternoon the evictions began. Scores of company guards fanned out through the two coal camps. They banged on the doors of houses with rifle butts, ordered everyone out, took special care to keep their guns trained on the children so their parents wouldn't fight back. They tossed furniture into the road. People salvaged what they could carry away. A woman named Betty Woolridge, nine months pregnant, laid down on a mattress and gave birth beside the road while her neighbor's dishes were tossed out and smashed beside her.

They arrived at Ermel's farm that night. The tents came two days later. In the meantime they slept on the ground and cooked over open fires. Ermel gave them food from his store. I promised him the union would pay him back.

When the tents went up with their peaks and circular towers, Ermel's cornfield looked like some Arab city you read of in books, made of canvas instead of stone.

THE STRIKE SPREAD. OVER 12,000 PEOPLE WERE LIVING IN the tent colonies. Many Kentucky miners signed up at an organizing meeting in Justice. By the end of the week Pond Creek was shut down, and a tent city grew up between Chieftan and Vulcan. Even Davidson miners signed up, so that Number Five closed down at once and I judged it would be only a few months before we would shut down the rest. Our demands were simple—freedom of speech, no Baldwin guards, union checkweighmen to guarantee a man got credit for the coal he mined, and recognition of the union. There was no mention of the land, but the union constitution called for the workers to receive the "full social value of their product," and C.J. seemed content that everything else would follow.

On May 10, 1920, I called out the miners at Jenkinjones. The next day, Isom came tearing up the stairs to my hotel room.

"They're here! Twelve of the bastards! And Jesus Christ, they got two of the big boys with them!" He pulled me to the window and pointed outside where a group of men with rifles slung over their shoulders strolled around the station platform beside the depot. "There by the baggage rack!"

Two men dressed in expensive-looking pinstripe suits and shiny shoes stood and smoked cigars.

"Hit's the brothers of the man that owns Baldwin-Felts. God, can you believe it? They just come in with those other thugs on the main Blackberry train up from Bluefield."

C.J. entered the room.

"I heard the local's whistle," he said. "It will be here any time."

Isom ran to the door, then back to the window.

"I cant arrest nobody. The word's gone out but the boys aint here yet. We cant arrest no twelve gun thugs without a lot of men."

"You got the warrants?" I asked.

"Daddy brung em down from Justice day before yesterday."

Outside the Jenkinjones local pulled in and the gun thugs, along with the two gentlemen in pinstripes, boarded the train.

"They're either goddamn arrogant and complacent, or they're scairt half to death," I said softly.

"They're arrogant," C.J. said. "They dont think nobody would dare touch em. Why else would old man Felts send his brothers in here?"

"Shall we try to foller them up to Jenkinjones, stop the evictions?" Isom asked.

"No," I said. "Hit's too late for that. But we'll be waiting when they come back."

Two score of miners arrived from Ermel's with their Winchester rifles. Isom sent them to the hotel windows overlooking the depot and into the hardware store that fronted the tracks. Antoine Jones had charge of the men in the hardware store. C.J., Ermel, Albion Freeman, Doc, Isom and I gathered in the hotel lobby. We decided that Doc and Ermel would remain in charge of the hotel.

"Where's your gun, preacher?" Isom asked.

"I aint toting one."

Isom looked at me and raised his eyebrows, said, "That's all right. I got this here under control."

We hung around the lobby and tried to make small talk about the new baseball season. Ermel, usually so careful of the appearance of his hotel, tapped his cigarette ashes onto the green patterned carpet. At 4:30 a miner stuck his head in the door. "Jenkinjones local's coming back down."

We tried to walk slowly out to the platform. We waited with our hands in our pockets, not looking at one another.

Talcott stepped up and tapped me on the shoulder. "I'm going to help you boys."

"Go on back to the hotel."

"Shit!" he said, and disappeared.

Isom paced the platform. It was strange to see him so agitated. I put my arm around him.

"Just arrest them," I said.

"Right. Then git drunk as hell."

C.J. kept glancing at his watch. The train whistle blew around the bend. Isom shook me by the shoulders.

"You got to git back. I dont want you messed up in this."

"Aw, I thought this here was settled."

"I just been thinking. They see you up this close, they might be tempted to shoot you. Go on! Git!"

He shoved me back roughly and I retreated to the doorway of the hardware store. I saw Talcott standing behind the depot. His hand rested on the brown handle of a pistol at his belt. I motioned to him to join me but he just grinned and waved back. Antoine handed me a Winchester.

"If you're going to stand in that doorway, hold this back behind you," he said. "Aint no sense to alarm em."

I waved at Talcott again. When he still ignored me, I sprinted to him just before the train pulled in.

"I didnt want you here," I said.

"You dont tell me what to do. This here is my fight as much as yourn."

The local pulled in and stopped, its engine grumbling to itself. The doors of the red passenger car flew open. The gunmen came down jauntily, with the pleased and impatient air of men who have done a job and are anxious to be home. They sauntered along the platform to wait for the Bluefield train.

Isom waited until the local pulled out before he approached. C.J. and Albion flanked him on either side. Isom set his hand to his badge to see if it was in place. Then he walked up to the two men in pinstripes.

"You gentlemen have been evicting people from their homes in Jenkinjones," said Isom.

They looked him up and down. Both had smooth, broad faces and thick fleshy lips. The taller one smiled at Isom while the other studied his brother's face expectantly.

"We've been removing trespassers from the property of the American Coal Company, Sheriff," said the tall one.

"I aint a sheriff," Isom said. "I'm chief of police. And you're under arrest."

They showed no signs of surprise.

"I got a warrant from the county seat," Isom continued.

"What's the charge?"

"Assault. And illegal possession of weapons. You aint got a permit for them guns."

"Since when do we need one?"

"Since last week," C.J. said. "City council passed an ordinance last week."

"And who are you?"

"I'm the mayor of this here town."

"Mr. Marcum, is that right? Well, Mr. Marcum, Mr. Justice, I'm afraid I've got some unpleasant news for you. It's really you who are under arrest. We're taking you both to Bluefield with us."

He reached inside his coat and brought out a piece of paper. I heard a clicking sound beside my ear. I turned my head. Talcott held his pistol cocked. Our eyes met.

"You cant do that," C.J. was protesting. "You got no right. This here aint no kind of warrant."

"I beg your pardon, but it's quite official. Drawn up in Mercer County yesterday."

"We aint going," Isom said. "Hit's a set-up."

The tall man's hand slipped back inside his coat, the butt of a pistol appeared, Talcott's gun roared beside my head. The man looked surprised, the weight of his gun dragged his hand down as he fired, and C.J. fell to the ground clutching his belly. Isom ducked and fired, my rifle was on my shoulder and I pulled the trigger, the short man fell, his hand tangled in his watch chain, Albion Freeman dragged C.J. backward, the gun thugs ran for cover. They shot back. The glass front of the hardware store exploded and the men inside screamed. The Bluefield train pulled into the station, one guard ran for it, Isom, kneeling and somehow unscathed by bullets, cut him down. The faces in the train windows flashed by. The train did not stop.

Three guards leaped at the caboose and clung desperately to the railing. One fell off and struck his head on a crosstie. Talcott strolled over to where the man lay writhing in pain. He raised his pistol in a salute to the retreating train, then leaned over and shot the man in the head.

I turned away. Isom still stood on the platform, surrounded by bodies. He carefully examined the barrel of his pistol. Albion Freeman crouched behind the luggage rack and cradled C.J.'s head in his lap. C.J.'s belly was a sticky mass of blood and flesh.

"Git Doc!" Albion hollered. "Hit's real bad."

I ran toward the hotel. Sam Gore yelled from the doorway of the hardware store, "Git Doc! Antoine, he hurt!" I passed two dead miners sprawled on the ground and met Doc, already on his way, his bag swinging from one hand and his coattails flying.

"C.J. and Antoine!" I cried.

"Lord, lord!"

He knelt beside C.J. first, put his hands over his face for a moment, then looked up.

"I cant do a thing for him," he said in a choked voice. "I could shoot him full of morphine but I dont expect he'll last long enough for it to take."

"Go tend Antoine," I said. I pulled off my jacket and laid it over C.J.'s midsection to keep away the flies.

"Papaw," C.J. said. Blood ran out of his mouth and Albion wiped it with his red bandana.

"Oh, papaw." C.J.'s chest heaved and he was still.

I squeezed C.J.'s hand and started to cry.

"We ought to take him to the hotel."

Albion Freeman put his hand on my arm. I shook it off. Between the two of us we got him inside and stretched him out on a couch just as Violet burst in. Her screams drove me back outside.

I met Carrie in the street.

"Albion?"

"He's all right," I said. "He's in the hotel with Violet. C.J.'s dead."

"Oh, Lord," she said. She looked toward the station. "I got to go. Doc's taking Antoine to the hospital and I got to tend the others." She took my hand. "I'm so sorry about C.J. I know you was close."

I pulled my hand away. "You better run to somebody that needs help."

I followed her toward the station and then I spied Isom. He was squatting by himself on the track rail, clutching his ankles. I sat beside him. His round face was streaked with tears.

"C.J.'s dead, aint he?"

"He's dead."

"He wont never git that land back."

"No, he wont."

"I kilt a man, Rondal. I kilt that one right over there."

"I kilt the short one in the suit. Leastways I fired at him right when he fell. They was shooting all around by then."

He wiped his nose. "They damn well deserved it. They pushed folks around long enough. How many did we kill?"

"Looks like seven maybe. Where's my brother?"

"Damned if I know. Last I seen he was heading for the creek."

Beside the toe of my boot, a piss ant struggled to escape from a spreading pool of blood. I offered Isom a pinch of snuff and he poked it behind his lip with one grimy finger.

"This here going to hurt your strike?"

I put my arm around his shoulders.

"Son, you kill a man in a suit, hit aint just a strike no more."

WE ERECTED A NEW SIGN AT THE TRAIN DEPOT THAT PROclaimed FREE ANNADEL in letters two feet high. Armed miners stood guard at every street corner. Only hours after the shootings we had moved into Jenkinjones like an occupying army. The red bandanas around our necks served as a uniform and we carried rifles on our shoulders. Many of the women were also armed. We went straightway to meet the newly evicted families, still gathering up their belongings beside the railroad, and told them to go back to their homes. Jenkinjones belonged to them.

The next day we held C.J.'s funeral in the main street at Annadel. We bore the coffin to the porch of the Alhambra Hotel, accompanied by hundreds of miners and their families. They came in their Sunday best, men and boys in suits and ties, women and girls in neatly pressed cotton dresses except for the Italians, who wore embroidered blouses and brightly colored skirts. Many of the children were barefoot.

Albion Freeman preached the sermon. Mostly he said the

same old things preachers say, about how a man must die because he is a sinner, about the next life and how sweet it is. But one thing he said caught my attention.

"Most of you got your guns there," he said. "Hit's a sin to have them. Hit was a sin to shoot down them gun thugs, even if they was bound to shoot you first. I'll not have a gun with me for the purpose of shooting a man, and I bid you to pledge the same. But I'll not condemn you for carrying those guns. You carry those guns in God's freedom. You make mistakes because you are alive and free. You cant escape your sin, so sin boldly and know God loves you. Only try to do good for the glory of God."

I thought these were strange sentiments for a preacher, although Doc said later that Albion was preaching straight from St. Paul. After Doc took over and launched into a tearful recitation of C.J.'s virtues and contributions to the struggle, I kept thinking about what the preacher said.

"This was a *good* man we lost," Doc said.

"A good man," I repeated, and thought of the road C J. had urged me down so many times, the road which lead to the place where we stood that day, a terrible place which would bring all the world down upon our heads.

Eight of us carried the coffin up the hill to the town cemetery for the burying. Isom walked alongside, supporting Gladys on one arm. Violet had already agreed that the two of them should marry.

"Look a-yonder," Isom said, and nodded up the hill.

A lone figure stood beside the open grave. I could just catch glimpses of him as we struggled up with the coffin for I had to keep a close watch on where I put my feet. But I knew who he was. He backed away as we approached, stood beside the fence like he might jump over it and run away. I looked at him steady as we set the coffin down, and he looked back. I studied him all through the final words—his rough hide jacket, his Indian brown skin, his long dark hair streaked with gray and pulled back in a ponytail.

He turned to leave before the last prayer was done, and I followed him into the woods. I doubt I would have caught up to him, but I called out "Uncle Dillon!" and he stopped and turned around.

"So you're that boy," he said.

We stood face to face and I searched my heart to know what I felt about him. What I found there inside me was anger.

"You come back just to leave again?" I said. "Without a word to nobody?"

"I aint much used to talk," he said slowly.

"I reckon not. You turn your back on folks, I reckon it's hard to know what to say to them."

He smiled then. "I see Ermel now and again, trade him a load of liquor for what I need. He said you was a mean one."

"Damn straight. You set the Evil Eye on me, according to Mommy. Not that you bothered much with me after that. Nor with my daddy when he needed you, nor with C.J. You been too busy living the old ways, aint that right? Living the pure ways, the dead ways."

He stood still as a statue.

"You could have fought back," I said. "A long time ago, before it was too late, you could have fought back."

"I fought back the only way I knew how." He spat on the ground. "And I'll fight a man that calls me a coward. Would you be a calling me that?"

I knew better than to take on a man that was all muscle and had cloudy brown eyes like an animal.

"Hell, no, I aint saying that. I just cant figure you out. I dont know you. Damn it, you come in here oncet in a while and see Ermel, and I dont even know about it. How come?"

"I didnt care for you to know. I made Ermel swear he'd not tell you when I come, or where I was. Wouldnt do you no good, nor me neither."

"Didnt you ever want to see your family? Didnt you want to see Daddy?"

"I loved your daddy but I never could abide that woman he took up with. Werent worth risking one for t'other."

"What about C.J.?"

He grinned and I saw all his teeth were gone. I wondered if he'd pulled them himself. "C.J. were a good boy. That's why I come down when Ermel sent word. C.J. allays had a silly streak. Dreamer, you know. I was fond of that. But he passed on from me to Ermel. He become a store man. That's all right. I wouldnt take nobody with me."

With that, the talk seemed to die between us. We looked at the toes of our boots.

"Why dont you come on down to the hotel, have a drink?" I said at last. "After all, hit's your liquor."

He rolled his shoulders around like he'd been carrying a heavy load. "I cant abide a room for long. I reckon you're a store man, like C.J. Reckon you like a room. Like all this ugliness too. Like all these outlandish folks that made it this a way. I seen em when I come to trade with Ermel. They live like sheep. They like to be ordered around. You pull them outen the fire, they'll jump right back in again. I cant abide em."

I had nothing to say back, not even a muttered hope that I would see him again. That was the last thing I wanted. For all these years I had known only what C.J. and Daddy had told me of him, and he had been something to dream about. It was a good thing to live on the land, to respect it and to hate anything that would tear it down. But Dillon was hoarding the land like a miser his gold, and he had nothing to give anyone. It seemed to me he was no longer among the living.

I dreamed of two men that night. Of C.J. alive and walking with me among the miners' tents. Of Dillon dead, a burnished skeleton lying on its back, the fingers of one hand curved and twined through the rib cage.

Sixteen

ROSA ANGELELLI

FRANCESCO IS BACK FROM THE DOCTOR. HE SITS BESIDE MY bed and talks with me. He brings me oranges.

Senore Davidson is not here. He goes to Carmello and Luigi, to see why they stay so long with the doctor. I stay in his house to watch over the butterflies.

The butterflies weep. Let us out, they cry. The glass case is so hot.

Mama tugs at my sleeve. Break the glass, she says. Let them go. They have been here so long.

I break the glass. I hit with the lamp. The butterflies scream. They are so frightened, but I whisper to them and they are quiet.

I cannot carry them all but Francesco helps. We must hurry, he says. When the butterflies are gone this house must burn.

But Chi Chi, I say, this is Senore's house.

It is God's house, he says. Smell. Like the incense.

Bambino, I say. He puts his arms around me. He doesn't speak.

Baby, I say in the inglese. You are my baby.

We run with the butterflies. Help them to fly, mama says.

Oh, mama, I cannot touch the wings. I hurt, I break.

But Francesco, ah! He picks up with his fingers, he is so gentle.

He throws and the butterfly is gone.

Again, I cry, again. Save them all.

He flings and they leap from his hand like purple and

gold fairies, their wings shine like precious jewels, they flash like the wine the priest pours. They go, fast.

Where do they go, I wonder.

Francesco smiles. To the angels, he says.

My mama is with the angels, I say. But she visits me. I squeeze his face with my hands. Bambino, let me wash your face. It is so dirty, and no one washes like your mama.

We kneel beside the river. The smoke does not choke us here. He gives me his red scarf and I dip it in the water. I clean the folds beneath his eyes, the tender skin.

I kiss his forehead. He presses my hand against his cheek.

I must wait for your brothers, I say. They will come to me. I must wait for Mama.

I will take you, he says. I know the place.

It is very clean here. Francesco comes every day and Mama makes my bed at night. Soon we will go to the angels.

Seventeen

CARRIE BISHOP

RONDAL LLOYD CAME TO MY TENT EARLY ONE SUMMER morning and shook me awake.

"I got to talk to you."

I sat up, wrapped my quilt around me and blinked stupidly at him. He smelled of burnt wood.

"Where's Albion?" he asked.

"He's with Doc standing watch over the Ledford baby. What you been up to?"

He pulled up the only chair and sat down. "We burnt part of Davidson last night. They was a big fight. I reckon they's at least ten men laying dead up there. But Number Five and Number Eight stood with us. Hit's Number Two that's kept working, but I think we got them scairt. They're staying home now."

He spoke easily of the shooting. But that morning there was such a look on his face. His was not the face of a man who has watched others die. His was the look of Moses who has seen the burning bush.

"I want to tell you what happened. I thought you'd know what I should do."

"Tell me."

"We set the big house on fire."

"Lytton Davidson's?"

"That's right. He took off for Philadelphy when the strike broke out, so we burnt it down. But just after we set the fire, I thought I'd best run in and see that they wasnt nobody in there. Sure enough they was a woman in a big room at the back. I learnt later on that she's an Italian that worked

198

for Davidson as a maid. Isom says her old man run off after the Number Six explosion and Davidson moved her into the big house. It appears she lost four sons at Number Six. Isom says one of them was a damn good baseball player.

"Anyhow, you wouldnt believe what that woman was a-doing. They was two big cabinets full of dead butterflies on pins. Davidson must have collected them. She was a-smashing them cabinets with a lamp. Jesus, the glass flew everwhere. She had a cut on her arm where a piece hit her. Hit's a wonder she didnt hurt herself bad. I hollered at her to stop, told her she had to git out of the house. And she turned and looked at me—slow like—" his eyes widened, "and she called me Francesco, says I'm her baby. I picked her up to carry her out but she was yelling that she had to take the butterflies with her. I tried to pull her away from them but she wouldn't budge so I helped her gather up them little panels with all the butterflies stuck on. And she headed down the hill with them, and then she made me pull all the butterflies off and throw them in the creek." He shook his head. "And then she made me sit there by the creek and she washed my face."

"That poor woman!"

He stood up.

"I didnt mind it," he said. "What I seen in her eyes— What am I going to do? I brung her up to the farmhouse and Annadel's got her now. But she's kind of looney."

"I'll go take a look at her."

I had to run to keep up with him.

"She thinks I'm her son. But I cant take care of no crazy woman."

When we reached the porch I grabbed his arm and swung him around.

"Why didnt you tell her you wasnt her boy?"

"Didnt have the heart. I'm turned upside down about it."

The woman sat in a rocking chair in the kitchen. She wore a white shawl about her shoulders. Her face was unlined, beautiful and peaceful. She spoke softly to herself. When she looked at Rondal, she gave no sign that she recognized him. I saw the disappointment on his face. He left me with her.

I learned by asking among the miners that her son Francesco had married and fathered a son before he was killed, and that the daughter-in-law worked in Ricco's Italian Bakery at Justice. I reached her by telephone and she agreed to take charge of her mother-in-law. She had not known the woman was ill, she said, for Lytton Davidson had assured her all was well. She would arrange for a bed in the Miners' State Hospital.

Rondal insisted on taking her to the train. She walked slowly as though she was under water. Before he handed her up to the conductor, he kissed her upon the forehead. She smiled up at him with the face of an angel, pressed his hand to her cheek.

"Francesco, you such a good boy."

IT WAS A GOLDEN SUMMER. WE LIVED IN TENTS, BUT THE weather was warm and the union sent us food. We had typhoid, but no more than was usual in the camps. Some of the mines still worked but our men blew up tipples and burned company stores. Some were killed, but no more than in the mines. Jenkinjones belonged to us. And whenever we walked to town we were greeted with a sign proclaiming FREE ANNADEL. The *Free Press*, black-bordered in memory of C.J. Marcum, ran articles extolling the American Revolution and the Declaration of Independence. On every corner, an armed miner stood sentinel with his red bandana knotted around his neck. The gun thugs called us rednecks. It was a name we accepted with pride.

There was no feeling like it in the world. I believed we could beat any coal company, any sheriff, any governor. So did everyone else. You could see it in the way people swaggered, hear it in the high-pitched laughter when they gathered over the cook-fires. I know now that Albion and Rondal were not so optimistic, that they hid their feelings for our sakes. I don't know how they did it. And sometimes, later, I cursed them for it. If we had known, would we have gone out, suffered like we did? I can hear them now, answering such a question.

"Hit aint the right question, whether or not we win," Albion would say. "The right question is, are we faithful? Ifn we strike just to win, we are lost at the start. We must

strike to please God, because nothing else will find favor in
His sight.''

Rondal? "A man does what he has got to." And he would
say nothing more, no matter how hard you shook him.

The miners were past arguments anyway. If Rondal had
tried to dissuade us he could not have. On the Fourth of
July, a vaudeville troupe came to Annadel. Isom persuaded
them to give a series of free shows. (No one asked what
means of persuasion Isom used.) They performed in each
camp, but Albion and I saw them at the Roxie. We hunched
together in the dark and held hands. A singalong time followed the last act. Slowly, rhythmically, everyone sang
"When Irish Eyes Are Smiling," rocking from side to side,
shoulders touching. I walked home with Albion in the
moonlight, swinging his hand in mine and softly sang, "In
the Good Old Summertime." Ahead of us in the camp,
firecrackers snapped and spat. Behind the tent flaps, men
perched on the edges of spindly cots and cleaned their rifles.

Two days after Labor Day, trainloads of strikebreakers arrived, accompanied by more Baldwin-Felts
guards. Miners on strike were fired and their names placed
on the blacklist. The scabs moved into the company houses
at Felco, Winco, Carbon, and all the Davidson mines. Only
Jenkinjones remained closed.

Rondal organized the men into small bands who took
turns laying out on the hillside and firing at the scabs as
they went to work. Some of the strikebreakers, especially
the Negroes, deserted. They hadn't been told that a strike
was going on. Most of them had nothing to go back to, so
they joined us in the tents.

Other strikebreakers stayed and tried to work. They were
immigrants from the cities who believed they would make
their fortunes digging coal, or they were farm boys from
Kentucky. Oh, my Kentucky. Their families would be the
poor ones, and they would have heard there was money in
the mines. They didn't know about how the companies had
taken the land, for it hadn't happened to them yet. They

didn't know about the union and they didn't like being told they couldn't work. They stayed on.

Albion lay on his cot with his long arms dangling over the side. He had just returned from shooting at scabs for the first time.

"They may have been Thornsberrys and Whitts and Slones out there," he said.

I tried to feel hard about them. "They claim they're just feeding their families," I said. "They think we aint got to eat? They'll break the strike. They'll sink themselves and us along with them."

"I fired over their heads," he said. "I kicked up the dirt in front of them. Everyone else was doing the same. You know how well our boys shoot. But they werent a scab kilt, only one hit in the arm. Sam Gore said hit werent like shooting at gun thugs. These fellers is just ignorant. Let them work a while and they'll learn. Anyway, I dont think I could never shoot one."

I knew Albion would never even shoot a gun thug. When I said once that gun thugs deserved to get shot, he answered that if we got what we deserved, God would mash us all flat like a passel of bugs.

He was tired all the time and he coughed a lot. He developed the cough in the mines and sometimes he spit up black phlegm. His cough worsened after we moved into the tents. Although the days were warm, the tents were wet with dew in the mornings. I fretted about the consumption. Doc Booker offered to let us move into his house, but Albion wouldn't hear of it. We must suffer what everyone else suffered, he insisted. We were all in this together.

He made rounds with Dr. Booker and me, and after we were done with each patient, he prayed with them while we moved on. In the evenings we ate supper together, usually soupbeans. Afterward we'd sit before the tent and talk while the gray twilight stole over the camp. Sometimes Rondal and his brother would pass by like ghosts, banjo and guitar tucked under their arms, on their way to pick on the Justice's front porch. Albion would watch them until they melted into the dusk.

In all our years of marriage I had never been pregnant. We both wanted a baby. Inside the tent, we often pushed our cots together and made love gingerly so as not to tip over onto the ground. But Albion always withdrew before we were done, frightened to have me expecting a child while we lived in such a state.

In mid-October the leaves turned and the nights grew colder. The tents in the morning were stiff with frost. Two scabs were shot to death at Felco, and the Number Eight tipple burned to the ground. The camp buzzed with rumors the next day.

"When the leaves fall we wont have no cover to shoot from," one man said. "Our women and babies will freeze. Hit's time to shit or git offn the pot."

His name was Cecil Nunally. He was talking to Dr. Booker while I bathed his little girl. She had a fever of 104. After I towelled her dry, her mother took her up in a blanket and pressed her to her chest. The lint from the woman's shawl clung to the child's dry lips.

ISOM JUSTICE SENT WORD THAT ALBION SHOULD COME TO his house at nine o'clock that night.

"You come too," Albion said. "Hit will be warm in the house."

"They may not want me there."

"Ifn they dont, you can talk to Gladys."

I went gratefully, for the nights were now so cold that the only comfort was to huddle close to those you lived with. The Justices lived in a solid brick house on the hill at the end of Main Street.

Rondal Lloyd stood by the fireplace in the sitting room. He acknowledged me with a brief nod. His brother was there, and Dr. Booker and Ermel. Gladys welcomed me in and took me to the kitchen for hot chocolate. I sat by the stove and shivered with pleasure.

I liked Gladys Justice. She had stiff brown hair wrestled into a bun at the nape of her neck, full cheeks, and dusty skin which looked like it should be freckled but wasn't. An oval picture of her dead father dangled on a chain at her neck.

The voices in the next room grew suddenly heated. Gladys

and I looked at one another, and without a word picked up our chairs and went into the parlor.

"How the hell would they find out?" Rondal was shouting. "Who would tell them?" He looked at Albion but said nothing further.

Gladys leaned over and whispered in my ear.

"Cesco Thompson called Isom on the telephone from his honky-tonk. Said some gun thugs had been to his place drunk and was talking loose. They knowed exactly where Rondal was going to sleep tonight and aim to kill him."

"I'll just have to sleep somewhere else," Rondal said.

"Hell you will," Isom replied. "You know what the rumors is. Word is, you're a dead man ifn you aint out of here soon."

"You're the goddamn chief of police! You saying you cant protect me no more?"

"That's exactly what I'm saying. This aint just a threat. Hit's like they got a contract out on you. You're going to git your ass on a train out of here tonight."

I had never seen Isom upset. His face was splotched with red and his scalp shone beneath the thinning hair.

"We knowed from the start it would be dangerous. I'm the leader of this here strike," Rondal said.

"Somebody else can be the leader," Albion said softly.

"You'd like that, wouldnt you, preacher? You'd like to be in charge yourself, wouldn't you? You'd like to stop the shooting; hit scares you. Besides, you got other reasons you want to git shut of me."

He looked straight at me as he spoke. I knew what he thought, that Albion was jealous of him, and I hated him for thinking it, hated his arrogance. "I aint caring for what you're implying," I said. "You better come right out and say it."

"Oh, Lordy, now I done got Miss Carrie riled. I'm saying somebody has set me up, and this here is the only feller in the room I cant trust."

"Now you're talking crazy," Dr. Booker said. "You been set up to be shot in a whorehouse. How would this boy know about that?"

Rondal continued to glare at Albion. But everyone else in the room was watching Rondal. And it occurred to me that someone else had called the meeting, that everyone, even Albion, knew what was about to happen. Everyone except Rondal.

"I'm the organizer here," he said as though to convince himself.

"You're the organizer," Albion said, "but they ought to be other leaders. Miners. We got to believe in ourselves. Ifn you're the leader and you git kilt, that would take all the heart outen us. We depend on you too much. You ought to pull back, for your sake and ourn."

"I aint leaving on your say so," Rondal said.

"Listen to him!" Isom said sharply. "Buddy, you know I'm the last one that wants to see you leave. But when it comes to what we're doing here, they's safety in numbers. Folks talk about you too much. You're starting to stand out."

"No! I aint leaving."

"You got no choice," Doctor Booker said. "Telegram come this afternoon. Union is pulling you out. They got other organizers."

Rondal leaned against the mantel and buried his face in his arm.

"You got to git, big brother," Talcott said. "But dont worry, Ruby wont be lonesome. She done took up with a gun thug already."

Rondal looked up. "What the hell are you talking about?"

Talcott laughed. "You stupid sonofabitch! Who do you think set you up? And you're blaming a damn preacher. But they do say love is blind."

Rondal swung at him, but Talcott dodged. Isom pulled Rondal away.

"Hit aint worth it, son," he said. "Ruby aint worth it."

"Damn straight, she aint," Talcott said. "I had a little talk with her on the way over here. Was her daddy put her up to it. She didnt even mind to tell me, long as she saved her own ass."

Albion said, "You aint going to hurt nobody, are you?"

Talcott laughed again. "Tell him, brother. Would I hurt anybody?"

"We aint got time for this jabbering," Ermel interrupted. "We got to git this boy out on the nine-thirty."

The nine-thirty freight always ran slow with an open box-car between Annadel and the camp, because the crew members were union sympathizers.

Rondal turned to me. "What do you say, Carrie? Should I leave?"

"I dont care what you do," I said coldly.

Isom handed him his coat. He took it and left so abruptly the others had to hurry to catch up with him. Albion wrapped me in my coat and walked with me down to the tracks. When we arrived, Rondal was standing apart from the others, refusing to speak to them. The freight rumbled through, rocking slowly and screeching. Ermel waved a lantern, and by its light I saw a red bandana dangling from someone's hand as the engine passed. Rondal ran alongside, leaped, and the dark doorway swallowed him. The train picked up speed, whined and disappeared.

"I hate him for what he said to you," I said fiercely to fight off the emptiness I felt.

"You know that aint so." Albion rubbed the back of my neck. "That poor feller lost everything tonight. Still yet, I'm glad he's gone. God forgive me, but I cant help it."

The next morning, Ruby Day found her father, Everett, slumped in a rocking chair on the porch of their house. He was shot once through the head from long range.

I TRIED NOT TO MISS RONDAL. HE WAS GONE, HE WAS SAFE, and it was easier to forget about him. I had Albion to fret over. Then Talcott brought Rondal's banjo to our tent.

"I got a message from Rondal. 'Give Carrie the banjo' was all he said. Reckon he meant it."

I laid the banjo beneath my cot so neither of us would have to look at it.

THE FIRST WE KNEW THAT THE GOVERNOR DECLARED MAR-tial law was when hundreds of state policemen swarmed through the tent colony in the early morning. Screams startled me out of sleep, feet pounded past the tent. Albion leaped up, struggling into his coat, and rushed outside. By the time I followed he had been wrestled to the ground by three policemen, his arms twisted and handcuffed behind his back.

"Run for Annadel!" he yelled as they dragged him away.

It seemed everyone in the world was running, as though we were all swept along by floodwaters. The men fled pell-mell for the hills, pursued by the policemen and Baldwin guards. An Italian woman wielding a broom tripped one of the gun thugs and he flew headlong into a pile of firewood. The other thugs chased her but she escaped in the maze of tents. I followed them on toward Annadel where they caught another Italian woman, this one pregnant, threw her to the ground and kicked her repeatedly in the belly. I hurled a rock at them. It struck one man on the back and he turned toward me. I threw again and he dodged. Then I ran, and prayed he wouldn't draw his pistol. From far up the mountain I heard the popping of gunfire.

I reached Annadel in time to see the police toss Dr. Booker into the back of a truck parked in front of the newspaper office. His forehead bled. Isom Justice stood nearby with three rifle barrels pointed at his neck. Shards of broken glass littered the streets like frozen puddles.

I could do nothing except return to the tents and treat those who had been hurt. The Italian woman delivered a stillborn baby and died herself the next morning.

THE STATE POLICE AND BALDWIN THUGS OCCUPIED ANNA-del. They turned Ermel out of the hotel and roomed there. The *Free Press* office burned to the ground and the FREE ANNADEL signs were tossed onto the fire. They burned several houses as well, including Talcott Lloyd's. Talcott escaped into the hills and Pricie moved back to the farm-house with her children.

Pricie asked what martial law meant. Ermel Justice said it meant the police ruled, that we had no more civil liber-ties.

"Coal miners never had nothing like that," said Pricie.

"But Annadel did," her mother said. "Now hit's gone."

I listened to them talk in the kitchen while I tended sick

people in the front room. They talked mostly of how to get
Isom and Albion out of jail. Over four hundred men had
been arrested, most with no charge. But Isom and Albion
were held for the murder of the Baldwin-Felts guards in
May.

At dinnertime they invited me into the kitchen for a bowl
of soup. The carrots, cabbage, peas and tomatoes were the
first I'd eaten in two months. Beads of fat glistened like
jewels in the broth.

"That preacher man of yourn never even toted a gun,"
Pricie said. "How can they call that murder? Besides, hit
were self-defense. Look what happened to Gladys's daddy."

Gladys swirled her spoon aimlessly through her soup.

"Ermel says he'll git Isom out of jail," she said. She
looked at me. "He'll git the preacher out too."

"Damn straight," Ermel declared. "Ifn it werent for me
that there judge would be slopping hogs up Coon Creek.
We'll git them out on bond, and after that, they aint no jury
in Justice County would bring in a guilty verdict. Them
boys will be back in your beds before long, younguns."

Gladys blushed and smiled at me. Annadel spooned more
soup into my bowl.

"Speaking of that," she said to me, "aint you freezing
to death in that tent by yourself?"

"Hit gits right cold," I admitted.

"Why dont you move in with us?"

"No, with me!" Gladys cried. "I git so lonesome in that
big house. We can talk about our men."

"Albion dont want me to put myself above the others,"
I said.

"Now aint that silly?" Annadel said. "And you a-sitting
up all hours nursing the sick. You'll do poorly yourself and
then you wont be worth nary a thing to nobody. You look
right peaked as it is."

I wasn't hard to convince. The first night at Gladys's
house, I took a hot bath. The enormous tub rested on four
porcelain lions' paws. I stretched out full length in the hot
water, pretended I was an Egyptian princess borne upon a
chaise, and fell asleep.

Ermel Justice traveled to the county seat each day to check

on Isom and Albion. Albion's face was bruised, he said, but they were fine otherwise. They would be out any day.

I was reassured but I couldn't rest easy until Albion was back. I feared that his very gentleness would be an affront to the guards, that they would take pleasure in abusing him. He was content to let God protect him. But sometimes I thought it was a point of honor with God to abandon the faithful ones.

Dr. Booker came home first, but only briefly. He was not a miner and, in the eyes of the state police, only a Negro who took up space in the jail. They ordered him to pack and leave Justice County or he would be sent to the penitentiary. I found him in his office, packing his medical books in a green suitcase.

"Child, I hate to leave you with all this," he said.

"I'll manage. I learnt a lot from you."

"You put these medicines in boxes and git somebody to help carry them down to the camp." He lifted his framed diploma off its hook, studied it with his forehead furrowed. "Howard University. I went to Howard all the way from Greenwood, Mississippi, where the delta start. I ever tell you about that?"

"No," I said.

"Had a uncle lynch in Leflore County. After that, I couldnt git away fast enough. Couldnt git far enough away from that place so I went all the way to Washington, D.C., and worked my way through Howard. That's where I heard about West Virginia. You know how this here state was started? It seceded from Virginia when Virginia joined the Confederacy. West Virginia didnt want to be no slave state. I heard that and I liked it. And I heard tell a Negro could vote in West Virginia, and they was lots of Negroes needed a doctor around these mines. So I come."

He sat on a white chair beside the examining table.

"Course they aint no paradise for a Negro. Every place but Annadel got the Jim Crow."

"Annadel is different," I said. "I wonder why."

"C.J. Marcum, he was here before the town was. Sometimes a good man can make a difference in a little place like this here." He sighed. "My old buddy C.J. He was a good friend, even if I never could git him to read Marx.

And they's other good men. That Isom is a fine one. Oh, they's only so far you can go, being friends with a white man. I know that. They's always things a Negro cant say or do, else he'll risk losing that friendship. Now, I'm not married. Suppose, just suppose, that I thought Violet Marcum was the finest woman in the world, and her a widow lady, needing a husband. Suppose—just suppose now—I took a notion to court her. Me, her dead husband's best friend, a respected doctor, the former mayor. What would Isom Justice say to that, and Violet his mama's cousin? I aint even sure how C.J. would have took to it.'' He leaned forward. "What would you say to it?''

"Well, I-I hadnt even thought about something like that. Hit wouldnt pass my mind.'' I twisted my hands in my lap, afraid I had hurt his feelings.

He grinned. "I know, honey. You was scared to death of this nigger when you first come here.''

"That aint quite true!''

"Not quite?'' He stood up and patted my shoulder. "I aint trying to make you feel bad. I aint trying to say anything against the white folks around here. I'm just trying to say goodbye to twenty good years of my life. It's easier to leave with all these questions tormenting me. If these aint the best people, maybe they's better somewhere else.''

"Where will you go?''

"Thought I'd head for Charleston. They's a Negro community there, and a Negro college nearby. I got friends there. It will be just fine.''

"You wont have no newspaper.''

He hoisted his suitcase. "Naw. Have to read somebody else's. But you know what? I may just find old Rondal up there. I bet he aint gone too far away.''

ERMEL RAISED BAIL MONEY FOR ALBION AND ISOM AFTER they had been a month in jail. Albion was pale and thinner, with purple bruises on his ribs.

On our first night back in the camp we managed to make love despite three layers of clothing. His face was gray in the moonlight, and cold to the touch. It was like loving a ghost, a memory.

* * *

WE DID EVERYTHING WE COULD TO PROTECT OURSELVES from the winter cold. We dug holes several feet deep inside the tents. A lucky few managed to find cast-iron stoves, which must be watched closely to keep the tents from catching fire. Bonfires were built at various places; the air around them shimmered and smoked.

It was difficult to sleep at night. Albion and I laid awake and shivered until we fell into a kind of faint from exhaustion. A few hours later we woke up numb. Then we took turns massaging each other until needles of pain stabbed our feet and the feeling returned.

The union tried to ship food from Charleston but the shipments were often intercepted by Baldwin-Felts guards and there was never enough. The Red Cross was supposed to send us aid, but the local chairwoman was the wife of a coal operator, and we never received a thing. We ate soupbeans for days on end and walked hunched over from bellyaches.

On Christmas Eve a delegation of Episcopal and Presbyterian churchwomen from Justice town visited us. They walked through the camp with a state police escort and hovered over crates of oranges to make sure only the children received them. They also left a small turkey and a bag of walnuts outside each tent. Then they gathered in the middle of the camp to sing Christmas carols for half an hour. I recognized Miles's wife in a red coat and hat. Her collar was some kind of fur with the animal heads left on, each one chewing on the tail in front of it in a circle of frozen viciousness. After singing, the women departed for the trains, blew on their gloved fingers as they stumbled over chunks of red dog in their heeled shoes, grimaced when they twisted their ankles.

We had no ovens so we brought out iron skillets coated with hard gray bacon grease and fried the turkeys like chickens.

The day after Christmas, the *Justice Clarion* carried a front page editorial expressing shock at the living conditions in the camps and condemning the union for its "monstrous inhumanity, as it forces women and children to suffer hunger and cold in order to advance its un-American and, ultimately, doomed goals.''

A FOUR-YEAR-OLD HUNGARIAN GIRL TOOK FROSTBITE IN
both feet. I wrapped her in blankets and carried her to Grace
Hospital on the train. At the hospital, both her feet were
amputated. During the operation I waited at the Tic-Toc
Grill on Court Street, drank two cups of coffee and fretted
because I had coffee while all the world was cold.

Miles entered the Tic-Toc. I ducked my head and hoped
he wouldn't see me but he sat down at my booth.

"Been a long time, Sis," he said.

"Whose fault is that?"

"For Christsake, can't we talk civil now?"

"No. I dont talk civil no more. I dont act civil. I'm a
troublemaking red agitator out to tear down civilization and
that's what I act like these days. You want civil talk, you go
home to that mealymouthed wife of yourn."

"Carrie, you look awful. You're just skin and bones. I
know what you been through."

"No, you dont. You dont know a thing about it. They's
a little girl named Sonia up in that hospital gitting her feet
cut off because of good Christian people like you, because
you dont know nothing about it, nor care."

"I saw Albion in jail. I went to see him once a week,
took him things."

"He told me. I werent interested."

"I let my people back in their houses for the winter."

That surprised me and I didn't know what to say.

"I couldn't stand it, seeing them in the cold. I opened
up all the Vulcan houses. And I let them dig coal for their
stoves."

"What about your scabs? Where they living?"

"Aw, I got a bunch of Italians in here that was redder
than Karl Marx. They worked two days and then they left."

I smiled.

"Boston wasn't happy," he said.

"I bet the whole damn city was heartbroke," I said.

"That isn't nice language, Carrie, not coming from a
preacher's wife. Next thing I'll hear you took up smoking."

"Only chewing," I said.

My head swam from all the coffee on an empty stomach, and I let him buy me the Blue Plate Special—baked steak, mashed potatoes and corn.

"So your heart was touched and you're trying to be kind," I said.

"We aren't monsters, Sis."

"No. But your people, as you call them, still aint got money for food. And they aint your people, Miles. They aint your kin. They are their own people. A miner shouldnt have to fret over whether his boss is a good man or not. Hit's all up to you whether that man freezes or keeps warm. Hit's up to you whether his family eats or starves. He's at your mercy. Why should he be?"

"Somebody's got to make the decisions," he replied. "A business can't make money if there's no chain of command, and those men won't have jobs if this mine goes under. Educated men have to say what's what."

"And make the money."

"Nobody will run a coal mine for charity," he said. He bought me a slab of apple pie. "Go back to the Homeplace, Sis. I'm worried sick about you, and so are Ben and Florrie."

"I got a husband on strike, and I got sick people to tend."

He drove me up the hill to the hospital in his car and left me at the front door. The child had come through surgery all right, so I returned to Annadel. Five days later I fetched Sonia back from the hospital. Her mother boiled water and wrapped the stumps of her legs continually with hot rags.

THE UNGRATEFUL, LAZY MINERS HELD IN THE JAILS WERE warm, and ate two meals a day at taxpayers' expense. The better sort of people grumbled about this in letters to the editor of the *Justice Clarion*. The men were released to a more fitting punishment, to freeze and starve, and to look into the faces of their wives and children.

We were not allowed to speak with one another outside the camps. Anyone who ventured into Annadel must do so silently, and shy away from any other person. To disobey was to risk a beating and arrest. But these restrictions did not apply to the better sort of people. They assembled daily to drill in militia companies and gathered freely to discuss the red menace in their midst.

I WALKED TO THE JUSTICE FARMHOUSE EACH DAY TO TEND the sickest people. The entire downstairs except for the kitchen had been turned into a hospital. Nine or ten people died each week and were buried in a new cemetery on the mountainside.

One morning I arrived to find Gladys in tears.

"Who died?" I asked.

"Hit aint that. Hit's what happened this morning."

"One of them gun thugs showed hisself to her," Annadel explained.

"Where was Isom?"

"He was right there," Gladys sobbed. "He was walking me over here. That man was yelling at me, saying Isom's werent as big as what hisn was, and what all he would do to me. And I knowed Isom wanted to kill him. But they wasnt a thing he could do. And he's the chief of police."

"Where's Isom now?"

"He went on back home. I'm scairt he might do something to git hisself kilt. Or if he aint done nothing, he's laying drunk up at the house because he's so mad."

"I'll send Albion to see."

"They wont let him go to our house."

That was true, but he was able to wander around town long enough to know that Isom hadn't shot anyone. For Gladys there was relief in knowing Isom had taken to a bottle instead of his gun.

The trial for Isom and Albion was not set for that court term, and so would not take place until summer. I could only think they had set the date so far away to prolong our worrying, but Ermel said it wasn't so.

"We done it a purpose," he declared. "Them operators want it over with, git my boy hung. Hit demoralizes them to see him free. Shows them they aint got all the power yet."

The circuit judge was Ermel's man, the only Democratic official in the county. The coal operators still controlled the sheriff's office and the rest of the courthouse. But Ermel had taken in hand a popular bootlegger from the northern part of the county, paid for him to study the law, and run him in the last judge's race. Northern Justice County had few coal mines. The people up the hollers still farmed, and "farmed in the hills," as Ermel called moonshining.

"They's still boys back in there can make as good as what Dillon Lloyd does. You git into politics, you got to know you some moonshiners. Hell, they was even Republicans in Justice town voted for my man for judge. They didn't want their liquor to dry up."

Ermel talked a lot. Annadel said it made him feel like he was still in charge of things. He was the only person who looked forward to the trial.

Albion mentioned the trial only once. When he heard nothing would be done until early summer, he said, "Leastways hit will be warm."

Albion Freeman at that time seemed to me the most precious person in the world. I loved him with the guilty love of one who has had to be convinced, and with a smothering love, for he would not watch out for himself. Worrying over him tired me more than my nursing. I was forever draping his scarf around his neck and cautioning him to stay near the fires. He never listened to me, but seemed not to mind my scolding.

I only saw him falter once, and that was at a preaching service. Albion preached twice a week, on Sundays and Wednesdays, to our camp, and the Negro pastor from Jenkinjones did the same for the families at the Annadel baseball field. Only the foreign miners were left out. The Catholic priest at Davidson was a company man who'd threatened excommunication for joining the union. The men did not seem to mind, but as we gathered for church on Sunday mornings, the women lingered in front of their tents, their rosaries dangling forlornly from their hands. Albion invited them to join us, but they never did.

On one bitter cold February morning, Albion preached from *Deuteronomy*. He yelled to be heard above the roaring bonfire.

"The children of Israel was forty year in the wilderness. And they suffered from hunger. And it werent cold, but lord, it was so hot they suffered as much as we do here. They died from the heat. But the Lord God preserved them, and led them home to the Promised Land. Only he had hard words for Moses. Now Moses led the children of Israel through hardship and suffering. But the Lord wouldnt let Moses enter that Promised Land. God required his life before Moses could enter. God said to Moses, 'Thou shalt not go over this Jordan.' Them is hard words after so much suffering. 'Thou shalt not go over this Jordan.' ''

His voice broke and he looked down. "Maybe we wont go over." He dropped his Bible into the snow and covered his face with his hands and sobbed. Someone moaned, "Sweet Jesus!"

Then Albion pulled himself together.

"But God let Moses see!" he cried through his tears. "God took Moses up on the mountaintop and Moses seen the Promised Land. Hit is there! And ifn we dont cross this Jordan, we may still yet see it. And ifn we see it, maybe our younguns will cross over. Maybe them younguns standing there in that snow drift a-shivering will enter the Promised Land."

He wept again in our tent. "Hit was you talked me into learning to read," he said. "I wanted to so's I could read the Bible. I aint so sure now hit's a blessing. They's hard sayings in there."

I heated a washtub of water and washed his feet. Then I put three pairs of socks on him and snuggled onto the cot beside him.

"Have you seen the Promised Land?" I whispered.

"I seen too much."

I BEGAN TO THINK IT WAS A GREAT JOKE TO CALL MYSELF a nurse. There was really nothing I could do for the sick. They weakened, took the influenza or pneumonia, we poured soup and whiskey down their throats, and they either died or survived to return to the cold. What they needed was food and warmth, and I could give them neither. Nor could the miners give these things to their families, and so they turned once more to their guns. Three scabs were killed on their way to work at Winco, and the state police returned to make arrests. They marched Cecil Nunally to the railroad tracks with his hands above his head and forced him to kneel.

"You've been identified," one policeman said. "You got anything to say for yourself?"

"Lord, have mercy," he said.

The policeman shot him in the back of the head while his wife and children stood by and screamed. Then the police threw his body on the back of a truck and took him to Justice town. We heard the local militia drove through the streets with Cecil's body on display.

Talcott Lloyd, who had managed to evade capture once more, jumped the slow train for Huntington that night. He planned to join Rondal, who was in Charleston, take a job in a union mine on Campbells Creek, and send for Pricie and his family as soon as he raised the money.

The day after the raid, one of the Negro children died. His mother, a tall, long-necked woman with her head wrapped tight in a yellow kerchief, carried him out of the farmhouse without making a sound or shedding a tear. She walked to her tent at the Annadel ballfield and laid him on a cot. An hour later, she returned with four hundred Jenkinjones women, all of them carrying iron skillets, broom handles, axes, hoes. They fanned out through the camp, stopped at each tent.

The Negro woman came to the farmhouse.

"We going to Felco," she said. "Yall come too."

Pricie snatched off her apron and threw it in the corner, went for her coat.

"I'm coming too," Gladys said.

Isom, who had come by for soup, stood up.

"You sit down," the Negro woman said. "They know what it take to beat you men. We doing this our own way."

"What if they shoot at you?"

"Wont they look brave?" She turned and left.

I looked at Annadel.

"You go on," she said. "I'll watch here."

The women milled around the tents. They had on shapeless wool coats worn smooth to the threads. A few had scarves and gloves. The Italian women wore black lace hairnets over tightly wrapped buns. The tall Negro woman strode through them, down the creek. We followed her bob-bing yellow head, drifting at first, then closed ranks and walked faster as the bottom land narrowed and twisted. The day had warmed just enough to melt the snow, and we traipsed through black sludge to the tops of our boots. The air smelled like the remains of a wood fire that has been doused by rain. No one spoke. No one sang. We walked, and listened to the squishing sounds of our feet.

Two state police cars blocked the road just above Felco, and armed men waited behind them. But the yellow head still went forward. We pounded our hoes and broomsticks on the ground as we walked, and stamped our feet. The sound gathered in the narrow hollow and echoed from the hillsides.

They were two dozen policemen, and we were over a thousand.

A man's voice carried in the crisp air. "What do we do? Can we shoot women?"

A hoe hung suspended above the yellow kerchief, then dropped with a crash and a tinkling of shattered glass. The policemen fled down the road and on out of sight. The women in the front beat on the cars, then rocked them back and forth until they trundled clumsily down the creek bank, snapping bushes and small trees as they went, and came to rest on their roofs. We stumbled, bumped into one another, but went on.

We passed by the boarded-up houses of upper Felco and Hunkie Hill, by the iron bridge and the new grade school, past the red brick superintendent's mansion with its white pillars, gardens and ponds, reached the company store. Without any words being spoken, we seemed to agree that this was our goal. A machine gun squatted on the concrete front porch, an iron spider balanced on skinny metal legs. No one tended it. It was midday and the scabs were all in the mine; the Baldwin guards had been replaced by the state policemen, who were nowhere in sight. We picked up hunks of red dog, flung them at the plate glass windows and clapped excitedly at the noise. The door was forced open and women poured inside.

They grabbed as much food as they could carry and hur-ried back outside. Italian women and hillbilly women bar-

tered, offering cans of yellow corn for sardines and hard
cheese. By the time I made it inside many of the shelves
were clear. The board floor smelled of oil and coal dust.
Rank after rank of dark wooden display cabinets lined the
walls. Most of the glass doors on them had been broken. I
pushed toward the walk-in freezer where they were hauling
out slabs of bacon and sides of beef. Pricie grabbed me by
the arm. She had Gladys with her.

"Daddy's got food," she said. "Let's look for them guns.
I bet they keep them in the basement."

"I'm scairt to," Gladys protested. "Where is everbody?
They may be hiding down there."

"Ifn they are, they're scairt to death. Hit's just old men
and women that work here anyway."

I snatched up a small side of bacon and a sack of flour
before I went downstairs. Ermel may have food, but Albion
did not. I caught up this booty in my skirt. Then I edged
my way down a wooden stairway and into the pitch darkness
of the basement. Pricie heard me and yelled, "Do you know
where they's a light switch?"

"I seen one at the top of the stairs."

"Go turn it on. They's guns here. Shells too, and another
machine gun. Go git some more of the girls to help carry
them."

I groped my way back and found what I thought was the
door to the stairway. When I yanked it open, I heard a sharp
intake of breath. Then a woman's voice pleaded queru-
lously, "Go on and leave us be. Please leave us be." Someone else sobbed softly in the dark.

"Yes, ma'am," I said, and closed the door gently.

I found the right entrance and rushed upstairs, tripping
on my skirt and hitting my knee painfully. I turned on the
light, but I couldn't bring myself to follow the ones who
went down after the guns. I went out onto the porch. Women
ran back and forth on Felco's lone paved street, the street
of big houses where the doctors and bookkeepers lived,
dragging pillowcases filled with food. Cecil Nunally's
widow emerged from the doctor's house with a chocolate
layer cake.

I heard the whine of motorcars approaching from down
the creek. I ran to the machine gun and sat down behind it,

careful to place my food on the ground close beside me. Three state police cars churned up the road through Colored Bottom. I swung the machine gun back and forth, surprised at how easily it moved. The metal trigger froze my finger clear to the bone.

The cars drew up below the store. Black sludge clung like icing halfway up their sides. The doors swung open and policemen jumped out. I squeezed the trigger, spun the gun wildly back and forth, kicked up globs of black mud at their feet. The first men out whirled around, tackled those behind them, piled back into the cars. They backed up and sped away, the rear ends of the cars waggling as they slid back down the road.

I sat still. My body buzzed from the racketing of the gun. I smelled burnt oil. Straight ahead, across the railroad tracks, I could see the row of houses where I had lived. Hundreds of women gathered there, too, so far away they appeared to walk on water. Scab miners came from the drift mouth to see what was happening. The women met them, beat them about the head with their sticks and frying pans, swiped at them with axes, and the men fled behind a row of empty black coal cars.

I gathered up my food. The bacon had been sliced and wrapped in slick butcher's paper, perhaps waiting to be picked up by the paymaster's wife. Even now she might be cowering in the basement.

Pricie and Gladys struggled out the door, carrying a machine gun between them.

"I hear shooting?" Gladys asked anxiously.

"Mmmmm," I answered. I was counting the bacon strips. Twenty-four slices. Enough for ten days if I could keep it frozen.

I LAY STIFF BESIDE ALBION AND COULDN'T SLEEP. HIS HAND rested inside my dress, upon my breast. I raised it to my lips, kissed it, and sat up.

"What?" he mumbled.

"Cant sleep. Got to walk. I'll be back in a little while."

I pulled on my cracked leather boots and went outside. The moon was full and the sky littered with stars. I wandered toward the railroad track, met Sam Gore, who stood sentry on the edge of the camp. Sam's house had been burned by the Baldwin guards and he lived with us now.

"What you doing up?" he said.

"I had to walk." I studied his gun. "You kilt anybody yet, Sam?"

"No. But way I feel right now, I wouldnt mind to."

"I almost did today. I shot a machine gun at some state police."

He grinned. "Yeah, I done heard tell of it. That there would have been something to see."

"I didnt know how to aim the thing. Didnt know nothing about it. I could have blowed their heads off as easy as what I did. Didnt really care, neither." I hugged myself and bounced on my toes to keep warm. "My brother used to take me hunting when I was a youngun. First time I kilt a squirrel I cried for hours. Wouldnt eat it or nothing. But I got used to it and went hunting all the time. I wonder if it's that way with killing people. I wonder if you can git used to it."

Sam nodded. "It be like a war, I reckon. Aint nobody care for it, but it be here on us. Me, I'd rather be playing baseball than toting this here gun."

I smiled. "I seen you play baseball. Seen you pitch. You beat Davidson."

"Yeah, we sure enough did beat Davidson."

I walked on down the track.

"Dont go too far now, hear?" he called after me.

I waved at him and walked the rail, setting one foot carefully in front of the other. It was comforting, as though keeping my balance on the rail would make everything all right. The rail vibrated. I looked up, surprised because there was no sign of a headlight, and slipped off onto the gravel track bed. Then I heard the engine. It sounded like the slow train, but it was too late for that. Well, I thought, if no one is leaving the camp, someone may be arriving. Suddenly I was sure that it was Rondal, that he would leap from a swaying boxcar and be with us again. I ran down the slope of the track bed and walked backward, never taking my eyes off the approaching train.

"What the hell is that?" I heard Sam yell.

Then the engine drowned him out. It still did not show a headlight, but the smoke from its stack gave off a light of its own. I searched the darkness in vain for a hand dangling a red bandana. Then the engine was past me and I saw the iron boxcar with its door slightly ajar. I ran toward Sam.

"Hit's Rondal come back," I called, and turned back to see if it was so, to watch him leap. I caught a glimpse of dark metal, and then the boxcar spat fire.

I fell onto my back and hit my head in the gravel. I saw Sam Gore kneel and fire his rifle. Then he jerked backwards like a rag doll and lay twisted and still. I tried to scream but the clatter of machine guns was deafening. Bullets ripped open the tents with great tearing sounds; those closest to the tracks collapsed.

I wept at the pain in my arm. A pool of blood spread darkly across the ground near my shoulder. I turned my head so I wouldn't see it. The gravel was sharp against my cheek. Then I passed out.

I RECALL ALBION'S FACE NEAR MINE, AND A NUMBNESS IN my arm, which I later learned was from his belt wrapped tight to stop the bleeding.

I must have questioned him, for he told me Sam was dead and he had seen several other bodies. My next memory is of a hospital ward. Albion and Miles stood beside my bed and argued.

"You going to pay for everbody else that got shot up?"

"You can't deny her medical care if I'm willing to pay for it."

"Didnt say I would deny her. But it aint right for the hospital to put folks out that has been shot."

"—can't answer for the hospital. I suppose they're over-crowded."

"She wouldnt want to go with you. I hate to say it, but it's true."

"—not in any shape to be particular."

"—take her myself, but I cant leave the county until the trial."

Ben Honaker's face hovered over mine. His fine blond hair looked soft as a baby's.

"Honey, you want to go home?"

I tried to smile and nod my head.

"—wrap her up good."

"Aint cold no more," I whispered. "Hot."

I saw my room at the Homeplace, the familiar oak chest, the gray checked wallpaper. Aunt Becka put spoons to my mouth, Flora bathed my face. I slept, and was content.

I TOOK THE PNEUMONIA ON TOP OF THE GUNSHOT WOUND. I was near death for over a week and slept for most of a month without memory. Then I woke to see the window standing wide open. The white curtains flowed like water. Flora perched on the edge of the bed, set her hand to my cheek.

"Hit aint even April yet, but it's turned unseasonable warm."

"Hit's lovely," I said.

She started to cry and called for Aunt Becka.

By early April I was able to sit on the porch in the afternoon sun wrapped in one of Flora's quilts. I wondered about Albion, how they were in the camps, if the warm weather had heartened them. I stared for hours at the folded mountains. The trees were white as bones and tipped with red buds, as though they had been turned upside down and dipped in blood.

ALBION WROTE THAT THE TRIAL WAS SCHEDULED FOR JUNE 12. He urged me to stay away until then. "Nothing you can do here. Medicine is about gone. The warm weather is keeping the pneumonia down. Twenty families have left, moved away. Funny how they put up with all that cold, and then it's the warm that breaks them. But most everybody else is dug in. Folks keep saying the worst is over. I pray to God they are right."

I missed him terribly and longed to tell him so. But it was useless writing to him, for the strikers' mail was intercepted, read and destroyed. I couldn't quite bring myself to go to him. After an initial period of strangeness the Homeplace had begun to assume magical proportions, as though

I had never seen any of it before, as though it were a mythical kingdom I had stumbled upon after years of weary wandering. They wouldn't let me do heavy work. I passed lazy hours on the riverbank, fishing and reading Ben's books, until Flora called, "Carrie! Supper!"—her voice clear as a bell. Then, after the fried trout and potatoes and shucky beans, Flora and I gathered up the children, Jane, Luke, Mabel, John Henry and baby Rachel, and we went to call the cows home.

The path took us past the Aunt Jane Place, empty now. I'd often say, "When that strike is over, I'm going to bring Albion Freeman back here and live in that house. You see if I dont." Flora smiled and led the way to the meadow on Scary. We caught a granddaddy longlegs, asked it which way the cows had gone and followed the waving of its leg. We heard the tinkling of the bells before we saw anything.

"Old Bess!" Mabel would cry, and Jane and Luke ran ahead swinging their sticks and leaping over hummocks of weeds on their long slender legs.

It was impossible to explain to Ben and Flora what Blackberry Creek was like. I wearied of saying, "Hit's coming to us," and hearing Ben reply, "I hear there's no coal on Grapevine anyway."

"Who says so? Miles?"

"Carrie!" Flora said. "That aint a tone of voice for talking about your brother."

"Things will change here too. You wait and see."

"They already changed some," Ben said. "Folks with big families, their homeplaces cant support all of them. Used to be some would move on to new land. But the land is all taken up now. What are they supposed to do? The world will move on." He shook his head. "This violence, I dont understand it."

"Hush!" Flora said. "Carrie aint needing to be reminded about all that."

Aunt Becka seemed to understand better than the others.

"I was just a little child during the War Between the States," she said, "but I recollect a few things about it. Everbody was hungry back then, because the soldiers took everything. They was a whole family up Scary kilt by the Yankee men. Even the younguns. We was mostly Yankee sympathizers, but everbody said how terrible it was. Still they werent nothing done to stop it. Both sides shot men while they worked in their fields. Shot them dead in front of their families. Then they was Alec May, kilt because he wouldnt fight. Hit was terrible times, and folks was so mean to each other.'' We rocked on the front porch and listened to the peepers. ''Alec was an abolitionist,'' she continued, ''but he couldnt see killing. Said the rebels was barefoot boys like him. That's why the Yankees shot him, left Jane with a baby to raise by herself.''

''My mama.''

''That's right. Your mama. It was a hardship on Jane, but I cant say Alec done wrong. He done what he had to. Live by what you believe is right and you bring the world down on your head.''

I felt ashamed. ''I shot at people,'' I said. ''That aint like Uncle Alec.''

''Aint like Carrie Bishop neither,'' she said gently. Then she patted my knee. ''When the world's turned around, sometimes up looks like down. I dont recall much about Alec. I was just a youngun when he was kilt. But I heard enough of him to know that you're Alec May's granddaughter and he wouldnt mind to claim you.''

She hugged me. She smelled like woodsmoke from standing by the fireplace.

''Child, child, what will become of you? But you wont go back on your raising.''

I saw her then, walking fifty miles through the rain to reach the Homeplace after she left her husband, her hair hanging in wet clumps and her drenched skirts slapping her legs.

I JOINED ALBION AT THE MINGO HOTEL IN JUSTICE ON THE evening before the trial. Isom and Gladys stayed in the room across the hall. It was all Ermel's idea. The Baldwin-Felts people and the coal operators took up two whole floors of the Carter Hotel on Main Street. He'd not have his boy arriving at the last minute, rumpled and tired from the train, while the coal operators strolled up the hill in newly pressed suits.

Albion had little to say until we were alone in our room. Then he pulled me down beside him on the green chintz bedspread.

"I missed you so much," he said. "I been so worried. I knew if anything bad happened, Ben would git word to me. But still—"

"I'm fine. I had it easy. My arm gits a little sore is all. But you, you're still yet so thin. Who's doing your cooking for you?"

"I done some myself," he said proudly. "And Annadel Justice fed me some."

"You dont say. Well, you dont need me around."

He laughed. "That aint so."

I pulled his shirt up and ran my hands up and down his back. I felt the mole on his left shoulderblade and rubbed it with one finger, rejoicing in its familiarity. "I know something Annadel Justice aint done for you."

He kissed me. "I been hungrier to taste your mouth than any kind of food," he said.

He was restless that night, finally sat up in bed.

"Sorry," he said. "I know you had a long trip today. I reckon I cant git used to a bed after them cots."

"Hit's all right. I wasnt sleepy no way."

"I been going over everything in my mind."

I twisted my fingers in the short curly hair of his chest and buried my nose in the soft flesh of his underarm.

"We got to face the worst," he said. "They may convict."

"We dont have to fret about that yet. The trial will take a while, and you'll be out on bond the whole time."

"But that trial will be crazy, Carrie. They's newspaper people coming, and they's already folks pestering me on the streets. We aint going to have much time to ourselves."

"Aint had none anyway since the strike."

"I know it. And that's why we got to say some things to each other. They could put me in prison for life. They could hang me."

"They wont," I said quickly. "Ermel says even ifn they convict, the circumstances aint right for first degree. The judge will make them reduce it."

"They brung the charge," he persisted.

"They wont do nothing like that," I said.

"Ifn they do, I want you to promise me you'll go back home. I know how much you love that place. Hit was such a joy to see you git offn that train today, to see the color in your cheeks, and your eyes bright. I know what put the life back in your face."

"Hit was seeing you again."

"No it werent. It was the Homeplace. If they convict, I want you to go back there. I cant bear the thought of being in prison and knowing you're in that tent. I want you back on your land with your people. Promise me, Carrie."

"Only if you promise you'll go back there with me when the strike's over. Leave the coal mines, go back there and be there for good."

He lay back on his pillow and didn't speak for a very long time. I put a finger gently to his lips and he kissed the tip.

"I cant see that far ahead," he murmured. His lips moved against my finger. "After the trial." He turned his head toward me. "Hit's like the refiner's fire, this here trial. Hit will leave everything clear, if I do like God says. They'll be gun thugs at that trial, Carrie, and the brother of them two that was shot. And they'll be hating me and Isom. They'll look at me and I'll see that hate in their eyes. I got to look back at them without hate. I got to be able to smile and speak gentle, and when the lawyers ask me questions, I got to answer with respect. And ifn I can do that, maybe I can live at the Homeplace."

I shook my head. "I dont understand. What does living as perfect as Jesus Christ have to do with the Homeplace?"

"Dont you see, Carrie, the Homeplace is lost."

I stiffened. "Dont say that."

"But hit's true, and we got to face it. I dont mean this year or next year, or even ten year from now. But you seen all this and you know it's true. Because the Homeplace aint Heaven, Carrie. Hit's part of the creation and hit's fallen and hit suffers just like we do. And the only way to live on it happy is to love everthing else that's fallen. And ifn I cant love them gun thugs, God wont call me back to the Homeplace, because I'll love all the wrong things about it, I'll love it because they aint no gun thugs there and because there I can turn my back on all the suffering, and I'll make an idol outen it, and worship it."

He had raised up while he talked and turned from me, and set his feet on the floor. I touched his back. It was damp with sweat.

"I love you," he said. "I love you so much."

WE DRESSED AS SOON AS IT WAS LIGHT, THEN SAT ON THE side of the bed, quiet. Most of our clothes had been lost when we were evicted from the house at Felco. I wore a new dress Flora made me before I left home, pink cotton with tiny white stripes sprinkled with red rosebuds. Albion had on Ben's suit that I'd brought with me. It was a little short on him, but not too noticeable.

We went downstairs for breakfast. Isom and Gladys were already there. Isom stood up and motioned us to join them. A red carnation peeked from the pocket of his pin-striped jacket. His hair was curly and long in the back.

"Eat up, younguns," he said. "Hit's on Daddy."

"Ermel and Annadel done gone up to the courthouse," Gladys said.

"Daddy wants a front row seat, and you know that there place will be full as a tick's belly." Isom flipped a cloth napkin so hard it cracked, settled it across his knees. "I got me a telegram."

He dug into his pocket and pulled out a crumpled yellow paper. "From Rondal." He tossed it across the table. I read, "Hog-eyed man fiddles too fast for thugs." It was signed "Sally Ann."

Isom laughed his short, hacking laugh. "I used to call him Sally Ann all the time. It's his favorite fiddle tune. I know it's killing him to miss this."

A waitress brought heaping platters of fried eggs, ham and redeye gravy, biscuits and sourwood honey. She lingered by the table.

"Yall the ones being tried?" she asked shyly.

"That's right." Isom smiled proudly at her.

"I just wanted to wish yall luck. My daddy was a miner. He was kilt up at Carbon Number Two, ten year ago." She fidgeted with a button on her white blouse. "Them gun thugs had it coming. Everbody says so, excepting the big shots.''

Gladys nodded her head. "That jury wont convict," she said.

"Not a Justice County jury," agreed the waitress. "Yall need anything else? I'll bring some more coffee."

Albion cut his eggs into tiny pieces. The yellow yolk ran into the red-eye gravy and he sopped it all up with a biscuit.

"Aint this nice?" he said. "I dreamed of fresh eggs for months now."

"We got to thank your daddy," I said.

"Didn't want your belly to growl in court," Isom said.

The waitress poured fresh coffee. Isom studied his watch. "Half an hour yet," he said and winked. "We dont have to worry about no crowd. We got seats saved."

When we stepped outside it was already hot. "I hope they got paper fans," Gladys said.

We crossed the street and walked alongside the high courthouse wall. The gray stone building with its single tower crowned the top of the hill. A flight of steep steps led up to the lawn, where a crowd of men stood about.

"They's some aint got seats yet," Gladys said. "Law, I'm commencing to git nervous."

"A lot of them fellers hanging around up there is Baldwins," Albion said. "I seen some of them before."

There was something about the way they stood that marked them—hands on hips and dark suit jackets pulled back, legs apart like they stood in the camps. Albion's hand was moist in mine. "Here's where it starts," he said.

Isom stopped, looked up at the men. He wiped his mouth with the back of his hand. Then his face cleared. "Oh, what the hell," he said. "Come on."

He pulled Gladys along with him. She looked over her shoulder at me, worried. She had a folded pink parasol clutched tightly in one gloved hand and held across her waist instead of down at her side, and when she turned to climb the steps, she poked Isom in the side with it.

"Damnation!" he exclaimed. "Them bastards try to git smart I'll just let you stab one of them."

We must have climbed two dozen steps and I was breathless at the top. The Baldwin men stared at us. Albion took my hand, placed it in the crook of his arm like we were at a dance. Isom spied someone he knew, raised his hand, grinned. The Baldwins stepped forward, pulling guns from inside their vests. When I cried a warning, the guns grew larger, the noise they made filled the whole world.

A wet spray struck my cheek. Albion's arm stiffened beneath my hand and he stumbled and fell. I tried to hold him up by the arm but he fell away so the arm was twisted behind him and I feared I had broken it. Each time I screamed another crimson gash ripped through his chest. In the ringing silence that followed I cried out for help. People ran from the courthouse, but they stopped short when they spied us and turned away with their hands over their faces.

Isom lay face down beside Albion in a pool of blood. Gladys knelt over him, her face frozen and contorted. She stared straight ahead, the pink parasol open in front of her like a shield. One of the gunmen, a short man with a long, curled moustache, strolled up. He leaned over, put his gun to the back of Isom's head. Gladys swung the parasol wildly.

"Dont shoot him again! Please dont shoot him again!"

I pulled Gladys toward me so she wouldn't see, and the gunman fired. A piece of skull struck me in the face and opened a cut on my cheek. Gladys screamed and struggled against me.

Then Violet Marcum was there. She knelt, gently took Gladys from me and wrapped her arms around her.

"Oh, Mommy, Mommy," Gladys moaned.

Violet smoothed Gladys's hair back from her damp forehead and rocked back and forth with her daughter in her arms.

"Where's Ermel and Annadel?" I asked.

"In the Courthouse. Annadel took a spell and passed out. Ermel's still with her." She touched the cut on my cheek with the tip of one finger. "Dont be fretting over them right now. You got to cry too. Go back to yourn and cry."

I stared at her. For a moment I had thought I might turn from their sorrow to seek comfort from Albion. But he lay still, staring at the sky. I stroked his cheek.

"Please wake up," I pleaded. "Dont be gone from me."

The force of the blows he had suffered gave his face a look of anger that had never been upon it in life. I raised his head to my lap. My hand came away wet with blood and I soon felt the dampness soak through to my thigh.

"I love you," I whispered. "You allays knowed that."

My throat closed tight and I sobbed. A forest of legs blacked out the light. Strong arms lifted me up. I kicked, struck out with my fists.

"Murderers!" I screamed. "Bastards!"

The men holding me laughed. Two others put a pistol in Albion's hand and carefully wrapped his limp fingers around it. A man in a blue suit with a camera snapped pictures. Then they took the gun away and left.

Someone leaned over me and said, "God in heaven."

I looked up into Miles's ashen face.

"I swear I never knew anything about it," he said.

"Git away from me."

"Oh, God, Sis, let me get you away from here. You got blood all over you. There's nothing can be done for him now."

"Dont you touch me," I hissed. "Hit's you needs doing for. I hope you burn in Hell."

He stared at me. "I swear—" He stood up. A man in a black suit was with him. "You can't tell me the Association didn't know about this," Miles said.

The man shrugged, looked away. "I suppose Tom Felts didn't trust the court. He lost both his brothers, you know."

Miles turned back to me. "Sis, we got to send for an undertaker. I'll help you take him back to the Homeplace."

He had his arms around me, pinned me to his chest. The smell of him was familiar, like sweet mown hay in the summer. Then I cried, with great racking sobs so that I couldn't breathe. I clung to him, terrified, struggled for breath while my throat closed as though I were being strangled. I heard talk of a doctor and I felt a stinging on my arm.

WE BURIED ALBION AS CLOSE TO ALEC MAY AS WE COULD. Miles stayed two days, then packed to return to Justice.

"You aren't going back to those tents?" he asked me. "I'm not sure it's safe for you. This was all a message, you know, that they won't be challenged anymore."

"Albion wanted me here," I said. "And I heard tell the union has sent another nurse."

"Good. There isn't any more you can do. I'm sorry, but that's the way it is. Coal is here to stay and the sooner folks cooperate, the sooner we'll get back to normal."

He carried his suitcase to the wagon where Ben waited. Flora and Aunt Becka followed him, hugged him. I stayed on the porch.

"Carrie," he said.

"Quit that job, Miles. They's other things you can do."

"Carrie, I've got two children now. I've got a good future with the company. They're not a bad company, not like some of the others. I can't just throw everything away. If the union will just quit pushing, things will be all right. I'll try to get to the bottom of all this. Those men murdered Albion and they ought to be punished. I promise I'll look into it, even though I won't be too popular for it. I promise."

I went into the house. Flora followed me into the bedroom. "He's your brother. Try to forgive him."

I turned on her. "Goddamn you! You sound like Albion! How can I forgive somebody that aint sorry?"

She turned pale and fled. I threw myself across the bed and lay there until I heard the wagon rattle off into the distance.

Miles wrote me from Vulcan to say that no one had been arrested for the shootings. He'd had no luck asking questions and made a few people angry. The state police were gone and hundreds of Baldwin-Felts guards roamed the hollers. Even he was afraid to say anything more. The union must see that it was hopeless, he said, they must let things be or the guards would remain and there would never be peace.

No one wrote to me from Annadel, and I was left to imagine how Gladys must grieve, how Ermel would be old and broken, how hungry they all must be.

Part Four

Eighteen

CARRIE BISHOP

No one had lived in the Aunt Jane place for years. Weeds grew close and dense in the yard and hung in tangles beneath each of the front steps. Inside, spiders draped their webs over the rough-hewn rafters and dustballs caught on splinters in the floor. I was so pleased when I moved in. I craved the roughness and untidiness.

I could see the headstones of the May family cemetery from my front window—Alec May, my mother, Aunt Jane, baby Orlando, Albion. The man who preached Albion's funeral spoke of the worms splintering the pine wood of coffins and devouring flesh, of sin and corruption. His words were oddly comforting. I couldn't have abided silliness from him.

Flora's children stopped by every day, just as Flora and Miles and I had visited Aunt Jane. I fed them blackberry pie and buttermilk, and told them stories about Uncle Albion. Once a month on Sunday we walked the eight miles to Tater Nob, to visit their Papaw and Mamaw Honaker. And in the evenings we popped corn, made fudge, pulled molasses candy, read aloud or told stories by the firelight. Often visitors stopped for the night. Flora and Aunt Becka were excellent cooks, and the Honaker farm gained a reputation as a good resting place for travelers. Ben had added a fifth room to the house, and if it was still crowded, Aunt Becka walked up Grapevine and spent the night in my big featherbed.

One evening in early August we had just sat down to supper when there came a knocking on the screen door.

"Company!" Jane called. Luke knocked over his chair as he ran to answer the door. When he came back his eyes were wide.

"They's a man on the front porch with a funny hat. He wont come in. Says he wants to talk to Aunt Carrie."

"Whoever could it be?" Flora circled the table, spooned mashed potatoes onto each plate with a sharp swatting motion.

"Dont let your supper git cold," Aunt Becka warned. "Bring him on in here."

Even with his back turned I knew him at once. He wore overalls, a red plaid shirt and a cloth cap. His dark hair curled over his collar. I pushed the screen door open and he turned around.

"Aint you a sight?" he said, and grinned.

"What are you doing here?"

"Come for my banjer."

"Then I'll go fetch it."

"And I come to see the meanest woman in east Kentucky. They kilt my fiddle player and they kilt the preacher. But you're still yet here. I had a hankering to see you."

I wrapped my arms around a porch post and looked out across the river.

"Besides that, I need nurses."

"I knew you wanted something," I said, "else you wouldnt be here, hankering or no."

"Maybe," he said.

"Carrie?"

Ben stood in the doorway, the warm yellow light of the kitchen behind him.

"Everthing all right?"

"Course it is. This here is a friend of mine from West Virginia, Rondal Lloyd. This is my brother-in-law, Ben Franklin Honaker."

Ben did not smile, and I remembered that he knew the name, that once I had spoken of how Rondal hurt me. Ben stood aside and held the screen door open.

"Yall better come in and eat before it gits cold."

"I just stopped by to say hello," Rondal said. "I werent meaning to put nobody out."

"In this neck of the woods, they aint no such thing as

putting people out," Ben said. "Florrie's done set a place for you."

We took him in the kitchen.

"You all, this here is Rondal Lloyd," Ben said. "He's from West Virginia."

"Pleased to meet you." Flora stuck out her hand.

Aunt Becka set an extra chair between her and Luke. "You're welcome," she said.

The children watched him expectantly while his eyes roamed the table. Except for fried bacon and hunks of corn-bread, everything was fresh from the garden—corn on the cob, new potatoes, green beans, kale, slices of red tomato as thick as slabs of meat.

"Yall know how to eat," Rondal said. He cut a slice of tomato slowly with his fork, but he chewed fast.

"Mister, that there sure is a funny hat," Luke said.

"They dont see nothing but wide brims," I explained.

Rondal pulled the cap from his pocket and set it on Luke's head, tugged on the bill so it came down over Luke's eyes. Luke giggled and glanced at Aunt Becka. Aunt Becka didn't even allow hats in the house, much less at the supper table. But she didn't say anything.

"Yall know that banjer I got up at the Aunt Jane Place?" I said. "That there is Mister Lloyd's banjer. Maybe if I fetch it after supper, he'll pick for us."

"I dont care to sing for my supper," Rondal said.

"Do you know our Aunt Carrie?" Jane asked.

"Sure I do. I knowed her longer than you have."

"No you aint. I knowed her all my life."

"That so?" He winked at her. "Reckon you got me beat then."

Ben pushed back his plate and propped his elbows on the table. "Where'd you come from?"

"Oh, lordy, I been all around Henry's barn. Took the train from Charleston over through Huntington and up to Louisa, walked to Inez, rode a mule for a feller I know into Shelby, sold it and sent him the money, then walked all the way up here."

"Just to pick up a banjer," I said sweetly.

"That's right." He stopped eating and looked at me. "Hit's a special banjer. My Uncle Dillon made it for me when I was just a baby like that one there." He pointed at Rachel, in Flora's arms.

"You got any stories to tell?" Jane asked. "Lots of strangers that come through tells us stories."

"They been spoiled," I said apologetically. "They come to expect it. You dont have to."

"That's all right. I reckon I might come up with a story. I could tell one about when I was an organizer out in Colorado."

I looked at Ben, who raised his eyebrows but said nothing.

"What's an organizer?" Luke asked.

"That's somebody that gits other folks doing things together. Like when you and your buddies is outside and one says 'Let's go pick berries' and figures out where to git the berries and how many buckets to take. That there is an organizer.

"Well sir, I went to Colorado to be an organizer. Colorado is one of them states away out west."

"I heard tell of it in school," Luke said. "They got big mountains."

"And lots of dust," Rondal said. "Anyway, I went to be an organizer with the coal miners. Only they is some rascals out in Colorado that cant stand an organizer. They cant bear to see folks get together. They are just plain mean and they want folks to be all spread out sos they can just pick them off, one by one." He grabbed Luke by the collar. "Like that!" Luke jumped, then giggled.

"Like the booger man!" Jane exclaimed.

"That's what they are," Rondal said. "Booger men. They aint nothing they like better than to sink their teeth into a nice, juicy organizer for breakfast. Any how, I went to be an organizer in a town called Trinidad. Now aint that a pretty name? And you best believe I was keeping a sharp lookout for booger men.

"I went to organizing, and I was doing such a fine job that I knew the booger men would be after me before long. Sure enough, one day I was in my hotel room, just minding my own business, when I heard a automobile drive up outside my window, and everything got real quiet down on that street. I looked out the window and what did I see but a whole car full of booger men—big ole fellers with green scabby skin and pointy teeth.''

"Yuck," said Mabel.

"Next thing I knew them rascals was coming up the stairs to my room. Coming slow up the stairs. Thump. Thump. Thump.'' He struck the tabletop with his fist. "Then I heard them outside my door breathing real heavy. 'Organizer,' they said. 'Organizer. We know you're in there.' 'That's right,' I answered. 'You come to git me?' 'We're going to bite off your toes and suck out all your blood,' they said.

" 'Well now,' I says, 'that's all right. But before you do, I got one last request.' 'What's that?' they say. 'Seeing how they aint nothing I'd rather do than organize, I'd like to organize one more time before you suck my blood.'

"I could hear them snickering on the other side of that door. 'Aint nobody here to organize but us,' one said. 'You'll do just fine,' I replied.

"They just hollered laughing when they heard that. 'How you going to organize us? One thing you can say about us booger men, we are already organized.'

" 'You may think you're organized,' I said, 'but I'm the best organizer they is and you aint met me yet.'

"About then, I pulled out my pistol and pointed it at that door. 'I'll tell you what,' I said. 'Before yall suck my blood, yall got to come through that door and git me. Now I got me a gun in here. First booger man comes in that door, I'm going to shoot. Second booger man through, I'll likely shoot too. Wont be until the third booger man comes through that somebody gits to suck my blood. So you got to git together. You got to git organized. You got to decide which booger men will be the first ones through that door, because them will be dead booger men.'

"Well, I heard them shuffling around and muttering out there. I waited and waited. After while, I hollered, 'Booger men. Oh, booger men. Yall got organized yet? Ifn I aint organized you, I'll be mortal disappointed.'

"Then I heard this buzzing and squeaking, you know how booger men do when they're just so riled they're like to bust. And I heard them bang back down them stairs and drive away in that car. And I knew I hadnt been able to git them booger men organized. But sons, I'll tell you, I lit out of Trinidad right now.''

He leaned back, looked slyly at me. "And that there is my story. Git your Aunt Carrie to tell you about how she saved an organizer from booger men over at Vulcan.''

"Tell us!'' they clamored. I said lamely that he was pulling their legs, and glared at him. He grinned back at me.

Ben took him into the front room after supper, like he always did with guests, while I helped Aunt Becka stack the dirty dishes. Through the doorway I saw Ben draw close to Rondal, speak to him. Rondal looked at him, nodded his head. A few more words passed between them, then they stared at one another briefly, before Ben motioned that they should sit down.

Flora came in from taking the children to the outhouse. They headed straight for the front room.

"Dont pester that poor man,'' she warned them.

Aunt Becka poured a pail of boiling water into the washtub. "That there is a rascal ifn I ever seen one.'' She waved her dishrag at me. "Go on in there with them. Me and Florrie will take care of this here.''

"I might walk up and fetch that banjer,'' I said.

When I told Rondal where I was going, he insisted on coming along. "I want to see where you live,'' he said.

"I want to go,'' Luke cried.

"Stay here!'' Ben said sharply.

We strolled along the edge of the cornfield. Rondal kept looking toward the river.

"Damn, I'd love to fish that thing,'' he said.

"What did Ben say to you?''

"When?''

"In the setting room. I seen him talking to you.''

"He asked if I had a gun. I said I did, and he said dont show it to the younguns or say nothing about it. I said I wasnt planning on it. That's all.''

I pushed open my door and he stepped inside. The banjo stood alone by the hearth.

"Place of honor,'' he said.

"You would think so.''

He picked it up, ran the back of his finger over the strings. "You let it git bad out of tune.''

"I aint paid a lot of attention to it. I dont know nothing about it."

He twisted the knobs, strummed, narrowed his eyes. Then he launched into Old Joe Clark, but stopped in the middle of it. "That's where Isom should come in," he said. He set it down, looked around the room.

"You git lonesome?" he asked.

"I got my kin. You git lonesome?"

"Me? Naw. Too busy."

"What you doing these days? They aint much you can do for the strike in Charleston, is they?"

He smiled. "That's what you think. Me and Doc and some other boys, we got big plans. We're going to overthrow the government." He whooped and slapped his leg. "I wisht you could see your face, Miss Carrie!"

"Well, what kind of crazy talk is that? You aint serious!"

"Never been more serious in my life. Come on, let's git back so I can pick for them younguns. We'll talk about it later."

All the way back up through the cornfield he kept snatching lightning bugs out of the air, then letting them go.

"How in the hell are you going to overthrow the United States government?"

"Carrie Lee! Such language!"

"You answer me!"

"I aint talking about the United States government. I'm talking about this government around here." He waved his arms in a wide arc. "I'm talking about that son of a bitch sheriff up in Logan County, and them Republicans in Justice County, and the gun thugs and the state police and maybe even the goddamn governor of West Virginia."

"I knowed you long enough to know you aint no fool. You cant believe they'll let you git away with that."

"I didnt say we'd git away with it. I said we'd try. Hit's like old Thomas Jefferson said. Hit's the course of human events."

They waited for us on the front porch. Rondal played Dusty Miller and Cripple Creek, Shady Grove and Soldiers Joy. Then he played and sang My Old Kentucky Home. We joined in the chorus.

Weep no more my lady, oh weep no more today.
We will sing one song for my old Kentucky home,
For my old Kentucky home far away.

After awhile Ben stood and stretched, said it was bedtime and corn to be hoed in the morning. Rondal offered to help and he agreed.

"You can have my bed tonight, Mr. Lloyd," Aunt Becka said. "I'll go up yonder and sleep with Carrie."

"Oh, no ma'am," Rondal said quickly. "I aint aiming to put nobody outen their bed. I'll just sleep in the barn."

"You'll do no such thing. We dont treat company that a way."

"But I love sleeping in barns. I love to smell the hay. I'm just like an old hobo, ma'am. I'll be right at home there."

"Nonsense."

Flora looked from me to Rondal. "Let him sleep in the barn," she said suddenly. Aunt Becka looked startled. "He should sleep where he's most comfortable," Flora said firmly. "Let's not fuss over it. Now kiss everybody goodnight, younguns, and wash your faces."

I said my goodbyes and Rondal asked if I would show him the barn. When we were up the road a ways, he said, "You reckon I could take a bath up at your house? I aint had one in a while. Hit sure would be relaxing."

I didn't answer and he walked on beside me. We didn't speak until we reached the house.

"You fetch the water from the well," I said. "I'll start a fire in the stove."

After the water boiled, I went out onto the front porch and sat on the steps. I heard him splash around, heard the cascade of water as he stood up to dry himself. Then he came outside with only his overalls on, rubbed the towel over his wet hair, sat down beside me.

"Dont I smell sweet as a rose now?"

I felt faint with the smell of him. I looked away. "You'll stink like a barnyard in the morning."

"Ifn I sleep in the barn," he said.

I turned on him. "You think you can just walk in here after all these years and—" The words died in my throat, strangled. He put his arms around me, kissed me lightly on the mouth.

"How long has it been?" he asked.

"Eight year," I whispered. "Eight year."

He kissed me again, unbuttoned the front of my dress. I put my hand on his.

"Rondal, somebody might come up here and find us."

"They wont. Your sister Florrie knows what's going on."

I knew it was true. I leaned my head on his shoulder and kissed the soft skin of his neck, even before I had decided whether I should. We took a long time with our lovemaking, two old friends getting reacquainted after many years apart. It was good to be a woman with him, instead of the frightened young girl of so long ago. I loved him hard, and knew I could bear whatever might come afterward.

We clung to one another in the featherbed.

"How was it?" he whispered.

"Hit just aint the same without the cast on your leg."

He laughed.

"I dont know what you must think of me," I said. "They aint nobody else I carry on with this way."

"Dont you fret. One thing I'd never take you for is a loose woman."

"I loved my husband."

"I know it. But he's dead, Carrie. Like Isom's dead, and C.J., and Sam Gore, and my daddy and brother. Me and you, we're still yet alive."

I tickled his mustache with my fingertip.

"I never stopped loving you."

"I know that too. Hit scairt me oncet, and maybe it still yet does. But I seen how easy things can be lost. Hit seems silly to push them away when it will all be took soon enough."

"You still aint said you love me."

"I aint sure I do. And I aint one to say things I dont mean. But I need you. I need you right now." His arms tightened around me. "Now that there is something I understand, needing somebody. But love—they must be something wrong with me, but I just dont know what it is."

"Didnt you love C.J. and Isom?"

"Them two, that's different. They was just allays there,

like the mountains is allays there. All I ever knowed of the world had C.J. and Isom in it. But with a woman it would have to be different, wouldnt it? It would have to be clean and pretty and clear, like that river running yonder, like this place here. I aint never lived in a place like this. I dont know it. Coal camps is home to me. Hit's like a baby duck when it's born, it takes the first thing it sees for its mommy. A baby duck spies an old ugly sow first thing, hit thinks, 'That there is home.' Hit's the same with me. I look for an old rattling coal tipple, or a house covered with the black dust. I look for things to be tore up. I seen so much of death and destruction they feel like home to me.''

I couldn't let him say any more. I put my hand to his mouth and then I kissed him until we made love again. I knew Albion did not mind. He was not dead to me, but murmured benevolently from the graveyard.

IN THE MORNING, I FRIED UP EGGS AND POTATOES AND BA-con, cut slabs of cold cornbread spread with apple butter. We ate quietly like an old married couple, then went out on the porch to smell the dew.

"I'll leave tonight for Charleston," he said. "I want you to come with me. Mind, I aint asking you to marry me. We need nurses."

"What makes you think I'd marry you?"

"I'm just checking. Be sure and bring your uniform."

"I aint even said I'd go."

He hugged me. "They's one thing in the world I trust right now."

While he hoed corn, I killed two chickens and fried them, baked fresh cornbread. I stuffed underwear, a dress and a nurse's uniform into a pillowcase. Then I put on an old shirt and a pair of overalls.

Flora stopped by on her way to call the cows.

"You're going, aint you? You aint never been good at hiding how you feel."

"Florrie, dont think hard of me."

"Honey, I dont. When you love somebody, you got to stand by them."

I started to cry. "I aint sure whether to be scairt or happy."

"You cant pull them two apart," she said. "Now you go on. Just promise you'll be back."

"You know I will."

We left as soon as it was dark, walking down Grapevine by lantern light. The full moon was out. Rows of weeping willows leaned and trailed their leaves like the trains of giant ladies-in-waiting. A rim of light glowed behind the black curve of the mountains and a night breeze rushed from the mouth of Bearwallow.

We stopped toward dawn and slept on a high rock above the river. I dreamed of fairies and Wuthering Heights and great adventures. One night, outside Louisa, we flagged down a slow train, a "redneck special" Rondal called it, heading for Charleston. He leaped into a boxcar and pulled me after him. Moonlight flashed between the wooden slats. We made love to the rhythm of the rails, and afterwards fed each other fried chicken.

Nineteen

RONDAL LLOYD

SOMETIMES I THINK I HATE HER. IT'S NOT HER FAULT. ALL in all, she's one of the best women I know, right up there with Annadel Justice and Violet Marcum. But a certain look on her face brings the anger up in me, a look of such assurance that I can't abide it.

She put that look into words only once. We were in bed at the Fleetwood Hotel. She pressed up against me despite the heat.

"I love you like my own kin," she said.

I was glad I couldn't see her face in the dark. I knew what it looked like, the lips pressed together, her gray eyes lit with expectation. Nobody I know expects as much as she does.

"Kin aint got a thing to do with this," I said. I can still hear the impatient edge of my voice. "Hit's like water running and cant nobody hold it back. But when it's gone, it's gone. That aint like kin."

My impatience melted like ice when she pulled away at the tone of my voice. That's when I know she's just like the rest of us, that she's not any stronger, that she's not like Mommy, who can't be hurt by anyone but Jesus. I can come close to loving Carrie then, after I've hurt her.

TALCOTT WAS WORKING AT A UNION MINE AT POINT LICK, on Campbells Creek near Charleston. He came into town often to talk things over with me. He was in charge of the men from his mine. They met every other day for drill, hid

246

their guns afterward. Talcott has been in the Army, knows what war is like.

He knew I didn't like to go up Campbells Creek with Mommy around. I went up to Point Lick once, took Carrie along just because I knew it would make Mommy mad. She'd stayed seated when I introduced them, but still managed to look down at Carrie. Her nostrils quivered like the gills of a fish.

"I know what kind of woman takes up with this boy," she said.

Poor Carrie was so earnest. She wore her good green dress and her hair was pinned up neat on top of her head.

"I'm a widder woman," she said. "My husband was a preacher."

"Do declare?" Mommy's eyes narrowed. "What persuasion?"

"Hardshell Baptist."

"Them's all lost," she said.

"If my husband is lost then they aint no God," Carrie said.

"With that kind of heathen talk, you and this youngun of mine must git along just fine."

On the train back to Charleston I said, "She thinks the wrong boy got kilt in the mines."

Carrie looked out the train window. We passed a tugboat pushing bargeloads of coal down the green Kanawha River like a scissor slicing through velvet.

"I talked to her some more while you and Talcott was drinking beer on the porch. She said she'd burn in Hell for all eternity if she could only have her boys back again." She touched my sleeve. "Rondal, she didnt mean just the one."

I was furious. "Hit's none of your goddamn business, none of it," I said fiercely. "My kin aint got nothing to do with you." I got up and moved to an empty seat at the front of the car.

It was the worst moment we had in our two weeks there. I waited for her on the station platform but she walked right past me. I let her go, bought a cup of coffee inside the depot. From the restaurant window I watched her disappear across the curve of the bridge, swallowed by the buildings of downtown. She didn't come to the Fleetwood that night. Doc Booker called me the next morning. We had often visited him in his house on Shrewsbury Street, and Carrie had spent the night there. I found her drinking coffee in the kitchen.

"I should have gone back to Kentucky," she said. "I got enough money for a ticket."

"Why didnt you?"

She blew her cheeks out full like she does when she's being stubborn. "I wont do you like you do me. I'm better than that."

I sat down at the table and Doc went into the front room.

"What's going to happen when this is all over?" she said. "Will you just go off?"

"I dont know." I picked up her hand that lay beside the coffee cup, turned it over and traced the lines of her palm with my finger. "I dont want you to depend on me too much."

She pulled her hand away.

"You want me to put you on the train?" I asked. "I wont think hard of you."

"You want me to go?"

"No."

I knew she wouldn't leave.

In the meantime we got word that martial law was declared once again in Justice County. Hundreds of miners were in jail. There were reports of murders, rumors that women were being raped. Many of the reports were exaggerated, but I knew enough were true. We passed on the word.

Twenty
CARRIE BISHOP

I'VE NEVER KNOWN HOW IT WAS PLANNED, OR WHO WAS IN charge. They were pledged to silence, and they keep their word even today. What I do know is that Rondal was gone most nights to the miners' hall on Summers Street, or on the train to a local union hall up some holler. I never expected to be with him in the evenings.

Summer evenings in the city had a special charm. A cool breeze from the Kanawha River blew the daytime heat from the sidewalks, and the air softened. People came out to stroll along the brick streets and children flew by on roller-skates or played hopscotch. I liked to walk up Kanawha Street, past the elegant Ruffner Hotel and the three-story stone mansions set back beneath the trees. Rondal said they were mostly coal operators' homes, but I liked to look at them anyway.

If I didn't feel like walking far, I sat on the riverbank and watched the boats, looked in the store windows downtown or went to the stone library near the state capitol building. I didn't have any money, but Rondal had a small salary from the union and he gave me quarters for ice cream sodas. On my birthday, he took the entire day off. We walked around the corner to Majors Book Store and he gave me a copy of *Bleak House* for a present. Then we took the streetcar to Luna Park, rode the merry-go-round and ate hot dogs. We ended the day with vaudeville at the Burlew Theater. I loved to be with him, but I didn't mind being alone. He was happier than at anytime I had ever known him.

He did tell me a little at night when he came in worn out

but unable to sleep and I bathed his face with a cool cloth and massaged his back. He spoke of Sheriff Don Chafin of Logan County, the meanest man in the state of West Virginia.

"He's got secret police like that Czar had in Russia. He's got hundreds of deputies, and the coal companies pay all their salaries. In Logan County, folks disappear in the middle of the night. And ifn anybody at the Huntington depot buys a train ticket for Logan, the secret police tail him, no matter who he is, or what his business is. The union aint never even got a toehold in Logan County. But we got to go through there to git to Justice. We'll have to hang that bastard Chafin."

He brought in a case of Pabst longnecks and drank three bottles every night.

"The local boys at headquarters are gitting nervous. The federal boys in town know something's up. Everybody's scairt."

"How many men you talking about?" I asked.

He sipped his beer, studied the bottle. "Ten thousand," he said.

"Lord in heaven," I said.

He gave me a U.M.A. headband to sew onto my nurse's cap. It covered the three black stripes that stood for the Grace Hospital.

Word went out on August 22. At dawn of the next day, Rondal took me by Dr. Booker's little red brick house with the white porch posts. Dr. Booker carried his black bag and a roll of blankets. He wore his old gray suit and wide-brimmed hat and a red bandana knotted around his neck instead of a tie.

"Where's the rest of your uniform?" He pointed at my overalls and plaid shirt.

"Uniform's in my bedroll. I didnt want to git it dirty yet."

"She's got on her redneck uniform," Rondal said. He pulled a bandana from his back pocket with a flourish. "I even got her one of these here."

He tied it around my neck, touched my earlobe and then my chin.

"Aint she one hell of a brave girl?" he said.

"I always did think it," Dr. Booker replied.

We walked with our bundles down Hale Street. The streets were sticky from a recent rain. On the sidewalk, gray

pigeons with pink bills poked at a mound of shattered pea-
nut shells. The downtown buildings closed in over our
heads, like mountains near the head of a holler. We paid
the toll and walked up the long curve of the bridge. An
early morning streetcar clattered by. Rondal waved his bandana at the moustachioed conductor, who tipped his hat.

"You know we got to win," Dr. Booker said. "You know
what will happen if we dont."

Rondal took my hand. "Be a relief to have it done with,
one way or the other."

We took the train to Marmet, the jumping-off point for
the road to the southwest. At Marmet thousands of armed
men milled around outside the depot. Most were clad in
overalls, but some wore faded military uniforms. Each man
sported a red bandana tied jauntily about his neck. Some
were already armed. One group of rawboned mountain men
carried long rifles that Rondal said dated back to the Revolutionary War, and I even saw a Greek with a curved
sword. A Ukrainian man wore a faded painting of St. Vla-
dimir on his back, sewn there by his wife as a talisman of
good luck. Welshmen, camped along the railroad track, sang
of building Jerusalem among dark satanic mills. Trains kept
arriving with men standing in the aisles, and trolley cars
from Charleston so full that passengers hung outside on the
steps. They gathered around the brightly hued banners of
their union locals, formed companies in the main street of
the town and marched off. Some were Justice County men
who had escaped to safety, but most of them were union
miners from the Kanawha and New River coalfields. Rondal
left us at the station and we waited until Talcott came from
the ferry with three hundred Point Lick men.

Rondal returned soon with a big grin on his face.

"We're set up at the mouth of the creek," he reported.
"They're checking passwords and handing out guns. They
even sent two machine guns through that they stole from
company stores. And there's ammunition and medical supplies waiting in Danville. I got to check when we git there."

"When did the boys first take out?" Talcott asked.

"Early. Some will be at the head of the creek by now.
And the line stretches all the way back to here, with fellers
still yet coming. God damn, we really done it!"

We joined the march. Townspeople lined the main street. Some only stood, their faces long with disapproval, but most clapped and waved. The men hoisted their rifles to their shoulders, swung their arms. We sang "John Brown's Body." Some Italians in front of us sang a marching song in their language. Doc said it had to do with a man named Garibaldi. Rondal held my hand and swung my arm high in time to the music. He laughed. "Jesus, I wisht C.J. and Isom could be here."

We quieted as we started up Lens Creek. Dr. Booker whistled the Internationale softly. Cicadas buzzed far up the dark green hillsides. At the checkpoint, Talcott approached three automobiles parked across the rutted dirt road.

"I'm in charge. Point Lick, Local 124."

One of the men made a mark in his notebook.

"Password."

"I come creeping."

"Stand around here and watch each man that passes through. Point out anybody you dont know."

"Who's the lady?" one man asked, his voice high with surprise.

"Nurse," Rondal said. "See her cap?"

"Honey, you got a long way to walk."

"I'll make it. I'm going toward home."

"That right? All I can say, you sure do pick bad company to travel in."

"You're jealous, Cantley," Rondal said.

Cantley laughed and waved us aside. We waited while those who had come unarmed received their rifles from the back of a truck. Then we marched off up the creek to a distant drumbeat from one of the locals behind us.

The day was scorching hot, even for August, and it took the longest and hottest part to reach the head of Lens Creek. I trudged along, worn out after the first few hours and hard put to keep up. I was not used to the long heavy overall material on my legs in such heat; I wondered how men could bear it. My spirits rose whenever the road joined the creek. Then I had an excuse to splash and wet myself down. Once I fell on purpose and flung cool water on my face and neck. My nurse's cap flew off and floated downstream where

Rondal retrieved it. He helped me up and set it crookedly on my head.

"You all right?"

"Fine," I said.

The sun was high for a while before we stopped to eat. I took a ham sandwich Rondal pulled from his knapsack, and mulled chunks of it around in my mouth. It was difficult to swallow.

"How far?" I asked.

"Two more mile to the foot of the mountain, maybe."

He leaned over and rolled one of my pantlegs above the knee.

"Rondal, I cant show my legs with all these men around."

"Hell you cant. I'll speak to the first one says anything."

I went on gamely in the afternoon. It took about an hour and a half to reach the foot of the mountain. Here the road was rougher, narrower. Naked roots and gouts of brown dirt hung along the roadside. Rondal gripped my wrist, pulled me along after him. Finally I stumbled, my feet dragged through the dust. He stopped, wiped his brow.

"Goddamn, I'm tired," he yelled. "Boys, let's rest a minute." They muttered a bit but crouched on their haunches. They tipped up water jugs and drank. The dust was itchy up on my legs. Rondal knelt beside me, pulled off my shoes. Both of my heels were bloody. He poured water from his bottle, rubbed my feet gently.

"Doc, git some bandages."

I bit my lip to keep from crying.

"You're so damn brave," Rondal said. "I sure am proud of you."

I counted each step up the mountain, lost track, and started over again. Going down, my legs felt as though iron rods had been soldered inside from my ankles to my thighs. Rondal carried me the last half-mile to Racine, all the way to the river bank, where we settled in the shade of a willow. I was embarrassed. I had always walked, sometimes ten miles at a stretch, but never in such heat and in such heavy clothes.

"I'm so sorry," I mumbled when Rondal set me down.

"Hit's all right. I'm plumb tuckered myself."

"Cause you been toting me."

"Naw, before that." He lay back, covered his face with his hands. "Damn Isom. Why couldnt he git hisself kilt in October?"

"Rondal!"

He laughed helplessly and pulled me down beside him. Soon we were both laughing like idiots, hugging and rolling on the ground. He kissed my forehead, my eyelids, my mouth. Then he jerked and yelled. Talcott stood over us, had kicked Rondal in the back. He dropped a cigarette butt near my face.

"Thought I'd remind yall they's other folks around and you look like damn fools."

We sat up. Rondal's face was red. I rolled down my pant-legs. Rondal helped me up and I hobbled beside him toward the river.

The bottom, once a cow pasture, had been transformed. Here and there a tent had been set up, but most of the men spread bedrolls out in the open, so that the whole ground was blanketed with varicolored cloth. Men sprawled on the blankets or stood in groups cursing and gesturing, or wending their circuitous way from one place to another. They lined up beside trucks drawn up at the edge of the field to dispense soupbeans and cornbread, or stood in circles, sharing bottles of liquor. Children from the nearby town dashed back and forth and dogs wandered in search of scraps of food.

Rondal left me the rest of the evening, and I thought he was angry. I shared supper with Dr. Booker. Then he went off with some friends to pass out socialist newspapers and I was left alone with Talcott. I spread out my blanket and laid down. All around me the Point Lick men laughed and cursed, speculated on which boss man was the meanest, played poker, tipped up tin cups of homebrew. Off in the distance I heard the singing of hymns.

"Damn missionaries followed us out here," Talcott grumbled.

"Naw, they's a preacher man digs coal at Bull Push that vowed to hold services every night we camped," someone said. "He's all right. He's union and he preaches burning hell for the operators."

I soon fell asleep despite the commotion. But Rondal shook me awake, whispered, "I found us a place," and picked me up, bedroll and all.

"Where you been?" I mumbled.

"Had to check on some things. We set up a big comissary tent for breakfast tomorry."

He stepped over sleeping men, carried me inside a tobacco shed. I could see the stars through the gap along the bottom of the roof. He fumbled with the snaps on my overalls.

"Damn, these are hard to git into," he muttered.

"You'll figure it out."

His scalp was wet with sweat and his skin tasted of salt and gritty dust. His rough denim overalls scraped against my belly. Then he stood up and undressed.

"Too hot for clothes anyhow," he said and laid back down. "You dont have to worry about walking tomorry." He kissed my neck. "We found us a train."

A COMMISSARY TENT WAS SET UP DURING THE NIGHT. COOKS served bacon, biscuits and milk gravy. I stared at the plate Rondal brought me, thrust it back at him, and ran to the river to vomit. When I returned he had eaten my bacon, but gave me the biscuit.

"Stick that in your pocket. You might keep it down later." He put his hand to my forehead. "You all right? Maybe you should go back to Charleston."

I had begun to guess what was wrong but was afraid to tell him. He would have sent me back for sure.

"I aint going back," I said. "Hit's the heat and excitement, that's all."

"Let's go git you that train."

"How on earth did you git a train?"

"We aint took it yet, but the boys is keeping a sharp eye on it. Hit's setting on a spur around the bend."

The train consisted of an engine, tender and four flat cars. I trailed along behind when Rondal, Talcott and the others approached it. They surrounded it, their guns pointed in the air with the butts resting easy on their hips the way a woman will hold a baby. A man in a blue cap stuck his head out the engine's window.

"Got her fired up yet?" Rondal asked casually.

"Almost."

"Where to?"

"St. Albans."

"How's about taking us to Logan first?" Rondal's voice sounded like he was asking for a cigarette.

"Boys, I'm with ye," the engineer said, his voice full of smiles. "Time to clean things up, aint it. But if I haul yall to Logan, hit's my job, son."

"And if we kidnap you and make you haul us?"

The man raised his hands. "Cant argue with no rifle, now, can I? No, sir. Yall climb on. I'll have her fit in ten minutes."

Talcott climbed into the cab with his rifle and the others clambered on board. Rondal ran back to me.

"Come on, while they's still yet room."

I was suddenly frightened. "You're coming with me, aint you?"

"Sure I am. You think I'd walk when I can ride?"

Dr. Booker yelled at us from the last flat car. Rondal hoisted me up, then climbed up himself. We sat with our legs dangling over the side. The train jerked, then moved slow and smooth. I smiled at Rondal, happy to be so close to him. But he was looking across the bottom at the miners breaking up camp.

"Take a heap more trains," he said.

WE STOPPED IN DANVILLE AROUND NOON. SOMEONE HAD decided we could take on cars there and pick up more of the men who had already made their way to Coal River. Dr. Booker and I entered a restaurant with a crowd of miners while Rondal went to see about the train. We squeezed around a table in the corner. The owner hovered uncertainly in the middle of the room, tried to walk in two directions at once, then called out in a voice that cracked, "Listen here! Listen! I dont serve no colored in here. Yall go on back outside."

A dark Negro at the lunch counter swung around on the stool. He made sure the man saw him lay his pistol on the counter.

"Mister, yall going to serve this here colored, or else I going to serve myself. And I guarantee, I'll give myself a bigger helping than you would."

"We're all rednecks!" someone yelled from the back.

The man retreated to the kitchen.

"Better go make sure he dont do nothing to the food,"

another Negro said. He and a companion followed the man into the kitchen. One of them returned shortly with a telephone in his hand, displayed the frazzled ends of its wires.

"I carried me away a little souvenir," he said.

We applauded. The food began to arrive soon after, trays of hamburgers, sandwiches, and fried potatoes. We paid for everything we ate, and the Negroes at the counter left a tip.

AT DANVILLE WE TOOK ON TWENTY MORE FLATCARS AND twelve boxcars. Men rode up top of the boxcars because of the heat. They seemed to float in the shimmering air, their hair smoothed back like birds' feathers by the wind.

I gave up trying to keep my cap on my head, and crushed it inside the bib of my overalls. It was speckled with cinders from the smokestack.

We passed through the middle of a large coal camp. Rondal yelled that it was called Ramage. Children raced alongside the train on long, skinny brown legs and waved their arms above their heads. They were lovely, their eyes large, their faces narrow, their gait awkward as they navigated across the jagged red dog on their bare feet.

A row of peeling dark green houses slid past across the creek. Their jumbled back porches were immodestly laid bare to passing trains. Washtubs hung on the walls and gray laundry flapped from wires strung between the porch posts. A spindly yellow dog charged across a footbridge, tossed its head. The noise of the train drowned out its yapping.

At the last house a woman leaned over the porch rail beside a row of potted plants. She waved at us. Then she ran down the steps and across the road to a green frame post office. She yanked the American flag from its bracket beside the door, tucked the pole under her arm and loped across the bottom, her skirt held high and her ponytail flying. We rounded a long curve beside a baseball diamond and she met us on the other side, planted her feet wide apart, and whipped the flag back and forth, beating the air to cream. We cheered like we were at a baseball game. A man near me, who wore an army helmet, flat like a saucer, snapped to attention and saluted.

The woman was lost to us around the bend.

Twenty-one

RONDAL LLOYD

ALMOST AS SOON AS WE ARRIVED AT THE FOOT OF BLAIR Mountain, we got word that we had to turn back. We were ordered to a meeting with the District 17 leadership at the baseball field in Danville to learn why the march was called off.

The men were in an uproar, and I was furious. Blair Mountain was all that stood between us and Logan, and Logan was the gateway to Justice County. I had no intention of returning to Charleston. But when the men heard the District was backing down, they got nervous. Talcott and I went to Danville to try to get things going again. Carrie and Doc Booker stayed behind because Carrie was so weary of traveling. I put her up in a hotel at Clothier and Doc boarded with a colored family nearby, the hotel being Jim Crow. I figured they were safe enough, for the union boys from Ramage and Sharples were in control there. We loaded the train, backed it up and returned to Danville.

They are good men, the District leaders. Two of them are even socialists, friends of Doc's. But they just didn't know. They always wanted to talk strategy. I admit that strategy is important. But they had lived in Charleston too long and couldn't understand that things had gone beyond strategy.

Frank Keeney, the District president, stood at home plate on the Danville diamond with his hands in his pockets and jiggled his legs nervously. Miners filled the bleachers behind the batting cage, packed the infield, hunkered down along the baselines. Talcott and I pushed through to get in close. I knew Keeney would be looking for me.

"Boys," he was saying, "Don Chafin's got four thousand men on top of Blair Mountain in concrete bunkers. He's got lots of machine guns. He's been waiting for something like this and he is prepared."

"We already know that, Keeney!" I yelled. "We got ten thousand men. Hit's a goddamn army, son!"

Our eyes met. His were soft with apology, pleading. "I'm sorry, boys, but it's no good. President Harding has sent a telegram to the governor. He's sending in the U.S. Army. He's calling this an armed rebellion."

"Damn straight it is!" Talcott hollered.

"I just talked to a U.S. Army general," Keeney shouted, "and I'll tell you his exact words. He says there are several million unemployed in this country and they're afraid this might assume proportions that they couldn't handle. Those are his words, not mine. It's the U.S. Army, boys. They're bringing in airplanes with bombs, the 88th Air Squadron. They intend to drop those bombs. You start questioning who runs this country and the big foot comes down."

Men had been pushing all around me, talking among themselves so it was hard to hear Keeney, but now they grew quiet.

"We cant go agin the federal government," someone called out. "We cant lick nothing that big."

"I got me a newspaper," a colored miner answered, "quotes a coal operator. Says we got a bunch of niggers turned loose with high-powered rifles. This here nigger aint setting down this rifle without a fight."

There was scattered applause, but most of the men were wavering, I could tell.

"Hit's a trick!" Talcott yelled. "The U.S. government dont give a damn what goes on down here. When has the government ever cared about this place? They dont even know we're here."

"Hell they dont," Keeney answered. "They knew where the Philippines was and where Cuba was. We're right in their backyard. You can be damn sure they know what's going on here. They know it all. And boys, they'll call it treason."

"So what?" I cried. "Hit's a lousy bunch of Republicans is all it is. Hit's a rich man's government and hit's a coal

operators' government. We dont have to take nothing offn
it. Aint yall never heard of the Declaration of Independence? Hit's our god-given right.''

An Italian in the bleachers began to sing in his language
and others joined in, clapping their hands. Keeney pushed
his way through to me, took my shirt in his two hands.

"I want this as bad as anybody," he said. "But they want
it too. Rondal, we heard things. We think one of the boys
that talked this thing up is a company agent. They want us
to attack because they know they'll win and they'll call it
treason and they'll have an excuse to break us all over this
state."

"They got to win first," I said. "Back off and you're
done broke."

"I want to say go on, but I can't. What I said has to be
the official position."

We stayed on that ball field and argued for over an hour.
Some men drifted off, like they were reluctant to leave but
had lost sight of the craziness that had brought them there.
Others stood with their arms folded, ready to march if only
Keeney said go. The Italians sang for a while, then lapsed
into a sun-beaten silence. One Italian who wore a uniform
I'd never seen before came over to where I stood arguing
with Keeney. He shook my hand.

"You say good things," he declared. "My papa, he come
to this country for the freedom. He can't find the land to
buy. Then he get crushed in the roof fall, poom!" He
clapped his hands. "Now, where I go to find the freedom,
huh? Alaska? Pah! I tell my wife, I have to keep look here,
you know?" He turned on Keeney, jabbering in Italian, and
flicked his fingers beneath his chin the way the Tallies do
to show they're disgusted.

"What the hell kind of uniform is that?" Keeney asked.

The man drew himself up to his full height. "Italian
army," he said proudly. "My papa's uniform."

"Shit," Keeney said. He shoved back his hat, looked at
me cockeyed, shook his head and smiled. "Before I took
over this district, the leadership was so careful they looked
ten ways before they pissed."

"I know it. I aint thinking hard of you, Frank. But me

and my brother left folks in tents at home. We aim to go back there.''

In the end it was out of both our hands. Talcott and I were ready to order our train back to Blair when men came running from the ball field, calling at us to wait for them. Two men had arrived on a railroad handcar, calling that the state police had crossed Blair Mountain and shot up the mining camp at Sharples. Scores were dead, they claimed, including women who were kidnapped and forced to march as a shield in front of the policemen. I spied Frank Keeney on the station platform just before we pulled out.

"Send the boys back that have started home!" I yelled.

He waved his hand and let it drop as though he hardly had the strength to lift it. A dark wet patch spread under the arm of his light suit jacket.

"Come on with us!"

"I got to go home and pack," he replied. "I reckon I'll be in prison for a spell."

CARRIE AND I SPENT THE NIGHT IN A BARN ON HEWITT Creek that belonged to a Holiness preacher who'd joined our fight. They are tough old birds, the Holiness, not scared of a thing. This one had been in the sun so long and worked so hard he looked to be made out of rope. We told him we were married and he offered us his bed but we said no, we'd not put him out. In fact, we wanted to be alone. But although no one else was in the barn, I touched her self-consciously. I was aware of the men camped around us, ready to climb the mountain in the face of the machine guns. I heard them breathe, felt their hands supporting me as I rolled atop her. Afterward I waited, quiet, for her to speak, to fret aloud over the danger I was in and beg me to be careful.

Instead she asked, "What's your idea of heaven?"

It was a typical Carrie question, and just the sort of thing I didn't want to think on right then.

"Never considered it before," I said grumpily. Then I relented, remembered the thrill of fear when it occurred to me on the train that she might be one of the women endangered by the police and the gun thugs.

"What do you think about heaven?" I asked, not really wanting to know.

"Heaven is where everyone you love is all in one place." She said it quickly, like she'd thought about it before.

"Sounds like a damn cemetery," I said.

She nipped my ear lobe with her teeth and I yelped.

"Ifn you're so smart-alecky, how come you're scairt to answer my question?"

"I might die tomorry," I said. "I dont like to think on it."

She pressed her face against my shoulder. "I know it."

A tenderness filled me. I kissed her hair and it clung to my dry lips, tickled.

"Hit's this here," I said. "Heaven is this here. Hit's all these men together, and you, and knowing this here is the way we was meant to do. But it only lasts a minute. Then hit's gone."

She kissed me. "I love you," she said.

The response leaped to my lips and died there. I turned my head away, shamed.

Her thin arms around my chest never loosened their hold. "You dont have to say. I know as much as I need to."

She never did beg me not to go. It was then I knew what I had in her. She'd throw out no snares to trip me and slow me, to keep me from giving everything up to what was coming. It takes a hell of a woman to be like that.

Twenty-two

CARRIE BISHOP

THE HOTEL AT CLOTHIER WAS QUIET UNTIL WORD OF THE shootings at Sharples. I was stretched out on my bed reading *Bleak House*, the black-trimmed window frame wide open to the Sunday morning sunshine. I heard men yelling from the direction of the train depot, then loud voices in the lobby below. When I went downstairs I saw a crowd outside listening to a short, curly haired man who stopped talking often to catch his breath in great sobs.

"Hit were the state police and Chafin's thugs! They shot up our houses with the younguns still yet inside. They caught the women and held them out front so's we couldnt git off a shot. They's three good men laying dead up there." His hands went to his face. "They hit my baby in the arm. Doc Lewis had to cut it—"

No one cried out in anger. They listened in silence now, and when one of the man's friends led him away they shouldered their rifles and began walking toward Logan. I went over to Doctor Booker.

"They'll all be coming back," I said.

BLAIR MOUNTAIN WAS ONE OF THE MOST POWERFUL MOUNtains I'd ever seen. It sprawled the length of Hewitt Creek and thrust out its arms to push away the punier hills. Shadows rolled across the folded slopes to mark the time of day, and sometimes the folds opened into a cove, seductive, that promised a way across. But there were no passes through.

"How will you go over?" I asked Rondal before he set out with the Point Lick men.

"We aint sure," he admitted. "Some will try over to Sharples, but we hear the road's guarded pretty good. And the blackberry and mountain laurel is growed up too thick to pass over the ridge in places. We'll have to hunt and peck for a place to cross."

"You should have waited for the cold before you marched," I said.

"But they's cover for us when the leaves is on the trees. Besides, you got to go when your time comes."

He buttoned me into my wrinkled white uniform and walked me up the creek to a one-room schoolhouse that would serve as our field hospital. Then he left me without a word, with only the most casual wave of a hand. I went cold with fear. There was something about the back of him as he walked toward the creek with his slight limp, something that said even if he crossed Blair Mountain he would keep on going to God knew where, but it would be out of my life.

I ran into the schoolhouse in a panic. Dr. Booker was already there, opening boxes of supplies.

"I got to do something! I wont never see him again!"

He put his hands on my shoulders and squeezed tight. "They's plenty to do right here. And that's all you can do, child."

"But I'm going to have his baby," I blurted out.

He shut his eyes and shook his head.

"You aint told him?"

"No," I whispered.

"Good. You're strong that way, you'll be just fine. Now help me with this here place before the shooting starts."

We carried the students' desks outside and set them beneath an elm tree. I poured water from the creek into a jar, dropped in a metal ball filled with English tea I'd bought in Charleston, and set it in the sun. Light brown currents swirled through the water like liquid marble. Inside the school we pushed a table next to the teacher's desk to make an operating table, emptied the bookcase and set out medicines, scrubbed the floor and the window sills, pumped water and built a fire.

At dinnertime we ate ham sandwiches and sipped tea cooled in the creek. A Dr. Mason joined us. Dr. Booker met him the day before at Clothier. Dr. Mason claimed no politics but said he was once an army doctor and knew how to dig a bullet out of a man. He said it with such relish that I shuddered. His white hair was greasy and he smelt of alcohol, but we let him stay.

"I was over in Logan two days ago," Dr. Mason said. "The place was crawling with armed men."

"Who are they?" I asked. "Where do they come from?"

"Well, lots of Baldwin-Felts guards, of course. Sheriff Chafin's deputies. Townspeople from Logan and Justice, Welch, Bluefield. Bankers, lawyers, doctors. A few American Legion Posts. Saw their flags. And college boys down from Morgantown on their summer vacations. Boys who were too young to fight in the big war, I suppose."

"I reckon they think they missed something," Dr. Booker said.

"They're all armed to the teeth. In fact, one of them already got drunk and shot his own man accidentally. But they've got plenty of machine guns. And they're building bombs."

"What?"

"That's right. Got a regular factory in an old warehouse over there." He shook his head. "I don't know what these miners think they're going to do. Even if they make it to Logan and Justice, do they think they can run things? Of course, they probably wouldn't do any worse than the rest of these hillbillies." He laughed heartily.

I stood up so fast I spilled my tea, and turned my back on him. Just as I did there came a loud tearing sound from the ridge that spread the length of the holler, as though the jagged edge of the mountain top had caught on the sky and ripped it open.

We froze, our eyes turned upward. The gunfire continued without ceasing.

"I served in the war with Spain," Dr. Mason said slowly, "and this gunfire's as heavy as anything I heard there. How many of these medical stations do the miners have?"

"Three," Dr. Booker said.

"They'll need them," said Dr. Mason.

A company of about eighty miners passed by in their blue overalls and red bandanas. They bore the bright blue banner of their local union hall, embroidered by their wives, emblazoned with two American flags and a golden eagle, hands clasped in solidarity, and the slogan, "United We Stand, Divided We Fall." Unlike the men on the first day out of Charleston, they did not joke or call out, but trudged silently, their faces set. We had watched companies just like them pass by all day.

Within half an hour, a dead miner, a Negro shot through the head, was carried down to us. Shortly after, the first wounded men arrived.

Twenty-three

RONDAL LLOYD

THREE DAYS ON THE MOUNTAIN, AND I KNEW WE COULD break through at Crooked Creek gap. Three days since, frightened and already weary from days on the march, we walked up the mountain in the quiet of the morning, no sound except our breathing and the snapping of twigs, no sound until we could see the blue sky above the ridge and the machine guns opened up on us. Three days back and forth, I scarcely slept and scarcely ate, and the briars ripped my clothes to shreds. I was everywhere, on Spruce Fork and Beech Creek and Hewitt.

Blair had the worst of it. The gun thugs waited in force at Blair, where the main road crossed. We soon decided it would be impossible to breach the defenses, and kept up a steady fire only to occupy the defenders. At Sharples I met a company of men just arrived from Pennsylvania. I sent them to the head of Hewitt, where Talcott was in charge.

Talcott and his men had taken over an abandoned mining works down holler from Crooked Creek gap. Besides his own Point Lick men, he had a company of Negroes all the way from Northfork in McDowell County. I joined him on the evening of the second day. We talked about Blair.

"The damn machine guns never stop," I said. "The men git up the nerve to make a charge but they just git pinned down. Cant charge straight up the hill no how because of the goddamn bushes."

Talcott spat. "Here too. Hit's like the trenches only upside-down. Hit's like climbing a damn wall, except they aint no place to git a toe hold."

Above us the gunfire was more sporadic.

"They're gitting tired," said the man beside Talcott.

"Want to try again?" said Talcott. He waved his arm. "Come on, boys!"

We poured out of the rusting tin sheds, climbed over rotting timbers, reached a slippery pile of slate. Immediately the bullets kicked up the top of the slate pile. The man beside me fell wounded. Flying slate cut my face. The others ran back to the sheds. I followed, dragging the wounded man by the leg.

Inside, I leaned against the wall in the semi-darkness, breathing hard. Talcott handed me a canteen.

"Hit will be dark soon," he observed.

"How do we go up?" I said.

"Damned if I know."

"You were in the goddamn army."

"Hell, you think I'm General Pershing?" He leaned closer. "You know what hit would take to breach that there hill? Ever man we got, going up in the face of them machine guns, knowing full well that half of them will git kilt in the charge. Then hand-to-hand combat at the top. And the only thing that will make a man do such a durned-fool thing is ifn he knows for sure they's a firing squad waiting ifn he disobeys. That there is how they drug us outen them trenches and that is the only way."

"Then what can we do?"

He shrugged. "I'm thinking on it."

The firing continued heavy that night, for the defenders feared we might use the darkness to cover an attack. The mountainside was alive with explosions of orange sparks. We took shifts, some spreading out along the hillside to return the fire, others sleeping under cover. I slept two hours. Then I woke, and the air in the sheds was too close to fall back to sleep. I went outside, crouched behind a tipped-over railroad sidecar and sucked on a cigarette. I stayed there watching the moon float behind the clouds and wondered briefly about Carrie. She was busy, likely, and wore out, but safe. The defenders could pass by us no more than we could break their line. Again I studied the flashing lights on the mountainside.

"Beech Creek," I said aloud, then shook my head. The

shooting was heavier there. I threw down my cigarette butt in disgust.

"Big brother," Talcott called from the shed, "come on in here. I got someone I want you to meet."

A skinny man with thin blond hair cowered in the corner while the Negroes who had been on patrol trained their rifles on him. He wore a dirty white armband, the badge of Don Chafin's volunteers.

"Dont k-kill me," he whined, his words so slurred as to be barely understandable. "Oh, lordy, dont sh-sh-oot. I'm just a poor ole miner like you."

"You're a scab," Talcott said.

"No! I work over to Ethel camp. They wont let us join no union there. I would ifn I could. You know how it is, boys."

One of the Negroes poked him with his boot, easy, but the man jumped liked he'd been hurt.

"Aint got no union in McDowell," said the Negro, "but we're fightin on this here side."

"You're fighting for them," Talcott said.

"Oh, no!" The man wept, his mouth wet and bent like it was made of rubber. "They made me. They come pulled us outen the mine. Said we had to plug up Crooked Creek Gap. Said they was short of men there."

Talcott looked at me and grinned. "You smell anything?" he asked.

"He smells like he took a bath in liquor," I replied. I looked around. The others were smiling, watching me expectantly. I hunkered down beside the man.

"Buddy, what's your name?" I asked in a friendly tone of voice.

"Junior," he said gratefully. "Junior Stamper."

"Junior. Yall having a party up on that there mountain, Junior? Got lots of liquor up there?"

"Oh, yeah. Old man Collins that owns the hardware store, he bootlegs on the side, you know?"

"His boys up there selling?"

Junior licked his lips. "Oh, yeah. They started out giving and then they commenced selling. And some of the boys has commenced taking. But old man Collins, he'll git his money outen them one way or tother."

"Boys laying drunk up there?"

"Oh, yeah. And shooting their guns."

"They're shooting their guns at the wind in the underbrush," Talcott said.

I took him aside. "How'd we find him?"

"Think he wandered away to take a piss and then decided to run for it when he saw nobody was paying him any mind. Only he was so drunk he didn't know which direction to go in. Run right into our pickets. Except he werent running, he was more like crawling when they found him." He lit a cigarette. "We could create a diversion somewhere else."

"We need more men. We need to call the boys over from Beech and Blair. We got to have all of them."

"No time. Hit will be light in a few hours."

"Then we'll send out word. Sit tight tomorry, make them think we're still holding out. Start pulling back at dusk. They'll wonder ifn we're giving up. They'll keep on drinking, maybe heavier."

"Chafin will plug Crooked Gap."

"With what? He wont dare pull men out of Blair. He done sent his reinforcements, and a distillery along with them."

"He'll stop them drinking."

I looked at Talcott steady, with my eyebrows raised. After a moment he started to giggle.

"Hell," he said. "He aint General Pershing neither."

I SENT OUT THE WORD TO COME TO THE HEAD OF HEWITT. Some came before dark, quiet, not so that you would notice, but then there were more of us.

And then Talcott.

I was up the hill with a group of about forty, all of us within their range but hid behind trees. We were shooting less, making them waste their bullets, laughing at the wildness of the racketing above us.

Talcott hunkered down beside me, offered me a bottle of water and I swallowed some.

"Some new boys are up from Madison. The Army's coming in."

"Tell me something new," I said.

"Hit's the real thing this time. They give us a last warning or they'll treat us like traitors. They're sending in airplanes with bombs. Some of the boys is already leaving. The leadership's in the field, pulling them out personal."

"No. We're going over tonight."

"Rondal, we cant beat the U.S. Army. I been in it and I know. They say the newspapers is full of this here. They say hit's a revolution and they wont stand for it."

I flung the bottle down the hill and it busted on a rock. A burst of machine gun fire answered me up the ridge.

"They got poison gas!" Talcott whispered fiercely. "They're a fixing to use it. I seen that, brother. Hit burns. Hit rots out the inside of a man's head."

"So what are you going to do? Turn tail?" I pushed him away and he toppled over backward. "You're supposed to be so damn tough," I mocked. "But you got your limit, dont you?"

"I seen the gas," he pleaded. "Jesus, I was in that Army."

"You turned tail!"

"Hit's them that's turned, not me. They aint no Americans."

I snatched up my gun and ran from him, up the mountain. I dodged a stand of mountain laurel. Bullets picked chunks of bark from the oak beside me. Then a weight hit me in the belly and I fell. The mountain laurel caught at my arms, held them up.

Legs came toward me like giant scissors. Bits of dead leaves stuck to the blood on my shirt. I was strung out tight, like a hog to be gutted, like a squirrel to be skinned.

Twenty-four

CARRIE BISHOP

I WENT TO THE PUMP TO REST FIVE MINUTES AND SAVOR A dipper of water. I sat on the ground with my back against the rough wood of the housing. When I shut my eyes the ground beneath me became unmoored and carried me off into space. A loud crash up on the mountain brought me back to earth with a jolt. I looked around, frightened, but saw nothing.

I heard the motor as I walked back to the schoolhouse. Then the airplane crawled across the blue sky above the ridge, following its own sound like a dog tracks a coon. A graceful tilt of its wings brought it directly above us. I thought what a pleasant thing it was, then realized it must be spying out the movements of our men. The magic disappeared and I went inside.

Doctor Booker looked up from stitching a bullet wound in a man's arm.

"Almost out of bandages," he observed. "They better send more from Charleston."

I nodded wearily and bent to rummage through a box of supplies when a deafening explosion shook the earth. The windows opposite me blew out, showered us with glass and dirt. I stretched prone on the floor and stared stupidly at my bleeding hands. My ears hurt terribly.

Dr. Booker rose from the debris coughing and flinging his arms through the dusty air.

"I told you they had bombs." Dr. Mason sat on the floor beside the blackboard. He smiled like a child who has outdone the grown-ups.

I raised up carefully. The stinging wounds on my hands and face seemed to be scratches and I could see all right. I crawled to the doorway, pulled myself up. Dr. Booker stood outside.

"Sons of bitches!" he screamed. He looked skyward.

I heard a buzzing and wasn't sure if it was my ears or the airplane returning. I felt drunk and sat back down again. "Is this how they do now?" I asked.

We had ten wounded who had not yet been sent back to Charleston. Dr. Booker examined them. After a while my head cleared and I went to one of them, a boy of about eighteen. He was sobbing. "Did the whole mine go?" He had a shoulder wound and had lost a lot of blood. I brushed the dirt from his bandage, picked the slivers of glass off his clothes.

We carried the wounded outside and cleaned them as best we could, then washed ourselves at the pump. Next to the building I saw a crater deep enough to stand in up to the waist. It steamed as though the land was a live thing with a hunk of flesh torn out, and rivers of loose earth ran down the sides.

"And that was just Sheriff Chafin's bomb," Dr. Mason said triumphantly. "Wait until the regular Army gets here. They've been refining the whole procedure."

WE TREATED SCORES OF WOUNDED AND I COUNTED AT LEAST thirty dead. I glimpsed other bodies carried past the schoolhouse by grim, silent men. They would bury their own.

Then word came that the men were pulling back. Volunteers came from Danville to carry our wounded to the train that would take them to Charleston. We only had two minor casualties left on that last afternoon, and Dr. Mason went home. I had trudged to the pump for what seemed the millionth time when I saw a small knot of men up the dusty road moving fast toward us. One of them waved.

"Call Doc! He's hurt bad!"

I tried to convince myself it was not Talcott Lloyd who yelled.

"Dr. Booker!" I called, "they's a man hurt bad."

He stood in the doorway and wiped his face with a handkerchief.

"That looks like Talcott," he said. Then he dropped the

handkerchief and ran toward them. They carried the
wounded man on a sheet of canvas. When Dr. Booker
reached them they set him down. Dr. Booker bent over for
a moment. I shook my head and whispered to myself,
promised myself it would be someone I did not know.

"Put the water on to boil!"

Dr. Booker ran alongside them, held the man's limp arm
by the wrist.

I went inside and set the large kettle on the cast-iron
stove, added some lumps of coal. I heard them carry him
in and hoist him onto the table. I knew without looking that
it was Rondal.

"He's conscious," Dr. Booker said softly.

I went to him then. His face was turned toward me and
he watched me with his long blue eyes. I put my hand to
his cheek. His skin was dry and hot, and the stubble of his
beard pricked the cuts on my hand.

"Carrie, I cant feel my legs." He was like a child, pleading. "Hit's like the bottom half of me was shot away."

Dr. Booker probed the wound. "Not as much bleeding
as there might be," he said. His voice was low and calm.
"Talcott, you and these boys go on outside. Nothing you
can do in here."

"He going to make it?" Talcott demanded.

"Go on out," Dr. Booker said. "I got to examine him
first."

I held Rondal's hand. "The Army's coming," he said.

"I know it. We heard this morning."

Dr. Booker pulled off one of Rondal's boots, poked his
foot with a needle. No response. He looked at me and shook
his head. "We'll just stop this bleeding," he said softly.

Rondal gasped for breath. His chest heaved.

"No, son, dont you do that!" Dr. Booker emptied a syringe of morphine into his arm.

I bent close to Rondal's ear, said his name over and over.
After a time he breathed more easily and his hand relaxed
in mine.

"We're going to put you under with the ether," I said. I
brushed the hair from his forehead with my fingers. "We
got to see what's hurt inside of you."

"What difference?" he mumbled. "We done lost it all."

I soaked a piece of gauze in ether. "I got something to tell you," I said. "I never told you before because I didnt want to trouble you. I'm going to have a baby. And I want that baby to have a daddy. So you still yet got to fight."

"Aint it the preacher's baby?"

"No. Hit's yourn, Rondal."

He swallowed hard and his forehead wrinkled. "Hit's daddy is in one hell of a shape."

I kissed his forehead. "You'll be just fine." I covered his nose with the mask.

"I aint made it over that mountain yet," he murmured.

"You will," I said. "I'll git you there. Now you count backwards from a hundred."

He sighed, counted only to ninety-one and the ether carried him off.

Dr. Booker found the bullet quickly, dropped the dark red plug into a bucket.

"Spinal cord stopped the bullet," he said, "and it's snapped clean in two."

I craved fresh air but I couldn't remove my mask.

"Nothing else in bad shape. How's his pulse?"

"Steady."

"I'll close up fast. Let him come back around. And better insert a catheter."

He stripped off his mask and gloves and went outside to speak to Talcott. I wiped Rondal's face, then my own, with a cool cloth. Then I inserted the catheter, pulled his overalls up over the bandage around his midsection, hooked the galluses over his shoulder. I looked out the window. A steady stream of men passed down the holler, retreating before the Army arrived.

Talcott and Dr. Booker came inside.

"One thing sure, he cant stay here," Talcott said. "Even ifn it is bad to move him."

"Who can say what will happen if he's moved," Dr. Booker answered.

We watched in silence until Rondal came out of the ether. His eyes fluttered and he turned his head but seemed to look past us.

"Hey, brother," Talcott said uneasily, "me and a couple of the boys will tote you back to the train in a little bit."

"No!" I said sharply. They looked at me. "He wants to go on."

"He aint in much shape to want, is he?" Talcott said.

"He dont want to go back to Charleston," I insisted. "Just because his legs is paralyzed, that dont mean his mind is."

"You think me and him could survive Justice County? Why, they'd shoot us in a minute. Assuming, of course, that Don Chafin didnt. Aint that right, Rondal?"

Rondal stared.

"I'm taking him to my Homeplace in Kentucky," I said.

"You're a-taking him? A little slip of a gal?"

"They's got to be a wagon around here someplace, and a team of mules. I'll take him right over the road."

"Be a hard trip," Dr. Booker said.

"No harder than getting him to Charleston." I realized that I was crying and wiped my face with the back of my hand. "I'll get him on the train in Logan."

"Dangerous for a woman."

"Anybody stops me, I'll tell them he's one of theirn. And I'll carry me a gun hid. But I aint going back to Charleston, no more than he is. You know me, Dr. Booker, and you know I mean it. He's the daddy of my baby, and I aim to take him home."

"This here is crazy," Talcott said.

"Ask him!" I was screaming. "He aint deaf! He's a-listening to you! Ask him what he wants to do."

Dr. Booker stepped close to him. "Rondal, listen to me. You understand me?"

Rondal nodded his head.

"I be straight with you, because I know you want it. You aint never going to walk again. It aint likely you'll live long, but I cant say for sure. You could git the breathing problems on you and go just like that." He snapped his fingers. "Or you could hold on a while. Could be a few years. Maybe the influenza will carry you off. But nobody knows for sure. Trip be hard either way you go. You'll be susceptible. I'll leave it up to you, son. You want to go with Carrie or you want to go back to Charleston?"

Rondal didn't answer.

"You hear me, son?"

Rondal nodded. He closed his eyes. "Carrie," he whispered. "Carrie, take me."

Talcott threw up his hands. "Then I reckon I'll have to come too, git myself shot at."

"Hit will be safer for all of us ifn you dont," I said. "I got my own way of doing things. You go on back to your wife and younguns. You can come visit him when things quiet down. Now if you want to help, go on and see if you can buy a wagon and a team of mules offn some farmer. And git me a jar of applesauce or something else soft while you're at it." I turned my back to him and pulled some money out of my dress, all Rondal had given me in case of an emergency.

He went out slinging his arms to show his disgust.

"You better take some morphine," Dr. Booker said. "I'll fix you up a bag."

"What kind of life," Rondal mumbled. "The blood sucked outen me . . ."

"We'll do the best we can," I said.

"You wouldnt have come offn that mountain," he said. "You would have stayed with me." He lost consciousness again and I laid down to sleep before we set out.

TALCOTT RETURNED WITH A WAGON AND TEAM OF MULES, sold reluctantly and at a high price by a nearby farmer. Rondal was still alive but senseless when we set out before dawn. I endured another argument with Talcott, then Dr. Booker burst into tears as we were about to leave. He looked old and shrivelled in the gray light.

"Will you stay in Charleston?" I asked him.

"I got no place else."

"Write to me. The post office is Henryclay, Kentucky. I'll let you know how he does."

They rigged up a sheet across the wagon bed to shield Rondal's face from the sun while I changed into a faded green cotton dress I'd brought along. I strapped a pistol to my calf with a pair of bandages. Dr. Booker and Talcott carried Rondal out on a board. After they lifted him into the wagon I untied the red bandana from his neck, found a pocket in his overalls and stuffed it inside. I inspected the mule team. They seemed to have pleasant enough dispositions for mules.

"Gert and Myrt," Talcott told me. "Both of them old, or he wouldnt have sold them. Gert kicks from the left sometimes. Think you can handle them?"

"I've drove more mules than you seen," I said.

I settled myself onto the buckboard and took up the reins. I felt the cracked leather straps with my fingertips, lifted them to my nose. They smelled like home.

"Geeeyaah!" I shouted and cracked the reins sharply. The mules lurched forward and I waved but never looked back.

We reached the mouth of Hewitt by the time dawn broke and turned up the main road. It was choked with rednecks headed in the opposite direction. They largely ignored us in their haste to flee before the Army arrived. A few yelled, "Where you going, honey?"

"To shoot Don Chafin," I'd answer, and they'd laugh.

I stopped below Sharples at mid-morning and pulled back the sheet. I was afraid to look for fear Rondal would be dead, but he was awake. I gave him some water, spooned some applesauce down his throat, gave him some more water.

"You hurting?" I asked.

He nodded his head, tried to speak. I took a syringe from the bag beside him, filled it with morphine.

"I put your bandana in your pocket," I said.

"All right," he croaked. Already his eyes were fluttering shut. I emptied his catheter and turned him over on his stomach. When I kissed his hand, his fingers curled around my thumb. I yanked the sheet back over the wagon bed.

When we started our ascent of the mountain we were alone for a time. It was slow going. The wagon tipped from side to side as the wheels rimmed the deep ruts. Dusty blackberry bushes whipped at Gert's flanks and scraped the sideboards. Gunfire crackled occasionally off to the right.

In a great curve of the road we met three armed men. Two wore the white armbands of Don Chafin's volunteers and the third was a state policeman. I spied them above and behind me when I first entered the curve, and I forced myself not to watch them as I maneuvered the team through the hairpin turn. When I finally faced them they were leaning on their rifles and grinning.

"Where you going, sweetie?" one of the volunteers said. "Whose legs is that sticking out of that wagon?"

"Hit's my husband," I said in my best plaintive voice. "He was out working his corn and a stray bullet hit him. Come offn the mountain there, I reckon. I tried to tell him not to go out with all the shooting, but he said the corn had to be got in."

The man strolled over and flipped back the sheet with his rifle barrel.

"He's in a bad way all right," he agreed. "Where's he hit?"

"Took in the back," I said. "He cant move his legs none. I'm taking him in to Logan to the hospital."

The man walked back around and stood near one of the mule's heads. He fingered her bridle. "Can't move his legs? Why, he won't be no good to you at all, now, will he? Can't hoe the corn and can't cut the mustard."

The other men laughed.

"Where you come from?" the other volunteer asked.

"Hewitt Creek," I said.

"That right? Yall had a nest of rednecks over there lately, ain't you? Been helping them out?"

"They stole from us," I said.

"That right? Most of you people over on Hewitt are red yourselves, that's what I hear."

"I dont know nothing about red," I said. "My man aint no miner, he just farms. I got to git him to the hospital. Will you let me by?"

"Why don't you forget about him?" said the man closest to me. "He can't do a thing for you now. Come on over beside the road and I'll show you what a real man can do."

They laughed except for the state policeman. He was only nineteen or twenty. I looked at him and he looked away. The man came closer. I leaned over and brought the pistol from under my skirt. It trembled as I pointed it at the man. He laughed.

"Darling, what can you do with that old thing? You can't even hold it straight."

"That's right," I said. "I'm so scairt, I might just aim at your feet to scare you and shoot off your pecker by mistake. Now you let me pass."

His smile faded and he backed up. I held the pistol more steadily and pulled back the hammer with my thumb.

"Let her go," the state policeman said. "This thing is over anyway."

"That's the hell of it," the man said. "Pretty soon there won't be any more fun." But he stepped aside sheepishly.

I kept my gun on him, facing backwards and letting the mules go forward on their own, until they were out of sight.

At the top of the mountain so many men were in the road that I had to stop. They all wore white armbands. They stood in clusters and talked, drank what I suspected was whiskey from tin cups. Many others had started walking down the mountain, and while I was grateful that they paid little attention to me, I could not get by them. They walked slowly as though to prolong their adventure, stopped frequently to wave their hands and laugh.

Then, after what seemed an eternity, I passed the car.

It was a large dark green touring car with a spacious back seat. A man and woman stood beside it, pads and pencils in their hands. I was surprised to see the woman. She wore a stylish gray suit and hat, and looked cool despite the heat. She smoked a cigarette.

I pulled up beside them.

"Who are yall?" I asked.

"Press," the man said. "New York Times and the New York Tribune. Yall ever heard of them there?"

The woman flicked ash from the tip of her cigarette and gave him a withering look.

"That yall's car?" I asked. "Yall going to Logan anytime soon?"

"Right away," the woman said in a strange, clipped accent. "It appears it's all over up here."

"I got a man in my wagon, hurt real bad. I'm trying to git to Logan. Will you ride us in your back seat?"

"Certainly," the woman said.

The man sighed and looked at the wagon with a dubious expression.

"Wait," I said. I jumped down and went to Rondal. Unconscious, pulse slow but steady.

The woman looked over my shoulder.

"What happened to him?"

"He's shot in the back. He's paralyzed."

"Is he—"

She saw something in my face and didn't finish her question.

"Please," I whispered. "Ifn somebody here recognizes him, they'll kill him sure."

We lifted him out, board and all. I hated to move him again, but told myself the damage was already done. I had to turn him on his back and bend his knees before he would fit in the car.

I quickly sold the wagon and mules to a dozen men who wanted to ride off the mountain, and returned to the car.

"You want to sit up front?" the woman asked.

I shook my head, self-conscious because it was so hot and I had not been able to bathe for days. I squeezed into the back beside Rondal and rested his head in my lap. He mumbled but didn't wake up. I stroked his temples. When I looked up, the woman had turned and was watching me. I blushed and looked away.

"I'm sorry," she said.

Tears slipped down my cheek and I cried. The car moved forward and the man blew the horn to clear a way. The men in the road scattered, probably assuming we were someone important.

They told me their names but I forgot them at once. I gave them mine but wouldn't tell them who Rondal was. They both lived in New York; the man was originally from Baltimore.

"You going to tell our side?" I asked.

"She will," the man said. "She's practically a damn Bolshevik herself."

The woman laughed. She had taken off her hat and her hair was black and curly.

"We aren't Bolsheviks," I said, careful of my grammar. "We're all kind of things."

The woman took out a pad and pencil. "Why don't you tell me about it? I won't be sending this out because they're censoring us in Logan, and listening in on our telephone calls. But I'll hide my notes and write them up after I return to New York."

I was glad to talk, to keep the worry away. Sooner than I

expected we came down off the mountain, drove through the coal camp at Ethel. Then we reached the outskirts of Logan.

"You say there are people here who might recognize your friend?" the woman asked.

"Oh, yes. There's lots from Justice County up here, we heard. And the Baldwin-Felts guards, some of them know who he is."

"Some men were murdered in the jail," she said. "They were ordered up on the mountain to fight but they wouldn't take up arms against the union. So they shot them."

I was frightened but said nothing.

The man shook his head. "This is a hell of a place you've got here."

"Who made it that way?" I said sharply, tired of his smart-aleck attitude.

"Not me," he said.

"Leave her alone, George," the woman said. She turned to me. "What will you do now? Put him in the hospital?"

"I'm scairt to. Hit's the coal operators' hospital. Besides, I want to take him home to Kentucky. I got a brother with a coal company. I figure he's in town. I aim to find him."

"If he's with the operators, he's probably at our hotel. That's where they all are. The Aracoma."

We couldn't park in front of the hotel. Downtown Logan looked like the Fourth of July, there were so many people, and American flags everywhere. We finally found a place near the railroad depot. A train filled with brown-shirted soldiers had just arrived, and the people in the street stopped to applaud.

"Fortieth Infantry," said the man. "We were told they've got mortars on that train, and 37 millimeter guns, big ones. Knock holes in these hills of yours."

"Why dont you go look for your brother?" the woman said. "We'll stay here with your friend."

I was frightened to leave Rondal. But it occurred to me that anyone who saw him in such a fancy car would assume he was one of the coal operators' men. I walked down Cole Street to the hotel.

The hotel lobby was packed with men eating supper. It was home-cooked food served up by stout, beaming ladies. Miles was nowhere to be seen. A clerk at the desk told me he was in Room 311, and that was where I found him. He had been sitting on the bed reading a book.

"Carrie! What on earth are you doing here?"

"I need your help, Miles. I need it real bad."

He led me to a stuffed chair.

"Sit down here and tell me what's wrong."

"Hit's Rondal Lloyd. You recall Rondal? The organizer you kicked out of Vulcan eight years ago?"

He frowned. "I'm afraid that I do. Jesus, Sis, you aren't messed up with him again! You aren't—" He looked me up and down. "You've been on the mountain. Why didn't Ben tell me?"

"Because he thinks I'm still yet in Charleston. Miles, I'm desperate. Rondal got shot and he's real bad off. He's paralyzed. I got him out in a car near the depot. They's some New York reporters looking after him. You got to help me git him out of here before somebody recognizes him. Help me git him on a train for home."

"Oh, Lord. How do you get in these messes?"

"I aint got time for no lectures. He's a-laying there in that hot sun."

"I wasn't planning on leaving until tomorrow morning. Last regular train left about an hour ago. But I could go tonight. Lytton Davidson has a private train pulling out around eight-thirty. But getting an organizer on there, I don't know."

"You can say he's one of your employees. They'll take your word for it."

"Well, we can try."

I threw my arms around him. His hair was neatly trimmed close to his ears and his neck smelled of cologne.

We stopped outside the ballroom downstairs.

"You had supper?"

"I aint et since this morning."

"Plenty of food in there."

"I wouldnt eat their food."

"But you'll ride on their train."

"That's different. Hit's for Rondal."

We went into a restaurant and bought sandwiches, and soup for Rondal. At the depot, the woman said, "He's awake and asking for you."

I introduced Miles and they shook hands all around. Then

we lifted Rondal out of the automobile and laid him in the shade. I knelt beside him and felt his forehead, rummaged through my bag for a thermometer.

"The train's over on the siding," Miles said. "I'll go see if we can take him on board."

"We'd better be going," said the woman. She took my hand and smiled. "Good luck."

"I cant thank you enough."

"Well," said the man. "Happy Labor Day."

"What?"

"Labor Day. Tomorrow's Labor Day. Isn't that ironic?"

Rondal's temperature was 103. I poured water on a cloth and wiped his face.

"Dont give me no more shots," he said.

"But the pain—"

"Hit's settled down some. Hit's tight in my chest is the worst part. The rest dont feel at all. Please. I'm scairt I might die while I'm asleep."

"You're holding up real well. Maybe you aint going to die."

"Up on the mountain there, I wanted to die. Just for that moment, I wanted it. And now I dont, even with my legs gone. Aint that funny?"

His voice faded, even without the morphine, and he slept again. Miles returned with another man and they carried him to the train.

"Why dont you keep him in the hospital here?" the man asked. "He looks about done for."

Miles looked at me.

"Doctor's seen him and said they done all they can. And he wants to go home. I reckon he's got a better chance there anyway."

"Legs don't work, huh? Poor bastard."

They carried him to a car toward the back of the train that was done up like a setting room and laid him on a desk. I tucked a blanket around him.

"More room here," the man said, and left. I sank onto a chair beside Rondal.

"Who was that?"

"Works for Malcolm Denbigh, Davidson's number two man." Miles smiled. "Denbigh's English and that fellow is his interpreter."

He unwrapped a turkey sandwich and handed it to me.

"Will you be in trouble?" I asked.

"Naw. I told them Rondal was one of my men who volunteered. They've got no reason to disbelieve it. In fact, they were impressed. Even gave us Lytton Davidson's study here to stretch out in. Davidson's not here. He went to White Sulphur Springs when things got hot."

"Water," Rondal said.

I jumped up to give him some and helped him sip tomato soup through a straw. I scarcely noticed when the train left the station.

The door opened and a tall man in a brown suit entered. He had a long heavy head and a wide nose.

"So this is the brave fellow," he said loudly, as though Rondal was deaf. Rondal turned his head and stared.

"This is Malcolm Denbigh," Miles said. He looked uneasy. "This is my sister, Carrie. She's been on the mountain today nursing our boys."

"My dear girl! Do you mean they wouldn't let you stay in town to perform your duties?"

"Someone had to go," I said. I glanced at Rondal. To my surprise he was smiling. I looked away quickly.

"A genuine Florence Nightingale," Denbigh was saying. "I do admire your courage. My own wife thought it a chore to see me off on the train at four in the morning. But here's the truly brave fellow." He strolled over to Rondal. "What a shame you had to take a bullet. But I'll bet you gave those reds a rough time of it. It is an honor to shake your hand."

He stuck out his hand. Rondal looked at it.

Miles twisted on his chair. "He doesn't move his arms well," he said in a high voice.

Rondal reached into his pocket and fished out his red bandana, laid it across his chest. Then he pumped Denbigh's hand before the astonished man had time to move.

"You're a motherfucking son of a bitch," Rondal said. He smiled sweetly.

Denbigh dropped his hand and backed away.

"What is this?"

"Oh, lordy," Miles croaked.

I stood in front of Rondal in case Denbigh called a gun thug.

"Bishop, did you know about this?"

"This is my sister's—my sister's—"

"I'm carrying his child," I said.

Miles stared at me.

"I was going to tell you. And I dont apologize. I'm proud of it."

"I want him off this train!" Denbigh demanded.

"I can't put my sister off."

"She can stay, but he goes."

"I go where he does," I said.

"Bishop!"

"I can't put my people off this train," Miles said.

"This is Lytton Davidson's train," Denbigh said grimly.

"I don't care if it belongs to the President of the United States," Miles said. "That man is gravely wounded. If you put him out and he dies, I'll swear out a warrant on you."

Denbigh stood in the middle of the room and cracked his knuckles.

"You're as ignorant as the rest of them," he said. "I wouldn't trust a goddamn one of you. I think I'll post a letter to Boston. The good gentlemen who own Imperial Collieries will be interested to know where your sympathies lie. Then you can go back to slopping the hogs."

He turned on his heel and left.

Miles pointed a finger at Rondal. "Who gave you the right to do that? After what I've done for you."

"I done saved your soul," Rondal said. "Even the preacher didnt do that."

"You're raving!"

"No, hit's you. You stood up there and testified." Rondal's fingers plucked restlessly at his blanket. "That man done murder when he was the boss man at Winco. I seen it with my own eyes. He had a Negro tossed into a furnace."

"God."

Miles flung open the door of the car as though to leave, but then he stood there.

"I can't face them," he said.

"You can be here with us," I said. "You could work in that bank. You could start up a store. You could teach at a school, or run for office."

"Don't talk to me any more. I just want to think."

Rondal's breathing was more labored and I bent over him. "You want another shot?"

He shook his head and worked his lungs, his mouth open. Finally he relaxed and shut his eyes, and I thought he slept. But when the train stopped at a station he opened his eyes.

"Where are we?"

I looked out at the lighted platform, empty save for two guards with rifles, read the sign.

"Annadel," I said. My throat hurt. "We must have come through Peelchestnut Tunnel. We're at Annadel."

The train moved forward.

"I want to look out the window," he said. "I want to see one last time."

"Rondal, hit's nighttime. Hit's dark."

"Please."

Miles stood up wearily and helped me move the desk close to the window. The train window was a rectangle of flat blackness. Then the car swayed with us and a pinpoint of light blinked like a fallen star.

"There's the farmhouse," Rondal said. "We just went through the cut and that there's the Justice farm. And the tents over yonder." He smiled.

He fell asleep before we reached Davidson. His temperature rose to 104. I checked his pulse, then settled into a chair with his hand in my lap.

"Are you really going to have a baby?" Miles asked from the corner.

"Yes. Probably in the early spring."

He lit a kerosene lamp on the table beside him. His face was a white mask with large black hollows for eyes.

"You remember when we were younguns?" he asked. "Remember when I kilt that dog?"

Twenty-five

CARRIE BISHOP

HE WAS BITTER AND HATEFUL MUCH OF THE TIME. He spoke harshly to Flora's children when they came to visit. They called him "the mean man," and little Rachel was frightened of him.

Sometimes he could be kind. From his bed he watched me drag my heavy belly around while I cooked and cleaned. He fretted because I must do so much.

But something would break inside him when I went to turn him, or to help him into his wheelchair.

"Well, you got me right where you always wanted me," he'd sneer. "Right under your goddamn thumb."

He asked for whiskey and at first I gave it to him, hoping it would ease him. But when he drank more and more, and threw an empty jug at me one night, I kept it out of the house. He berated me for that, too.

I wanted to have him carried down to the Homeplace from time to time for a visit, but he wouldn't go, not even at Christmas. I spent Christmas Day listening to his stubborn silence, and crying to myself. Ben and Flora brought the children for a visit but he was so disagreeable that we were all uneasy. On Old Christmas Eve, I decided to leave him and walk to the Homeplace by myself.

"What the hell's Old Christmas?" he asked as I was preparing to leave. "I aint heard of it."

"Hit aint observed much these days," I said, "but Aunt Becka allays did like it. Hit's the day the wise men brought their presents to the Baby Jesus. And the night before, that is, tonight, the animals go down on their knees in homage.

Some even say the animals talk on Old Christmas Eve. Once when I was a youngun I went out to the barn at midnight. And the animals did kneel. I saw it myself. It was like a miracle.''

His lip curled scornfully and when I bent to kiss the top of his head he looked away. I went on, determined that he would not ruin my evening. When I returned a few hours later, he said, ''Let's go out to the barn at midnight.''

''What?''

''I want to see them animals kneel. Ifn they can kneel, maybe I can stand up.''

''I dont think—Rondal, hit will be so cold, and you're up late already.''

''We can wrap up warm. And I aint tired.'' His eyes challenged me. ''You're the one claims it happened. Well, I want to see it. I want me a miracle.''

I dressed him in two layers of clothing and wrapped several quilts around him. At eleven-thirty I wheeled him out the door and down the ramp Ben built for his chair. We only had a milk cow, because I borrowed Ben and Flora's mules. I positioned his chair near the cow's head. I expected more backtalk from him but he ignored me and watched the cow intently. I sank down into the hay and shivered, wondering what had possessed me.

He fell asleep well before midnight, his chin dragging on his chest. I looked back and forth from my watch to the cow. She still stood and nuzzled her feed bag at ten after midnight. I wheeled him back inside and dumped him into his bed.

When I woke the next morning he was already awake and watching me across the room. I scuttled across the cold floor, my teeth chattering, to build the fire.

''Werent that something?'' he said.

I paused at striking the match.

''What?''

''You must have fell asleep,'' he said.

I was weary to death of his mocking. ''I dont see your legs moving,'' I said, astonished at my cruelty even as I spoke. I turned back to the stove.

''I seen what you seen,'' he said stubbornly.

He was quiet all the day. He read *Life on the Mississippi*

and fixed a wobbly chair for me. When I put on my night-gown he said, "Sleep over here tonight. I want to feel that baby kick."

I went to him, laid my head on his shoulder and twined my fingers in the hair of his chest. The next morning, slowly and awkwardly, we made love.

WHEN OUR SON WAS BORN IN APRIL, RONDAL WANTED TO name him Dillon.

"I reckon I ought to marry you," he said. "Make you and the boy respectable."

He said it like I should be grateful.

"No," I said. "I want him to have Albion's last name. Albion deserves that much."

He looked surprised, then suspicious. "Hit aint because I'm a cripple?"

I kissed him and held his face in my hands. "I think you're worth ten of any other man I know."

The wrinkles on his forehead smoothed away.

"Dillon Freeman," he said. "Dont sound too bad."

He loved to tend the baby while I was out working the garden. He changed diapers, and rode around the cabin in his chair with the baby in his arms, its head craned back and its eyes open wide to take in every detail of the room. When both of them tired, Rondal hoisted himself onto the bed, lay on his back, and stretched the baby out on top of his chest. They slept that way for hours.

They were asleep when Rondal was taken with one of his breathing spells. From the vegetable garden out back, I heard him gasp. By the time I reached him, he had stopped breathing. The baby was snoring peacefully, one hand wrapped tight around Rondal's thumb.

I sat by them until evening light, when Dillon woke and cried to be fed. Then I went to the Homeplace to tell Ben and Flora and Aunt Becka. I walked past the cemetery where Rondal would at last have a place of his own. The head-stones did not stand in tidy rows on that slope beside Scary mountain. They were placed companionably, as people will sit together and talk—Aunt Jane beside Uncle Alec, Albion facing them beneath a spreading oak, Florrie's dead baby at his feet. The elements had already worn the names from the older stones and they leaned at gentle angles as though conferring with one another. Butterflies and honeybees tended the violets and sweet clover that grew over the graves.

It was a tranquil place, but no one could ever imagine a quiet slumber for the dead in that earth. They are not a people made for eternal peace, and even if they were, the mountains would not let them rest. The mountains are conjurers, ancient spirits shaped by magic past time remembered. The dead walk abroad in the shaded coves, or writhe in their graves, pushing up with strong arms and legs, waiting for the day.

AFTERWORD

AFTER THE BATTLE OF BLAIR MOUNTAIN, THE LEADERS OF U.M.A. District 17 were arrested and tried for treason. Their trials were held at Charles Town, in the same courthouse that saw the conviction of John Brown. Popular sentiment was on their side and they were eventually acquitted, but the union was broken throughout West Virginia, even at mines that had once been organized. Justice County's miners endured another winter in the tents before drifting away, defeated. Not until the administration of Franklin Roosevelt twelve years later was the union given the freedom to organize and the mine guard system abolished.

Dr. Toussaint Booker died at Institute, West Virginia, in 1931. Gladys Marcum Justice bore a daughter after Isom's death. She continued to live at the farm. My Uncle Talcott and Aunt Pricie lived on Campbells Creek until 1934, when the Justice County mines were organized. They moved back to Blackberry Creek that very year and settled at Winco.

Rachel Honaker, Ben and Flora's daughter, my first cousin who was more like a sister to me, married a grandson of Rosa Angelelli and set up housekeeping in the coal camp house at Winco where the Lloyd family once lived. By that time the mines had been mechanized and Winco had been reduced to ten families. Rosa was ignored by her own family, and only Rachel, who was a nurse, went to see her. Once I went along to visit Rosa in the state hospital where she was kept for so many years. I wrote down her story as I remember she told it, her mottled brown fingers gripping my arm, her long fingernails digging into my flesh as she called me by the name of a long-dead son.

In 1929, my uncle Ben opened a general store at the mouth of Scary Creek near the Aunt Jane Place. The store failed in the early years of the Great Depression. Not long after, Imperial Collieries claimed to have purchased all mineral rights to the land the year that Orlando Bishop was killed, and laid claim to the Homeplace. Uncle Miles, who had gone to work at his father-in-law's bank, could do nothing. My mother, Uncle Ben and Aunt Flora were forced to move, and lived at five different places in Paine and Justice Counties until their deaths. Aunt Flora suffered a stroke after the third move in the early 1940's, and died in 1957 at the age of 71. Uncle Ben passed away in 1962.

Although the timber was clear-cut, coal was never mined at the Homeplace. The land was purchased by the federal government to build a dam, which was constructed in 1969. But the floodwaters never reached the Homeplace and it stands empty to this day, held for some unknown reason in the control of a distant power beyond our ken. The houses are gone and I can only find the site by searching out a row of willow trees.

In Justice County, I am president of my local union. American Coal refused to honor the latest United Mine Workers contract, and we have been locked out for over a year. I have used the time, when not on the picket line, to put together this story from the yellowed newspaper clippings of articles written by C.J. Marcum and the journal where my mother recorded the events of her life and the stories of my father. Last month, scab miners were brought in to take our place. The young boys who laughed at the old-timers' stories of Blair Mountain are applying for food stamps.

Carrie, my mother, lived into her eighties. She never re-married. The companies still own the land.

—Dillon Freeman, 1987
Winco, West Virginia

The Random House Reader's Circle presents . . .

SAINTS AND VILLAINS
by
Denise Giardina

In the charnel house that was Europe in the
Second World War, there were few instances of
shining moral courage, let alone secular sainthood.
Dietrich Bonhoeffer, the German theologian and
Nazi resister, was the exception. This emblematic
figure risked his life—and finally lost it—through
his participation in a failed plot to assassinate
Hitler and topple his regime.

Saints and Villains gives us this exemplary
life in a sweeping narrative that is bold in
conception and utterly convincing in its power of
imaginative reconstruction.

 Look for the reading group discussion
guide at the back of this book.

Available now in bookstores near you.
Published by The Random House Publishing Group
in trade paperback.